GIFT OF THE AMULET

Book 1
Shattered Worlds

BY

Michael Anthony Cariola

Prologue

Seven Wizards.
Four Elementals.
Two Worlds.
One Destiny.

The Grand Arch Wizard, Eternal King of his people, stood upon the highest peak within the open-air temple—the Heart of Aralia. He trembled with sorrow, stricken to the core for the magnitude of their betrayal. His friends—his trusted advisors—had sunk to unimaginable depths, a darkness from which there was no return, and now their treachery was complete. With unquenchable grief, the Grand Arch Wizard sank into bitter despair—his agony and guilt so great he had nearly consigned an entire race to oblivion. Of the Six, their enchantment over him had been subtle—so insidiously deceptive, that he, the greatest, most powerful wizard in the entire world had failed to see it.

Failure, like acrid bile, crept its way into his soul. It enveloped him, threatening to tear the very heart from his chest. His purpose— to divert the Elven race and the race of Men from the precipice of war, to prevent the blood that once spilled would taint the pure Magick of his world—had been thwarted by the cold calculations of the Six he had loved as brothers. And thus, the Grand Arch Wizard sank to his knees and wept his despair.

The Dark Presence—the Lord of Death—had been raised from the pit by traitorous sorcery. The Six held it bound by forbidden Magick and kept it under their control. Either the Eternal King would battle the beast, or he would consign himself to an oblivion from which there was no return—rather than destroy the race of men. The Grand Arch Wizard had raised the Four Powers from the cardinal directions of his world and stood fused to their indwelling might. If he did not release the accumulated might—the sum of their power to complete the ritual, it would consume the world. But he could not—would not—as an alternative, consign men to such a heinous fate. For all their faults, he had seen goodness in them. They were undeserving of such punishment.

He turned the combined powers of the Elementals upon the Dark Beast. Goaded and under the command of the Six, it raised its black leathery wings and belched fire—ready to strike the Grand Arch Wizard down. Knowing that Death could not be defeated by Magick or any other means, he nonetheless drew his ancestral sword. At his touch, it erupted with power and a scorching, blinding light.

He struck a mighty blow at the Dark Beast, and it bellowed with rage as the pure scourge of the Sword—the Lightbringer—blasted a scale from the heart of the great dragon. With one more blow, the Arch Wizard would do the impossible: destroy Death.

But it was not to be. The Elemental Dragons would not permit the destruction of their brother.

In silence they conferred, halting time and motion until the Four Elementals and the Beast arrived at a decision—one that would alter the course of the universe and the future itself. Instead, they took the destruction upon themselves, choosing to be eternally bound and imprisoned rather than destroy the world—and the Eternal King, whom they loved.

With a mighty rending, Aralia—and the endless space from which it was affixed—split in two. In the monumental cataclysm that shook the cosmos to its very foundations, all that existed shattered and rejoined—diminished in power, yet preserving the lives of both elves and men.

Two worlds—two dimensions—now existed side by side, but separated by a chasm that could not be bridged by conventional means. And it was at this moment that the One Destiny was born of the destruction.

In the aftermath, the Arch Wizard—the Eternal King—was bound to the new world as were the Six who had betrayed him.

Diminished, he would face this new hostile, untamed planet stripped of its Magick—and live out his years in hopes of righting the wrong.

It was then that the Arch Wizard examined the stars and read the prophecy written there.

There would come a time—hundreds of generations hence—when one of his line would be born to heal the rift separating the two broken worlds. This Child of Destiny would reunite the worlds to one—or they would remain forever apart and fade to ruin.

Of necessity, it would be the Son of Luminance—the awaited one—who would restore the universe to its former balance. The One Destiny would be born with the power to heal Aralia and return Pure Magick to its rightful place—or there would be no other.

Gift of the Amulet

Chapter 1

She stared thoughtfully across the kitchen table at her son, as she had done so many times before. He had so many questions lately; at times, she was simply lost for words. This was a difficult question, and it required a concise answer.

"My son, many of Earth's visionaries across the ages have written about it, dreamed about it—some had even come close to the truth—but they never understood the true nature of their imaginings. In their heart of hearts they sensed the subtle, hidden realities of this world, the power of thought itself, but their lack of faith inevitably kept them in shadow. They understood this world's peril, and perhaps even knew how things had changed from ancient times to the present, but never quite grasped what had happened in the first place—what had set it all in motion. So always remember you are part of this world, but not of it." Abelene Kingsley smiled tenderly at Azriel. "Now wash up and get ready for dinner. Your uncle will be over soon and rumor has it, he's bringing you a very special gift. After all, It's not every day my young man turns thirteen!"

Azriel beamed at his mother. He made his way to the bathroom and lathered up his hands. He scrubbed meticulously, rinsed, and wiped the excess water on his jeans. At thirteen years old, Azriel was a tall, wiry boy with dark hair and striking grey eyes. He had inherited his comeliness from his mother, and anyone seeing them together could have no doubt that Azriel, was her son.

As in any small town, gossip was the favorite pastime in the tiny hamlet of Harden Lake. The tightly knit women of Harden Lake would often clustered together, whispering and clucking like old hens, wondering about Abelene. Stunningly beautiful, her flowing, black hair framed a cherubic oval face. Her grey eyes, flecked with gold, could pierce through any lie, and her regal bearing kept most folk at a respectful distance even if they weren't consciously aware of why. Nonetheless, the townspeople thought it scandalous, murmuring among themselves, wondering why she wasn't married or what had happened to the boy's father. She didn't go to any of the local churches, and she was deeply secretive. There was an aura of mystery about her that kept the locals guessing. Some even suspected that she was different—not unpleasantly so, but exotic in a way that made the men leer, and their wives grow jealously cautious of her. As a result, Abelene had few people she considered friends and even fewer she trusted. Only those who knew her could detect the underlying aura of sadness about her, as if she harbored a terrible secret, or had suffered a heartbreaking loss.

Azriel helped his mother set the table—place settings for three. Earthenware plates, cups, and two fluted goblets for wine. Uncle Nick always brought a bottle or two when he visited. With Silverware and napkins placed properly, the table looked cozy and inviting, and Azriel was famished. He hoped Uncle Nick would arrive soon so they could eat dinner.

Azriel wondered with excitement what his great-uncle would be bringing him. Like every other kid in his class, he wanted the latest gaming station with lifelike computer graphics. The new gaming system featured a helmet that put the player directly into the virtual world with intense three-dimensional graphics and contact electrodes that stimulated certain parts of the brain to activate scent and touch for an enhanced experience. That was what Azriel wanted, and that was what Abelene had firmly put the kibosh on the whole matter.

"I will not have my son's brains scrambled into mush." She crossed her arms sternly the last time Azriel asked. "Besides, you will need all your wits about you for the challenges you'll have to face in *this* world, not a fantasy one."

But Azriel didn't worry too much, for he knew that Uncle Nick would likely bring him what he wanted. Uncle Nick had a weak spot for his nephew and often indulged Azriel's desires, even if it sometimes meant locking horns with Abelene.

On one occasion, his uncle had given him an authentic sword. He said it was from the Middle Ages; but Abelene dragged Uncle Nick into her private study and slammed the door so Azriel wouldn't hear their argument. Of course, Azriel stood by the door and heard everything.

"What are you thinking, giving my son a bladed weapon—particularly, *that* one," Abelene fumed. "By Shenach, it's bigger than he is!"

"Dearest Abelene, you exaggerate," Nick placated, "And besides, I did what you asked," he said with humor. "You made me promise that I would hold onto it until your son was ready."

"Well he's not ready yet for that burden. He's only a boy!"

"Soon to be a man," Nick countered firmly. "You can't protect him forever. His destiny has already been imprinted upon him. That happened when you gave birth to him. It's time to let Azriel know what that destiny entails, and it begins with his father's sword!"

Those words sent an electric thrill down Azriel's spine—and the first pang of resentment toward his mother. His father's sword? Abelene never spoke much about Azriel's father, only that he had been killed in a terrible war in a place called Aralia. What else was she hiding, and why was she protecting him? He listened more intently.

Abelene's voice grew husky with emotion. "Nicodemus, I have told him many stories of the realm—of Aralia. I am preparing him."

"Certainly not enough, my dear. To him they are just stories. They will mean nothing to him until he knows the truth."

"The truth," Abelene muttered bitterly and suppressed a sob. "I just want my little boy a while longer."

"I know," Nicodemus softened his voice, trying to comfort her. "But you know you can't protect him forever. He needs to be prepared."

"Prepared? Prepared for what! To be placed in danger? To battle this world until his heart breaks? What else then? To age—to grow old and die? Nicodemus, this world is a dagger through my soul. I don't know how much longer I can do this. The land cries out and suffers from the abuses of men and I feel every bit of it. Please let him be a child a little longer." Abelene finally broke down and wept.

"A little longer then," Nicodemus conceded, and from the sound of Abelene's muffled crying, Azriel knew that Uncle Nick had embraced her to offer solace.

That was the extent of the conversation, but since that time, nearly a year ago, Azriel often pondered the exchange between his mother and uncle. He didn't have enough information to draw his own conclusions, and asking about it would only reveal the fact that he had been eavesdropping. It would do nothing but earn him a serious tongue-lashing from Abelene. The sword he kept safely stored under his bed. Every so often, however, he removed, trying to make sense of its meaning.

His father's sword.

Upon examination, the sword bore strange cursive writing down the length of the blade on either side, a script Azriel had never seen before. Stranger than the odd language was the blade itself, fashioned from an unusual metal that glowed violet in sunlight. The hilt, however, was beautiful. It appeared to be carved of gold, with an intricate design of interwoven aspen leaves. On the pommel was embedded a strange black stone that though highly polished, reflected no light. All in all, it was a superbly crafted sword. Not that Azriel would know, but it certainly seemed to be of fine craftsmanship.

Azriel tried to pry more information from his mother about the weapon—and about his father—
but she remained mum on the subject. She never spoke much about Azriel's father, but became sad and withdrawn when pressed on the issue. Concerning the sword, she claimed that Nicodemus had purchased it at an antiques market in Europe some years ago, but Azriel knew that she was being purposefully deceptive. And Abelene had never lied to him before. It angered him to think that his mother would try to deceive him. That point alone began the first stirrings of distrust he'd ever felt for his mother.

Azriel thought about all this while waiting for Uncle Nick to arrive. He stared out the window waiting. The path leading to his house, many would consider idyllic. Natural and unpaved, it wove its way through the first five acres of woodland to a smallish cottage set back into a clearing. Stone and stucco with dark wooden beams, it was the perfect definition of an English or European home, except oddly, it was built in the back hills of northern Idaho. Because of its remoteness, after the original owner had died, it remained vacant for several years like a hidden treasure before Nicodemus secured the title to the property for Abelene to dwell, and transferred ownership to her. Acquiring the parcel ensured her safety and privacy, which Nicodemus considered paramount.

Azriel loved the place. Certainly, he had been on a few field trips with his class, but no natural setting seemed to be quite as beautiful as his own backyard. The total twenty-five acres were abundant with wildlife and a diverse array of vegetation throughout the forest. If one walked the full length of the acreage, the traveler would come to a stream defining the back boundary of the property. He often spent hours roaming and discovering, an exercise Abelene encouraged. It gave the boy an affinity for the natural world which she hoped he would retain in later years when setting out on his own to face the challenges of his destiny. He would need it.

At last, the old man drove up in his favorite car—a Ford Model T. He was dressed in a driving coat with his long white hair sticking out over his collar. He kept his white beard closely cropped, and wore a ridiculous pair of driving goggles that had been out of fashion since about 1905. Azriel ran out the door to greet Uncle Nick. The car sputtered and popped once before it stalled and bucked forward a few feet. Azriel choked back a giggle as Nick grumbled and opened the side hood panel. Quite oblivious to Azriel's amusement, Nick removed a screwdriver from a toolbox in the trunk and began tinkering with the carburetor, adjusting the air-gas mixture. Azriel looked into the engine compartment and remembered a recent conversation he had with Abelene. He had learned a new word and asked his mother what it meant. She hesitated for a few moments, trying to come up with the best explanation she could muster, then smiled with a mischievous twinkle in her eye.

"*Eccentric* is the perfect word to describe your uncle. He does things his own way, much to the consternation of his friends and neighbors. But you see, if he were merely a poor old man, by this world's definition, he'd be considered nuts—crazy!" Abelene smiled wryly. "But since he's wealthy he's allowed to be eccentric!"

Thinking of that, Azriel continued to watch, fidgeting impatiently.

"Uncle Nick?"

"Hmm?" he answered, absently immersed in the mechanics of his car. He pulled out a handkerchief from his back pocket and buffed away a smudge of oil from the starter coil.

"Why do you keep this old junker?"

"Junker!" Uncle Nick suddenly straightened and looked down at Azriel with a scowl, making quite a show at being insulted by the question. "Junker, you say! Boy, I purchased this car right off the assembly line in 1906, and have since restored it twice! It's a fine piece of machinery and I see no reason to replace it with something I can't fix! The old man's eyes suddenly softened with humor. He winked at Azriel and tussled the boy's hair. Azriel squirmed and rolled his eyes. The car had been built in 1906. There was no way Uncle Nick could have purchased it new. That would make Nick well over a hundred years old. And it was obvious that Nick was no more than perhaps fifty.

"You're full of it!" Azriel retorted.

"You think so, don't you, clever boy! Well, here's a piece of advice. Don't always trust what you see. Appearances are often deceiving."

"Yeah, right." Azriel smirked and smiled. He risked a peek in the back seat of Uncle Nick's car, hoping to see if a wrapped present sat there waiting to be opened. Sure enough, a rather large box with shiny holographic paper tied in green ribbon gleamed and sparkled in the ray of sunlight filtering through the side window. Azriel tried to act as if he hadn't seen it. He didn't want to seem too anxious. But he couldn't help himself. It would be a personal victory to be the first one in his school to have the latest system. Even better, to be able to shove that tasty morsel into Eddie Breck's arrogant face. Eddie's parents had money and he always loved to brag about every new thing he got.

"Sneak!" Nick opened the back door and tucked the gift under his arm as he headed toward the front door.

"Abelene!" Uncle Nick called as he entered the house.

"In the kitchen," she called back.

Nick let himself in and made his way to the kitchen, with Azriel tagging close behind. Nick plopped the alluring package onto the countertop and grabbed Abelene by the waist. He kissed her affectionately on the forehead. With his mother and great-uncle thus occupied, Azriel took the opportunity to finger the beautiful wrapping paper and lift the box to ascertain its weight. It felt heavier than he expected.

"Azriel!" Abelene scolded. "Not until after dinner."

"Aw, Mom."

She gave him *the look* that required no explanation. He quickly placed the box back on the counter.

"Where have you been, Nicodemus?" she asked.

"Traveling."

Abelene gave Azriel a furtive glance. "Have you located what you hoped to find?"

"Not entirely. We must talk later about it." He peeked in on Azriel, who had gone into the other room and was now planted in front of the television. Satisfied the boy was out of hearing range, he risked saying what he was sure would rankle Abelene's nerves.

"It's time," Nicodemus whispered. "In your heart of hearts you know that."

Abelene sighed with resignation.

"Yes, I do. But it doesn't make it any easier."

"My dear, letting go never is."

She looked down at her feet.

"Azriel must become acquainted with his birthright—and his true origins. You should have told him sooner," he chided. "It will now become much more difficult, for already he's immersed in this world. Azriel begins to doubt what he feels in his heart. This world has a way of doing that—and you know that to be true."

"I've tried to keep him grounded, told him the stories of Atlantis and Lemuria…"

"Those events were only a backlash to that fateful event." Nicodemus retorted with more annoyance than he meant. Abelene looked up at him sullenly. He quickly lowered his voice in apology.

"Azriel will hate you for a time, but that will pass. He needs this time to grow into power and knowledge. He will reject it all at first, but in the end he will become strong and powerful—equal to the task that has been placed before him. The stars were in a position of power at the moment of his birth. He is the one."

Abelene rested her head on Nicodemus' shoulder. "I'll need your help. You're often gone for long periods of time. It gets lonely—and you're the only one who understands. Please stay and help me through all this."

"I will do what I can, my dear. Now, if you don't mind, I'm quite thirsty. Let's drink."

Nicodemus opened one of the kitchen drawers and rummaged through the various kitchen gadgets until he found a corkscrew. Smiling, he said, "The key to happiness! A most useful human invention." Jauntily, he removed a dusty old bottle from a cloth sack and wiped it clean. He stared at the label and mused. "Muscatel from the south of Spain. 1807—a very good year. I've been saving this bottle for a special occasion. Have you any wine glasses?"

"Of course." Abelene smiled with humor. Good wine was one of Nicodemus' weaknesses. The old man often drank to excess, but never got mean or unruly. He'd only get jolly and boisterous and wind up snoring loudly on the sofa.

The bottle opened with a loud pop. Nicodemus poured a scant inch in both glasses and handed one to Abelene. Swirling the contents gently, he examined the color—a deep claret—and sniffed heartily of the wine, his nose plunged firmly in the glass. He smiled with satisfaction.

"To the reuniting of our worlds!" he raised his glass with Abelene, and she added, "To peace."

Sweet warmth spread from Abelene's stomach to her extremities, and she smiled. "Oh my!" she giggled. "That is quite wonderful. Are you trying to get me drunk?"

"Never, my dear. Just sharing in a little happiness. Now I think it's time to eat."

After a sumptuous meal of richly seasoned roast chicken with potatoes and shallots, Abelene quickly cleared the table. Azriel stood to help his mother, but she smiled warmly. "Not tonight, sweetie. You just stay here."

Azriel waited in anticipation for what he knew was coming. His mother was an excellent cook, but when it came to baking, no one in the world could make a birthday cake better than Abelene. It wasn't just the secret ingredients that, to consternation of others, she refused to reveal, but something else. Eating her cake was like eating happiness right down to the core of one's being—simply magical!

She emerged with a beautifully decorated cake. Unusual patterns crisscrossed the top and sides, interspersed with roses and leaves cleverly shaped from the icing. Gaily lit candles sat atop the cake. Abelene proudly placed the cake before Azriel.

After the obligatory birthday song and the usual ceremonial extinguishing of the candles, Abelene cut three sizeable wedges, handing one each to Azriel and Nicodemus before serving herself. She took a large forkful and closed her eyes in delight.

"From the old country," she said. "Only some ingredients have to be approximated. Some herbs are just not available here." Abelene glanced knowingly at Nicodemus. Azriel caught the exchange and suppressed a slight pang of annoyance. Where exactly *was* the old country? As always, Abelene had been vague about it. What was she hiding? All Azriel knew was that he seemed to be the focal point of a big deception. He would think about it later, however, since Abelene left the room and returned with a stack of gifts.

Upon opening the first one, Azriel made a show of being pleased with the gift—a new pair of jeans. The next package contained two shirts. Azriel thought to himself as he suppressed a sigh. *"Looks like it's going to be another practical birthday."* Not that he blamed his mother. Lately she complained in jest that she couldn't keep up with his growth. The clothing she had purchased for him only six months prior he had already outgrown.

Abelene smiled knowingly. Of course, she knew her son would want some fun gifts, and she kept them for last. Azriel opened a rather sizeable box and smiled in delight. Inside it was a spanking new baseball glove and the most beautiful Louisville Slugger he had ever seen. Also, a box with three Major League baseballs lay nestled in the corner. Azriel loved baseball—a love also shared by Abelene and Uncle Nick.

"You missed something." Abelene said, as Azriel tried on the glove for size. It felt good, but would need to be oiled. He peered in the box again. An envelope was taped to the side. Of course it would be the compulsory birthday card. He peeled the tape and opened the flap. His eyes widened with joy when he held up four tickets for the Seattle Mariners. Looking closer, he noted that they were box seats on the first-base line.

"Mom! How did you ever get these?"

"I have my sources." She grinned as Azriel gave her a hug. Abelene savored his affection, since those hugs came less often as Azriel had grown. "There are four tickets so you can bring a friend, okay?" Abelene added, enjoying his delight.

Azriel nodded with approval.

"Now, one more thing." Abelene dug into her pocket and removed a beautifully carved wooden box that filled her hand. Odd cursive designs were etched into the black and red grained wood. Azriel had to admit it was beautiful. Nicodemus, however, peered at Abelene and raised an eyebrow. This was unexpected, though not entirely unwelcome. It would probably help the boy attune himself to the gift Nicodemus had brought.

"Go on, open it!" Abelene's mien suddenly changed. Her jovial expression morphed to one far more solemn. Azriel flipped open the lid and stared at the pendant tucked inside. His eyes narrowed with curiosity as he lifted the chain and examined the small treasure. The medallion was cast from a most unusual metal. It appeared to be woven of silver and gold, yet it had an indigo tinge he had seen on only one other item. Strange symbols and designs festooned the four interlocking dragons, each one unique in its own way.

He became quiet and introspective as he brushed the dragons with his fingers. His hand tingled and he pulled it away in surprise.

"Mom, what's this?"

Abelene sat quietly for a moment as she gathered her thoughts. She knew he would have questions, but she still hadn't figured out just how much she would reveal to him. The talisman was an object of tremendous power, forged when Azriel was still in the womb. Abelene had commissioned the piece for her son. The greatest high mages of the day were present at its creation. They had poured their energy and purpose into its forming, destined to be worn by a man of power—her son, Azriel. He would grow into it.

She sat Azriel down and waited until she had his full attention. "What I tell you must always be kept in your heart. It is knowledge for you only. Never reveal what I am about to tell you."

Azriel stared back at her. He knew he was about to hear another of Abelene's fantastic stories—stories he'd heard since he was old enough to remember. Stories of a place his mother had come from, a place where she was a queen and he a prince. Abelene spoke of her realm as an *earth* very similar to this world, but more powerful and potent. Magick abounded, energizing her world with strength and purpose. That was Magic with a "K," not the silly stage magic of fakery and illusion, but Magick of the most effective kind that sprung from the powerful emanations of heart, will, and mind. This, Azriel barely understood. But he nonetheless enjoyed his mother's stories as something exclusively between them. It was their special bond.

Abelene sat opposite Azriel and locked eyes with him. This was important, and required his full attention.

"Before you were born, I had this amulet made for you so that someday you may wear it proudly and take your place in our society, but—that never happened. I crossed over to the world of men to protect you."

"Mom, you told me this already…"

"Don't interrupt. This is important! The high wizards and mages knew you were destined for greatness and that you would be the one to unite both worlds. Some feared the reintegration of the worlds and would have had me killed. And you, in your unborn state, would have died with me." She gently extracted the amulet from Azriel's hands as he swallowed down his sudden fear. This story was far more intense than her usual tales, which were usually fun. Abelene continued as she pointed at the amulet. "These four represent the dragon elementals that keep the worlds from falling into chaos. They are Earth, Water, Air, and Fire. They carry within them the unalterable laws of nature, to be used in your defense should you ever need it. The symbols over each dragon are their sigils—their secret names, which should never be uttered frivolously. They can be called upon in times of dire need. But know this—that it takes a man of unusual power to control them and to keep them from destroying the world."

"What are their names?"

Abelene hesitated and looked up at Nicodemus. He shook his head imperceptibly.

"Those, you will learn when you are ready. I cannot reveal them to you. The names must be earned." Abelene placed the chain over Azriel's head, and the amulet draped down below his chest. He looked up at his mother with a bemused expression. "It's a little large, isn't it?"

"You'll grow into it." The intensity of her expression softened, and she kissed him on the cheek. "Now always keep it safe and hidden away until you are ready to assume the responsibility for it. I've protected it for the past fifteen years. Now *you* must."

Behind them, Nicodemus nodded with tacit approval. It had taken courage for Abelene to gift her son with the amulet. For something seemingly insignificant, it was the first step of letting go and allowing Azriel to grow into his destiny—something many a mother is loath to do. But she had done it well by stepping back and permitting her boy the way to becoming a man.

"Now," Nicodemus said with levity, lightening the somber mood. "It is time for my gift!"

Azriel grew excited as Uncle Nick handed him the large elaborately wrapped package. He stared at it knowing what lay hidden inside. He couldn't wait to plug in the new system. It would certainly put his old system to shame. The kids at school would be so jealous!

"Go ahead, open it."

He was almost sad to tear open the beautiful paper, but Azriel made quick work of it and lifted the lid. Looking inside, however, he couldn't contain his disappointment and looked up at his uncle as if he had been betrayed. Nicodemus pressed his lips together to prevent himself from bursting out in laughter.

Azriel lifted out the huge tome and placed it on the table. The leather binding, though ornate and beautifully embossed, was cracked in some spots. It smelled of great age.

"You got me a book?" His voice revealed his lack of joy with the gift.

"That's not just any book, boy. It survived a most dangerous journey. In it, you will find who you are and where you came from—that is if you have the smarts and courage to learn how to use it—so don't be an ass!"

Behind Azriel, Abelene stared at Nicodemus and shook her head. Tears were beginning to form at the corners of her eyes. She would have been happier if he had given her son one of those brain-scrambling gaming stations. Anything but that book. He wasn't ready for it. She turned away, but not before giving Nicodemus a scathing look of accusation.

Azriel shrugged and opened to the first page and frowned with consternation. Written in a language he had never seen before, the characters, though cursive, were shapes unrecognizable to any modern tongue.

"I get it. This is a joke, right?"

"No son, my jokes are far more elaborate," Nicodemus smiled. "But you will need this." He reached into the box and moved the tissue. He lifted out a nearly transparent stone tablet. Etched along its borders were runes carved into the crystal plate. "This is a transformation crystal from your mother's world—and yours. Place it over the page."

Azriel did as instructed, and the odd characters slowly shifted and swirled into readable English. The title page read, "*The Complete History of Aralia*".

Azriel was intrigued. "Okay, I'm impressed."

"Supposedly, that's only the first thing the crystal plate can do. Beyond that, your mother won't tell me. Though to my understanding, its secrets reveal themselves when the student is ready."

Abelene gave Uncle Nick a scorching look. "Nicodemus, we need to talk—now!"

Azriel snapped a glance at his mother and then at Nicodemus. Interesting—his mother's reaction to the book. For that reason alone, he now felt more inclined to read it. Obviously, it had information within that Abelene didn't want Azriel to know—which made it all the more appealing. Before Azriel could react, Abelene snatched the book from under him and grabbed Nicodemus by the arm like a naughty boy, dragging him into her private study before slamming the door.

"Why *this* book?" She fumed.

He sighed with frustration. "Abelene, do we really need to have this conversation again? His knowledge of your world is sadly lacking. How do you expect him to understand the forces he will be up against? By osmosis? It is time to begin his training."

Abelene opened the book and flipped through the pages until she found one of interest. She placed her hand over the page and muttered an incantation, then slapped the book closed.

"By Shenach, there are things in here no child should see."

"Mene's blood, woman! In whose opinion?"

"Mine! I'm still his mother. This time you've overstepped your authority, Nicodemus." She suddenly softened her stance. "Dear, dear Nicodemus, I owe you so much. If not for you, I never would have made it through the transition to this side. But this—this, I can't bear." Abelene's gray eyes darkened as they glazed over with tears. "He will hate me."

"That's why I've decided to begin his training. Other than you, who else is more qualified to teach him than me? You know the places I've been and the secrets I hold. He is at an age where he will receive it from me, but not from you."

"Why not!" Abelene spun around, nearly shouting.

Nicodemus' shoulders sagged. He didn't want to hurt her any further, but she needed to appreciate this delicate time. "Because you're his mother, and as much as he loves you, he is at the age where he begins to doubt. As he grows, he will go through a period of rebellion. He hasn't a father to kick his backside when he needs it, and you, my dear, won't have the heart to. That is why you need me at this crucial time. Do you understand?"

"Only in my mind, not in my heart."

"Then that will have to do."

"His training begins now. Are we agreed?"

Abelene exhaled forcefully. "Yes," she grumbled.

Then, come June, pack his things. We will be going on a trip this summer. You'll need to prepare Azriel, and you will need your passports."

"Neither is a problem. Besides, he's not as clueless as you think."

"Good," Nicodemus replied affably, "I hope you'll be okay with flying. Time is of the essence. We need to be there for the solstice."

"No—I hate flying. Being cramped in an unpredictable mechanical beast for eight hours isn't my idea of a good time. I prefer the old ways of traveling."

"I know, dear. But that form of high Magick seldom works in this world—and it's too easy to trace. We have enemies. You know that."

"Of course I do. Just let me grumble a bit. It makes me feel better."

Nicodemus chuckled heartily and gave Abelene a peck on the cheek. Holding his index finger to his lips, he motioned to the door. Abelene tiptoed over and quickly pulled it open. Azriel, whose ear had been firmly planted to the keyhole, stumbled forward and fell awkwardly on his face. He looked up sheepishly and grinned broadly.

Abelene folded her arms and looked down at him, clearly displeased. She pressed her lips together with exasperation.

"So where are we going, Uncle Nick?"

"To the British Isles."

20

Chapter 2

Harden Middle School was one of the first schools to be built in the tiny rural hamlet. It sat nestled in the far corner of town, separated on one side by a chain-link fence and on the other side by a dense stand of conifers. The old school still had hardwood floors that creaked with age and classrooms in dire need of an upgrade. Still, it was cherished by the members of the community and would likely be restored rather than replaced if funding ever permitted. Azriel took the bus with only four other kids of his age group since his home and theirs were furthest from the school. Much to his chagrin, he rode "the short bus" with his closest neighbors, whose farmhouse was two miles down the road. Albert and Jasper Cunningham were lively boys with golden hair the color of ripened wheat and an abundance of freckles on their cheeks. Though inseparable as siblings, they often fought more than got along, usually over the pettiest of issues. Beside them rode the youngest of the Cunninghams, Julia, a sweet but rather naïve girl in pigtails and ribbons. Because of her naiveté, her brothers teased her mercilessly. And being so trusting, she often fell prey to their pranks. She wasn't entirely defenseless, however, since on more than one occasion, when pushed too far, Azriel had heard of her getting back at her brothers in the most ruthless of ways. Like the time she smeared crazy glue on the toilet seat. Jasper had been stuck to the seat for two hours before his mother figured out a way of removing him from the toilet with solvent and a cooking spatula.

In the back of the bus, Camille McElven, a rather secretive girl, scowled as she stared out the window. Thin and waifish, with unremarkable black hair and striking blue eyes, she always remained by herself for reasons no one seemed to know. She had moved to Harden Lake a third of the way into the school year. Therefore, being the new kid and an outsider, most of the others avoided her, thinking her either too aloof or simply peculiar. They often whispered horrible things about her and treated her as if she were diseased. Azriel felt bad for her, since she didn't seem to deserve the abuse she often received. But as children frequently mimic the biases of their parents, Camille was at the bottom of the pecking order, merely for being labeled as "different".

Albert plopped down next to Azriel and poked him in the ribs. "So did you get that the gaming console from your uncle?"

"No," Azriel slapped Albert's hand away and sighed. He now wished he hadn't said anything about it. But Azriel had been so certain he was getting one. He hated appearing stupid.

"So, what did you get for your birthday?" Jasper asked.

"You know, the usual stuff. Some shirts and pants…"

"Boring…" Albert and Jasper chimed.

"…a book…"

"Lame," they intoned.

"I did get a new mitt and a Louisville Slugger!"

"Well, that's pretty cool." Albert nodded with approval. "It's about time. You're always stealing *my* mitt. Where is it?"

"I left it home. It's being oiled."

Azriel didn't tell them about the Mariners tickets, since he liked Albert and Jasper equally. It would give rise to a problem that would likely lead to a fight between the two.

Before the school bell rang, the schoolyard teemed with excited adolescents running to their favorite hangouts. Azriel sat with a few of his friends on the bleachers, watching an impromptu softball game. Though he tried to remain cheerful, as was his usual demeanor, he couldn't help being in a grumpy mood after learning that Eddie Breck, the school bully and loudmouth, had gotten a new gaming console from his father for no reason at all. Eddie, a chunky troll of a boy, delighted in making the other kids jealous of all the things his absent father would bring him from frequent business trips. Since Eddie's father spent extended time in Japan, his connections always allowed him the luxury of getting all the best electronics that Japan had to offer before being available on the American market.

Eddie strolled up to Azriel with his posse close behind. The three other boys, Bernie Claxton, Dirk Platt and Cory Ames, hung onto Eddie's words as if each one were a new revelation. It was debatable whether they truly liked Eddie, but they were certainly attracted to all the neat stuff he always had. They also liked the fact that Eddie had little respect for anyone or anything. Azriel had, on a few occasions, witnessed firsthand the boy's cruelty. He had harassed another classmate for two semesters before the boy, tired of the persecution, transferred to another school. On another occasion, he and his gang of young hoodlums had treed a raccoon and kept throwing rocks at it as it hissed down at them. Truth be told, Azriel despised Eddie and his moronic friends so much that he hoped all four would fall off a cliff or be squashed by a rogue meteor.

Eddie stood, his feet firmly planted, and faced Azriel with an arrogant sneer. "Hey Ass-real, or is that *Real Ass*! I heard you didn't get what you wanted for your birthday!"

"Yeah, you heard right. Are you done?"

"Well, I got one from my father, and it wasn't even my birthday. Oh, I'm sorry. I forgot—you don't have a father."

The three boys behind Eddie laughed in derision.

"So what! My father died in a battle. He was a hero—more than I can say for your father. All he does is buy you things. That's probably so he doesn't have to spend any time with a loser."

Azriel must have struck a raw nerve. Eddie straightened his back and postured, drawing closer with a threatening stance.

"Wanna make something of it—jerk?"

Within moments, Jasper and Albert were by Azriel's side, ready to rumble should the situation require. But before the argument could escalate, Mr. Jacklin, Azriel's English teacher on yard duty, strode up.

"Is there a problem here, Mr. Kingsley?"

"No sir," Azriel replied cheerfully and smiled, just to further annoy Eddie.

"Well?" Mr. Jacklin turned and stared down Eddie.

"No sir," he muttered, but glared with cold hatred at Azriel.

"Then line up for class." Mr. Jacklin shook his head with disapproval as he headed toward the main entrance of the school. The warning bell rang, and all the students jockeyed for position.

Eddie, however, leaned forward until his nose nearly touched Azriel's.

"You're dead, Ass-real. You'd better hope I don't find you alone."

"Yeah? Just try it, butt wipe!"

A sharp look from Mr. Jacklin, and the small group disbanded. As Eddie and his friends walked toward the entrance, he purposely bumped into Camille, the strange, quiet girl, knocking her books from her grasp.

Azriel muttered to Albert, "What a jerk. I hate that kid." He bent down and helped Camille gather her books and papers.

"Sorry," Azriel shrugged. "He's an idiot."

Camille didn't reply. Her eyes began to well up, but she gave a hint of a smile before blushing and running to the main entrance.

"Geez, what was that?" Jasper grimaced comically.

"What do you think, you moron." Albert replied. "She's sweet on Azriel."

"No, she's not!" Azriel defended hotly.

"Yeah, well, either way she's just—weird. She never says a word. Doesn't talk to anybody."

"That's true, but maybe you'd be the same way if you were always being picked on. She has no parents. I heard they were killed in an accident." Azriel suddenly thought about his own father, whom he had never met, and felt a twinge of sadness.

"Yeah?" Albert said as they headed to room 109. "I also heard that she lives with her two aunts. They say that both of them are really strange."

"I don't know," Azriel whispered as he sat at his school desk. "Either way, I still feel bad for her."

The din of voices suddenly quieted when Miss Roberts walked in. She smiled cheerfully at her students and sat at her desk. Only a year out of completing college and her internship, she was young and pretty with curly blonde hair and sparkling blue eyes. Adored by most of the boys and girls, the eighth graders particularly liked the fact that she made every lesson interesting, taking great joy in discovery. It was the best of luck to be in her class. Not like Mr.

Ortega, the other eighth-grade science teacher, who was old and close to retirement. Jasper, the older of the two, had the misfortune of being in Ortega's class. Being only ten months apart from his brother, though in the same grade, prevented them from being in the same class. He told Azriel that Mr. Ortega was boring and hated kids. It was also the reason why Jasper more often than not wound up in detention. He couldn't help but ruffle Mr. Ortega's feathers at every opportunity.

Miss Roberts quieted the class down and waited as the PA crackled and hissed before Mr. Wilson, the school principal, ordered all to rise for the Pledge of Allegiance. After the usual announcements, the loudspeaker went silent with an annoying click. Miss Roberts waited for Eddie and Dirk to stop whispering. Their heads were together while Dirk pointed at something Camille was wearing.

"Mr. Breck and Mr. Platt, is there anything you wish to share with the class?" Miss Roberts said firmly.

"No ma'am," They mumbled.

"Hmm. Eddie, I want you up front where I can keep an eye on you."

His face red with humiliation, Eddie exhaled forcefully before moving to the front row-seat directly before Miss Roberts's desk.

"Now I have a wonderful announcement. I've canceled Friday's science quiz."

The room suddenly erupted with cheering.

"Shh, shh!" Miss Roberts smiled, quieting the class while gesturing with her hands. "Instead, we'll be going on a field trip. I have received special permission for this class to hike through Holloway Nature Preserve. I will need to have these permission slips filled out and returned by Wednesday. You will also need good hiking shoes and a warm jacket. I've been told it can get chilly there. Miss McElven, would you hand these out?"

Camille's eyes went wide with anxiety. She always preferred to remain hidden in the back of the room, hating having attention drawn to her. It would also mean having to go near Eddie Breck.

She sullenly took the slips from Miss Roberts and quickly passed them out. She bristled as she came close to Eddie's desk.

She quickly dropped the slip on his desk but was so nervous that the paper fell to the floor. She bent down to get it and her necklace—a silver star within a circle—fell from her blouse. With a blush, she nervously tucked it back in.

"Weirdo." Eddie whispered and sneered.

Frightened, Camille quickly finished her task and returned to her seat in the back of the room.

It was lunch break, and the students had a choice of eating in the cafeteria or sitting outside, since the weather had turned unusually warm for an early spring day, and most took advantage of their good fortune. Azriel sat at his favorite spot on the bleachers with Jasper and Albert. On the opposite side of the bench, Camille sat quietly, eating her lunch while reading a book. But every so often, she would surreptitiously peek over at Azriel. It made him uncomfortable, particularly since Albert and Jasper now had something new to tease him about. It wasn't that Camille was ugly or anything like that; in fact, Azriel secretly thought she was kind of cute, but being considered the most unpopular girl in the eighth grade made anyone who even spoke to her a target of ridicule. Azriel already had enough to contend with.

After eating, Jasper pulled out two baseball gloves from his backpack and tossed one to Azriel. Likewise, Albert removed a glove and ball from his satchel and soon the three were having a lively game of catch.

As they tossed the ball to each other, Azriel couldn't help but notice that Eddie and his band of hooligans had strolled up to Camille and surrounded her in a somewhat threatening manner, for the sole purpose of giving her a bad time. Azriel couldn't help thinking of wolves on the prowl, circling their prey, but immediately repented of it. Wolves were far more noble creatures than Eddie and his stupid friends. He drew closer and kept an ear out as he threw the ball back to Albert.

Camille stood to leave, but her way was blocked by the four boys. Azriel stopped to listen, leaving Albert holding the ball. Sensing trouble, Jasper and Albert walked up to Azriel and observed.

"What's this you're wearing?" Eddie grinned maliciously as he grabbed at the chain around Camille's neck.

"Nothing. Leave me alone!" She backed away, pushing him off, but Cory flanked her, preventing escape. Before she could tuck the pendant back in her blouse, Bernie grabbed her by the wrists.

"Hey, look guys, it's a pentagram. My mom says that it's a bad symbol! What are you, some kind of freak, Camille?"

She attempted to wrestle from his grasp, but he was bigger and stronger.

"I know," Bernie laughed, "She's a witch. "At my church, they say witches are evil. People who matter say they mess with things they shouldn't."

Camille began to cry. "Stop it! You're hurting me."

"Hey Dirk—I bet she's an atheist." Cory snickered.

"What's an atheist?" Dirk asked.

"Means she doesn't believe what everybody else does, stupid!"

Eddie came even closer to her as she squirmed in fear. "You an atheist, witch? I bet you don't believe in any of it, huh? You know what that means? Means you're wrong—and everybody knows it."

Watching her humiliation, Azriel couldn't refrain from coming to Camille's defense, even if it meant being teased by the other kids. Eddie's actions were wrong and inexcusable.

"Hey! Leave her alone, jerk!"

"What's the matter, Ass-real, she your girlfriend?"

"No, you're just an idiot and a bully. And I don't like you!"

The boys turned their attention from Camille to Azriel. Jasper and Albert were on each side of Azriel ready to fight should the need arise.

Eddie grabbed Azriel by the collar. "Now it's time for your beating, you friggin' cockroach."

Azriel shoved hard and broke Eddie's hold, but the larger boy pushed back and Azriel nearly lost his footing. He was about to charge head-on when Mr. Jacklin came from the front of the yard. He held Eddie and Azriel apart.

"Break it up, boys. You know the rules about fighting and rough play. Next time, it's down to the office for both of you. Is that clear?"

"Yes sir," they both muttered hotly.

"Good," Mr. Jacklin snarled. "I don't want you within twenty-five feet of each other, understood?"

"Yes sir."

"Are you all right, Miss McElven?"

She nodded.

Mr. Jacklin ushered the boys away leaving Azriel, Jasper and Albert with Camille.

It didn't stop the other boys from pointing and laughing at Azriel.

"Idiots." Azriel shook his head. "I'm sorry about them."

"Why? They're not your responsibility." Camille sniffed and wiped her tears with a sleeve.

"Yeah, you're right. I just feel bad. And I'm tired of seeing them pick on you. Are you okay now?"

She nodded. "Thanks for helping me."

From several feet away, Eddie gestured wildly to the amusement of his friends. He pantomimed giving loud, sloppy kisses and hugs, trying to get a rise from Camille and Azriel.

"Moron!" Camille scowled. "I wish a big ol' bird would drop a fat, wet turd on him."

Azriel thought about that image for a moment and couldn't help but laugh. "Yeah, that would be great."

As they agreed wholeheartedly, a rather sizeable seagull flew overhead and circled Camille and Azriel. Oddly, it seemed to wink at them before swooping toward Eddie. It planted a large wet mass of crap squarely on the boy's head.

Eddie felt around his scalp with horror and disgust. "Ugh!" he grunted. "Gross!"

Watching, Camille covered her mouth with surprise. "Oh my!" She giggled. Azriel laughed too. The coincidence was astounding.

But soon the seagull was joined by several more. Magpies, hawks, ravens, crows, starlings—they all flew from the stand of conifers adjacent to the school yard and began circling Eddie and his buddies. As one, they all dove and launched turds on the boys to their humiliation—and to the amusement of every other kid in the school yard. The birds continued to chase the boys down as everyone laughed and hooted, pointing at the spectacle. Humiliated, Eddie screamed as he tried to cover up his face with his arms.

"Get them off me! Get them off!"

The birds continued to dive-bomb the four boys until they were completely covered in white slimy goo. The punishment concluded only when the boys made it to the safety of the school entrance.

The other kids moved out of their way, laughing in derision, holding their noses.

Camille and Azriel looked at each other with amazement. How in the world could anything like that happen? Wishes generally didn't come true, and when they did, not with such immediacy.

"That was great!" Azriel laughed. "My mom will never believe it!"

"Neither will my aunts!" Camille's eyes sparkled. It was the first time Azriel had ever seen Camille happy.

"You should do that more often." Azriel said.

"What?" Her grin faltered.

"Smile. You have a nice smile."

Camille blushed as the bell rang. They headed back to class.

The class lined up as three o'clock approached, buzzing with anticipation. The bell rang, and Miss Roberts released her students, though not without calling out one last reminder.

"Remember to get your permission slips signed and returned by tomorrow," she called out cheerfully. Her eighth graders poured out the door and headed to their respective buses. Azriel found his seat by the window next to Albert and Jasper. Julia filed in behind them and as usual, Camille sat in the very back, apart from the others. Azriel glanced tentatively toward the rear of the bus, then back at Jasper and Albert.

"What are you doing?" Albert whispered.

"I think we should invite her to sit with us." He whispered back.

"Why?" Albert wasn't at all happy about it. "She's weird!"

"So are you! We're all weird! Besides, she's really kind of nice." Azriel called out. "Hey Camille!"

Eyes wide, she looked at Azriel, suspicious and startled by being addressed at all. Her words nearly caught in her throat. "Are you talking to me?"

"I don't see anyone else here named Camille!" Azriel said with a wry smile. "Of course I'm talking to you."

"What do you want?" She asked quietly, suddenly afraid that Azriel was going to make fun of her.

"Why do you always sit back there by yourself?"

"I don't know," she said in a small voice.

"Then why don't you come sit with us? It's no fun being by yourself."

"Really?" Her voice sounded hopeful.

Azriel smiled. "Yeah, really!" He elbowed Albert in the arm.

"Yeah, come join us," Albert said with feigned enthusiasm.

Camille grabbed her backpack and happily took the seat next to Julia.

"Hi." Camille said.

"Hi yourself," Julia smiled. "Pretty cool what happened to Eddie Breck and his idiot friends. How'd you do that?"

Camille shrugged. "I didn't do anything. It just happened."

"That's not what I heard." Julia said. "Azriel told me you made a wish and it happened just like that!"

"Honestly, I didn't do anything. It was just a coincidence."

"Sure it was!" Albert interjected. "Hey—is it true you're a witch?"

Azriel punched Albert in the arm.

"Ow! What was that for?"

"No, it's okay," Camille answered. "My aunts follow the Wiccan path and are teaching me the craft. So I guess I'm a witch. Does that scare you?"

"Not really. I think it's kind of cool. Hey, can you turn Jasper into a newt, or frog, or maybe something really repulsive?"

"No," she giggled. "It really doesn't work that way. Besides, if I could, I would've done that to Eddie Breck a long time ago!"

They all laughed at the thought. Before long, the bus rolled to a stop at the long driveway leading to the Cunninghams' house. Albert, Jasper, and Julia filed out, leaving Azriel and Camille sitting in adjacent seats.

The bus lurched forward again, nearly bouncing Camille out of her seat as it struck a massive pothole in the dirt road. Camille looked at her feet, masking her shyness, and blushed through the silence.

Azriel broke the ice. "So, Camille, do you like baseball?"

"Who doesn't?" Her face screwed up with chagrin.

"What's your team?"

"Mariners, of course."

"Cool." Azriel thought for a moment, then cleared his voice. "How would you like to come to a game next week? I got box seats for my birthday."

Her eyes widened hopefully and then narrowed. "Are you messing with me? Why didn't you ask Albert and Jasper?"

"Because I only have one extra ticket. Besides, I think you're nice!"

"Well…"

"Look, it doesn't mean you're my girlfriend or anything like that. I just think it would be fun."

"Well, okay. I'll have to ask my aunts first, but I think they'll be all right with it."

"Good. Here's my stop. I'll see you tomorrow."

"Okay."

Camille stared after Azriel, trying not to melt in her seat. He was the nicest boy she had ever met. She wondered why they had never spoken before—until now.

Upon returning home, Camille placed her satchel of books on the dining room table. She found Aunt Penelope stirring the contents of a sizeable cast-iron pot. Sanitized jars were laid out on the counter, while lids and rings boiled in a colander, submerged in a huge, enameled pot.

"Glad you're home, dear. My arms need a break." Aunt Penny kissed Camille on the forehead. "Would you mind stirring this for me? It's almost done, so don't let it burn!"

Camille sniffed at the mixture. "Mmm! Fruit butter. Pears, plums, cinnamon, sugar, honey."

"What else, dear? You missed something," Aunt Penny quizzed. "Go ahead—taste!"

Camille took a spoonful and blew on it before tasting. She knitted her eyebrows, trying to identify the subtle missing ingredient.

"Hmm," she mused. "A touch of basil?"

"Good!" Aunt Penny bubbled. "Anything else?"

"I'm not sure. There seems to be something... "

"Use all your senses, child—your inner ones as well."

Camille hesitated to answer. What was that phantom flavor, she wondered.

"It's too hard, Auntie. I don't know."

"Now, child, remember what I've always told you."

"Yes," Camille rolled her eyes and repeated her aunt's usual words, even using a good approximation of Aunt Penelope's squeaky voice. "A good witch is not merely born. A good witch is made!"

Penelope giggled at Camille's parody. "Naughty girl," she said.

Camille finally made the connection. "Cardamom!" she said proudly. "It's cardamom."

"Do you know why?"

"Basil is to bring wealth. Cardamom is to spread love!"

"Excellent, dear! We'll make a good witch of you yet. Now don't stop stirring."

"Auntie Pen, where did you get plums this time of year?"

"I had them shipped in from California. We were down to only one jar in the cold cellar. I just *had* to make more!"

"I thought I heard talking in here!" Aunt Daphne strolled in, laden down with a huge basket of wild mushrooms.

"My, my, my!" She chortled happily. "The woods are just loaded this spring with morels and chanterelles! They will be perfect with dinner tonight!"

"Hi, Aunt Daffie!"

"Hi, pumpkin! How was school today?"

"Wonderful!" Camille smiled broadly and began to hum a lively tune as she stirred the pot. Every so often, she smiled to herself as if remembering something joyful.

Daphne and Penelope glanced at each other with wonderment. Camille seldom had anything good to say about school. They knew that, for the most part, she was unhappy with the arrangement. The kids at school were generally mean to her; Penelope had even considered homeschooling Camille, but didn't feel she was qualified to teach her anything other than the arcane arts. Penelope was a master of herbal lore and potions. She also was a genius at spellcrafting. Daphne, on the other hand, had a knack for astrology and divination. Many from her inner circle would come from miles around to have her read their cards. She also had one of the finest collections of tarot decks in the world, some dating back to the fifteenth century.

Looking at the sisters, no one would ever suspect that they were related—except when hearing them speak. Both spoke with a thick brogue. Penelope was short and stout, with rosy cheeks and a lively, easy smile. In comparison, Daphne was tall and gaunt, with a rather severe, pointy nose. Her soft eyes, however, hinted at the gentle heart she kept inside. Another difference between the sisters was that Penelope had flaming red hair, while her sister's hair was dark brown, nearly black, like Camille's. Both, however, were unusually kind and shared a mischievous sense of fun. As a result, Camille was most comfortable when at home.

Camille continued to hum happily, and her two aunts stared at her with amusement.

"You look like the cat that ate the canary. So out with it—what happened today?" Penelope demanded.

Camille's eyes glistened with glee as she recounted the tale. It didn't take much coaxing on Daphne's part to get the full story.

"So what you're saying, child, is that a swarm of birds just swooped down and attacked those mean boys? Amazing!"

"Aunt Daffie, did I do that? Did I make it happen?"

Daphne mused for a moment and shook her head doubtfully. "I don't think so. Your skills aren't that well developed yet. It would take years of psychic work with animals to make that happen. Tell me about this boy you met."

Camille smiled. "Well, it's not like I've just met him. He's on the same bus as me. It's just that we finally spoke today. He came to my rescue when that jerk, Eddie, was saying awful things to me. Azriel almost got into a fight with him to protect me. He was so noble!"

"What else did he do?" Auntie Pen asked, amused at seeing Camille so clearly smitten.

"Earlier, he picked up my books when Eddie knocked them out of my hands. He was so nice to me. He's really cute, too. He has dark hair and dreamy grey eyes. They're kind of different, too, with little spots of gold in them." Camille's face took on a faraway expression as she spoke.

"Oh, my, my! You've got it bad, Camille. Penelope, I think our niece is in love!"

"Am not!" Camille defended. "He's just—nice!"

"Of course he is!" Penelope and Daphne said in unison. They smiled knowingly at each other.

"Well anyway, when I said that a big bird should drop a turd on Eddie, Azriel agreed and said it would be great. Then it just happened! Pretty neat, huh?"

"Pretty neat, indeed." Daphne said and looked at Penelope with an expression that silently conveyed their need to discuss this phenomenon.

"He also asked me if I would go to a Seattle Mariners game with him."

"Really?" Penelope nearly gasped.

"Can I go?"

"Of course you can go. We'd like to meet this remarkable young man."

"Auntie, it's not like he's my boyfriend."

"Nevertheless, child. It's our duty to make sure he's not a scoundrel!"

"Auntie Pen!"

"Those are the rules." Penelope giggled impishly then pulled Daphne into the adjoining room. She peeked into the kitchen at Camille stirring the fruit butter, then quietly closed the door.

Penelope whispered, "Could the boy be the one we were told about?"

"Well, it *is* why we were sent here—to watch for the one who would come—the one who would bring Magick back into the world. The Magus told us so!" Daphne said with excitement. "The coven will be so pleased."

"Now let's not be hasty, sister. We really need to see the boy before we say anything—and before we speak to the High Magus."

"Then it's agreed. We must see this young man before we say anything. But I must say I've been missing Ireland all too much lately. If he is the one, then our job is done. It will be nice to go home. I feel like we've been exiled." Daphne smiled ruefully.

"It's only temporary, Daffie. Besides, it was a good thing we were here, not with Camille losing her parents like that! The poor dear. Why they ever decided to go on that stupid African safari, I'll never understand. Flash floods—bodies never found. So sad." Penelope choked back the onset of tears. "I sure miss our baby sister. And Shelly was such a talented witch! Do you think there's ever a chance they might be found—alive?"

"Not likely. I'm only glad that Shelly left Camille with us when they departed, otherwise she would have had no one—an orphan."

"Aye, sister. That she would have."

"So put it out of your mind, Daffie. We aren't going anywhere until Camille is ready to be on her own. We owe it to her—and to Shelly. Besides, Camille has finally found a friend. We'll not be taking that from her. We're staying put!"

"Aye, Penny. You're right—you're right!"

Azriel sat at the kitchen table while Abelene diced asparagus and cheese for a baked pastry. He opened a book to begin his homework, but found himself distracted by the day's events. As he thought about it, he couldn't help but smile.

Abelene placed the knife on the counter and sat opposite Azriel. "I know you're just dying to tell me what happened at school today, right?" She waited for his response.

"Mom, do you remember me mentioning that quiet girl on the bus?"

"Uh huh," she nodded, rolling out dough for the pastries.

"Well, that idiot Eddie, and his moronic friends were really roughing her up today. It really pissed me off, so I went to her defense—even though you've told me time and again not to get into fights."

Abelene's face softened. "Oh, honey, there's a time for everything. Sometimes taking a stand is necessary. So what happened?"

"Mr. Jacklin came and broke it up before anyone could throw a punch—and believe me, I really wanted to. Matter of fact, I've wanted to for a long time. Someone needs to put Eddie Breck in his place. Anyway, that would have been the end of it—except for what happened next."

Azriel explained in detail how Camille made a wish and how the birds immediately attacked Eddie and his friends in retaliation for their mean behavior.

Abelene giggled. She nodded, staring at Azriel thoughtfully.

Azriel asked, "Mom, Camille admitted to being a witch. Could she have made that happen without knowing how?"

"No, dear—you did." Abelene said with certainty. "Though I'm surprised your talents would have emerged so soon."

"Huh?"

"Son, haven't you learned anything? All those things I've told you since you were old enough to understand are not just stories. Camille is human, and though humans possess some magickal ability that can be learned, you are Ferrishyn!"

"Yeah, I know. It's my true surname, and I've kept that secret for as long as I can remember!"

"And that is well. Ferrishyn is your race. *Kingsley* is the name I've taken—and given you—so you always remember you are of the royal line. In the world you come from, we Ferrishyn are the most powerful of the elfin realm. We have a natural affinity with magick, nature, and woodland creatures."

"Then why haven't I seen you work these wonders around here?"

"Oh, I do—in my own subtle way. That's why our woods are so special. It's just that humans fear what they don't understand. Just like that boy, Eddie. He's already learned fear from his church. His teachers and parents have taught him that magick and witchcraft are evil, so he acts out his fear on people like Camille. Don't forget— our identities must remain secret. We are fugitives in this world!"

"So you won't work any magick because you don't want to scare our neighbors?"

"Partially. I won't because I want to protect you from harm. Perhaps I should have told you sooner. The last thing I want is for you to become a target."

"So how did it happen—you know, the thing with the birds?"

Abelene smiled impishly. "The best explanation is that you leaked!"

"Leaked?" He glanced down at his pants. "Did not!"

"No, not that, silly. Your brain leaked! When Camille suggested that a bird should crap on Eddie, you were already in an emotionally heightened state, having nearly gotten into a fight. When you agreed it would be great to see, you unwittingly caused it to be!"

"Really?"

"Of course!" Abelene grinned. "The birds heard your thoughts and acted on them."

"So I can affect any animal?"

"More or less…"

"And people?"

"No. That's harder—and also forbidden."

"Why?"

Abelene sighed. "Azriel, all creatures have a right to exist on their own terms. It's in a bird's nature to fly, sing, and well, poop!" she giggled. "But you see, it's not in a bear's nature to, say, knit a sweater. So you couldn't direct a bear to do so. He wouldn't be able to. But you *could* have him bring you a comb of wild honey."

"I think I get it. I'd have to give a suggestion based only on what that creature is capable of doing."

"Now you get it! But the thing with humans—they are as intelligent as the Ferrishyn and the Elven folk—in fact, all magickal folk. They just think in different terms. To compel a human to commit an act, regardless of intent, is evil and forbidden because you've taken away his free will."

"So I couldn't compel Eddie to, let's say, jump off a cliff?"

"No—and I know you'd like to, dear—but his own self-preservation would prevent that. You also couldn't compel a person to kill another—unless it was already in that person's nature to do so. Therein lies the danger. One could never know the depth of a person's sense of right and wrong. A person without a moral center could become a monster."

"I see."

"No, you don't, Azriel. You must never—ever—use your abilities on anyone, even if you think you are acting out of good. Your actions can have dire consequences. Very dire! Aside from being wrong, people are unpredictable. What you expect may lead to a far different result. Are we clear on that?"

"Yes, Mom." Azriel nodded. "Can I try something?"

"As long as it doesn't harm anything! You'll need to learn to control your ability."

Azriel smiled and released a thought. Within moments, a hummingbird flew through the open kitchen window and hovered before Abelene's eyes. She slowly lifted her outstretched hand, and the tiny bird alit on her finger. Abelene laughed with joy, then released the bird with a thought. It flew back to the open woodlands.

"You exhibit quite a natural talent, son. We will work together to develop it."

"Oh, Mom? Camille is coming with us to the game tomorrow. I invited her."

"Did you!"

"Yeah, she's kind of nice."

"Well, she's more than welcome to come."

Azriel returned to his homework while Abelene completed rolling the pastries and slid the pan into the oven. He finished his assignment and made his way into his bedroom, the wonderful aromas of Abelene's cooking wafting through the house. He needed to think about this new talent he had and soon realized he really knew nothing of his own heritage, despite the stories his mother had often told of his world. The huge tome that Uncle Nicodemus had given him still remained unopened on his desk. Azriel stared at the voluminous book for a long moment before deciding. He picked up the crystal plate lying beside it and opened the book to the first page.

Gift of the Amulet

Chapter 3

Much to Azriel's surprise, Camille arrived an hour earlier than expected. He waited out front for Uncle Nick to drive up, fully anticipating the distinctive sound of the old man's Model T engine echoing through the trees that lined the dirt driveway. Azriel nearly jumped when he felt a tap on his shoulder. He turned to find Camille grinning broadly at him. Her hair was tied back in a ponytail pulled through the adjusting band of her Mariners baseball cap.

"Hey—where did you come from?"

"I cut through the woods."

"My woods?"

"Well, sort of. Haven't you ever wondered what's beyond the stream on your property line?"

"No, not really."

"Humph." Camille furrowed brow, feigning disappointment.

"What?" Azriel said, slightly annoyed.

"Bet you didn't know I'm your closest neighbor. If you take the path from your back door to the stream at the end of your property, then hop the fence, you'll come to another stream. If you follow the stream to the left, you'll see a wooden bridge. Cross that bridge, keep going, and you'll eventually come to my house!"

"That's your place? I thought it was vacant. And where did the bridge come from?"

"I built it," Camille said proudly. "You're not very observant, are you, Azriel Kingsley?"

"Yeah, well I've had a lot to think about lately. Come on. I want you to meet my mother."

Azriel led Camille through the front door and into the kitchen, where Abelene was putting the finishing touches on four sandwiches. Camille scanned the kitchen in awe. It was so similar to her aunt's kitchen that it could have been cut from the same mold. Bunches of wild herbs were tied and hung from a central wooden beam. Clay jars upon clay jars were lined up on various shelves. An eclectic collection of pottery—none of it matching—nonetheless felt perfectly at home in the cozy room. Abelene had slices of black bread—obviously home-baked—laid out on the table. They were heaped with savory cuts of roast beef and spread with French brie. She sprinkled generous handfuls of alfalfa sprouts and a sprig of cilantro on each, finishing the culinary masterpieces. Camille watched, fascinated. Azriel hadn't told her that his mother was so beautiful. She appeared stately and poised; even while performing the simple task of making sandwiches, she carried a regal air.

"Mom, this is Camille," Azriel said, breaking the silence. Camille blushed.

"Azriel has had much to say about you, dear," Abelene said with a smile. "Would you help me finish boxing these lunches? It's a long drive, and we're certain to get hungry. There are a few pretty rest stops along the way to Seattle."

"Yes Ma'am."

"Oh, you don't have to call me Ma'am—Abelene will do. Get four pears from the bin beside the fridge. Azriel, grab a handful of cookies."

Abelene packaged everything into a sizeable wicker basket, along with a half gallon of juice and a bottle of wine.

"There—all set to go. So, Camille, would you like a slice of cake?"

Although she had just eaten breakfast, she couldn't resist. Abelene cut three slices of spiced cake and sat across from the girl. Camille took a large bite, and suddenly her face lit up with joy.

"Mmm! This is delicious. Hmm, I taste clove, catnip, honeysuckle, witchgrass and..." Camille took another bite and closed her eyes to heighten her sense of taste. "Ah! Meadowsweet!" She smiled proudly. "All of them are for bringing happiness!"

"Interesting..." Abelene said with amusement. "You're quite talented! Who taught you to identify herbs—particularly meadowsweet? It's quite rare in these parts."

"My aunts Pen and Daffie, are teaching me the basics of the herb lore."

"Well, my dear, your talent is far from basic—but you missed one!"

Azriel gave his mother a peculiar look as he watched the exchange; she was normally quite private about her arcane abilities.

"Go on," Abelene coaxed. "Take another bite."

Camille nibbled off another piece and concentrated on the flavor. "Yes, I do taste something different—strange. Sort of tangy, with a slightly bitter aftertaste. It's subtle. What is it?"

"It's a secret." Abelene teased.

Camille glanced down, pretending disappointment. She looked up at Abelene with the poutiest eyes she could muster.

Abelene giggled. "Okay, I'll tell you. But you must be sworn to secrecy."

Camille smiled shyly.

"Come on—pinkie swear!"

Abelene and Camille hooked fingers together and twisted.

"The secret ingredient is called Tienchi! It's not native to the area—only grows in China—so I cultivate my own. I'll give you a cutting if you wish, but you can't share it with anyone else, promise?"

"Promise," Camille said resolutely.

"So, what other skills do you have, dear?"

"Well..." Camille was uncertain how much she should reveal, particularly to one she had just met, but Abelene seemed so trustworthy. Yet her aunts had always warned her to be secretive about her knowledge of the arcane arts. For one, it gave Camille a particular advantage over non-magick users.

"You can trust me, dear. I also practice the magickal arts."

"I kind of thought so..."

"Really?" Abelene replied with amusement.

"Yeah. It's your woods. They sort of...glow!"

"Indeed. Very few actually can see that unless they're attuned. What else can you see?"

"I see spirits and other things. There are actually quite a few fairies and sprites that make their home in these woods—yours and mine."

"Yes dear—I invited them. They protect the forest!" Abelene's eyes sparkled with delight. "I think you and I are going to become fast friends. Azriel, you make sure to bring this lovely young lady around anytime you want. She's a natural. Now go outside and wait to greet your errant uncle."

Azriel and Camille left the house and sat on the porch swing.

"Your Mom's nice," Camille said with candor. "Do you use magick too?"

"Yeah, it's sort of a natural ability in my family."

"How come you never told anybody?"

"The same reason you didn't. The kids at school wouldn't understand."

"Do Albert and Jasper know?"

"I think they suspect it, but are afraid to ask."

"Maybe we should teach them."

"Are you crazy? Both are—as my mom says—loose cannons. They'd probably hurt themselves."

Camille giggled just as Uncle Nick drove up in a 1959 pink Cadillac convertible.

"Wow! Cool car!" Camille's eyes widened with delight.

"Ugh…" Azriel grumbled. "Why does it have to be pink? It's a girl's color."

"I like it!"

"Yeah, you would."

Uncle Nick stepped out of the car wearing the Mariners team colors of navy, teal and silver. He tossed Azriel a baseball.

"Here, you keep that safe. It's pretty rare."

Azriel glanced down at the ball and read the signature.

"No way!" He smiled in disbelief at the name boldly signed in blue ink.

"Let's see." Camille stood close wide-eyed at the name *Babe Ruth* scrawled across the aged creamy white surface.

"Yup. The Sultan of Swat signed that very ball for me the opening day of the 1923 World Series at the Polo Grounds."

Azriel sighed and rolled his eyes. Camille glanced at him and giggled. "Don't believe him—he does this all the time. Uncle Nick would have you believe he's a thousand years old!"

Nicodemus laughed and roughed up Azriel's hair. "Well, maybe I am," he said before thrusting out his hand. "And who's this lovely young lady?"

"Camille, sir." She extended her hand for a proper handshake, but Nicodemus kissed it like a nobleman. She grinned and blushed.

Just then, Abelene strolled out the front door with the basket hooked into the crook of her arm. She wore a straw hat tied with a black ribbon beneath her chin.

"Are we all ready to leave? I'd sure like to have enough time to spend at Pike Place Market. I need a few items I just can't get anywhere else."

Nicodemus opened the passenger side door with an eloquent bow. "Madam, your chariot awaits." He parodied a thick British accent.

"Nick, you're such a dear!" Abelene patted his cheek tenderly as she settled into the front.

Azriel screwed up his face and acted as though he was going to gag amid Camille's laughter.

"Just get in, dummy! Uncle Nick pushed Azriel toward the back seat. Camille climbed in next to him. With the press of a button, the convertible top suddenly lifted and folded itself into the receptacle behind the back seat.

"Neat!" Camille smiled and looked up into the sky as the car sped off.

All around the box seats and behind, T-Mobile Park was filled to capacity. The Mariners had struggled through eight innings against their bitter rivals, the New York Yankees. It was top of the eighth and the Mariners were tied with the Yankees, four to four. At the plate, Yankees top slugger, Mel West faced two outs on a full count with runners on second and third.

The moment was tense as Azriel watched in despair while pitcher Joe Philippe hurled a screaming fastball. West's bat connected with a loud crack, and the ball soared into an open gap between left and center field. By all appearances, it was impossible for either fielder to make the play. Without warning, however, a stiff breeze blew in from the north, and the ball suddenly arced toward left field—straight into the waiting glove of the Mariners outfielder. The crowd roared with joy as the side was retired.

Abelene glanced sideways at Azriel with suspicion. Was it possible her son had manipulated the weather? It wasn't likely. That skill usually didn't emerge until a much later—usually in one's thirties. She kept a close eye on Azriel.

In the bottom of the eighth, Yankees hurler, Bill Grant, faced the Mariners toughest lineup of hitters. After a line drive down center put a man on second, he struck out the next batter. But now he faced Tim Frankel, who had been hot the entire game. He opted for an intentional walk. The crowd around Azriel booed and hissed. With the inning tense, Grant hurled two perfect curveballs at Mariners slugger Isao Mataguchi, running the count to 0–2. But on the next pitch, low and inside, Mataguchi slammed the ball down the right-field line for a triple. Two men scored with Mataguchi now on third. With the Mariners ahead six runs to four, the crowd was on its feet in a cheering frenzy. Camille, seated next to Azriel, jumped up and down with delight; she impulsively gave Azriel a hug and hooted wildly. Abelene, though pleased, bent close to Azriel. "You had better not be doing what I think you're doing," she scolded.

"Me? I'm not doing anything," he avowed, but his smirk told a different story.

Now with two outs, shortstop Ben Willis approached the plate. This wasn't a particularly good development, since his batting average for the past three games had been terrible. He took a few practice swings and waited for the perfect pitch. Two balls and a strike, Bill Grant threw his signature fast ball right down the center line. At 101 miles per hour, his fastball was nearly impossible to hit. Willis, however, connected, and the ball soared toward center field, seemingly destined for the waiting glove of the center fielder pressed against the back wall. Again, however, a gale-force wind blew the ball just two feet further, past the wall and out of reach—

for a home run. The Mariners advanced 8 to 4 over the Yankees. Though the crowd went wild, Abelene glared down at Azriel. She was furious.

"I know you did that."

"You can't prove it," he retorted.

"I felt it. That's cheating, and you know it."

"Yeah? So what are you going to do about it?" Azriel stared at Abelene defiantly. "Are you going to tell the baseball commission? They'll never believe you."

Abelene couldn't believe her ears. Azriel had never exhibited this kind of disrespect. Now that he knew of his natural talents, he was flexing his mental muscle. Abelene needed to put him in his place.

"You'll see what I do about it."

For nearly fourteen years Abelene had kept her abilities in check and never used them to determine the outcome of an event, but Azriel needed to learn a very vital lesson.

"Creenach, veth Chronos!" Abelene shouted. The stadium suddenly grew silent as all activity ceased. Every fan and every player stood frozen, as though Abelene had pressed a pause button on reality. The ball hovered midway between the mound and the plate. Only Abelene and Azriel were aware of the stoppage of time. Even Nicodemus and Camille had been frozen in place. Azriel's face went pale.

"Do you wish to defy me, Azriel?" Abelene stood tall, her face flushed with anger. "I have held my magick in check for your safety, but what you have done today is unconscionable. You are never to use your emerging powers to change what will be—particularly for something so trivial—no matter how slight it is. You may influence, but not manipulate."

"But the Mariners were losing!"

"Then that would have been their fate!"

"Well, what's done is done." He replied belligerently.

"Oh, you think so! You have no idea what I am capable of doing. Let this be a lesson to you!"

Abelene lifted her arms and called out. "Chroneth ish'ma reverti!"

Azriel's skin prickled with the sudden onrush of power blasting through his mother and surging onto the field. In moments, all the actions of the past half hour rewound to the instant when Azriel had manipulated the wind.

It was once again top of the eighth, with two outs. Mel West faced a full count. The Yankees and Mariners were again tied. West slammed the ball into center for a double. It drove in a run.

In the bottom of the eighth, and the Mariners were unable to rally. Three up, three down, and the side was retired. In the top of the ninth, the Yankees scored another run. The Mariners were unable to surge ahead in the ninth, and the Yankees won the game by two runs. Azriel stared in disbelief at the final figures on the scoreboard and then angrily at his mother. He was ready with a caustic comment over her interference, but she suddenly fainted and collapsed back into her seat when she rose to leave. Abelene's face went pale and began to perspire. The release of so much power without preparation had drained her of vital energy.

Nicodemus immediately tended to Abelene, patting her cheeks and helping her revive. He glanced at Azriel, whose guilt-ridden face betrayed his involvement.

Uncle Nick leaned close to Azriel and whispered, "What have you to say, boy?"

"Nothing. I didn't do anything." Azriel defended unconvincingly.

"We'll see about that."

Abelene shook herself awake. For the sake of Nicodemus and Camille, she assured them the episode was past. "I haven't been feeling well," she said. "I just need to drink more water. I've been a bit dehydrated."

Nicodemus wasn't convinced. He knew all too well of Abelene's constitution. Ferrishyn were immune to all illnesses. The proof was evident in Azriel as well, who had never suffered so much as a cold. He let the incident pass fully intending to address the matter later.

The ride home was quiet and a bit strained. Camille thought it was merely due to the Mariners having lost the game. Abelene put on a good show of being a charming hostess to Camille, offering light conversation and good food. Her attitude toward her son, however, remained decidedly frosty. Azriel knew not to expect a thaw for at least a day or two. Not until he made some form of amends.

It would have been difficult to explain to Camille why he was in such a dark mood, so he did his best to lighten his mood for her sake. Midway on the ride home, Camille fell asleep on Azriel's shoulder, but he didn't mind as it would give him some time to reflect on what had occurred. If his mother had the power to abruptly stop time and reverse events, what might he be capable of doing? It was exciting and frightening at the same time. How had Abelene managed to refrain from using her goddess-like powers for the thirteen years of Azriel's life? And why hadn't she ever told him?

Of course, he knew the stories she had recited since he was old enough to understand, but part of him had always doubted, and so the stories took on the form of wild fantasy rather than his true ancestral history. Irrational as it was, Azriel couldn't help but resent the fact that she hadn't told him. Even more so because of what these abilities meant. For one thing, he wouldn't have had to put up with Eddie Breck and his stupid friends. Azriel smiled to himself at the thought of being able to make Eddie's life miserable.

As they approached Harden Lake, Azriel gently nudged Camille awake. She yawned and stretched, then blushed at having used Azriel as a pillow.

"Sorry." She said, smiling self-consciously. "I didn't drool, did I?"

Azriel made a show of wiping his shoulder, then smiled. "Nope—clean as a whistle!"

The pink Cadillac rounded the curve past Azriel's home, and Camille gave directions to her house. A cozy two-story Victorian stood nestled between two sizeable rowan trees in a clearing surrounded by a white picket fence. It did nothing to deter a deer, which ran off at the approach of the car's high beams.

From behind the porch light, Camille noticed a curtain shift as Aunt Daffie peek through.

After the car rolled to a stop, Camille stepped out and smiled. "Thanks so much for such a wonderful day."

"You're quite welcome, dear." Abelene replied graciously. "Now, make sure not to be a stranger. You're welcome anytime. I'd love to meet your aunts, too. Tell them I'll invite them for tea soon. Maybe we'll swap recipes."

"I sure would like that. Thanks, Uncle Nick. Thanks, Azriel. I'll see you at school, okay."

"Sure, I'll see you Monday."

Nicodemus waited until Camille was safely inside before circling around and driving back to Azriel's home in silence. Once inside, Azriel was about to retreat to his room to brood in privacy, but Abelene ordered him to sit at the table as she put up a pot for tea.

She began speaking without preface. "Do you think this has anything to do with a stupid ball game, Azriel? It doesn't. It has everything to do with you!"

Azriel looked up sulkily at his mother. Nicodemus, however, glanced between them with confusion. "Would you mind telling me what's going on?"

"Yes," Abelene fumed. "My son manipulated the game so the Mariners could win!"

"But they didn't," Nicodemus retorted.

"Yes they did—in an altered reality. I reversed it so it never happened. That's why you don't remember it."

"I see. Although it would have been nice to see them win!" He winked at Azriel, who smiled back. Abelene shot Nicodemus a stern glance.

"Stop it. This is serious," she snapped then leveled her gaze at Azriel. She softened her stance, however, and sat opposite him. "You aren't even aware of the power you possess, and perhaps that is my fault for not telling you as much. You see, Azriel, if you were in Aralia right now, you would already be preparing to take the Vow of Peace and Prudence—non-interference. All Ferrishyn take this vow when they turn fifteen years of age. This is done because of the devastation one of our ancestors caused many thousands of years ago, when our world was split apart. Aralia is a potent place. If not for the Vow, our worlds would crumble into chaos and destruction. During the time of the split, a few powerful wizards remained in the world of men and manipulated events for their own selfish desires. Over time, many either destroyed themselves or were hunted down and silenced by Hunters—Avatars from our world. They sacrificed themselves for the safety of both worlds. But some of their quarry escaped and remain hidden in the world of men. Because of that, I've kept you concealed for your safety. Whether you know it or not, son, there are forces out there that would want you and me dead."

Azriel paled, but Nicodemus interrupted Abelene. "Then you did a very foolish thing, my dear, by altering time—even if only for briefly. Those dark lords may now be alerted to your presence."

Abelene looked down, sullen. "True. I lost my temper, and for that I'm sorry. There's no excuse." She rose and poured out three cups of tea, then returned to her seat across from Azriel and took his hand. "You think I've been telling you all the stories of Aralia for your amusement? This is a dangerous world, son. There are men who would wish to harness your abilities and use you for their own gain. That is not why you are here in the world of men. If they can't control you, they will seek your ruin."

"Who are these men, Mother?"

"If I knew where they were hidden, I would have already sought their destruction. Powerful wizards they are! I know *what* they are but not *who* they are."

"Mom, are you sure you're not just being paranoid?"

"Paranoid?" She retorted, half amused. "No, son. This is the real thing." She looked down. "I've not been a good mother. I've hidden things from you."

Azriel tilted his head slightly, his face filled with compassion. He had never seen his mother seem so vulnerable. It made him sad—and uncomfortable.

"Mom..."

"No, you must listen. There are things I've done. Dark things—terrible things. But only to keep you from harm. Now I can no longer protect you. I was hoping to tell you when you were older, but you must know now. Yours, Azriel, is a powerful destiny. It's your task to set things right and reunite the worlds. This burden was placed on your shoulders because you are the last prince of our bloodline. If not for you, the worlds will forever remain split and flawed. Men will destroy this world, and Aralia's magick will fade. Only by restoring balance to both worlds will they be safe. That can only be done by healing the rift—by making them one again."

"And this is my task?" Azriel tried to refrain from sounding petulant, but it was too much to swallow. "Why me?"

"Because you're the last—the last of our line. The potency of the Ferrishyn is fading. It took me many years to conceive."

Azriel fell silent as he tried to absorb all this. Suddenly the Mariner's losing the game didn't seem all that important.

"What if I don't want to play?"

"I'm not sure you have a choice in the matter." Abelene smiled sadly. "I didn't. There are things I can't tell you yet. I'm not ready—and neither are you."

Azriel couldn't hold down his agitation. Why all the secrecy, Mom? Why is everything so shrouded in mystery? Abelene read Azriel's emotions and wanted to cry for the pain she was causing her son.

Nicodemus sought to diffuse the tension. He spoke softly. "Son, there are many things you must learn before that time comes when you must face your destiny. It begins with the book I gave you. Your mother had me keep it safe when she crossed over to be in the world of men. It's also the reason why we are traveling next month to Great Britain. Some things will become clearer to you. In the end, any action you take will be your choice. Have you begun reading the book?"

"Only a little."

"Then I suggest you hop to it, boy. You can't remain in ignorance forever."

Azriel nodded contemplatively. He had the feeling this was larger than he ever could imagine. He needed to think. Before heading upstairs to his room, he embraced his mother tenderly. With Azriel out of sight, Abelene finally allowed herself to cry. She wept on Nicodemus' shoulder.

Chapter 4

A dark SUV slowly made its way up a narrow service road that wound through the Allegheny Mountains of West Virginia. In a remote area of the Dolly Sods wilderness, most local folk were unaware that the road even existed as it wended its way through regal stands of birch and alder. Further up, a high plateau skirted Mount Porte Crayon, the highest peak in the immediate area. The forest growth was thick in some places, and twice the driver had to stop to remove fallen trees from the path. If it had been winter, the only way in and out of his destination would have been by helicopter, but well into spring, the road became passable—though not without difficulty. It was always advisable to carry a chainsaw for such emergencies. Though the driver could have used magick to move the annoying log, he didn't want to waste his power on something so trivial. The driver returned to the vehicle and headed further into the forest, where it seemed almost like twilight despite the midmorning hour. Again the driver had to slow to a stop as a bevy of wild turkeys strutted across the road.

The dense stand of hemlocks finally cleared, and opened onto a gated field marked as a restricted government facility. Directly next to the cinderblock-built bunker stood the towering spire of a repeater antenna. Further beyond was a concrete slab with a bright orange circle and crosshairs that served as a heliport. The driver sniffed at the air, sensing the distinct stench of aircraft exhaust. The helicopter must have arrived only recently.

Altais walked slowly toward the low bunker, his ornate cane tapping against the tarmac with every stride. He removed a key card from his wallet and inserted it into the receptacle. It unlocked a keypad that required a ten-digit code for access. With a faint click, the reinforced steel door swung open to reveal a rather drab and indistinct control room. The radio equipment seemed old and outdated—an obsolete transmitter-receiver that still functioned, but only barely. Behind the massive gray control console, an elevator seemed an anachronism, out of place in the low-tech, World War II bunker. The elevator also required key access. Altais slipped in the card and entered another string of integers before the door slid open. Inside, only two buttons glowed—one pointing up, and the other pointing down. The sublevel arrow flashed red, and Altais gave it a perfunctory jab. He was not at all happy to be called away from his work, but he understood the significance of being summoned. If Rastaban, the head of his order, required his presence, then something of importance had occurred.

The elevator to the subterranean level took a full twenty seconds to complete its descent. Altais didn't know how far underground the meeting hall lay. All he knew was that for years he had remained an active participant in a grand subterfuge in which the world had no knowledge. Here was where the true power base of the planet revealed itself. The door opened onto a richly appointed chamber with the ornate symbol of his order emblazoned on the far wall beyond a massive mahogany conference table. The symbol consisted of a serpentine dragon in a figure eight, consuming its own tail. Above the Ouroboros, the word *Draconis* had been carved into the wall in cursive script, nearly indecipherable to the untrained eye. Beneath it lay another portal that descended into a hidden chamber deep in the bowels of the earth. The vault remained sealed behind a great iron door. Altais stared nervously at the vault. Upon entry into the order, he had endured several encounters with what remained hidden behind those doors—and each time he hoped he would never have to face it again.

Rastaban greeted him with the secret handshake of their order and offered him a drink. Altais nodded, and Rastaban poured a generous measure of Cognac into a sizeable snifter from a beautifully hand-cut crystal decanter. He offered it like a gracious host, but Altais sensed an underlying menace emanating from Rastaban. The leader of the order poured another for himself before taking his seat at the head of the great conference table. Altais took the seat to the side.

Rastaban sipped thoughtfully while Altais waited for him to speak. But the leader remained unreadable, the depths of his mind unfathomable. His deep-set eyes lost in contemplation; something had disturbed him enough to call a face-to-face meeting.

"I have felt a stirring," Rastaban spoke succinctly. Altais nodded. He had felt it too.

"I concur," he replied.

"Have you located the source of the disturbance?"

"No, my Lord, only the approximate location. Somewhere on the Northwest Coast—Seattle, I think. It was almost indecipherable, but I sensed a slight displacement in time. I believe the Avatar is here."

"Undoubtedly." Rastaban's smile was grim. "But this was not unexpected—only sooner than we thought."

Suddenly, a slight tremor emanated from below, startling Altais. Sweat beaded on his brow and he stared fearfully at the iron vault.

"Yes," Rastaban nodded. "You feel it, don't you? The dragon stirs. It has also sensed the Avatar and now seeks release from its prison. You know we cannot allow that. He is the source of our power, and his release would destroy this world—and us! You must narrow your search, Altais."

"I have tried, my Lord, but I have felt interference, as though my probing is being blocked—deflected. I am certain the source is human."

Rastaban raised an eyebrow. "That is not good news. I thought we had hunted down every one of the Earth Wizards. That renegade, Eltanin was a fool to impart magick to these mortals. The effects of his actions have been felt for untold centuries. And yet for all that time, we have had no idea whether he is dead or alive. That uncertainty alone is cause for concern."

"That is true. He created a dangerous precedent by imparting the Rede to mortals. They are as unreadable as they are unpredictable. If events are allowed to unfold as foretold, all we have worked for will come to naught. We cannot allow the reintegration of the two worlds. What do you command, my Lord?"

Rastaban reflected on the dilemma. "Only one of our kind can fulfill what has been prophesied—can reverse what has been done. That was set forth at the beginning of the schism. As you know, with any ritual of such magnitude, the key to reversing its effects must be written down. You must find where it is written and destroy it. The formula must never see the light of day."

"My Lord! You give me an impossible task!"

"Difficult, yes. Not impossible," Rastaban countered. "You will have help. Hold out your hand."

Altais hesitated. He shuddered with dread knowing the consequence of disobedience could be dire. He held out his hand with trepidation.

The High Lord placed a small golden cube into the palm of Altais' hand. It immediately began to burn with intense heat. Altais tried to throw it off his hand, but the cube had already begun to absorb into his flesh. He fell to the ground screaming in agony as the dark magick burned its purpose through his blood stream like lava. Finally, as the pain abated, the purpose settled within his eyes.

Rastaban explained. "All human wizards who have passed the many tests of Alchemy, upon completion, partake of the elixir of life— if they have the wisdom. Those human immortals emanate an aura of power, invisible to most creatures. You, my friend, now have the ability to locate that emanation. You will also be able to raise fell creatures from the very bowels of the Earth. They will follow your command and do your bidding. Find the Wizard and you will locate Eltanin—if he still exists. We need to be certain. Find Eltanin's resting place and you will find the spell to reverse what he has done. Destroy the spell and we shall remain in power. Do not fail me," Rastaban added ominously. "Seek out the hidden. Search out magickal places and obliterate them. Human magick must be bent to our will—or annihilated. Only *we* must preserve the power."

Altais breathed deeply, awed to be entrusted with such a mission and terrified of failure. "Yes, Lord Rastaban. What will *you* do now?"

"Now we wait. Our colleagues will be here shortly."

Another slight tremor vibrated through the marble floor, this time a little stronger. Rastaban glanced nervously at the vault. It was the first time Altais ever saw his Lord display any fear. Rastaban removed an object from his pocket. The carved stone was pyramid shaped, nearly clear, with a golden penumbra surrounding its base.

The leader stared into it and muttered an incantation. The rumbling beneath the floor abated and fell silent.

"My Lord!" Altais gasped.

"Yes." Rastaban smiled wickedly. "I have mastery over the dragon. He will not break free."

"Are you sure? His release would spell our doom."

"Trust, my friend. He has been imprisoned for twenty thousand years. He will remain so for another twenty thousand. Where is your faith?"

"My Lord, with respect, we once had faith in Eltanin. Where did that lead us? The ritual meant to free us instead imprisoned us, nearly leading to our ruin."

"You forget, dear friend, that Eltanin was a fool. He did not foresee our plan until the very end. Our only mistake was that we underestimated his power. Alas—a fool, but a powerful one. Our folly, perhaps."

"But My Lord, we are trapped here."

Rastaban laughed, his voice cruel. "That depends on your point of view. Trapped, maybe. But never forget that we are the ones who control this world. Everything else is an illusion. You live quite comfortably, do you not?"

"Of course, my Lord. I have more wealth than I need. But if I may be so bold, after twenty thousand years, our powers are fading. You know it to be so. As this world continues its plunge into chaos, magick is waning. That was the reason we tried to separate ourselves from humans in the first place. These humans," Altais spat the word with contempt, "continue to destroy this planet at an exponential rate. And because of Eltanin's incompetence, we will never return home. All the wealth in the world is meaningless if we have no world left to control."

"My friend," Rastaban countered, "Never underestimate these humans. They are quite resourceful. But more so, do not underestimate Eltanin. He was the most powerful wizard of our order. That is why we must learn the truth about him. Amazing that for all his bumbling incompetence, he managed to elude us for so long. If he is dead, then we need to prove it. But if he is alive, we need to draw him out."

Altais paused to reflect on Rastaban's words. However, the silence was broken by the sound of the elevator door opening.

Four men filed out and greeted Rastaban with formal nods.

"Nodus," Rastaban said as he returned the salute and shook his hand.

The remaining three, Edasich, Thuban and Giausur—took their seats in order of rank at the great table. Nodus, third in command, was visibly annoyed as he sat next to Thuban. Altais moved to the second seat.

"What troubles you, Nodus?" Rastaban asked.

"My Lord, that mechanical device troubles me. If that elevator ever loses power, we'll be trapped. I do not like being closed in. It was far easier when we were able to travel by portal. I have no trust for human invention."

"Yes, brother. The loss of our ability to create portals has been… inconvenient. That is true. Sadly, we must use what is available to us—for now. That is why we must continue to thwart human knowledge and aggressively curtail human invention. Their scientific devices grow more powerful by the day—and less controllable. I don't care if they destroy themselves—but I will not be destroyed along with them."

The others nodded in agreement.

Rastaban decanted drinks for all present, and then sat at the head of the table. "So, Thuban, what have you to report?"

Thuban, a tall man with a dark complexion, sat erect in his seat. He answered obsequiously. As fourth in command, he often struggled with feelings of inferiority and tended to whine.

"My Lord, our plan is working marvelously. Oil supplies are waning as China and the U.S. vie for control of the resources. Soon, we will have another conflict. It will quiet the dragon."

"Just make sure you divert several billion dollars back to North and Central America. We want conflict, not an all-out war. You must destabilize the Chinese stock market. As prices plunge, wealth will increase in the States. After destabilizing the Shanghai market, we need to disrupt the Japanese market as well. I will put that in your capable hands, Giausur."

Giausur, a robust man with golden hair tied at the nape of his neck, nodded in agreement. "Yes, my lord. As always, destabilizing the world economy will keep us powerful, and probing eyes away from us." He chuckled.

Rastaban added, "Yes, my friend; that is the power of Money Magick. We do not need to expend our magickal energy. We must save it for the time when we will require it. Therefore, we will continue to shift money here and there to restore order. We also need a few more natural disasters to create more turmoil. And," he chuckled, "we are deliciously close to ecological disaster. The momentum is building, and we need only sit back and observe!"

Edasich spoke up. "Yes, my Lord. A tsunami will rage through the Pacific in about a week. The estimated death toll is about three hundred thousand—not nearly enough, though."

"True, but it has to appear natural."

"Yes, my Lord."

Nodus asked in all seriousness. "Lord Rastaban, will it be enough? The dragon continues to grow restless."

"My brother, the dragon ever feeds on conflict. There is enough dark energy in the world to keep him sated. Do not worry. All is going according to plan. Now we must go about our business and meet back here in a month. Is that agreed?"

They all nodded their assent and rose to leave.

60

Chapter 5

Camille waved as the car circled out of the driveway. "I'll miss you!" She said, grinning broadly. Azriel waved back and smiled. "Keep my mom company!"

Abelene looked down at Camille and handed her a basket. She had been clutching it nervously in her hands. Abelene had never been separated from her son since his birth and suppressed the pang of sadness creeping into her heart. As much as she would have liked to accompany Nicodemus and Azriel to England and then to the Isle of Man, she knew in her heart that coming out of hiding could be dangerous to herself and her son. Recently, she had begun having premonitions of danger and decided it would be best for Azriel's sake that she remain at home. Despite Nicodemus's assurances of Azriel's safety, her decision was also based on her knowledge that the challenge he would have to endure was best faced alone. She would be too tempted to assist. Nicodemus, she knew, could be stubborn and ruthless to a fault. But he would also be fair. Abelene sighed and turned away.

"Come, Camille. We have a few things to gather. Your aunts will be here later."

Camille was happy to spend the morning with Abelene. After school was dismissed for the summer, Abelene had finally met her aunts. They had gone together for ice cream to celebrate the end of the school year. Daphne and Penelope were in awe of Abelene's knowledge of the magickal arts, and likewise, Abelene was glad for the companionship. It was a lonely existence for Abelene to be unable to share her knowledge with worthy recipients. It turned out that Daphne and Penelope came from a long line of witches. They had been lucky in the fact that their ancestors had barely escaped persecution from the witch hunts that had plagued Western Europe some three hundred years before. Much ancient knowledge had therefore been preserved in Daffie's Grimoire and Book of Shadows. The three women were happy to share secrets, knowing the mysteries would be safe with each other.

Today, she would teach them the formula and spell for invisibility. Not true vanishing from sight but rather a way of becoming imperceptible to their enemies. Abelene deemed it necessary to protect Camille and her aunts, as she sensed to the core that they would soon become targets. There were signs. Lately, she had perceived a stirring in the woods, as though someone or something had tried to penetrate the shield over her property and the surrounding area. Whatever it was had almost succeeded, but she had awakened suddenly in the middle of the night with an overwhelming sense of exposure. As furtively as possible to avoid detection, she called upon the woods to emit an aura of confusion toward anything that would attempt to break through. Only after the feeling passed could she rest easier, but she promised herself to remain ever diligent.

"Now this is what we're looking for." Abelene handed Camille a sprig of amaranth. "We need to gather a bunch, but only those in flower. We also need raven feathers."

"How are we going to find raven feathers?"

"I have already asked. The woods will provide." Abelene nodded in assurance.

They headed out to the thickest section of the woods. Camille scanned the ground as they walked. "Oh, look! Trillium. Aunt Pen asked me to find some while we were here." She bent down ready to pick them, when Abelene stopped her.

"Magickal herbs should never be picked. You must cut them properly and give thanks." Abelene instructed and handed Camille an oddly crafted knife. Its handle was carved of white bone, with magickal symbols etched into the design. The keen-edged blade curved inward like a crescent moon. Camille glanced up at Abelene curiously.

"It's called a boline. It should only be used for harvesting herbs and spell components. It is for cutting. Not like an athame. An athame is for directing energy."

"It's pretty."

"It was given to me by my great grandmother when I was no older than you." Abelene smiled, remembering. "I miss her." She smiled, remembering. "Now cut only half of it, so the remainder may grow back."

Camille made swift work of it and put the plant in her basket. Walking further, they located a stand of amaranth. Soon they harvested a goodly amount.

They continued beyond the thick of the woods and came to a small clearing. It seemed to Camille as though something had prevented the trees from further incursion into the grassy knoll. A stone bench had been erected along one side and a standing stone beside a fire pit jutted up from the center. Abelene cleared a few leaves from the bench and sat. She patted the seat, inviting Camille to sit beside her. After a few minutes of sitting in silence, when she could endure it no more, Camille finally asked, "What are we doing here?"

"Shh, you must be patient," Abelene whispered. "I have already requested audience."

Camille scrunched her face in incomprehension, but knew she would get no further explanation. In her short time knowing Azriel's mother, she knew that it would be futile to ask. Abelene's instructions always took on the *wait-and-see* approach.

Abelene sat tall and closed her eyes as she raised one hand to the sky. As she did, Camille heard cawing in the distance. It approached with great speed. From behind the perimeter of the clearing, the largest raven Camille had ever seen descended and alit upon the standing stone. It eyed Camille and Abelene with curiosity.

Abelene opened her eyes and smiled broadly, addressing the magnificent bird. "Thank you Mother Raven, for the gift of your presence."

The raven chattered and quorked. She seemed to bow her head before emitting an ear-piercing caw.

"We require assistance from you—a boon."

"I don't understand," Camille whispered.

"Nothing from nature should be taken. Her feathers must be freely given for the cloaking spell to be effective."

"Oh, I see. Hey, look!" Camille's eyes widened in wonder.

The raven began preening itself as it perched on the rock. Soon, four feathers floated down, having been neatly plucked from the great bird's tail.

"I thank you for your gift, Mother Raven. We will use them wisely." Abelene bowed her head in gratitude.

The raven bobbed its head again and spread its massive wings. As it flew west, Camille called out, "Thank you, and I hope we meet again."

In the distance, the raven cried out in response and disappeared.

Camille looked up at Abelene. "How did you do that?"

"It is a skill that can be learned. It's not that hard once you know how. Soon I will teach it to you. But now we must be off. Your aunts will be here soon."

The ferry coasted into port, skirting the city of Douglas. Though the capital city of the Isle of Man, it was only recently that it had been named as such. To the south, the ancient city of Castleton was far older and the small island's first capital. That was where Azriel and Uncle Nick were heading—on foot—much to Azriel's annoyance.

"I'm tired. Can't we just take a cab? It's not like I didn't notice a taxi stand at the dock!" Azriel complained. Nicodemus stared down at the boy, shaking his head. He growled, "The modern world has made you weak. In my day..."

Azriel rolled his eyes, knowing what was coming. He braced himself for another one of Uncle Nick's outrageous yarns.

"In my day," Nicodemus continued, "I rowed with a band of Vikings all the way from Norway, over a thousand years ago. We faced gales and storms! Rugged men they were, and never did they complain one whit!" Nicodemus stopped to adjust the huge trunk on the wooden cart he had procured from a local merchant. He gave it a shove and continued with his tale. "Aye, but they were a fearsome bunch, looting and pillaging these poor people. Had I known, I never would have shown them the way here, but I suppose I'll have to live with that. It wasn't until Godfred Croven brought peace to this troubled land that these people were finally left alone. I fought by his side to preserve the oldest parliament in the world. It's called the Tynwald by the Manx, having been established in 979 AD, though I can't say it did much good until Godfred came along. Now if you want to know a place, you need to feel the ground under your feet, so quit your grousing, boy. We're walking, and that's that!"

Castleton would ultimately be Azriel and Uncle Nick's destination, but first they needed to journey to a small hamlet beyond the city on the southern tip—a town called Cregneash—where a dear old friend of Nicodemus resided.

They veered off the main road and followed a narrower path. The gnarled, misshapen ancient trees bordering each side of the trail were laden with hanging moss. The pathway seemed to go on forever though in truth they had walked only a mere six miles. Azriel huffed with exertion, as he had taken over pushing the cart for Nicodemus. A slight rise in the narrow road led to an even narrower bridge. As they approached, Azriel stared in wonder at the numerous notes, letters, trinkets, and gifts left by the foot of the tiny bridge. Curiosity aroused, he was about to pluck one of the notes off the bridge railing when Uncle Nick stayed his hand.

"Leave it."

"Huh?"

"They're for the faerie folk and best left alone. Travelers set them there either as gifts or blessings, or to ask the wee folk for a boon."

"What is this place?"

"Indeed. It's the Fairy Bridge—the real one. You see, there are two of them. One in Santon for the tourists, and then there's this one—and this one has stood far longer than the other."

Azriel shrugged and was about to cross the bridge when Uncle Nick held him back. "Careful, boy. You never cross this bridge without offering a greeting to the faeries guarding it. If you get on their bad side, there's no telling what they'll do to you. They'll harass you and make your life miserable until you make amends."

"Sounds like a ridiculous local superstition if you ask me."

"Well, I'm not asking you, am I?" Nicodemus retorted. "Already this world has you fooled. You must learn to see with other eyes—the ones you were born with."

"What do you mean?" Azriel asked defensively. "I see just fine. It's an old bridge in need of repair. Maybe we should be more concerned with rotting wood than a bunch of cranky faeries."

"See, that's exactly what I mean. You're so mesmerized by the wonders of the new world—the marvels of machinery and powerful electronics—that you've forgotten the old world—the one you came from. You, boy, are Ferrishyn. A powerful race you come from, yet already you would settle for the mundane. Look at your mother, for instance. A grand woman she is. Abelene sees beyond the physical. She manipulates the world around her. You have this power too—though undeveloped. You're not here on this ancient isle for a vacation. You're here to be tested for your worthiness. I know your mother has told you that you are *in* this world but not *of* it. Now you need to learn that lesson. You must awaken what has remained asleep—rouse the power that has lain dormant for eons. That is your quest. The test you will face, dear Azriel, will be easy in comparison to what lies before you. This I do not say lightly." Nicodemus growled ominously, "Heed my words, boy." Azriel bristled, fear shadowing his expression. He swallowed it back down. Uncle Nick's stance softened and he smiled with understanding. He tapped Azriel's chest. "Here is where you'll find your courage. Your heart beats with the blood of kings. It is a good heart, forged with the fortitude of countless generations—powerful wizards that shaped your world, Aralia, from the very beginning. Trust that strength within you. It will not fail you."

Azriel steeled his resolve and straightened his stance, staring at the bridge. It seemed ordinary. Mere wooden planking overlaid a precarious span of ancient timbers, but on closer inspection he noticed a subtle glow, as if magick held it together. His approach was tenuous, and he stammered. "I... greet you, great faeries, who guard this bridge. Um, honor and blessings to thee, so I may cross this bridge safely and unharmed." Azriel smiled at his own wittiness.

Nicodemus shook his head. "That was a bit verbose. Come on then, let's go." He nudged Azriel forward and then called out to the unseen sprite guarding the bridge, "G'day to you, my friend."

The span seemed a bit rickety, but it stoutly held their weight as they crossed to the other side. The path opened before them, and soon they were traveling at a good pace toward Cregneash. On either side of the road, the landscape gave way to lush emerald fields, ripe with forage for the grazing cattle and native longhorn sheep. In short measure, they were upon the ancient town of Cregneash. Many structures appeared to have risen from the native granite, others whitewashed and topped with simple thatched roofs. Dark grey buildings of mortar and stone surrounded St. Peters Church, a simple peaked edifice with a squat bell tower gracing its crown. Winded after twelve miles of walking, Azriel began to slow his pace, clearly in need of a breather. A cozy thatched inn sat opposite the church, with music and pleasant aromas wafting through its slightly open door. Azriel gazed longingly at the inviting inn, hoping for a place to sit and eat. Nicodemus peered down at Azriel, only slightly repentant at having pushed the boy through such a journey for which he was clearly unprepared.

"Well now, I guess this place is as good as any." He parked the cart with his belongings by the entrance and led Azriel inside. Worse for wear at having been tortured by his uncle, Azriel slumped down dramatically into a chair at a table by the door. The room itself sported great oaken crossbeams, darkened and aged through decades of smoky fire from the blazing fireplace. Behind the bar, the source of the great aromas perched—a cast-iron cauldron bubbling with herring and potato stew. The deep-bellied pot sat on the fire pit with cheery coals that provided warmth and comfort. A few locals sat at the bar and around the various tables. But all conversation ceased when Nicodemus and Azriel seated themselves; a few surreptitious glances followed, and slowly the conversations resumed.

Suddenly uncomfortable, Azriel glanced up at Uncle Nick. Reading his unspoken concern, Nicodemus commented in a low voice. "Not many tourists come to these parts, so the locals tend to be a bit mistrustful."

The innkeeper, a jolly man with red, pocked cheeks, approached and greeted the strangers. "What'll ye be havin'?" he asked in a thick brogue.

"The herring and potatoes seem just fine. Some black bread, ale for me, and milk for the boy," Uncle Nick answered. Azriel sighed with contentment finally able to rest. "So how much further?" Azriel asked.

"Just another two miles or so. Ahh, here we are!"

The innkeeper quickly returned with a tray of food. The large earthenware bowls were filled with a dark brown broth, heaped with savory fish and potatoes. The black, crusty bread had a large knife thrusting from the rounded loaf; on the side a small dish of fresh creamery butter. He served his guests with pride and returned with a sizeable flagon of ale and a serving of local milk.

Azriel gingerly tasted the rich soup and smiled with pleasure. Its heartiness chased away his fatigue, returning warmth back into his chest and stomach. He began eating in earnest. The black bread was unlike anything he had ever tasted. He thought of Abelene. "Mom would love this!" he said with his mouth full.

"Aye, indeed she would! It's very much like her home cooking. This place is as close to her home as she tells it. As a matter of fact, I'll have a secret to tell you when I'm ready to! There's more to this little isle than meets the eye. Don't ask the locals, though," Nicodemus whispered, "Their memory doesn't go back that far. The secret is in that book I gave you."

"Yeah, the book…" Azriel paused tentatively. "Uncle Nick, tell me about Eltanin."

"So you've finally begun reading it, have you? It's about time. I'll tell you the story in due time, but not here. It's one for the road, out of earshot of the locals. Don't want to get lynched, you know." Uncle Nick chuckled as Azriel suppressed a shudder and rubbed his neck. They continued eating the hearty meal in silence. Nicodemus drained the remainder of the brown ale and squelched a burp that rumbled up from his belly. "Well, best be going. Another place to visit before we head to my dear old friend's abode."

"Who are we seeing, anyway?" Azriel asked quietly.

"Ah, yes. Should have told you—thought I did." Nicodemus rubbed his chin absently. "Ah, whatever. Her name is Amaryllis McBrae."

The room suddenly quieted. Though the townsfolk pretended not to be eavesdropping, they had apparently been furtively monitoring every word. An old man perched upon a barstool jerked a hard stare at Nicodemus.

"We'll not be mentioning that name here, if'n you know what's good for ye, laddie! A dark sorceress, she is, comin' and goin' as she will. She's the sea hag!"

"Nonsense!" Nicodemus countered. "Nothing but old sailors' yarns told over too much ale!"

"Oooh, and like you would know, would ye—a foreigner like you!" the old man retorted, his temper flaring. "I tell ye, I seen her doin' her mischief, then disappearin' just like that." He snapped his finger for effect. "Vanished into the rock by the coast. Now ye wouldn't be callin' me a liar now, would ye?"

"Wouldn't think of it," Nicodemus responded pleasantly hoping to diffuse the situation. "Here, let me buy you another round."

"I'll not be acceptin' anything from the likes of you, consortin' with witches. You'd best be takin' that young scallywag with you and leave here—if'n ye know what's good for ye."

Knowing when his welcome was about worn out, Nicodemus promptly paid the innkeeper and left with Azriel. He grabbed his cart and took the north road out of town. When far enough from the inn, Uncle Nick slowed to a more comfortable pace.

"What was that all about?" Azriel glanced up at Uncle Nick with concern, and then quickly peeked behind him.

"Anyone following us?" Nicodemus asked.

"Nope."

"Good. Bunch of old fools," he muttered. "Amaryllis McBrae is anything but an old sea hag! Beautiful she was in her day. Though I fear she's losing her touch. I must tell her to be more careful. No telling what trouble these locals may cause her if they catch her."

"I don't understand."

"No, I don't suppose you would. See, Azriel, Amaryllis has been in hiding for years—many years." Nicodemus's tone became quite serious. "There's much you don't know—even more you wouldn't believe at first. For what I'm about to tell you, you'll have to unlearn everything you think you know about this world. Fortunately, you haven't been too spoiled yet by all of man's wisdom, or at least what passes as knowledge and wisdom. Suffice it to say, these humans only think they know everything. Truth is, they've only scratched the surface. If they knew what I knew, the knowledge would burn them alive." Uncle Nick shrugged. "Or just turn them into raving lunatics!"

They continued to head north until they came to an escarpment of stone overlooking a cliff that led down to the ocean. The road suddenly ended, and Uncle Nick lowered the cart. He found a jagged, fist-sized rock and wedged it between a wheel and the ground to prevent the cart from rolling down the hill. They continued walking parallel to a stone fence erected from native rock. Several hundred years before, the troublesome granite was cleared from the fields and used as barriers to define the local farmers' property lines. Finally, Uncle Nick stopped and peered down the hill.

"This is our first destination."

"This place? There's nothing here for miles." Azriel scanned the horizon. It appeared to be a desolate, rocky coastline. A few gulls cried out with agitation in response to the sudden intrusion. Jutting out from the Irish Sea, huge spires of striated stone stood defiantly against the beating waves. Dangerous chasms, some hundreds of feet deep, punctuated the pathways, making the walk to the coast a treacherous affair.

"Use your eyes, boy. You'll see it."

It took a few minutes, but soon Azriel fixed his eyes upon a circle of stone that seemed oddly out of place in this remote setting. Where other boulders and jetties appeared naturally shaped and worn away by time, these were deliberately placed—though not recently.

"Come, Azriel. That's the place. We'll stop here, and I'll tell you a story." Nick led Azriel down the steep incline to the ancient site. Dense shrubs held their ground in the rocky earth, their tenuous existence shaped by gusting winds and continuous erosion. They stood in the center of the stone circle, and Uncle Nick motioned for Azriel to sit. Nick also joined him on the ground, facing the sea.

"The Manx call this place Cronk Karran. They would have you believe this site is the remains of a stone hut or a burial circle, but that's not the truth." Uncle Nick began. "Thousands of years ago, this place was the stage for a terrible desecration that literally tore this world apart. You see, Azriel, a great temple once stood here at the very ground you sit upon, and it was here a ritual had been performed that changed the course of human history—a dark and terrible rite that nearly destroyed this planet and even rent a hole in the very fabric of time and space. You asked about Eltanin—who he was, why he is mentioned with such hatred in the Book of Aralia. Betrayer, desecrator, infidel—they called him. Well, I'll tell you that as powerful a wizard he was, Eltanin, by his own admission had been naïve—not realizing until the very culmination of the evil rite, that he had been duped into believing he would help the world and protect his people. Yes, dark forces used Eltanin, for without him, they didn't have the power to achieve their sinister ends. In the end he managed to thwart the plans of the Clave of Wizards, yet not without nearly destroying the world. Now this island is all that remains of the mighty continent of Aralia." Nicodemus sighed heavily.

"Seriously?" Azriel asked doubtfully.

"Without question."

"How can it possibly be that this small island was once a great empire?"

"Aye, indeed. It's a complicated story. But we have time. Tell me, Azriel, how much you know of Aralia?"

"Only what I've read."

"Then that's a good place to start. Tell me what you know."

"It's not much. Only that a new people had come to Aralia and somehow made all Ferrishyn afraid because their ways were different. The Clave of Wizards attempted to teach them the ways of Magick, but they wouldn't learn. In the end, they decided to keep Ferrishyn and Human apart. In time, the humans all but forgot about the Faerie realm—the Ferrishyn. Today, there is little contact between them."

"Well," Nicodemus chuckled, "That's the official story, but the truth is much darker—far more sinister." He shifted his weight to get more comfortable and removed a pebble that was jabbing into his thigh. He tossed it aside. "Azriel, you Ferrishyn were once a proud and noble race, born with the elements of Magick written within your very core. You achieved great things, building grand structures with the power of your minds and hearts. Your world was a perfect place, filled with harmony and light—a golden time when there was peace and plenty. Art and music abounded. Creation was only a step away from imagination. Your people understood the balance of nature well, working with it instead of against it. And there were dragons living among them. They were great beings—gods with stores of ancient wisdom, readily imparted to your people. But there were also four of the greatest—the Dragon Elementals. They were the embodiment of Air, Earth, Water, and Fire. One could not see them in their entirety without being stricken mad, for a single mind could not contain their enormity. When seen, they appear only as a projection of their vastness—an extension of their true form. It is indeed a blessing to see them at all. They wouldn't bother showing themselves to any ordinary man. They were not always understood, since they have the power to create and destroy, but nevertheless they remained benevolent toward the Ferrishyn. All was well, and the foreseeable future was bright.

"But then, around twenty thousand years ago, as humans reckon time, a change took place that the Clave of Wizards did not foresee. The first humans suddenly appeared on the scene, and everything changed."

"I don't understand, Uncle Nick. They don't seem any different from me. Like Camille, Jasper and Albert—they're just kids like me."

"True. Side by side, you wouldn't be able to tell Ferrishyn and Human apart—at least here, on this planet. The difference is up here." Uncle Nick tapped his own cranium. "There's the fundamental distinction. Humans and Ferrishyn are wired differently. Ferrishyn have abilities humans will never achieve. Oh, for sure, some skills can be learned—but never truly mastered. Some humans have come close—Merlin was one; Rasputin was another, but he was warped and evil. I was happy when he died.

"Now it was never truly understood how the first humans arrived on Aralia, but the common consensus is that they had come quite by accident—either in a great ship or by some temporal anomaly, maybe even a dimensional shift—who knows. Nevertheless, they arrived in great numbers and began shaping their world in ways that beat against the laws of nature. First it was little things, like destroying meadows to plant fields, and then it grew into harvesting trees to build their homes. There was no end to their cleverness. For everything the Ferrishyn achieves through magick, humans can mimic by mechanical means. They destroyed mountains to mine metal; they dumped waste into the water, making it undrinkable; they erected monuments to themselves with little regard for those around them who had been there thousands of years earlier."

"Doesn't seem much different than now," Azriel commented.

"Exactly my point. Just look at the condition of this planet. It's a mess. In time, the Clave of Wizards had devised a solution—an evil plan to rid themselves of the human problem. There was only one catch. They needed Eltanin, the greatest wizard of all time to pull it off.

"Six in all there were, the most potent wizards of the day—who had plotted behind Eltanin's back. Their names are Rastaban, Altais, Nodus, Edasich, Thuban, and Giausur. Together, they cast a spell of deception over Eltanin to mask their duplicity. They designed a powerful ritual meant to send the humans back to where they came from. In that way, they would not be harmed. As you know, a wizard sworn to the Path of Light can do no harm to any living creature, himself included. The plan for a time seemed a good one and Eltanin was none the wiser that the spell had a deliberate flaw—an enchantment had been placed over him. He was blinded by the Clave and ignorant of their dark design.

"After months of preparation, the day of reckoning finally arrived. It would require summoning the four Dragon Elementals from their slumber and using their combined power to create an energy vortex potent enough to encompass the human settlement. If successful, it would turn back time to before the human journey began, thus repairing the tear in the fabric of space-time. Only a most formidable wizard like Eltanin could control such forces. A test of will and concentration would be required. Therefore, Eltanin had sequestered himself for a month, denying his body food, and only taking enough water to survive. Once purified, he could achieve this ponderous task.

"From the four corners of Aralia, the purest elements were gathered. For the Earth Dragon, soil dug from the Elysian Fields; for the Water Dragon; Ice from the Glaciers of Montesardt. For the Air Dragon, the rarest incense, born from the resinous blood of Yggdrasil, the First Tree. And for the Fire Dragon, Electrum smelted and refined thirteen times in the fires of Thuramin. These would be offered to the Dragon elementals as recompense for disturbing their eon's-long slumber.

"With bold humility, Eltanin summoned the Elementals and bared himself to their scrutiny. They sensed no guile in him and accepted his gifts. In exchange, they would create the vortex to send the humans back from whence they came, but suddenly as the vortex was forming, from out of the void, the Dark Dragon of chaos and destruction appeared in their midst. Horrified, Eltanin realized he had been deceived, for the Clave had struck an evil bargain with the Lord of Chaos. Only through the elemental vortex would the Dark Dragon be able to consume the souls of the humans and enslave them to his own purpose. It was thus that Eltanin realized the flaw he had missed in the ritual. No one knew from where the humans had come. Without that knowledge, there would be nowhere to send them, and they would disappear into the void, where the Dark Dragon could wreck his havoc upon them. Too late, Eltanin could not call back the power he had summoned. If he did not release it, the whole of Aralia would be destroyed."

Azriel sat breathless, his eyes wide with horror at the enormity of the tale. "So what did Eltanin do?"

"Ah, yes!" Nicodemus smiled. "What the Clave didn't perceive was just how powerful Eltanin truly was. In fact, Eltanin underestimated himself. He could not allow the destruction of humanity, so instead, in grief and passion, he sought to take the destruction upon himself. To do so, he would have to weave a spell of imprisonment on each dragon, so in battling it they would turn on Eltanin and destroy him. But then a strange thing happened. The Dragon Elementals saw into Eltanin's heart and perceived his purpose—that he, the most powerful wizard in all of Aralia, would sacrifice himself for the sake of the humans. Instead, as one, they accepted their imprisonment and bound the Dark Dragon as well. In doing so they knew that in their fate, they would doom Aralia as well, and magick would eventually fade from the world.

"The vortex collapsed as the Dragon Elementals disappeared one by one, but in its wake, Aralia was transformed. The rift in space-time tore even wider, and Aralia, indeed, the entire world, was split in two. One world vanished into the rift, and Aralia remained, albeit broken and reduced in size and power. In the aftermath of creation and destruction, Earth was born from Aralia, and the humans remained safe on the transformed world—though thoroughly confused."

"What happened to the Dragon Elementals?" Azriel asked.

"They are here—on Earth—but hidden. Not even I know where they are."

"And the Dark Dragon?"

"Hidden as well—no one knows. As your mother tells it, Magick in Aralia did indeed fade as the influence of the Elementals waned over time. Eltanin vanished with the humans and remains in hiding."

"In hiding? Why?" Azriel stared up at Nicodemus, puzzled.

"Why, indeed! The Clave was not destroyed. Those who betrayed Eltanin are still alive. They have vowed vengeance upon him. Just recently, over the past two hundred years, their influence has begun to be felt again upon this world. They have not given up their evil plans. Either they will dominate this world or they will destroy it."

Nicodemus paused in his tale and looked down, suddenly fatigued, as if something weighed heavily on his heart. He carefully reached into Azriel's shirt and extracted the amulet the boy wore. The four dragons, fashioned from the strange indigo metal, were intertwined in a circle. Uncle Nick sighed. "You must learn their names, Azriel. Only then will you begin to have mastery over them. That's your destiny."

"Me? What can *I* do? I'm just a kid."

"You'll grow into your destiny. For now, you must learn all there is to know."

"How am I supposed to do that?"

"First you start by letting go of everything you *think* you know. This entire world is real enough, but it's only a veneer for what lies beneath. Soon enough you will learn to tap into that power—that is, if you begin to trust yourself and believe you can do it. It all starts there."

Nicodemus glanced up. The sun had passed its zenith and hung lower in the sky. There were still a few hours of daylight, and it was time to move on. He rose, brushed himself off, and waited for Azriel to follow suit. They headed up the steep incline and followed a little-used path that skirted the coastline. Some of it was tough going, and more than once, Azriel needed help pushing the cart through some harsh terrain. The path circled around a rocky cove, and soon they came upon a place where the grassy fields gave way to a rock-strewn abutment hugging the coast. Stopping to look down over a steep incline to the sea, Uncle Nick pointed to a large, roughly rectangular boulder jutting up from the barren rock. Its crown was shaped much like a crusty loaf of bread, and beyond it, the waves splashed against stone in a perpetual battle for dominance—neither victorious, nor giving way in this ancient setting.

"There!" Nicodemus pointed. "There is our destination!"

"You're kidding. Here?"

"Yes, that's where we're staying tonight."

Azriel sniffed the air in disbelief. Already, the temperature had dropped, and a cold breeze blew in from the coast.

"And where exactly are we supposed to bed down? We'll freeze to death." Azriel crossed his arms, clearly annoyed. "How are you going to explain to my mother that I died of exposure out here?"

Nicodemus stifled a laugh. He stared down at the boy. "So sure you are—trusting what you see. You need to look beyond your sight and feel the place. Use your instinct!"

Sighing, Azriel hoped this wasn't another of Uncle Nick's tricks. It wouldn't be the first time Azriel had fallen victim to one of the old man's pranks. Nevertheless, he headed down the cliff only to discover that a rough-hewn staircase lay cleverly hidden from view. He wasn't sure whether it was an accident of nature or if it had been carved by man. Either way, it seemed ancient and led to the base of the massive stone block rising before him. Nicodemus grabbed a few of his belongings and tossed a knapsack down to Azriel. He left the huge traveling trunk on the cart and headed down, meeting Azriel at the bottom.

"Well here we are."

Azriel pulled his jacket closer and shivered. "Please tell me we're not staying here tonight. I'm freezing."

Nicodemus grunted with exasperation. "Good grief, son. Use your eyes for once."

Clearly confused, Azriel threw down his knapsack with annoyance and stared up at the sheer surface of the blue-gray granite block. Nearly featureless, it defied logic. Though clearly natural, it seemed to have been placed on the slick surface of the ocean-carved jetty. On closer inspection, however, a nearly invisible thin wisp of smoke rose from the top of the domed rock. To the right, a fissure rose up twice the height of a man, like a scar on the flat surface of the giant boulder.

"It can't be…" Azriel approached the split in the rock and stared deep into the fissure. He held onto the rock for support and peered inside. Suddenly the crack shifted and pivoted on a central point, allowing access to the massive stone interior. His eyes widened. "That's amazing!" he said.

Nicodemus chuckled. "Too easily impressed, you are. You have much to learn."

Furtively glancing behind them, Nicodemus led the way into the roomy interior of the strange domicile. To the far corner, a cozy hearth was filled with glowing embers. To the side, a sizeable, black tailless cat—a Manx—dozed lazily on a stool by the fire. "Hello there, Felisa," Nicodemus stroked the cat, and she rolled over, emitting a soft purr. A sizeable pile of driftwood lay stacked against the rough stonework. Uncle Nick picked up a few pieces and tossed them into the fire, stoking up the embers with an iron poker that hung from the mantel. From an adjoining room, he heard labored breathing. Pointing to another seat by the hearth, Nick spoke quietly. "Wait here."

Nicodemus gently tapped on the door and let himself in. The room was small, not nearly large enough for the massive, framed bed and dresser. To the side, an oil lamp sat precariously on the edge of a small night table. Nicodemus pushed it toward the center. A diminutive old woman lay on her side, nestled in a thick comforter, shivering. She turned her head and peered up at Nicodemus. Amaryllis smiled wanly.

"I've been expecting you, old friend." She coughed, and her body shook with a sudden spasm.

Nicodemus stared down at her with compassion. Amaryllis had lost her youthful glow. Her eyes were sunken in with fatigue, and her once-cheery, oval face had grown wrinkled and sallow. Her white hair was dingy and matted. "You don't look well," he said. "You should have contacted me sooner."

She smiled wanly and blinked through heavy eyelids. "Ah, my dear old friend, it appears that time has finally caught up with me. I no longer have the strength to create what I must in order to survive. It's time for me to die. I'm tired, and I welcome it."

"There's time enough for death, but now is not your time," Nicodemus replied sternly. "I've brought the boy."

"So soon?" She shifted uncomfortably.

"There has been an ominous stirring in this world—I have felt it. You have felt it too—I know you have. It's time for him to be tested. Abelene has given him the amulet."

"Will he have the fortitude?"

"Yes, he will—he must."

"And if he fails?"

"Then both our worlds will come to ruin. There is no other way."

"Our fate, then, rests in the hands of the young man. Does he know yet?"

Nicodemus sighed, troubled. "I haven't the heart to tell him everything—how much our survival hinges on his success. He's too young to know. Azriel must grow into his courage; otherwise, the knowledge will terrify him into inaction. Small steps, Amaryllis— small steps…"

She rolled onto her side, and a tear slid down her face. "I'm tired. It's too great a matter for me. Let me die."

Nicodemus raised his voice, speaking sternly. "The time approaches when all must be set right. If not, both this world and Aralia will fade into oblivion, and all will be lost."

"Maybe we should let it!" Amaryllis retorted with vehemence. She seemed to regain some of her strength; her eyes pierced his. "You have seen history unfold, Nicodemus. We both have lived too long. We have watched men destroy this world and all that is good and just. They grasp for power. Battle—death—destruction. They will not learn. Even with all my sorcery and all your wizardry, we have made little progress. Peace here comes at too great a cost, and our people just live their lives oblivious to what's around them, not knowing what's at stake. They kill, maim, and ruin their world for temporary gain. They die, and their children repeat their folly. They grow in intelligence and knowledge, yet they still will not learn. We are among the last, brother. The Order of the Ankh is all but done. So many of our brothers and sisters—lost—murdered—hunted down. Six thousand years is too long for any mortal to live. I've seen too much." Amaryllis wept. "I've lost faith."

Nicodemus's stance softened and he stroked her silver hair. "Dear sister, dear friend, we cannot give up. There's too much at stake. Draconis is rising again—I have sensed their presence. They are searching for the boy. True enough, it would be better for this world to die as nature would have it, but that is not what we foresaw. You know that. Instead, both worlds wax toward evil. Humankind and Ferrishyn alike will be enslaved, and freedom will fly in the face of oppression."

"They're slaves already, Nicodemus—only they don't know it. They're slaves to their ambition, their self-centeredness. They have no sense of unity. Both races are contemptuous of life. They only seek out what benefits them individually, but not what's good for the whole."

"I have more faith than that, Amaryllis. Humans practice a strange form of brinkmanship. It seems only in adversity that they ultimately grow in wisdom."

"Yes, they play a dangerous game, brother. They can destroy their world several times over."

"But they won't. They will learn in the end. That has always been our purpose."

Amaryllis smiled at Nicodemus and shook her head. "Ah, brother, you have always believed in good triumphing over evil. I am not so sure anymore. I've become old—jaded. From the time of my birth, I saw Pharaohs conquering kings; kings oppressing their subjects; myriad uprisings and revolutions slowly reverting back to corruption and indifference. I should never have taken the elixir of life, my friend. I should have died a slave in Egypt. The Order of the Ankh has outlived its purpose."

"I refuse to believe that." Nicodemus smiled and tilted his head with empathy. "There is still time yet."

"You're an old fool."

"Yes, perhaps I am—but an honest one."

Nicodemus helped Amaryllis sit up in her bed. He raised the wick in the oil lamp to afford more light in the room.

"Please, brother, don't make me do this!" She averted her eyes, ashamed.

"You made a sacred oath. You cannot turn your back on it now. There's too much at stake!"

Amaryllis stared up at Nicodemus, her eyes pleading.

"You must, sister. There are so few of us left."

They stared each other down, a test of wills, but finally Amaryllis conceded and bowed her head. "Let it be done then."

Nicodemus nodded and smiled with sympathy. He removed a tiny box carved of black mahogany from his pants pocket. It appeared seamless, as though it were merely a block of wood. Lifting it up to his lips, he blew gently and whispered, "Open." Of its own accord, the lid lifted, and the contents glowed with ethereal light. Inside, the substance seemed to defy reality, as though it had mass but was strangely transparent. Attached to the inner lid, a miniature golden spoon released itself into Nicodemus's fingers. He scooped a small fragment of the magickal substance and held it out to Amaryllis.

As soon as he touched the elixir to her tongue, Amaryllis's body reacted with a spasm and arched in pain. The fire of immortality coursed through her body and singed her blood. She stifled a scream.

In the adjoining room, Azriel waited impatiently. Every so often, he heard Nicodemus's voice, but could barely make out any words. His voice was punctuated by another—clearly female but again indistinct. How many times had Azriel been admonished by his mother against spying? Yet eavesdropping had always been in Azriel's nature. How he hated secrets.

He decided to take a look around. First he walked to the section he supposed was a kitchen. He smiled with a sense of recognition. Glass and clay jars were piled haphazardly on several shelves, and bunches of herbs and other flora hung from hooks in the ceiling. Curious, he picked up a clay pot and lifted the lid.

"Ugh!" He closed the lid quickly, nearly puking from the vile smell. He placed it back on the shelf and wiped his hands on his pants. "Disgusting!" he muttered. Next to a wash basin, he noticed a mortar and pestle. In the bottom of the stone bowl was a white, powdery substance that glowed slightly at his touch.

"What the... " Azriel whispered.

He strode to the hearth and poked up the fire for more warmth. Hanging from a tripod in the fire, a small cauldron bubbled merrily with meat, potatoes, carrots, and turnips. Funny—he could have sworn it hadn't been there before. He also realized he was quite hungry. What was this place, he wondered? Azriel knew for certain that magick filled the room, much like his own home—but magick like he'd never seen. For one, a window faced the sea, and great oaken beams supported a thatched roof—yet all of it was invisible from the outside.

As furtively as possible, Azriel tiptoed to the room where Nicodemus spoke quietly with Amaryllis. With the door, slightly ajar, Azriel hid in the shadow and watched with interest.

Amaryllis appeared ancient and haggard. Her grey hair, streaked with silver, hung in unkempt mats. It was stained yellow from years of fire and smoke. Obviously old and infirm, she looked weak—dying. She and Uncle Nick seemed to be arguing about something, and Azriel thought he heard his name mentioned. Then Uncle Nick did something strange. He put something on her tongue, and suddenly the poor woman began to shudder as though in pain. Her trembling intensified, and Nick held Amaryllis down to prevent her from injuring herself. She suddenly stiffened and Azriel gaped in wonder, his eyes widening at the strange sight.

Amaryllis floated off the bed, hovering nearly two feet above the covers. An impossible transformation, frailty lifted from her body, sloughing off so much debris. She began to glow with blinding light, and Azriel had to shield his eyes. When the light waned, a younger woman lay on the bed, as vibrant and youthful as his mother. Amaryllis had been altered into a striking woman with classical features and golden skin. No longer was her hair a rat's nest of tangles; rich black tresses now flowed to her shoulders in a cascade of curls. Having gone through the crucible of transformation, the glowing subsided, and Amaryllis smiled impishly at Nicodemus.

She jerked her head and spoke with amusement. "We're being spied upon!"

"Azriel!" Nicodemus blustered. "I told you to stay put! What did you see?"

"I've seen enough," he replied heatedly. Azriel suddenly realized he knew nothing of his uncle. All those stories—those tall tales of Viking voyages, of cars purchased in the last century, of baseball games at the Polo Grounds—were perhaps true! Uncle Nick had said as much, but Azriel had found it all hard to swallow. And all the stories of another magick-laden world, he only half believed—though his mother had insisted that they were all true. His world—and everything he knew—seemed to be crashing down around him and Azriel bristled.

"What else have you hidden from me, Uncle Nick?" Azriel crossed his arms belligerently.

"Get in this room right now! I never lied to you, boy. Not once! You just never believed me."

"But how could I?"

Nicodemus laughed heartily. "Son, you think everything you see around you is the truth—but *that* is the big lie. What passes as reality is only a veneer for the Magick that lies beneath. You have only to tap into it to see the truth for what it is. Humans are quite content viewing their world as impotent and powerless. You have only to quit being human and embrace your past, boy. Then you will see the truth for what it is. Now come inside and meet my dear friend, Amaryllis."

Azriel gingerly stepped into the bedroom and bowed his head politely. "Pleased to meet you, ma'am."

"Oh, let's not be so formal. I'm Amaryllis!"

Azriel tilted his head. "How old are you—really?"

She smiled broadly, amused by the boy's candor. "Well," she said. "As you reckon time I'm about five thousand, five hundred years old."

"And Uncle Nick?"

"Older…"

"Impossible." Azriel scowled.

"Still you doubt?" Nicodemus interjected.

"But how?"

"I think it's time for a story," He answered. "But first some sustenance. Let's eat."

"Yeah, about that…"

"Yes?"

"I'm positive there was no food cooking when we first got here."

"So sure you are." Nicodemus rose, shooing Amaryllis and Azriel out into the main living area. There on the table sat four bowls heaped with a delicious-smelling stew. Spoons were placed on cloth napkins, and a loaf of crusty bread sat in the middle.

"How—" Azriel gaped at the table.

"How, indeed!" Amaryllis sighed dramatically and shook her head. "Nicodemus, does the boy know nothing?"

"Only what he's been taught."

"Oh dear—then he's an imbecile!"

"Hey, I take offense to that!" Azriel protested.

"Tut, tut, Amaryllis," Nicodemus scolded. "It's not his fault. He has so much to unlearn. He still trusts what he sees—never notices what's really there."

"Blind too, then." Amaryllis held the back of her hand to her forehead and struck a tragic pose, sighing. "Such a pity."

"I don't believe this," Azriel muttered mostly to himself.

"And therein lies the problem. Shall we eat?" Uncle Nick said politely.

"Yes, let's!" Amaryllis seated herself at the head of the table, while Nicodemus joined her. Azriel, however, stood with his arms folded scowling at both, clearly unhappy with being belittled.

Amaryllis giggled and chided him. "Sit down, son. Your dinner's getting cold."

Just then, Felisa brushed against Azriel, purring and sinuously circling between his legs. Then she nestled within a rumpled green cloth on the ground—her bed perhaps. He looked down and smirked. "Funny-looking cat. Where's her tail?"

To Azriel's shock and surprise, the cat transformed before his eyes. In moments, she had grown to Azriel's height, now wearing a green robe. Her features, though mostly human, had definite feline attributes. Pixyish, Felisa had a slender build with shaggy black hair from which delicate pointed ears jutted out. Her face kept Azriel spellbound. With large coppery eyes and a squat tiny nose, her whiskers twitched comically. She seemed more a fanciful caricature dreamt up rather than any creature one would expect to see on earth.

"And what makes you think I would even *want* a tail?" she said, clearly offended. She smacked his arm. Her childlike voice quavered with a musical lilt. Felisa turned away haughtily and sat at the table. She unceremoniously began to pick at her food. Azriel, for his part, still stared wide-eyed at the changeling, watching her eat.

Felisa, with controlled finesse, placed her spoon back on the table, annoyed by his scrutiny.

"Well, what do you expect me to eat—Purina? Yuck!"

"Um," Azriel stammered.

"What's the matter, boy? Cat got your tongue?" Felisa hissed. "Sit down and eat before I scratch you!"

Amaryllis stifled a giggle. "Now, Felisa, be nice to our guest!"

"Humph!" She turned her face away, refusing to acknowledge Amaryllis.

"Felisa, I'm talking to you."

"Well, I'm not talking to you." She looked down and pouted. Her lower lip began to tremble.

"Felisa?"

"You were going to leave me. You were going to die and leave me alone!" She started to cry and flew into Amaryllis's arms. The older woman embraced Felisa, stroking her head.

"I'm so sorry. I guess I was just being selfish." Amaryllis said contritely.

Felisa rubbed her face against Amaryllis's cheek. "Don't ever do that again!" She sniffled. "I wouldn't know what to do without you. Promise me."

"I promise." Amaryllis cooed.

"Good!" Felisa suddenly brightened and skipped back to her seat. She dug into her stew in earnest.

Azriel sat next to Felisa and began to eat in silence. He took a slice of bread from the center of the table and dabbed it into the bowl, sopping up the rich gravy at the bottom, and finished the superbly prepared supper.

"That was delicious!" Azriel commented feeling sated.

"Yes, Felisa is quite the cook!" Amaryllis smiled. "Now we need to talk, young master. I'm sure you have questions that need answering." She dragged a chair toward the hearth and sat ceremoniously.

"Now it's time for a story." Amaryllis waited for the three to gather around. Nicodemus seated himself next to her, while Azriel and Felisa sat comfortably on the richly woven rug by the fire.

"Where to begin…" She mused. "Ah! I guess at the beginning. My true name is Sekhet—the name given at my birth. I was born in Thebes, and at that time it was merely a small, unimportant city in Egypt. Born of slaves—alas, that was my lot in life. Whether by luck or fate, I was sold into service to the first true king of Egypt. His name was Menes—a great politician and conqueror. It wasn't so bad being a slave in his household; I had beautiful clothing and was taught by the finest scholars and magicians the world had to offer. I was poised to be an advisor to Menes. A mighty man he was, capable of great feats—like the time he had been out hunting and was attacked by his own dogs, which had been frightened by a lion. To escape them, he mounted the back of a crocodile that bore him to the other side of the Nile. There he established a new city to honor his escape and called it Crocodopolis. He built a great temple to the crocodile god, Sobek in thanks—and to Ptah the god of wisdom! But that's history you can read in any book. What the world doesn't know is that Menes had fallen in love with me—and would have taken me to be his wife. But as all pharaohs had done ever since, he was bound by tradition to marry his half-sister, Neithotepe. As a matter of course, she was jealous of our love. A king could have many wives, but to marry a slave? Oh, that was forbidden. Worse than that, most marriages were arranged for political gain and for alliances between the city-states—love had little to do with it. So it was that Neithotepe, furious that Menes loved me instead of her, plotted to have me murdered.

"Now there was a certain court astronomer who heard rumors of the plot. He was also one of my tutors—a dear man by the name of Nicodemus." Amaryllis glanced at him and smiled tenderly.

"As the mortal world fates men to their destiny, Menes suddenly died. It is said that he had been attacked and carried off by a hippopotamus while swimming in the Nile. Stricken with grief over her husband's death, Neithotepe's hatred from me knew no restraint, and she sent her guards to retrieve me—to executed me before her!" Amaryllis made a slicing motion with her index finger across her throat.

Azriel and Felisa, entranced by the story, both gasped.

"Ah, but Nicodemus knew of the betrayal and confused the guards, sending them where I wasn't. You see, Nicodemus had anticipated the queen's anger and had already packed stores for traveling. There, in the magician's old cart, I lay safely hidden. Quickly, we escaped from Crocodopolis. No one suspected that the court astronomer would betray his queen, nor was the cart searched when leaving the city. Of course, it's bad luck to anger a great sorcerer, and no one dared to search him!" Amaryllis laughed.

"Now the queen's rage knew no bounds, and she made Nicodemus and me outlaws with prices on our heads. But we eluded capture and headed east to Sumer—then to China."

"But that was over five thousand years ago. How can that be?" Azriel clearly couldn't grasp the thought that someone could live so long.

"You really don't know much about your uncle, do you, Azriel?"

"I guess not," he replied astounded by the enormity of the story.

"Then let me continue." Amaryllis shifted in her chair while Nicodemus poked at the fire. "We traveled to centers of learning throughout the ancient kingdoms—disciplines long forgotten by the modern world. Nicodemus protected me like a father, and for a time we could pass as such, since I was much younger than him. Now perhaps it's time for Nicodemus to finish the tale."

"Don't want to boast, Amaryllis?" Nicodemus chuckled.

"It wouldn't be seemly."

Nicodemus smiled and continued where Amaryllis left off.

"Well then," he cleared his throat. "Several years passed, and rumor had it that Queen Neithotepe died, leaving Menes's son Hor-Aha to continue the dynasty. You see, he had only been a boy when

Menes died, so naturally Neithotepe had ruled as Queen Regent. Fortunately, in young adulthood, Hor-Aha was a wise and tolerant man. He lifted the price on our heads and begged us to return.

"By this time, Sekhet—Amaryllis—had proven herself to be my brightest student, but alas, she had aged and I was now an extremely old man. So mighty a sorceress had she become that news spread, and her services—as well as mine—were heavily in demand. It was then that, after many years of absence, my old mentor suddenly reappeared back into my life. I hadn't seen him since," Nicodemus frowned, thinking deeply, "since before Atlantis sank into the ocean!"

"You see, Azriel, we Atlanteans are blessed with unusually long life, and it was there as a young man that I first came to be indentured to Eltanin."

"Wait," Azriel interrupted, "you mean the same Eltanin who split the worlds in two—the same guy who nearly destroyed the worlds?"

"Yes, the same. It was under Eltanin's tutelage that I learned the deep Mysteries—the hidden Magick of the Ferrishyn. It was from him that I learned of the ritual that nearly destroyed everything, and it was from him that I discovered one of the greatest secrets kept from man—how to create the elixir of life: the Lapis Occultus. Ah, it is a powerful magick—rarely achieved and not one for the faint-hearted."

"What exactly is it—this Lapis Occultus," Azriel asked.

"What it is *exactly*, I don't think even the greatest sorcerer in the world could explain—even Eltanin himself. The Lapis Occultus, or the philosopher's stone—as it is more commonly referred to— transcends matter. It exists somewhere between the mortal world and the world of spirit. No one can say where the formula came from—only that it is an exacting discipline that requires fortitude and commitment. Once down the path of the alchemist, one can never return. Secrets both ancient and holy are revealed to the alchemist—but also dark and forbidden ones. And once the sorcerer creates the Lapis Occultus, he faces an even greater challenge— whether to ingest it. For the Lapis Occultus can either save or damn," Nicodemus' voice lowered ominously, "it can bless or curse, set free or enslave, grant eternal life—or eternal death in a hell of one's own choosing."

Azriel shuddered. "So how *did* you choose?"

"Ah, yes," Nicodemus replied, "It was for that very reason the Order of the Ankh came into being. For nearly six thousand years we have dwelled among mortals, meeting in secret once every hundred years. Many throughout the ages accomplished the Great Work. From India, the mighty Dryaneshwar, from Persia, Jābir ibn Hayyān—who wrote volumes on the four basic qualities of hotness, coldness, dryness, and moistness, that which needs to be understood to create the Lapis Occultus. There was Albertus Magnus, Isaac Newton, Nicolas Flamel—all great alchemists in their own right— who understood the tablet that had been passed down all the way from Hermes the Great: the secret of immortality, the Emerald Tablet of Thoth!"

"Yeah, but aren't they all dead?" Azriel inquired.

"Alas—dead indeed. In their folly, they chose not to maintain their immortality."

"And you did."

"Aye, I did. But immortality is a blessing—and a burden. I have my own regrets."

"And you took it too?" Azriel stared at Amaryllis.

"Alas, I have. And I have kept my vow to use my immortality for the good of all—not for power or personal gain. That is the oath I took when I was inducted into the Order of the Ankh. Some day you must take the same oath, young master."

"Me?" Azriel replied with a bit more anger than he intended. "Why me?"

"Because you're the only one who can seal the breach—restore the two worlds to one."

"Great." Azriel muttered. "And what about you? What's your story?" He turned and stared at Felisa. She purred softly and smiled. Amaryllis answered instead.

"Felisa came about as a result of my selfishness. What I did was foolish—and wonderful—at the same time. Nearly four hundred years ago, this great boulder became my home. Shortly after settling here on this tiny isle, a little stray kitten wandered into my kitchen, looking for scraps. I knew she must be magical, for she saw through the illusion of the rock. Felisa was great company in my solitude. She lived for twenty-six years—a long time for a cat! But she became old and infirm. I couldn't bear the thought of her being gone as she lay dying in my arms, so in my grief and folly, I broke a very ancient rule. I gave her some of the Lapis Occultus. One could only partake of it if one has earned the right to take it. I was nearly expelled from the Order for my actions. You see, there are warnings about giving it to an animal—particularly a familiar. I placed her in my bed expecting the worst, but when I awoke, something unexpected had occurred. Felisa lay next to me—very much like you see her now. Oh, she was frightened—terrified to be in this new body! She would have attacked me, but something in her recognized me. Like any infant, she learned to walk and talk. Magick dwelt within her and soon, Felisa learned to transform back into her original form. She is a marvel—a changeling of the most wonderful kind!"

Amaryllis stroked Felisa's hair as she leaned against the woman's leg and purred with contentment.

"This is all too much!" In a huff, Azriel rose and walked outside to be alone. Nicodemus called after him, but Amaryllis hushed him. "Let him be, old friend. He just needs time to think."

Azriel walked among the strewn boulders of the ragged coastline. Confounded, he stared out at the sea. The tumultuous waves sprayed a constant mist into the air, and soon he was soaked to the skin. He sat on a convenient boulder and glanced down at the pebbles at his feet. Picking up a handful, he tossed them angrily, one at a time, into the waves.

Everything was getting too weird. His once-normal life was becoming increasingly abnormal, even for Azriel. Changelings— immortality—what next? And then a task he must perform. How could one person unite two separate worlds? A world of Magick and a world of men—it was too much to ask of anyone. Nicodemus had always spoken of a great destiny, but now Azriel resented it—

especially because he had no real choice in the matter. Azriel's thoughts darkened further with a strange sense of foreboding. He was certain this was only the tip of the iceberg. Much more still remained hidden—things Azriel was sure he didn't want to know; dangerous things that would cause his very soul to quake. He wasn't sure he was up to the challenge. What was it he'd overheard Nicodemus saying? If he failed, then all would come to ruin! Azriel hurled another stone into the sea, cursing under his breath.

Azriel suddenly had the itchy sensation of being watched. He turned quickly, looking behind him, and saw nothing but the rock-strewn beach.

"Who's there?" he shouted, but hearing nothing, he shrugged and peered back at the waves. Before he could react, Felisa flew at him, hit him square in the chest, and they both rolled onto the sand. He lay prone, with Felisa straddling him.

"Gotcha!" She giggled. Felisa stood offering her hand, and pulled him to a sitting position. She sat beside Azriel while he brushed off the sand.

"You could learn a thing or two from a cat, you know," she offered.

"Yeah, like what?" Azriel sulked.

"Like landing on all fours."

"Huh?"

"Of course. A cat can fall from a great height and still land on its feet. You're falling right now, so how are you going to land, Azriel? Are you going to dash your head against the rocks, or alight uninjured and shake yourself off?"

"Well..."

"Humans say cats have nine lives. It's not true, of course. It's just that a cat can save itself from harm because we are stealthy and sneaky." She clawed her hand and swiped at Azriel playfully. "We can wait in silence, unseen, and then attack when you least expect it."

"That's good to know..."

"And the Egyptians worshipped cats!" Felisa said proudly. "They honored Bast, the mother of all cats. They also believed cats capture sunlight in their eyes, allowing them to see in the dark. You must learn to see, Azriel."

"That's easy for you to say, Felisa."

"Oh, are you forgetting that I had to learn to be something other than what I am? That's a lot harder. You are so much more than you think. My cat sense tells me that—and a cat is a good judge of character!" Felisa smiled and yanked at one of her whiskers. "Ow! That hurts." She absently rubbed at the sore spot. "Here—this is for you." She handed him the gift. "This will keep you safe and give you good luck. It will also give you direction when you don't have any. Keep it safe! It's not a thing a cat does lightly—giving up a whisker." She stared at Azriel and blinked, then reached over and gave him a peck on the cheek. To Azriel, it felt a bit more like a lick.

Felisa giggled. "You're kind of cute for a human."

"I'm not really human—or at least that's what Nicodemus says. I'm Ferrishyn."

"Oh! Then you are powerful and capable, indeed."

"I don't feel like that at all."

"Give yourself time. You're still a kitten. You'll grow into your claws."

Azriel smiled briefly and shivered.

"Look at you! You're soaked to the skin. Come back to the house and curl up by the fire. It's one of my favorite things to do!"

He followed Felisa back to the cottage and found a cozy spot by the hearth. Nicodemus was already snoring comfortably in the adjoining room. Amaryllis handed Azriel a piping mug of hot cocoa, laced with a bit of rum. "Here—that will raise your spirits!"

Azriel tasted it and smiled. "My mom would not approve."

"It will be our secret, then."

It had the effect of fending off the chill, and soon Azriel yawned, suddenly feeling sleepy.

"Now, young master, you need to get some rest. You have a long day ahead of you and an important task to begin." Amaryllis said cheerfully.

He yawned again. "And what would that be?"

"Rest your thoughts, son. You'll find out in the morning."

Chapter 6

Camille loved spending the early morning hours walking in the woods. Her basket was nearly full of wildflowers and herbs she would need to help her aunts brew a healing infusion. Lately, Aunt Pen had been troubled with aching joints, and her supply of liniment was nearly depleted. Camille had spent many days with Abelene as well, learning magickal secrets even her aunts did not know. Though her summer was full, she missed Azriel, as did Abelene. It would still be a month before his return. It was good to finally have a friend—and sad to be separated from him. Part of her was afraid for Azriel, though she didn't know quite why. From bits and pieces she had gathered during her time with Abelene, she sensed that Azriel was embroiled in something vast, though what it was she could only surmise. Abelene remained mum on the subject, often aloof and secretive.

That morning, Camille thought to stop by and visit Abelene. Lately, Abelene had been teaching Camille animal lore—the secrets of understanding and communicating with earthly creatures. Though the denizens of the woods didn't speak—at least not in human terms—it was still possible to learn their ways and understand the messages they left, or the meaning of their sudden appearances. Certainly, Abelene exhibited remarkable skills that transcended even the most adept animal whisperers, and Camille hoped to someday be as talented. At first, Camille had to learn not to be afraid. It was the one thing she hadn't mastered yet.

Having arrived early, she tapped on the back door, where Abelene was packing a brunch for their hike in the woods.

"Good morning. Are you ready?"

"Always!" Camille replied cheerfully.

"Excellent. Today I wish to walk the boundaries of our forest. I've felt something unsettling and want to see if anything is amiss. One can't be too careful these days."

"What do you mean?" Camille asked, concerned.

"I have sensed a shifting as if something threatens our safety. Forces out there would come against me and Azriel—you and your aunts as well. Come, we'll talk on the way."

Abelene closed the door and whispered an incantation to protect her home.

"Why not just lock it?" Camille inquired.

Abelene smiled. "Locks are for amateurs. Spells are stronger!"

They headed east, taking their usual path into the thicker part of the forest. Huge, moss-laden spruces and tamaracks towered over them, and the forest buzzed with insects and birds squabbling in the canopy. They walked in silence for several minutes, giving Camille time to think and assess. By now she knew that whatever Abelene said carried deeper meaning than what hovered at the surface.

"Abelene," Camille asked timorously, "am I in danger? Are Aunt Pen and Daffie?"

A fallen log lay across their path. Abelene sat on it, and patted it signaling Camille to join her.

"Dear, we are always in danger—but rarely from where we expect." Abelene said evenly. "You have already chosen the path of the witch, as your aunts have. You are now entering a hidden world of which most people are unaware. What is bizarre to others is commonplace to us. Ours is the hidden world of spirits and natural forces beyond the comprehension of most people. Already you see things others do not. They label you weird or strange, do they not?"

Camille grudgingly agreed and nodded sadly. "Sometimes I get strange feelings, like I'm being watched. Yesterday I felt something in the woods as well. Something menacing."

"Hmm," Abelene mused. "You must never ignore a feeling. What did it feel like?"

"It felt as though Aunt Pen and Daffie were being threatened, but when I got home it was only Barclay."

"Who's Barclay?"

"He's the High Magus of Aunt Pen's coven."

"What's he like?"

"Tall, handsome—powerful. I don't know why, but he scares me. Aunt Daffie laughed when I told her. She said Barclay was harmless—at least to us. I think she's smitten."

"What is it about him that troubles you?"

"I don't know. He just seems—sneaky."

"Well you keep an eye on Daphne—and keep me informed. One can't be too careful."

They stood and brushed themselves off, and continued on their way.

Abelene clarified as they walked. "You asked about the woodland creatures, particularly predators. Well, the biggest thing you should know is they sense fear, and will use it to their advantage, much like a wolf pack hunts down a terrified elk. The elk being pursued is fearful and will likely make a fatal mistake that will cost it its life. Know when to hold your ground—and when to vanish." Abelene said. "Knowing which to choose is the key to survival. We should learn from them."

They paused again and Abelene cocked her ear, being alerted to something.

"Stay still. Be quiet!" She whispered. "Look! We're being watched!"

Deep in the underbrush a mountain lion crouched ready to attack in defense of her cub. Camille gasped, terrified.

"Make no threatening move," Abelene whispered, "and whatever you do, don't run! You're safe with me."

"Abelene, I'm scared."

"Don't be. I've known Kita since she was a cub."

"Kita?"

"Yes, Azriel named her. Her mother was killed by a hunter. Probably mounted on a wall somewhere," Abelene snorted in disdain. "I took care of Kita until she was old enough to be on her own. And now, look. She's a mama with her own little one!" Abelene said with pride.

"Kita," Abelene called softly. At first, the mountain lion's steps were cautious, tentative. Then she approached and pushed her massive head against Abelene's leg. Her cub lingered behind, unsure what to make of these two humans. He had already learned to be cautious of people. Kita nudged him forward with her nose, toward Abelene. She held out her hand so the cub could sniff and grow accustomed to her scent.

"Do the same," she instructed Camille. "Let them know you, and don't be afraid. Kita will not harm you."

Once introductions were made, the cub crawled into Camille's lap and playfully swiped at her face. Kita emitted a low growl, and the cub desisted. "What shall I call you?" Camille picked up the cub. Smiling, she stared him in the eyes. "How about Merlin?"

The cub wriggled in agitation clearly displeased, and Camille placed him back on the ground. He immediately caught a scent and fixed his eyes on a spot in the low brush. With one motion he bounded toward the brush and flushed out a rabbit. But being the quicker of the two, the rabbit escaped becoming dinner. A quick snort from Kita, the cub was back by her side. He dashed toward Camille and pounced on her foot.

"My, you're fast," Camille giggled. She suddenly thought of a better name. "I know! I think I'll call you *Hermes*—for the swift messenger god." The cub rolled on the ground, purring happily.

"Then Hermes it is," Camille said, smiling at his antics.

Abelene nodded in agreement. "A good name, I think."

Suddenly, Kita's ears pricked up. She stared into the trees, and a low growl rumbled from her throat.

"What is it, Kita?" Abelene stretched her sight and peered into the trees. She sensed—more than saw—something dart from one tree to the next. Kita followed the movement and roared in frustration.

"What do you see?" Camille asked, agitated.

"Nothing—and that's what disturbs me. It feels..."

"Menacing." Camille completed Abelene's thought.

"Let us leave. We should go to your house. I would like to speak with your aunts."

Kita lifted her head and sniffed at the air, catching a promising scent. With a soft parting growl, she disappeared into the forest, Hermes trailing behind. Camille, well acquainted with this part of the woods, found the path winding its way to her home. Within ten minutes, they came upon the majestic rowan trees guarding Camille's house. She led Abelene inside. Aunt Penelope and Daphne sat at the kitchen table, sipping tea and mixing up a rich chocolate batter for their special brownies. Camille stuck a finger in the bowl for a sizeable dollop while Aunt Pen playfully slapped her hand away.

"Yum!" Camille giggled, placing the basket of herbs and other medicinal plants she had gathered from the woods on the counter by the sink.

"Merry meet, Abelene!" Penelope said happily. "I've so wanted to see you again. Tea?"

"That would be lovely."

Daphne poured a cup and set a clay jar of honey on the table to sweeten the brew. Meanwhile, Penelope poured the batter into a greased pan while Camille knowing the routine scraped the remaining mix from the bowl with a spatula—but not without helping herself to another sizeable taste.

"Camille, you're going to blow up like a balloon the way you eat." Daphne teased. Of course it was completely untrue—Camille was far too skinny.

"Aunt Pen, where's Barclay?" Camille asked.

She hesitated before answering. "He's gone, dear. You know how he comes and goes like the wind. He visits, and then he disappears." She scowled momentarily, suddenly disturbed.

"What's wrong, Aunt Pen?"

"I'm not sure I can say…" Penelope seemed befuddled, as though her memory suddenly failed.

"Penelope, who is this Barclay?" Abelene asked.

Pen brightened as the cloud of bewilderment passed. "Oh yes. He is the High Magus of the Council of Covens."

"How many covens are there exactly?" Abelene asked.

"For this region? At least twenty. Possibly more. New covens are forming every day," she answered.

"Tell me more about this—Barclay." Abelene sipped her tea and stared levelly at Penelope.

"He's creepy," Camille interjected before Aunt Pen could answer.

"Hush, child," Daphne scolded as she washed the mixing bowl in the sink. "He'll be *your* High Magus, too, when you're ready to join the coven."

"Not if *I* can help it." Camille scowled. "Aunt Daffie, I don't like him. He's always skulking around like he's spying. He seems too secretive."

"Now, dear, that's the way of the mage."

"He gives me the willies." Camille shivered.

Penelope smiled at Abelene and shrugged. "She's young yet—not well acquainted with power."

Camille glared at her aunt, offended at being spoken about as if she wasn't there. She stormed off into the living room.

"Barclay oversees the Covens. I think he's charming," Penelope continued. "I've been told he comes from a long line of wizards—and a very old, secretive order I'm not privy to."

"So, what was the nature of his visit today?"

"Oh, nothing really. Just to chat."

"I don't want to pry, but what did you talk about?" Abelene asked delicately. "It's important. Something dark stirs in the woods today that, quite frankly, causes me concern." She brushed a stray strand of hair back over her ear. Penelope followed Abelene's movement, her eyes lingering on Abelene's ears. For the first time, she noticed the exotic nature of the woman's features. For one thing, there seemed to be an unusual protrusion atop her ear—a point, a beautiful contour, almost mythologically elfin. She made a mental note.

"Tell you what," Penelope said. "I'll answer your question if you answer mine."

"Okay." Abelene glanced at Penelope as she took another sip of tea.

"Where are you from?"

Abelene froze for a moment. She had never fabricated an answer to such an obvious question. The best she could do now was to mask the truth. "The Isle of Man," she answered quickly. In a way, it was the truth—but how could she explain that Aralia existed a dimension apart from this world?

Penelope eyed her suspiciously, then smiled. "Listen, dearie, all my kin hail from Ireland, so I've had occasion to visit the Isle of Man—and sorry to say, no one I've met looks remotely like you. Not that it's a bad thing, mind you. You're quite lovely."

Abelene blushed. "My parents died when I was young, so I never knew about my ancestry, other than that they had emigrated from another place." She hoped her little fib would suffice.

Penelope shrugged again. "Okay, keep your secrets, then. I'll tell you anyway. Barclay visits from time to time, just to check up on Daffie and me. He wanted to know…" Penelope's face clouded over again. "Funny… suddenly I can't remember. Daffie, what were we talking about?"

"Why we…" Daphne scowled. "Dear me, I think perhaps we're going senile, sister. I can't remember a thing." She chuckled.

"I see…" Abelene nodded. What were the chances that both would suddenly suffer a lapse of memory? She glanced at both of them and smiled. Something wasn't right. Abelene always kept her innate powers in check for fear of discovery—but she needed to know. She focused her sight beyond the physical and released a small fragment of her energy, muttering an incantation. Indeed, a dark mass seemed to hover above Penelope's head. It writhed and shifted like an evil mist. The same miasma had settled over Daphne as well. Abelene experimented.

"Penelope, try to remember. This is important."

As she tried, Penelope's brow creased, but for all her effort, her memory of just a few hours before wouldn't return. As Abelene watched, the dark matter above Penelope's head pulsed, growing stronger with every effort the woman exerted. Abelene had seen enough—she had seen it before. Such a spell could be exerted only by a most powerful wizard, to be so nearly undetectable. The only thing in Abelene's favor was that she was more powerful; otherwise, she never would have been able to see through the deception.

"Penelope, may I use your restroom?"

"Down the hall, dear." Pen said cheerfully, already forgetting the conversation. Abelene grabbed her purse and excused herself. Once inside, she hastily closed the door and rested her back against it. What to do? Releasing her magick could alert whatever presence hovered about the woods. She needed to be careful—not only for herself, but for her new friends. She didn't want to put them in danger. How she wished Nicodemus were with her for his advice in this matter.

She rummaged through her handbag. Though from all appearances, it was merely a purse, it contained magickal items for just such emergencies. She removed a small, ornate pentacle and a black candle. She also kept hidden a thin cloth—a veil she often used in ritual. She called to mind a revealing spell she had long committed to memory.

She placed the pentacle on the counter as she invoked the four elements, then lit the candle. Holding the veil before her with both hands, she began a low chant, whispering through the veil. Her purpose was to weave a cloaking mist over the house, invisible to the eye, yet powerful enough to push attention away from the area. Simultaneously, she reached out with her mind to stir the creatures of the forest, confounding whatever presence lingered there. In the distance, she heard the agitated chattering of birds, suddenly infused with her thoughts. That accomplished, she opened the door slightly and called out.

"Camille, could you come here for a second?"

Camille hurried over and peered into Abelene's eyes through the crack in the door.

"Are you okay?"

"Listen, Camille. I have little time to explain, but a Confusio spell has been placed over your aunts. I need to break the spell, but I need your help! Come inside." She handed the pentacle and candle to Camille.

"What's a Confusio spell?" Camille asked, curious about the strange word.

"A very powerful enchantment. No time to explain. This spell must be done quickly; otherwise, your aunts will suspect, and it won't work. The Confusio was placed by deception and must be broken by the same."

Abelene thought for a moment. She couldn't use her Elven magick; otherwise, she could alert those that would do her harm. Earth Magick, however, was potent enough to break the spell over Camille's aunts. She suddenly remembered she had kept a few packets of salt in her purse from the last time she went to a restaurant with Azriel. She rummaged through it until she found them at the very bottom. Camille looked on with curiosity as Abelene tore them open and placed the salt in the center of the pentagram. Passing the candle over the salt, she whispered a simple incantation.

"Reveal!" Abelene intoned with authority. A simple spell, but effective, however, she would need Camille to create a distraction.

"What are you doing?" Camille asked in a hushed voice.

"Shh! What are some of your aunts' favorite things of nature?"

Camille scowled as she thought, then brightened. "Bears, rainbows, hummingbirds..."

"Perfect!" Abelene smiled. "I will call them to your kitchen window. When you see them, call Penelope and Daphne over. I'll take care of the rest, okay?"

"Bears?" Camille's eyes widened at the prospect.

"No, silly—Hummingbirds!" Abelene reached out with her mind and called out to them, implanting a thought of luscious pollen-laden flowers by the windowsill. When she touched their presence, she sent Camille on her way.

"Just act natural. They will suspect nothing."

Camille quietly let herself out of the bathroom and headed toward the kitchen. She made a pretense of getting herself a glass of water while looking out the window. Just as Abelene had promised, a swarm of hummingbirds—more than Camille had ever seen in one place—gathered around the window, chirping and twittering. Some even tapped on the glass searching for the nectar they knew was there.

Camille called out excitedly, "Aunt Pen! Aunt Daffie! Look!" She didn't have to fake her sense of wonder. Penelope and Daphne crowded by the window to marvel at the unusual sight. At her cue, Abelene snuck behind them holding the pentagram in the palm of her hand. Before they could turn, she blew the salt in a cloud over their heads. Just beyond perception, they all heard a scream of frustration as the presence clouding Pen and Daffie's memories dissolved into the void. They both swooned as the power was released.

Daphne's face paled. "What in the world…"

"I apologize. It was the only way," Abelene said contritely.

The memory of the morning—and Barclay's visit—came flooding back as the Confusio lifted.

"Oh my!" Penelope held her hand to her mouth in understanding. "I remember now!"

Abelene glanced out the window at the myriad hummingbirds and smiled. "Thank you, my little friends. I release you!" The tiny birds dispersed and flew off into the woods.

Daphne placed her hand on Abelene's arm, suddenly frightened. "Dearie, we need to talk." They seated themselves back at the table and huddled close.

"Barclay cast a spell over you to cloud your memory," Abelene stated with certainty. "What do you remember?"

"He asked many questions," Penelope responded ominously.

"Like what?"

"He asked about you."

Abelene paled. "What did he want to know?"

"Nothing specific, but he was probing. He said there were rumors in the magickal community of a powerful sorceress and her son. He asked if we knew of anyone who fit that description. Said he wanted to invite her to be part of the coven."

"What did you tell him?"

"Nothing."

"Are you sure?"

Daphne paused thoughtfully, then answered. "I didn't like his line of questioning. He's a powerful wizard—powerful enough to seek and find anything or anyone he wants—so why can't he find you? I've always sensed there is something more to you than meets the eye." Daphne smiled. "I also know how close Camille and Azriel have become. You know, I must protect my own! Of course, I've never distrusted Barclay before, but something held me back—call it intuition."

"Well, you keep on trusting that intuition. It serves you well," Abelene said ruefully. She looked down, her face pensive. Perhaps it was time for the truth—but how much of the truth could she reveal? It had been so long since she had taken anyone into her confidence. The last time she did, her handmaiden and closest confidante was tortured for information, and it nearly led to Abelene's ruin. Tears came to her eyes as she thought of that horrible day. She vowed Azriel would never know what had happened—or why she had come to this world. Knowledge could be dangerous in the wrong hands—and worse even fatal to Abelene and Azriel if leaked to the wrong ears. Secrets revealed had toppled empires and caused strife among untold masses. She needed to make Penelope and Daphne fully understand the magnitude of her secret—as well as the consequences—if they let it slip what she was about to tell them.

"Dearie?" Daphne said tenderly, concerned by Abelene's sudden change in mood. "What's wrong?"

"There's something I must tell you. It's dark and evil, and you must not tell a soul!"

Penelope and Daphne stared at her, transfixed—and suddenly afraid.

"You must swear an oath that you will never reveal—or even discuss with each other—what I am about to tell you. Is that understood? That goes for you too, Camille."

The girl swallowed. Her throat had suddenly gone dry.

Abelene looked at each of them, her expression grave, until all three nodded.

"We must make a blood oath."

Camille's eyes widened as Abelene removed a sheathed blade from her purse. The handle, beautifully wrought in silver and bone—Daphne recognized it for what it was: a ritual boline, used only on the most solemn of occasions.

"Understand, ladies. This must be voluntary." Abelene said.

"I understand." Penelope held her hand to her heart and bowed.

"I, too." Daphne conceded and turned to her niece. "Camille?"

"Will it hurt?" Her voice quivered.

Abelene smiled tenderly. "Only for a moment."

"Okay, I will too."

"Something else you must know," Abelene added. "We will now be joined as family. It is an unbreakable bond—the truthbond of a witch!"

Camille straightened, a hint of pride and bravery in her stance.

"I need an incense brazier—and I need dragon's blood." Abelene said.

Daphne, glad to comply, strode into the adjoining room and returned with a small cast-iron pot in one hand and an ornately decorated vial. Knowing well what Abelene required, she removed a chunk of brownish-red resin from the tiny container and ground it with a pestle in a stone mortar. For good measure, she added a touch of wormwood to strengthen the spell. Penelope scooped out a goodly amount of hot coals from the fireplace and poured them into the iron pot. Camille then emptied the contents of the mortar onto the coals. A heady cloud of perfumed smoke wafted through the kitchen. As the sweet aroma of the dragon's blood spread to envelop them, Abelene began to chant:

> "Ancient spell, cloak of night,
> Keep us hidden, out of sight.
> Close the ears of all who hear,
> Banish those who linger near!"

She repeated the spell three times until the room felt completely private. Once sure of their concealment, she unsheathed her blade. She held the needle-sharp end to her sternum and pressed until a drop of thick blood seeped from the tiny wound. She ceremonially handed the boline to Penelope, who also drew her own blood. Daphne likewise did the same. She then handed the blade to Camille. She took the blade with trembling fingers and stared at the sharp point. For a moment she thought she might faint.

"I'm scared, Aunt Daffie." Camille's voice quivered.

"Would you like me to do it for you?" Daphne offered.

"No. She must do it on her own," Abelene said quietly but firmly.

Camille took a deep breath and winced as she pricked herself with the boline. "That wasn't so bad." She smiled bravely but her hand shook as she returned the blade to Abelene.

Abelene nodded with approval and dabbed her finger into the trickle of blood on her own chest. She then pressed it into the blood on Penelope's chest, saying, "My blood to your blood; my heart to your heart. That is the unbreakable oath I make." She repeated the ritual vow with Daphne and Camille. They in turn repeated the gesture to Abelene and to each other until they all had mingled their blood.

"It is done, then." Abelene said with finality. "My secret will now become yours."

They sat at the kitchen table facing one another. Abelene began to speak.

"This world is not what you think it is. Many thousands of years ago, to protect humanity, this world was split in two by the most powerful wizard who ever existed. His name was Eltanin. Not many know of this except a privileged few. My world is invisible to modern science, existing a dimension apart from yours. What you think you know is an illusion. This world—this planet—had been bigger once and most magick had been taken from it. The remnants of magick, however, still remain in places closest to the source of the breach.

"Daphne, you and your sister grew up in Ireland, and what I am about to tell you will be difficult for you to fathom—but understand it, you must! Between Ireland and England is the small island you call the Isle of Man. But it is all that remains of my home world—a mere remnant of the place of my birth. It was once the great continent of Aralia and the source of all Magick. Flanking Aralia, off its eastern and western borders were islands—present day Britain and Ireland. In the many years before the breach, my race, the Ferrishyn, had grown in Earth power and shaped our world to perfection. Peace and harmony abounded; there was no lack or want among my people. It was said that a strange occurrence took place at that remote time. A ship arrived, carrying thousands of people—humans. No one was quite certain where they came from. It was believed, however, that they came from the far future, seeking to escape a terrible calamity that had befallen their world—this world—though no one was certain. What *was* certain was that they didn't know how to live in our world and would not learn the ways of magick. Instead, they resorted to their powerful technology, mimicking our magick through destructive means. If allowed to continue, they would bring ruin to Aralia. It was for this reason alone that a terrible ritual was invoked, separating the world and tearing it asunder. The Elemental Dragons protecting my world were imprisoned on yours! On that terrible day, the earth shook to its very foundation. A new dimension was formed and the planet—now two—was reduced in size. When the dust settled, a great chunk had been torn from Aralia—its very heart. In time, it became a lake. On your world it is the Isle of Man. My people remained on Aralia, but its heart was gone—a dimension apart from us. Soon, the consequences of Eltanin's dark ritual became apparent.

"Over time, Magick began to fade from Aralia, for its heart was gone—unreachable."

Penelope interrupted. "Whatever happened to Eltanin?"

"No one knows. It is said that the ritual destroyed him. He disappeared into the newly created dimension. It's possible he still roams your world." Abelene paused, then added a new twist to the story. "You have a legend about the destruction of Atlantis and Lemuria. For what it's worth, the ruin of those civilizations could only have been brought about by the most potent magick and the most powerful of wizards. I'm guessing here, but I believe Eltanin had survived and tried to recreate his ill-begotten ritual to reintegrate the worlds. Again he failed."

Camille had become subdued. She asked quietly, "Abelene, are you and Azriel human?"

Abelene smiled. "Yes, to a certain degree—and no. In many ways, we are the same physiologically, but we have differences—like the ears." she pointed at her own playfully. "See this point? On my world, it's a bit more pronounced. We Ferrishyn live a long time—longer than mortal humans. Magick is ingrained within us. That is something I have kept hidden for fear of arousing suspicion—and why I mostly keep to myself. You see, I was born about 300 years ago, as you reckon time."

They all gasped involuntarily, but Camille blurted, "Can I learn your magick?"

"That depends…"

"On what?" She sounded disappointed.

Abelene giggled. "Why, on you, Camille. It depends on how open you are to accepting what couldn't possibly be real. But let me get back to my story."

"Okay—but I'm not letting this go."

"Camille!" Aunt Pen scolded.

"As I said before, Magick began to fade in my world. What was once child's play gradually could only be performed by only the most adept wizards and witches. Certainly, on this world Magick was all but gone except in certain places where it still lingers—but one must delve deep to find it."

Abelene paused. Now she was at the heart of the matter.

"There is a prophecy on my world—that one would be born who would reunite the worlds—bring about balance—restore true Magick. He would be born with all the powers of a true wizard— one as powerful as Eltanin. And he would be born of royal blood." Abelene looked down and quickly swiped at the tears forming in her eyes.

"You see, I am from a powerful line of wizards and sorcerers. My royal line has remained unbroken for fifty-nine generations and when I conceived—when Azriel was born—the stars were in position to herald his coming. It is Azriel who must bear this terrible burden."

"But Azriel…" Camille interrupted.

"Wait. There's more. Some among the powerful and elite did not want this change to occur. My husband, Berrill, the King, was among them. They feared more than anything the loss of their power over others. If the worlds again become one, all will change. Those who resisted the change," Abelene broke down and wept. "Those men—including my husband—plotted my murder! Kill me, and my child would never be born."

Penelope and Daphne stared, ashen faced, at Abelene, horrified, as the gravity of the situation became clear.

"There was only one thing I could do," Abelene explained darkly. "I invoked an ancient and terrible ritual to translate myself and my unborn child to your world." She shivered with remembrance. "My soul was shot out into the void. In my peril, I faced seven hells before my body reunited with my spirit. That's when I was found, near death—here in this world. Nicodemus had been waiting. As Earth wizards go, he is one of the most powerful. Somehow he knew where and when I would appear. Nicodemus nursed me back to health and even attended the birth of my son."

Abelene stared at all of them, her expression grave. "So you see, Azriel and I are in great danger. It is why I have remained hidden all this time—to protect him. Even on this world, there are those who seek his ruin! I have felt them and know they are searching. When Eltanin performed his ritual of desecration, there were six others present—powerful and mighty wizards. When he disappeared, they vanished with him and were never seen again! I believe they are on this world. That is why you must be ever diligent. Never reveal what you know!"

Chapter 7

The ocean was shrouded in thick gray mist. Still early, the sun hadn't yet burned off the morning fog. Having just awakened, Azriel stood by the doorway wondering where Nicodemus and Amaryllis were. Felisa lay curled up in the rocking chair, purring contentedly by the hearth. Peering into the misty coastline, he caught a glimpse of two figures walking arm in arm into the distance. The quiet was unsettling as Azriel still wrestled with his thoughts. Bigger things seemed to be afoot—bigger than even Uncle Nick was letting on.

"Good morning!"

Azriel nearly jumped out of his skin. So silently, Felisa now stood beside him and stretched.

"You scared the life out of me! I'm still not used to that!"

"Perhaps you need to sharpen your senses." Felisa smiled broadly.

Azriel sighed. "You could have warned me."

"It's not in the nature of a cat to give warning. Come and help me with breakfast."

Felisa stoked the fire and added a few pieces of wood to the embers. She pulled a small kettle from the kitchen shelf and filled it with water.

"The oats are in the cupboard. Measure out four cups," she instructed. "Some good oatmeal will be perfect for such a chilly morning. Amaryllis likes tea with her breakfast."

An iron rod was affixed to the hearth. Azriel hung the kettle from the center hook and sat by the fire, stirring the pot and impatiently waiting for it to boil.

"So today's the big day!" Felisa said cheerfully.

"What are you talking about?" Azriel retorted defensively.

"Oops!" She giggled. "I guess I just let the cat out of the bag."

Azriel rolled his eyes. "You enjoy that, don't you—all the cat references."

Felisa didn't respond. Instead, she laughed to herself.

"So what's going on?"

"You'll just have to wait for Amaryllis. She has a task for you."

"Fabulous." Azriel's tone was less than amicable.

Soon the mixture of oats and dried fruit came to a rolling boil. Felisa sweetened the porridge with a generous amount of honey and cinnamon and licked the spoon with contentment. She hung another pot of water over the fire for tea. As she noisily set the table with bowls, cups, and spoons, her ears perked up.

"Oh, they've returned. Just in time!"

Amaryllis and Nicodemus entered and sat at the table while Felisa doled out portions of the hot porridge. With tea poured, they sat facing each other and ate in silence. Azriel noticed Amaryllis staring at him and squirmed uncomfortably.

"I have a task for you, young man." She smiled amicably.

He bristled, not at all thrilled with the prospect.

"Now don't you worry about it, son. This is the easiest of the four challenges you will have to complete. Simple, really, if you keep your wits about you," Amaryllis assured.

"You know, somehow I don't find that very comforting."

"Quit your complaining," Uncle Nick blustered. "It's about time you learn some self-sufficiency. You need to grow yourself a backbone, boy."

Felisa piped in, "I'll go with you, if you want."

"No, Felisa, he must do this alone."

She looked down, pouting, and complained. "I never get to go anywhere."

Amaryllis handed Azriel a neatly tied package. It felt heavy in his hands. He looked up doubtfully at her.

"Go ahead, open it!"

Azriel untied the ribbon and stared down in disbelief. Within the wrapped paper, a pocked and cratered stone—blackened and misshapen—stared up at him.

"A rock? You're kidding me! What am I supposed to do with it?"

"Read the paper it was wrapped in," Uncle Nick growled.

"Yeah, I get it! Rock, paper—where's the scissors?"

Nicodemus leaned forward and smacked Azriel on the back of his head. Felisa giggled.

"Don't be an ass, boy. This isn't a game."

"Okay, I'll read it!" He rubbed his head and scanned the cursive writing scrawled across the page. Knitting his eyebrows, he sighed with consternation. Azriel hated riddles.

"Well, what does it say?" Felisa asked.

Azriel read aloud:

> In Castleton dwells the scaly man,
> Repulsive, malicious, and hard to behold.
> Weighed in the balance the secret plan,
> A lesson learned transforms into gold.

"So what does it mean?" Azriel scratched his head.

"It's a riddle. You're the one who has to solve it," Amaryllis said lightly. "That's your task for today. If completed successfully, you will learn the first of the four secret names."

"What names?" Felisa inquired.

Amaryllis reached over from the table and gently extracted the amulet nestled within Azriel's shirt, holding it before the boy's eyes. He stared at the four interlocking dragons. "The secret names of the elementals. Without them, you cannot hope to summon their power. But understand—their names are a gift not lightly given. You must earn them. Earth is the solid foundation." She pointed at one of the dragons on the medallion. "Soil, sand and rock beneath your feet— like the base of a pyramid, your footing must be firm; otherwise, everything you do will crumble under the weight. Learn the name of the Earth Elemental, and you will be well underway to your goal. Fail and the world will be doomed." The cast of her eyes intensified, and Azriel shuddered. Just as quickly, Amaryllis smiled impishly. "So, son of Abelene—that is your task. Do not return here until you have completed it. But be comforted—you just might have help along the way." She winked mischievously.

Azriel gaped, staring from one to the other. Nicodemus, Amaryllis, and Felisa stared back at him. "Wait, do you mean I'm going alone?"

"Of course!" She answered, "A quest is always done alone; otherwise, what good would it do?"

"But…"

"Well," Nicodemus grunted as he rose from the table, "you'd best be at it, boy. Time's wasting."

Amaryllis extracted a satchel from the cupboard and handed it to Azriel. He opened it and examined the contents. Various packed foods, a few utensils; a box of matches, warm clothing, and a sleeping bag filled the sack. The sight of the bedroll didn't help to fill him with much confidence. Obviously, this task would take longer than he expected. Resigned to his fate, Azriel hefted the satchel over his shoulder and set out to leave. He stuffed the note in his pocket and headed toward the door.

"Aren't you forgetting something?"

Nicodemus tossed him the rock. "You'll need that."

"Yeah, right. The rock." Azriel looked at it dubiously and stuffed it in his other pocket.

Felisa stopped him at the door and took his hand. "I wish I was coming with you."

Azriel hesitated and smiled grimly. "Yeah, me too."

He soon found himself on the road leading to Castleton. A wooden signpost pointed the way, and Azriel headed down the dirt road determined to be done with his task before nightfall. Still early morning, Azriel had the full day ahead of him. The sun burned off the remainder of the morning dew; here and there, wisps of vapor dissipated from the fields. The countryside panorama filled Azriel with a sense of wonder. Gentle and serene, his mind wandered, lost in the beauty of the landscape. It filled him with a peculiar feeling of longing, though for what he didn't know. His thoughts were of his mother and Camille. He missed them. Jasper and Albert, too. He figured they were probably out playing baseball right now and wished he were tossing the ball with them. In fact, Azriel's pitching had improved and he'd developed a reasonably good fastball. So immersed in his musings, Azriel was surprised to find himself approaching the Fairy Bridge he had crossed the day before. It led through a dense stand of woods, the path winding through a thick canopy of foliage. He absently headed toward the wobbly bridge. As before, the handrails and supporting beams were festooned with notes and gifts for the wee folk.

"That's just ridiculous." Azriel muttered to himself, amazed that people could be so superstitious. Refusing to heed Nicodemus' warning, he stepped onto the bridge without offering so much as a greeting, determined to prove the local legends a bunch of hogwash. The bridge shook unsteadily and Azriel had to grab the handrail to get his footing. He backed off the bridge.

"Idiot."

"Huh?" Azriel could have sworn he heard a voice. He looked around but the road on either side of the bridge was deserted.

He steadied himself and stepped back onto the first plank.

"Moron!"

"Who's there?" He spun around, nearly tripping. Answered by resounding silence, Azriel grumbled and continued on his way.

"Imbecile!"

"Hey! Knock it off, whoever you are!" He peered into the bushes on either side of the bridge, but his sight was hampered by the dense undergrowth. Now truly annoyed, Azriel purposely stomped onto the bridge. Suddenly a rock sailed through the air and rebounded off his skull.

"Ow! Dammit!" he shouted.

"Seems I can't knock it off. Your head's firmly attached!" a voice came from within the bushes.

Face red, Azriel blustered. "Show yourself so I can kick your ass!"

From within the bushes, a face suddenly appeared. Tangled red hair thrust out from the sides of a rumpled green cap that flopped down comically on one side. Hoary eyebrows framed deep-set piercing eyes; the creature's nose protruded, as bulbous as an old potato. The wizened gnome stepped out from beneath the shrubbery and rubbed his thick beard thoughtfully. He stood a caricature of a man, at least a foot shorter than Azriel. Turning around, he bent over and wiggled his backside.

"Go on then," he offered. "Kick me arse."

"Who are you?" Azriel growled.

"Nope! Only one request at a time. Go ahead, laddie. Kick me arse. I know you want to!" He wiggled his rump salaciously.

Having taken enough ridicule, Azriel wound up with enough force to punt the ugly little troll into the next county. He released his foot with as much strength as he could muster, only the little gnome and his rumpled butt disappeared with an audible pop. With nothing for Azriel's foot to make contact with, he fell on his back with a thud.

"Dammit!" he screamed in frustration.

The hobgoblin now sat on the guide rail of the bridge and laughed merrily, pointing at Azriel with ridicule. "Guess your aim ain't so good, eh laddie!"

Azriel thought of pushing the little pest over the side, but knew he'd only be fooled again, probably plunging himself into the stream below.

"All right, so who are you?"

"Pog's the name."

"Pog? Pog who?"

"Not who, just Pog."

"Yeah, well, what do you want?"

"A proper greeting would suffice," Pog answered as he picked his nose. He wiped a nasty looking booger onto the handrail. "There's a gift for ya."

"That's disgusting," Azriel responded heatedly.

"Aye, and pretty disgusting, the way you treated poor old Pog, not saying even a hello and good mornin' as you cross me bridge."

"All right then. Good morning! Can I cross now?"

"Suit yourself!" Pog shrugged. The air around him shimmered and he disappeared.

Azriel stood up and brushed himself off. He stepped gingerly onto the bridge and tested the wood. Carefully, one step at a time, he plodded along, not trusting the old structure; but halfway across, his steps were more confident, sensing that the bridge, after all, was quite safe. He took three more steps when a plank suddenly gave way. Azriel along with his satchel, plummeted ten feet below into the stream.

Azriel sputtered, spitting water, quickly retrieving his sack before it floated away. "Dammit!" He slapped the water angrily.

"As you requested!" Pog sat at the bank of the stream. Suddenly, a mass of sticks and branches rose from the water blocking its flow. From the center of the woody mass, a beaver popped its head from its lodge and squealed angrily at Azriel.

"Oh, for cryin' out loud." Azriel scrambled to dry land and sat next to Pog in a soggy heap. "Why are you bothering me?" He asked miserably.

"Bothering? Bothering! I'm here to help, and all ye do is hurt old Pog's feelings." He hung his head into his hands and shook it sadly. "A fine kettle of fish! Bothering, he says."

"Okay, I'm sorry."

"No, you're not." Pog sniffed miserably.

"Yes," Azriel held his hand to his heart. "I'm really, really sorry."

"Mean it?"

Azriel sighed. "Yes."

"Very well then." Pog's demeanor brightened. "Now, young master, what is your name?"

"Azriel."

"Azriel...who?"

"Azriel Kingsley."

Pog's eyes narrowed. "You lie! You're a Ferrishyn."

Azriel paled. How could the little pest know?

"Indeed! You can't hide from me!" Pog answered Azriel's unspoken thought. "You and me—we're kin!"

"That's not very likely. I mean—look at you, and look at me."

"Judge a book by its cover, would ye? Not very smart, are ye! I could help ye get smarter. I'm pretty good when it comes to fools!"

"Hey!" Azriel sputtered.

Instantly, a small bale of hay dropped from the sky and landed at Azriel's feet.

"What the hell..." Azriel sputtered.

The bale burst into a conflagration of flames and was, in seconds, reduced to ashes.

"Will you stop that!" Azriel shouted.

"Stop what?"

"Taking everything I say literally!"

"Then you should say what you mean, laddie."

"This is impossible," Azriel muttered darkly.

"No, it isn't. Nothing's impossible when you know how!" Pog poked at Azriel's shoulder.

"So what do you want?"

"Me?" Pog emoted, holding his hand to his chest. "I'm in need of nothing. Pog is only here to help."

"What are you anyway?"

"I told you! I'm a Ferrishyn, otherwise known as a fairy, elf, dwarf, leprechaun, gnome, hobgoblin, sprite—one of the wee folk; call me anything except late fer dinner!" Pog patted his belly and emitted a belch that resounded through the woods. "Ah, yes. Love to eat."

"You're a revolting little turd, aren't you!"

Before Azriel could take it back, a rather large bird flew overhead and released a massive stream of stinking excrement that splattered squarely on his shoulder.

"Ugh! Gross!"

Twelve cartons of eggs neatly stacked appeared at Azriel's feet. "There you go." Pog chortled, "Count them!"

"Huh?"

"One hundred and forty-four—exactly a gross!"

"Will you knock it off!"

"Tried that already—didn't work." Pog shook his head sadly.

"Why are you doing this?"

"I told you. I'm here to help!"

"Well, I don't want your help," Azriel responded darkly.

"But you need it—a fool like you on a quest!"

Azriel grumbled under his breath.

"So where would ye be going, laddie?"

"Castleton."

"For what?"

"Not sure really—maybe a circus or carnival?"

"None that I know of there." Pog rubbed his beard thoughtfully.

"Well, where else would I find an ugly scaly man except in a sideshow?"

"Gone soft in the head, eh? No such thing. So what will you do when you find this scaly man?"

"Don't know."

"Then you'll probably fail, poor, poor lad. If you fail to plan, then you plan to fail." Pog sighed.

"Look, you're a nice—whatever you are—but would you just leave me alone?"

"Can't do that." Pog shrugged and held up his hands.

"Why not?" Azriel squelched down his rising temper.

"Told you. I'm here to help."

"Then tell me where I'd find a scaly man."

"Hmm, scaly man—an ugly, scaly man—a man with scales." Pog's face perked up with a thought. "I know! You need an assayer. They have scales."

"I think you're grasping at straws, Pog. The riddle was explicit. It said to seek out a scaly man."

"And you're so bright, you can solve this riddle all by yourself, hmm?" Pog purposely provoked him.

"What a pain in the ass." Azriel mumbled.

Suddenly, a mule crashed through the brush, braying pathetically. An arrow protruded prominently from its backside. In its panic, it knocked Azriel to the ground as it galloped out of sight. He got up and brushed himself off.

"That's it! I'm leaving. Now bug off!" Azriel shouted.

"Suit yourself, then." Pog looked up in the air and sighed heavily.

Azriel headed off the path to Howe Road, the way leading to Castleton.

Pog followed several paces behind. "Well, at least ye be doing one thing right. Good sense of direction!" he said cheerfully.

Azriel did his best to ignore him, hoping he'd go away.

"But you're still an idiot!"

Azriel cussed under his breath.

"Such a vulgar tongue on a youngster—imbecile."

The harassment continued through the morning. From Station Road to Four Road, Pog followed behind, hurling insults at Azriel. The boy turned right onto Castleton Road when Pog let fly a new tirade of verbal abuse.

"Nitwit! Dolt! Pea-brain!"

Azriel spun around. "What!" he complained loudly.

"Ye be going the wrong way. Can't believe everything you read. Just 'cause the sign says Castleton Road doesn't mean it leads there—twit! Got to go straight on to Church Road. That turns to Old School Road, then you take right to Ballagawne Road."

Azriel ground his teeth and growled, clearly frustrated and close to losing his temper.

"Face it, laddie," Pog stated, "Without me, you'd be lost already—wanker!"

"Stop insulting me. You're really starting to piss me off."

"Good idea." Pog dropped his trousers and urinated off the side of the road. Disgusted, Azriel grimaced and turned away.

"Don't you have a shred of decency?"

"Not likely, not when dealing with silly dodders like you."

"I've had about enough of your insults!"

"Oh, have you, laddie? Perhaps you don't understand the King's English. How about Yiddish? Putz! Schmuck! Shmeckle!"

"Go to hell!"

"Been there. Didn't like yer mother's cookin'."

Azriel had reached the end of his limit with the impertinent little pest. He thrust his hand in his pocket and grasped the rock. He wound up with a mighty pitch and hurled the rock with all his strength. A perfect fastball, it promised to meet its mark and smack Pog squarely on the noggin. But quicker than Azriel thought possible, the old troll reached up and caught it, smiling deviously.

"Thanks!" Pog bubbled gleefully, holding up the rock as if it were a prize, and vanished with an audible pop.

"Finally, some peace!" Azriel spoke to himself and took the Church Road. Throughout the morning, and without Pog irritating him, Azriel was actually beginning to enjoy himself—and the quiet. The road passed many quaint houses and curved around at the small hamlet of Ballabeg. As he rounded the corner, a young man, perhaps a few years older than Azriel, pulled up next to him on a scooter.

"Where ye be heading, mate?"

"Castleton." Azriel answered.

"Hop on. I'm heading there myself. What's your name?"

"Azriel. What's yours?"

"Billy. Get on."

Azriel sat behind and soon they were coasting at a good pace. A short hop later, within ten minutes, they were in the heart of the town.

"Well, here we are, mate," Billy said cheerfully. "Where are you off to?"

"Not sure. I have to find something—someone."

"What exactly?"

"It's going to sound strange. I'm looking for a scaly man."

Billy rubbed his chin thoughtfully. "Can't say I know any. But there is a pet shop down the street. Maybe there? Matter of fact, the proprietor is an ugly old bloke. Face all mashed up—missing a hand—alligator, ye know."

"Where are you going?" Azriel inquired.

"I'm off to the open market. I'm working a concession today. It's somewhat of a tourist trap. Matter of fact, you're not from around here, are ye?"

"No, from America. I'm here with my Uncle."

"I'll drop you off by the pet shop. If you get hungry, stop by the market. We set up right at the quay near Castle Rushen. The shop is just up the street by the old House of Keys."

"A locksmith?"

"No!" Billy laughed. "Don't know much about local history, do ye? It was the House of Parliament before the Tynwald was moved to Douglas. It's just a museum now."

"Oh." Azriel hid his embarrassment.

"No problem. Just get on."

After a short ride, Billy let Azriel off by Castleton harbor and pointed to the House of Keys. He then pointed to the road beyond it. "That's where the shops are situated." He nodded toward the opposite side near the castle. "And that's where I'll be. Stop by for some bangers and mash."

"Thanks, Billy."

Azriel watched as Billy scooted off toward the castle entrance, quickly lost in the crowd of tourists and locals. He headed toward the street beyond the House of Keys, passing ancient buildings and quaint shops. Across the street, Castle Rushen loomed before him. Within a wrought-iron fence, a granite cross in the Celtic tradition stood guard over a well-manicured flower garden. It seemed a beautiful and serene spot, a counterpoint to the madness that had already marked his morning. Tempted toward diversion and a bit of rest, he considered lingering by the garden, but the pet shop was just down the street, and he wanted to complete his task and return to the relative sanity of Amaryllis' home. A few paces, and soon he stared up at the sign that read, *Creature Comforts* above the shop.

Azriel entered through the narrow door and instantly his senses were assaulted by a cacophony of squawks, squeals, bleats, howls, chirps, chatters—a veritable Noah's Ark of noise. An old man strode about, feeding and watering his stock. He suddenly turned around and glared at Azriel, a look of menace in his one good eye. The other was covered with a patch. Azriel stammered. Indeed, the old codger was perhaps the ugliest creature in the pet shop. His face was scarred along the right side, as though he had been viciously clawed. Where his left hand should have been, a mangled stump stared back; above it, a muscular arm completely covered with tattoos. Around his neck, a boa constrictor hung limply, peacefully asleep.

"Well, don't just stand there gaping. What do you want?" the shopkeeper snarled.

"Um, I think I'll just look around," Azriel replied, suddenly intimidated by the old man.

Looking from tank to tank, Azriel took in a menagerie of the most bizarre creatures he'd ever seen. Not your typical pets, there were exotic beasties from every corner of the world. Horned lizards, tarantulas, fruit bats, rodents, weasels, baby pigs and goats, strange outlandish birds—yet not one puppy or kitten.

"Find what you're looking for?" the shopkeeper said, startling Azriel.

"Um, no."

"Perhaps you don't know what you want, eh? How about a pig?" The old codger picked up the little piglet with his good arm as the poor thing squealed in terror. "This little guy is Herman. Try him out. Loyal, smart, good truffler—and if he doesn't work out, you can always eat him."

"Uh, no thanks."

"How about ol' Lucifer?" He pointed with his stump at the snake draped around his neck. "All you gotta do is feed him one sizeable rat every two weeks—alive, of course."

"Actually, sir. I have a question." Azriel hesitated. "Um, do you have scales?"

"Scales? Are you daft, boy? You want scales? Maybe you should play with Daisy here!" He pointed to a six-foot alligator behind a glass barrier. "Took my hand, she did. Lucky I didn't turn her into luggage! Scales! Dumbest thing I ever heard. I think perhaps you should leave before I sic Daisy on you. Now get out!" The old shopkeeper bellowed and shoved him toward the door.

Azriel found himself on the sidewalk again, his face red with humiliation. He spent the early part of the afternoon searching for any clue to solve the riddle. Having roamed about Castleton without being any closer to an answer, he found himself by the castle garden again and settled on a comfortable bench. Removing the note from his pocket, he reread the riddle. The second line both intrigued and baffled him. Azriel sounded out the line. "Repulsive, malicious, and hard to behold." He thought long and hard. The pet shopkeeper was certainly repulsive—a malicious old bastard—and hard to look at. The answer *had* to lie with him!

Frustrated and hungry, Azriel reached into his satchel and removed the food Amaryllis packed earlier that morning—only to find it waterlogged and ruined. Azriel cussed under his breath. He had forgotten the dunking he'd taken on the bridge. "Curse that Pog anyway," Azriel growled. He rummaged through the pack and found a few pounds of local currency folded neatly inside. Now quite famished, he decided to find the booth his new friend Billy manned at the open market. It didn't take too long to locate.

He waited in line, and soon he was the next one served.

"Ah, Azriel! You look a mite bit hot around the collar. Tough morning?" Billy inquired cheerfully.

"Yeah, you could say that. Let me try some of what you've got there."

"Right. One serving of bangers and mash. A bit of ale?"

"Billy, I'm fifteen."

"Won't tell a soul."

"All right."

"Here you go then. That'll be two pounds, five shillings."

Azriel handed Billy three pounds and took his change. Billy spoke to the fair-haired freckle-faced girl next to him manning the booth. "Liza, I'll be taking my break now." He loaded up a plate with food and followed Azriel to a table.

"So mate, what has you so hot and bothered?"

Azriel didn't immediately answer but dug into his plate. He couldn't help sighing with contentment. Sausages and mashed peas never tasted so good. He finally answered. "This is probably going to sound completely bonkers, but my uncle sent me here to solve a riddle."

"Aye, did he?" Billy mused. "Let me see!"

He scanned the paper handed to him and read it through while Azriel ate voraciously. He had trouble with the ale at first, tasting somewhat bitter. It revived him though, and in fact went to his head rather quickly. Azriel giggled.

Billy looked up and smiled. "Your first beer? Mary, Mother of God, yer a lightweight." He laughed. "Now this riddle? It's utter nonsense. Unless…"

"Yes?" Azriel looked up hopefully.

"Unless, maybe you're not looking for a man."

"Huh?"

"A man could be a woman, and a woman can be a man! Particularly on this island."

Azriel's face went blank.

"Kind of dense aren't ye. Isle of Man—get it?"

"That's crazy! And besides, who would have scales."

"And a stubborn bloke too! I know exactly who you need. Rosemary! Aye, she's lovely to behold, true to her name—as beautiful as a rose. She works in gold and silver at her father's shop."

"Yeah but the riddle says the person I'm looking for is ugly."

"Can't help you there, mate, but I'll tell you a little secret. Rumor has it that she belongs to a secret order. A high priestess I'm told. Some say she's sometimes seen in the forest on the night of the full moon, naked as the day she was born—doing strange things! But it's only a rumor, mind you." He sighed, "Aye, but I don't care! If'n only I could win her heart."

"You're crazy, you know."

Billy laughed. "Aye, as a crazy as a loon! Well, best be going back. Liza will be quite cross if'n I'm late from my break—and once her tongue starts waggin' there's no stopping it."

"See you, Billy."

"Aye, you can bet on it!"

Azriel wandered aimlessly without any direction and no closer to his quarry. He found himself back at the pet shop again and steeled his resolve. Entering the store, Azriel saw the old man seated at a desk, reading, with a rather unusual critter perched on his shoulder and draped over his head, napping. Its long, thick tail—ringed with darker bands—hung limply from a slender, catlike body. The shopkeeper looked up from his book and slammed it shut.

"You again!" He snarled.

"Yeah, me again. Look—sorry about the scales thing." Azriel looked curiously at the creature napping on the man's head. "Um, what is that?"

"Called an Olingo—from South America. Want to take him home? Only forty pounds."

"Sorry—no."

"Then what do you want?"

"I'm trying to solve a riddle. It's important."

The old man stared at Azriel levelly. "Son, what's your name?"

"Azriel, sir."

"The name's Parkins. That's Mister Parkins to you. So let me get this straight. You've been roaming around Castleton like a silly twit, trying to solve a riddle? You *must* be daft."

"Here, take a look." Azriel handed him the paper.

Mister Parkins read the note, eyebrows knitted as he nodded. "Ah, you know what this is?"

Azriel stared at him in anticipation.

"It's complete piffle!" he crumpled the paper and threw it in Azriel's face. "Now, it's a beautiful day. Go out. See the sights—but stop bothering me!" He pointed with his stump. "There's the door."

Azriel picked up the wrinkled note from the floor and made a hasty exit. Frustrated, he sighed heavily. He walked aimlessly down the street holding the note, and came to an intersection where the buildings seemed strewn about in a haphazard arrangement. The old grey structures, cut from local granite, seemed to have stood for centuries. Still holding the note in his hand, he stuffed it in his pocket when the whisker Felisa had given him slipped free and landed in a puddle at his feet. He was about to retrieve it when it began to behave oddly. It spun like the needle of a compass, and pointed to a narrow alley at the end of the street.

"Odd," he murmured. With no other clue, Azriel picked up the whisker and followed its direction. Within the tight passageway, tiny shops lined each side. One in particular caught his attention, not so much for its ornate window and glossy black doorway, but for the bronze statue perched on a pedestal beside the door. A beautifully cast mermaid sat upon sculpted rock, her fish tail hanging down the side; long, flowing hair seemed to whip about in an unseen breeze, framing a lovely face. In one hand, she cradled a conch shell; in the other, arm extended, she held a pair of scales. He glanced up at the gold lettering on the window. He read aloud. "Gold, Silver, Exotic Jewelry, Assaying—Purveyor of the Rare and Arcane." Azriel shook his head. "Couldn't be that easy."

He gingerly opened the door and peered inside. The store did not appear to be manned. Within antique display cases, beautifully handcrafted objects sat upon purple velvet. Pendants, crosses, amulets, gold and silver braided chains dazzled the eyes. In another showcase, chalices, beautifully wrought blades and daggers, ritual items were arranged for maximum presentation. Further in, adorning the walls, were icons, mandalas, medicine bags; on the shelf's numerous ornate bottles and clay jars labeled with names of incenses and herbs—a veritable hodgepodge of magickal items.

At the back counter, a tiny bell sat on the side with a sign that read, *Ring Bell for Service*." Azriel rang the bell, and a sweet tone resounded through the store. A few seconds later, the curtain concealing the back room swept aside. Azriel's jaw dropped. Perhaps the most beautiful woman Azriel had ever seen entered through the curtain. A cherubic oval face was framed with golden hair. Her green eyes sparkled merrily, and her full lips curled up into a smile. She wore a simple red-and-black peasant dress with a white lacey chemise beneath. For her beauty alone, her presence was altogether intimidating.

Azriel stammered, "You're not a man!"

She chuckled lightly. "Well, I should think not!" Her voice chimed like crystal, laced with a thick Irish brogue. "What were ye expecting?"

"An ugly old man."

"Ah, that would be me father. Hideous old codger—but a good and gentle heart. I run the shop now."

"I see." Azriel mumbled. "Hey, you look like that mermaid outside!"

"And why shouldn't I? Me father had it fashioned to look like me. Always going on about how I should have been born a fish, bein' I love the water so much."

"Are you Rosemary?"

"Aye. Ye must be Azriel." She looked at an antique clock on the wall and scowled. "I've been expecting ye. What took ye so long?"

"I kind of got delayed."

"Did ye, now. You'll never get very far in life dillydallying. Well, time's wasting. Give it to me then."

"Give you what?"

"You were supposed to bring me something to weigh. What am I supposed to measure—air? You're good intentions?"

Azriel paled. The rock.

"Well, where is it?" Rosemary demanded.

"I lost it—sort of."

"Well, that won't do. You'd best be finding it!"

"That might be a problem."

"Aye, yours, not mine. Off with ye then. I can't help ye if ye can't help me! Come back when ye find it."

Rosemary, without further ado, exited behind the curtain.

Afternoon quickly turned to evening, and Azriel sat on the beach beyond the docks in a quandary. He dared not attempt returning to the Fairy Bridge at night. Even for a small country, he could easily get lost in unfamiliar terrain. Azriel counted out eight pounds—certainly not enough to rent a room for the night. He had no choice but to sleep on the narrow beach, and already the temperature had dropped. He wrapped the sleeping bag around his shoulders for warmth.

The day had been a disaster. His chance meeting of Pog had really set things off badly. Now the little pain in the ass had the rock he needed to complete his task. Cold, miserable, and hungry, he brooded as he stared at the ocean.

"In a bit of a pickle aren't ye, laddie!"

Azriel jumped, startled. Pog suddenly sat beside him without warning.

"You again!" Azriel bristled. "Give me back that rock!"

"But you gave it to me! Not very mannerly to give a man a gift and then demand it back. How rude!" Pog remarked tersely. "What you need right now is food and warmth."

Pog produced a small cloth sack from his belt, no larger than a lunch bag. He reached in, his arm to the shoulder, and rummaged around. He removed an ornate chalice and placed it on the sand.

"Nope, not that." Reaching in again, he extracted a sizeable sword, impossibly large for the tiny sack. Azriel gaped as Pog placed it beside the goblet.

"Now where is that thing?" Pog muttered as he withdrew a wooden wand.

"Here, hold that, would ye, laddie." He tossed the wand to Azriel. "Ah, here it is!" He produced a flat, golden disc embellished with a five-sided star on its surface. Placing it between Azriel and himself, he held out his hand for the wand. Azriel complied.

Waving the wand with a flourish over the pentacle, he intoned. "Inferno!"

Suddenly, a huge flame shot out from the center like a blowtorch.

"Whoa!" They both jumped back.

"Extinguish!" Pog said quickly, a bit embarrassed. "Darn, wrong spell. Hmm, what was that?"

He pressed a finger against his lips as he thought. "Ah, yes! Fiero!"

With a flick of the wand, a warming flame emerged from the center of the disc.

"There, that's better. Now for some sustenance!" Reaching in the sack again, he pulled out two cups and a flask of brandy, a roast chicken already cooked, forks, knives, potatoes, carrots, plates, and a fluted vase with a spray of flowers. For effect, he clapped his hands and a grill appeared, magically floating above the flames. The chicken, potatoes, and carrots now sizzled over the hot surface.

"There you go, laddie."

"How'd you do that?"

"Magick, of course. Here, have a snort to warm yer cold bones!" The flask lifted off the ground of its own accord and poured a shot of brandy into each cup. One cup floated into Azriel's waiting hands.

"My mom would wring your neck for giving me this."

"Well she's not here, is she, laddie. Go on, live a little."

Azriel took a sip and nearly gagged at the strong drink, but warmth quickly seeped into his body. Pog cut the chicken into four quarters and served up the terrific meal. They ate quietly until only the bones remained. Fully sated, Azriel patted his belly and belched.

"Good one, laddie." Pog then released a belch that echoed throughout the beach and finished the eruption with a resounding fart. Azriel stared at him with a look of awe mixed with disgust.

"There, that's better!" Pog waved his hands with a flourish, and all the remains of the meal suddenly disappeared. The disc of fire, however, still rested on the sand.

Azriel felt better and a bit more kindly disposed toward the old gnome, even for all the trouble he caused earlier in the day.

"Um, Pog... Thanks for dinner."

He placed his hand over his heart and bowed with a flourish. "At yer service. Pog is only here to help."

"Really? Then give me the rock."

"Can't do that, laddie."

"Why not! I need it!"

"Aye, ye should have thought about that before ye tried to bean me old noggin with it!" Pog goaded.

"Well, I didn't know I'd need it."

"Sure ye did! Ye just weren't paying attention. I guess now yer screwed!" He looked up at the sky and sighed. "Know what yer problem is, laddie? Yer reckless, stubborn, and ye don't take anyone's advice. Tried to help ye, I did, and ye just ignored me. Denser than the Rock of Gibraltar. Other people tried to help ye today, too, but ye got so single-minded that ye can't see the forest for the trees. Rude, ill-mannered, dimwitted—keep this up and you'll never make a good sorcerer! Ye need to listen, laddie..."

"Are you done?" Azriel responded belligerently.

"Not even close."

"Look, just give me the rock!"

"Not a chance!"

"But you're supposed to be helping me!"

"And I do, in me own way. Well I best be off. Perhaps if ye readjust yer rotten attitude, Pog will reconsider! Ye know where to find me!"

Pog disappeared with the usual *pop*. The pentacle and flame disappeared as well, but in their place was a neatly stacked pile of kindling, driftwood, and a box of matches.

Azriel dreamt of mermaids—one in particular. He had been swimming and was pulled deep into the ocean by an undertow. Struggling, nearly drowning, he sank deeper and deeper when, inexplicably, he was suddenly lifted up out of the water, supported by a pair of lovely arms. She smiled at him and pushed him toward the shore until his feet found solid ground.

He awoke just before dawn. Disoriented, he remembered the events of the previous day and the disturbing dream. Glancing left and right, he was the only soul on the beach—or so he thought. Behind him, he heard a cheerful voice.

"Good mornin' sunshine!"

Azriel spun around to find Rosemary smiling brightly, drying off from a morning swim in the ocean.

"I dreamt of you." he said with wonder.

"Aye, I have that effect on people."

"Listen," Azriel hung his head. "I wasn't entirely truthful with you yesterday. I didn't lose the rock. In a fit of anger, I threw it at someone, and now he won't give it back!"

"A pity. Now ye have yer day cut out for ye."

"Great. Well at least I know where he'll be."

"Oh? And where would that be?" Rosemary wrapped herself in a sarong.

"The Fairy Bridge."

Rosemary suddenly laughed out loud. "Ah, you've met Pog! Annoying little bugger. Ye shouldn't have tangled with him."

"You know him?"

"We've spoken on occasion."

"Yeah, well, the little guy is a real pain in the butt. Takes everything I say literally."

"Aye, he does at that. Perhaps, Azriel, all you need to do is give him what he wants."

"And what would that be?"

"That's for you to find out."

"Is everyone on this island always so vague?"

Rosemary giggled lightly.

"Oh no," Azriel moaned.

"What, now?"

"It's him!" He grumbled. "That creepy guy from the pet shop."

Down the beach, Mr. Parkins strode at a good pace, walking Herman the piglet on a leash.

Rosemary quickly stood and ran toward the old man. She wrapped her arms around him and kissed his face. "Mornin' Papa!"

"This isn't possible." Azriel muttered to himself. "Open mouth—insert foot!"

Mister Parkins folded his arms and glared at Azriel. "What are ye doing here with me daughter? Yer not plannin' any mischief, are ye?"

Rosemary giggled. "Oh, Papa, leave the boy alone! He has enough trouble for the day without ye giving him more."

"I suppose," Parkins grumbled. "And where are ye headin' off to today? Still lookin' for the man with scales?"

"No Papa," Rosemary answered for him. "He's headin' back to the Fairy Bridge."

"Lord have mercy!" Parkins guffawed, laughing at Azriel in derision as he continued his walk on the beach.

"Good luck, laddie." He called out. "You'll need it."

Rosemary smiled, her dimpled cheeks pink from the morning chill. "Don't you mind him, Azriel. He's an awful tease. Now, here ye go." She handed him a paper sack with two scones neatly wrapped. "In case ye get hungry. Now off with ye. Time's wasting."

Retracing his steps wasn't terribly difficult now that Azriel had daylight. But he still had no clue how he would extract the rock he so desperately needed from Pog's possession. He thought over this dilemma and assessed the events of the previous day. He was starting to get the uncomfortable feeling that Rosemary and her father—indeed—everyone he met was part of a conspiracy—one in which he was the butt of an elaborate prank. Nevertheless, he appreciated the little help he had gotten. He munched on one of the scones while heading toward the bridge. It was quite tasty and filled the void in his stomach. Rounding a corner around midmorning, Azriel arrived at the Fairy Bridge. There, perched upon the handrail sat Pog, lazily fishing in the river below, beside him a bucket with two sizeable fish. Suspended from the line was the troublesome rock Azriel needed to complete his task. Suddenly, a huge fish leapt out of the water and clamped its jaws over the rock, refusing to let go. Pog struggled to pull it in. Once on the bridge, Pog produced a small club from his pocket and whacked the poor fish on the head. Releasing its hold on the rock, Pog swiftly tossed the fish in the bucket. He lowered the line again with the rock hovering just above the water.

"Hey, that's my rock!" Azriel bellowed.

"That's where ye'd be wrong, laddie. It's *my* rock!"

"Give it back."

"Come and get it then!"

Azriel dropped his traveling sack on the ground and reached for the fishing line. Goading him, Pog yanked the line out of the way. "Here, fishie, fishie!" He teased mercilessly. Azriel stretched out over the handrail to grasp the rock, but overextending his reach, plunged headlong into the stream. Sputtering water, he surfaced and glared at Pog.

"Now don't ye be lookin' at me like that, laddie. No magick here except the laws of nature. Ye did that one yerself."

Azriel crawled up the riverbank and back onto the bridge. Enraged, he leapt toward Pog, with all intentions of tackling him to the ground and wrestling the rock from his grasp. Except he wasn't there. Pog vanished and reappeared at the far side of the bridge.

"You'll never get me that way, ye silly twit!"

Azriel charged across the bridge but stopped short suddenly when a plank two paces ahead evaporated out of existence.

"Ah, learning, aren't ye! Best be replacing it." Pog waved his hands and the plank under Azriel's feet vanished. Again, he plummeted into the water below.

He looked up at Pog as he surfaced and shook his fist. "I hate you!" he raged.

"Ah, laddie. Hate is such a strong word." Pog cajoled. "Yer never gettin' the rock that way!"

Azriel trembled, a combination of anger and cold.

"Oh, dearie me! Yer going to catch a death of a cold. Here, let me help."

Pog removed a wand from his pocket and whirled it clockwise.

"Home!" he invoked.

With little transition, Azriel found himself wrapped in a blanket, sitting in a comfortable chair, surrounded by a cozy, albeit tiny room. Before him, a fire blazed, in which three gutted fish sizzled on a spit. Pog sat opposite him with his feet propped up on an ottoman. "There! That's better." Pog grinned.

Eyes wide, Azriel glanced around the room. He gasped at the piles of gold and silver, ornate chests stacked three high, glistening gemstones—some as big as a fist; indeed every conceivable treasure dazzled the eyes.

"Quite impressive, isn't it," Pog bubbled. "Now laddie, ye can have anything ye see here, but ye can't have the rock!"

Azriel glanced from pile to pile of riches, more wealth than he could ever imagine. He surged with a sudden, greedy desire to grab handfuls of the booty, but then paused. He realized he was being tempted away from his task. Pog was playing him. But why another test? The magnitude of what he was after finally hit home. What the culmination was, Azriel didn't have a clue, but whatever it was, Pog went through an awful lot of effort to distract Azriel from completing his mission. Azriel finally saw through the ruse. Whatever the end result, it must be more valuable than all the treasure in the room.

"No, Pog. I don't want any of it."

The little gnome stared at him thoughtfully as he scratched his beard. "Well, all right then." With a flourish he waved his hands and all the treasure in the room vanished. A small table, fully set with fine china and silverware appeared in its place. The fish, perfectly seared, now sat upon the plates.

"Time for lunch!" Pog rubbed his hands together and took a seat. Azriel sat opposite. The fish was quite tasty, crispy on the outside and buttery on the inside. They ate in silence helping themselves to other delectable treats on the table—turnips and mushrooms, bread with butter and honey, and a pitcher of creamy milk. They ate their fill, but as they dined, Azriel began to feel remorseful. Pog, for all his quirks, was really a fine host, helpful and caring.

"Pog?"

"Hmm." He answered, his mouth still full.

"I'm sorry for throwing the rock at you." Azriel looked down at his plate, repentant. Pog considered him in his sincerity.

"Think nothin' of it, laddie. I provoked ye."

"Pog?"

"Aye?"

"You say you only want to help. Now I need all I can get! Why won't you give me the rock?"

"Why, ye say? Well, laddie, it's because ye didn't ask! Ye just demanded!"

Azriel hung his head ashamed. "May I please have the rock back?"

Pog slipped out of the chair and walked to the other side of the table, placing the rock gently on Azriel's plate. "There ye go, laddie."

"That's it? All I had to do was ask?"

Pog sat back on his seat and faced Azriel levelly. "Son, no matter how big or small, how smart or stupid, people—no matter who they are—just want respect. If ye treat people with kindness, they will reply in kind. Amazing how much ye can accomplish if'n ye just ask."

"I guess I've been a bit of a—what did you call me—a wanker?"

"Aye, that and more, but it's all behind ye, laddie. Now ye must be off. There's a task for ye to complete." Pog held his hand up, and motioned slightly. Azriel found himself mysteriously returned to the foot of the Fairy Bridge.

Azriel stared at the bronze mermaid, wondering what would happen next. He hesitated by the black-framed door before making his entrance. He approached the counter, rang the bell, and waited, not sure of what to expect. He thought Rosemary would pass through the curtain behind the counter, but he was kept waiting. Azriel began to feel nervous. The anticipation was maddening.

"Azriel…" A musical voice resounded softly from a shadowed alcove he hadn't noticed on his first visit to the shop. Peering into the darkness, he could barely make out a figure. Within the recess, a candle was lit, illuminating the hidden woman.

"Come face me, Azriel."

As the candle grew brighter, he recognized Rosemary—but not as she had dressed the day before. She wore an elaborate black gown fringed in purple. On her head rested a silver crown lined with pearls; upon it, an upturned crescent moon.

"I am the Lady Rosaluna, High Priestess of the Holy Flame. Sit, Azriel."

He took the seat facing her and swallowed his sudden fear.

"Today you have learned a great lesson, Son of Luminance, for you have learned humility. You now know that no man stands alone. There is help for the asking if you know where to search and discern who to trust. Today your eyes will be opened further, but first you must be weighed in the balance."

From beneath the table, she extracted a pair of scales. She placed them gently on the black-clothed table and her eyes locked with Azriel's.

"Have you been successful in your journey?"

"Yes ma'am." He handed Rosaluna the stone. Placing it on one of the golden platens, it rose impossibly to the very top, though nothing filled the other plate.

"Er, Rosaluna, I think your scale's broken."

"No, Son of Light, I must weigh your heart. And I see it is heavy—troubled. Much heavier than the stone."

Frightened, Azriel held a hand to his chest defensively. Rosaluna's stance softened. "Do not fear, Azriel. No harm shall come to thee. I only wish to know if you are ready to embrace your destiny."

Azriel studied her face. It was as though her entire persona had changed. Gone was her thick brogue. Her speech was formal and even.

"May I ask a question, Lady? I thought your name was Rosemary. Why do you now call yourself Rosaluna?"

"It is the name I take in my role as High Priestess—my secret name. You must never reveal it to those undeserving."

"Yes Ma'am."

"Now, Azriel, why are you here?"

"To learn the name of the Earth Dragon—the first elemental."

Upon answering, the platen holding the stone lowered a notch, even though the left side was still empty. Azriel stared at the scales in awe.

"Who is your mother?" Rosaluna intoned.

"Abelene Kingsley, Queen of Aralia." Upon saying her name, Azriel finally realized that all the stories his mother often recited were the truth. The scale lowered another increment.

"And her true name?"

Azriel hesitated.

Rosaluna smiled. "It is time for trust, young master."

"Ferrishyn. Her name is Ferrishyn—as well as mine." The scale lowered another increment.

"Then are you a Prince—the one to unite the worlds?"

Azriel hesitated. "Yeah, I guess so."

The rock on the scale rose a notch, back to its former position.

"On this, you must be certain, Son of Light, for if you do not know who you are, then you cannot possibly fulfill your destiny. So I ask you again. Are you a Prince?"

He thought for a moment, letting the question sink in. Azriel had denied his importance for so long that he never allowed himself to accept the responsibility of what his life meant—the role he would play. And indeed, for months it had lain heavily on his heart.

He stared levelly at Rosaluna. "I am Azriel Ferrishyn, Son of Abelene, and Prince of Aralia." The scale lowered another notch, and then a little more.

"And Prince of Aralia, what is your purpose?"

Azriel knew the answer Rosaluna sought, but it felt partly false, because he didn't yet know all it would entail. This was only the beginning.

"Ma'am, I'm supposed to bring balance to the split worlds," Azriel said with a faint smile, "Like these scales." The platens wavered. "Somehow, I'm the one who's supposed to restore Magick to the worlds, but..."

"Yes?" she prompted.

"Well, Lady... I'm just not sure how to accomplish that. I mean, look at me. I sort of made a mess of things yesterday. This task I'm being nurtured for really scares me. I'm unprepared for whatever destiny I'm meant to embrace. I don't even know what I'm supposed to do! I could wind up making things worse!"

"You're the chosen one, Azriel. If not you, then no one else."

"Yeah... that's what terrifies me."

Rosaluna smiled and nodded, pleased with his response. The scales suddenly came into balance.

"See, Azriel, these scales measure your honesty. It is not for you to know how things will end, only to drink of the cup and partake of your future. You have just begun your journey, but know you will not stand alone. Many will come to help you. Do not spurn the boons that come your way, even if you do not understand the source. Now your heart has been unburdened with your admission, and you can finally proceed. Look and see."

Azriel peered at the rock. As he watched, the stone began to crack. Tiny fissures appeared, spreading from the bottom. The entire pitted surface fell away like chaff, revealing what had been hidden within. A tiny golden chest now sat upon the scales.

"Go on. Take it," Lady Rosaluna coaxed.

Azriel gingerly removed it from the platen and examined the box. Etched in delicate filigree, a representation of a dragon—the Earth Elemental—graced the lid.

"Open it."

He lifted the lid and peered inside. He read the name scrawled on the bottom.

"There!" Rosaluna grinned. "You now know the name! You are ready!"

"Ready for what?" Azriel looked up with trepidation.

"Come. Follow me!"

Azriel gasped when he entered through the curtain. In every corner of the room, tall candelabras were lit, casting a golden glow. Central to the room stood a finely cut stone altar draped in green velvet; above it hung the ancient emblem of the Ankh—the Egyptian symbol of life.

Lady Rosaluna faced Azriel with her arms raised in blessing. "Now, young initiate, is the time for you to embrace your destiny— if you have the courage."

From behind the draped curtains, robed figures emerged. The procession was led surprisingly by Pog wearing a black hooded robe lined in purple, much like Lady Rosaluna's. Azriel stared, his mouth agape. Following Pog, dressed much in the same fashion strode Mr. Parkins, then Billy from the market. They were joined finally by Felisa, Amaryllis, and Nicodemus.

His uncle approached and placed his hands on Azriel's shoulders. He smiled proudly at the boy. "Well done, Azriel. You have passed the test. All you see here are sworn to the Order of the Ankh. We have taken an oath to preserve life, to bring peace, and to restore Magick to the worlds. Our hopes rest in you, young initiate."

Azriel nodded in realization. "You were all part of this?"

Billy, robed in brown, laughed. "Aye, indeed, brother."

"You too?" He glanced at Mr. Parkins. The old man smiled tenderly at Azriel.

"Aye. Hope I wasn't too rough on ye."

Nicodemus turned to Amaryllis and nodded. She approached with a green robe draped over her arms. Nicodemus placed it over Azriel's head, dressing the boy. Like the others, it had a golden Ankh emblazoned on the chest.

"Receive the symbol of your order, young master. You are now an initiate of the Order of the Ankh, but understand, Azriel, this does not come to you frivolously. With it comes the responsibility to learn. You must study the ways of Magick and pass through the steps of becoming a wizard. The power is within you, but you must learn to harness your strength and use it wisely. Today is the first step to becoming an Adept."

With a nod from Nicodemus, all present took their positions around the altar. Pog took on the voice of command. "Azriel, enter within the circle."

He obeyed and faced the altar. On it he recognized the four objects he had seen the day before—the chalice, blade, wand, and pentacle.

"These are the tools of your trade, young initiate." Amaryllis spoke solemnly. "You will learn their uses in time."

Mr. Parkins then commanded, "What have you brought to the table?"

Azriel produced the tiny golden chest from his pocket and placed it on the altar. "I have brought the name."

"Reveal your amulet, Azriel." Nicodemus ordered.

Azriel removed it from within his shirt and let it dangle over his chest.

Rosaluna then stepped forward. As she did, all the others in the room raised their wands over the altar. "You must now speak the name," she intoned.

"Lagina-Tierra," Azriel spoke in a voice of command.

They all watched in awe as the tiny chest began to glow with ethereal light. A deep pulsing, more sensed than heard, resonated through the room. It rose from the box and swirled around Azriel like a whirlwind. Transfixed, it circled him, building in momentum. As it did, all present in the room began to chant in a language Azriel had never heard before. Their voices soared in unison rising in intensity as the whirlwind of power entered Azriel's heart. It held him immobile, filling his mind with knowledge and power. And as it absorbed into his being, the tiny chest that had contained the power faded from existence, its purpose fulfilled. The power found its focus within the amulet Azriel wore. It began to glow. Suddenly, the dragon of the north moved with the power. It reared its head and roared as it changed color, the strange violet metal from which it was wrought transforming to green. The other three dragons, however, remained inert. With a sudden realization, Azriel now knew, unquestionably, the power of Earth Magick. He knew the secrets of plants and herbs, of rock and creature—the subtleties of their existence and the ancient lore of nature.

Azriel stared at them all in awe, astonished by what he now knew in his heart. He looked down at the transformed amulet. The green dragon—the Earth Elemental—glowed slightly with power.

He was about to speak when suddenly, Azriel nearly jolted from the tremor beneath his feet. In his subconscious he sensed—more than heard—a roar of frustration. Dark and malign, it emanated from the bowels of the earth. Judging from the reactions of the others present, they all felt it.

Amaryllis gazed at Nicodemus, fear in her eyes. "The dark dragon stirs!"

"So soon?" Rosaluna added.

Pog closed his eyes and held out his hand, sensing the emanations. "Aye," he nodded. "Surprising, but not entirely unexpected. We knew it would awaken."

"Then we are no longer safe," Felisa added, her eyes wide with fear.

"There is time yet." Pog assured. "He knows of our presence, but not who we are, and where we are."

"What? Who?" Azriel asked, filled with anxiety.

"The dark dragon of death." Nicodemus answered. "I suspect it is being held captive somewhere on this world by the fallen wizards. I have spoken of them before, Azriel."

He remembered. They were the wizards who had made a pact with the darkness to thwart the great wizard Eltanin in his effort to restore balance to Aralia. Instead, they nearly destroyed the world with their defiance and their crime against nature.

Pog spoke to the group, but mostly to Azriel. "Now it begins. We must remain ever diligent in our cause. Many will come against us.

Always test the spirits of those we encounter. We will be pressed upon to battle the darkness."

"Now it would be wise for us to depart this place," Rosaluna added. "Have no fear, Azriel. We will be watching and protecting you. For safety's sake, you must keep your Magick in check for now. We do not want the dark wizards alerted to your presence. Learn everything there is to learn, for in knowledge is the power to overcome any hardship you will encounter."

Evening had set in. Nicodemus, Amaryllis, Felisa, and Azriel sat by the hearth sipping hot cocoa. Outside, a storm raged. Rain fell from ominous clouds, casting a pall over the turbulent ocean.

Nicodemus sighed heavily. "Well, Azriel, our task here is finished. It is time for us to return home. We leave at daybreak."

"So soon?" Felisa pouted.

"Yes, I'm afraid so," he answered.

"I'll miss you, Azriel," Felisa looked at him with doleful eyes.

"Yeah, I'm going to miss you too, but I think we'll be back soon." Azriel said, glancing at Nicodemus.

"Aye, you can count on it."

Tired from such an event-filled day, Amaryllis embraced Nicodemus and smiled. "Well, old friend. Until next time."

In turn, Azriel hugged Felisa. "You were right," he said. "I'm growing into my claws."

She smiled and purred.

Everyone had gone to bed, but Azriel lay awake, tossing and turning. Finally, he fell into a fitful sleep, perturbed by dark and troubling dreams.

Chapter 8

August flew by with lightning speed, and Azriel faced the challenge of a new school year—not only a new grade, but a new school. He still had the luxury of riding the bus to school. By the normal circuit, Harden Lake High School was five miles distant, but because it bordered his property line, he could shave four miles off the walk by cutting through the woods to Camille's house and walking the path behind the school baseball field. This he preferred to do while the weather still held.

Upon his return from the Isle of Man, Azriel had been unusually subdued, still absorbing the events that had changed him in some fundamental way. Abelene had wisely given Azriel the space he needed to grow into his new powers.

The day before school started, Azriel and Camille spent the afternoon together. She had missed his friendship during the month he had been gone. Her attitude toward him had subtly changed. During his absence, Camille had pined for Azriel's presence, and although she would never let on for fear of changing their friendship, the flame she carried for him burned a little brighter. And it's not that Azriel didn't notice. Camille seemed a bit clingier and unsure of herself. Of course, Azriel did his best to ignore it, hoping it would go away.

There were also new things to consider. He and Camille had shared the events of the summer during the time he had been gone. She had privately pulled her shirt down enough for Azriel to see the tiny scar where she had pierced herself above the heart to seal a blood oath with his mother and her aunts. The reason was indeed troubling. He told her of his ordeal and much of the history of Aralia, particularly the details concerning the Wizard, Eltanin, and the missing high wizards who had betrayed him. When Camille mentioned Barclay, he couldn't help but grow suspicious. Why now, he wondered. Could it have anything to do with his involvement with the Order of the Ankh? Azriel suddenly became acutely aware of his vulnerability. He was on his way to becoming a hazard to anyone who associated with him. Camille and her aunts, Jasper and Albert, his mother, and Uncle Nick—they were all in danger.

They walked along the path leading to Camille's house when Azriel paused in their conversation and stopped by the tiny bridge.

"Camille, I've been thinking."

"About what?" She reached down and picked a flower, absently sniffing at it.

"Being around me is dangerous. I don't want you to get hurt. Maybe we should just see each other at school."

Dropping the flower, Camille stared at him stricken—shocked and injured that he would even suggest it. Tears welled in her eyes, and she angrily wiped them away.

"You suck! How can you say that? You're my best friend!" She punched him in the shoulder. "I don't care about the danger! And you're not going to exclude me! You try to get rid of me, and I promise you, I'll stalk you!"

"Wow!" Azriel glanced at Camille with a mock look of horror. "Maybe I should be more afraid of you!"

Camille looked down and giggled through her tears, embarrassed by her outburst.

"Look, I'm sorry. I'll never suggest it again." Awkwardly he hugged her.

"You better not." Camille held onto Azriel longer than he felt comfortable with, particularly because of the unexpected feeling that came over him—one he wasn't prepared for. He released his hold and looked away. His cheeks suddenly flushed. Camille self-consciously blushed as well. They spoke nothing more of it and resumed their normal, candid conversation. But later on that night, lying in bed, Camille never forgot Azriel's embrace.

The following day, school started with the usual confusion. Baffling class schedules, getting acquainted with a new host of teachers—it seemed to Azriel he'd never get used to high school. He was comforted that in the least, Camille was in three of his classes, as well as Jasper and Albert. They sat together in a small cluster. Unfortunately, Eddie Breck and his gang were also in the same classes. Eddie had never forgotten the humiliation he suffered the previous year when he was attacked by a flock of birds. Knowing that Azriel and Camille had witnessed it in delight, he turned and gave them both a scathing look. Azriel returned the stare. With what he knew now, he was no longer intimidated by Eddie and his band of thugs.

At 2:30, Azriel waited by the front foyer, glad that school was over for the day. He had promised he would wait for Camille. Jasper and Albert waited with him as well.

"How was your first day?" Azriel asked Jasper.

"It sucked." He bristled, "They put me in all the advanced classes. I'm never going to get through biology and trigonometry. I have at least four hours of homework."

"You think you have it bad? Albert complained. "Maggie Thornton is in three of my classes. She keeps staring at me and whispering to her stupid girlfriends."

"That's 'cause she's in love with you. Kissie, kissie!" Jasper teased his younger brother, knowing his sore spots.

"Aw, piss off!" Albert punched his brother in the arm. Jasper, of course, punched him back. They began to go at it blow for blow.

"Are you two at it again?" Camille strode up, obviously perturbed about something.

"Hi Camille. What's wrong?" Albert asked, "Eddie Breck bothering you again?"

"Yeah, he's such a jerk. He kept asking me if I got to first base with Azriel yet. And he kept saying bad things about him."

Azriel looked steadily at Camille. "Just ignore him. He's a moron."

"Yeah, well be careful, Azriel. He really has it out for you." She added as they headed toward the back field. "Oh, crap! Speaking of the spawn of Satan…"

Eddie sauntered up with Dirk and Cory trailing behind.

"Let's go." Azriel whispered to his friends.

They headed to the back field of the school, where the trail through the woods began.

"Hey Ass-real," Eddie taunted as his friends egged him on. "Why are you so weird, hanging out with these losers?"

Azriel kept walking. But Jasper stopped in his tracks, his face reddening with anger.

"Ignore him. That's just what he wants," Azriel cautioned.

"Hey Ass-real, I'm talking to you." he continued. "How about if I knock your head in the dirt!"

They kept walking.

"Hey Ass-real, you doin' it with your ugly girlfriend?"

"Piss off, Eddie."

"Oh yeah? And who's gonna make me?"

Azriel turned around and faced Eddie squarely. "So, Eddie, have you had any run-ins with birds lately?"

Eddie and his friends looked up suddenly. He glared at Azriel. "Think you're funny, butt-wipe?"

Azriel smiled, taunting. He held his arm up over his head. "You have no idea who you're messing with."

Suddenly, a magnificent hawk swooped down from the sky and landed on Azriel's outstretched arm. It flapped its wings and screeched at Eddie. Jasper and Albert stared in amazement, but Eddie backed away, clearly frightened. Azriel produced a small piece of beef jerky from his pocket and offered it to the hawk. It gladly accepted the treat.

Eddie pointed. "You're crazy. You know that?"

The hawk flew toward Eddie, buffeting his face with its wings and gave him a sharp peck on the head. He and his friends scattered as the hawk chased them down. Camille laughed in delight, but Albert and Jasper gaped in awe.

"How'd you do that?" Jasper stammered. The hawk flew back onto Azriel's arm. He scratched the bird's head.

"Maybe it's time to come clean about some things," Azriel shrugged. He thanked the hawk for its assistance, and it flew off into the woods.

The trail leading to Camille's house was unusually quiet and subdued as they chatted. "There's something I need to show you when we get to my house," Azriel offered. "It'll explain a lot."

Walking further, the trees grew thicker in spots and the carpet of leaves crackled underfoot. Azriel halted and perked up his ears, sensing something. He motioned with his hand for the others to stop. "Don't move. Don't make a sound," he warned.

"What is it?" Camille whispered.

"Kita."

From beneath the dense brush, Kita stepped out cautiously, waiting for Azriel to approach.

"Holy crap!" Jasper froze, terrified.

"It's okay. She knows Camille and me."

"Knows you? Are you nuts?" Albert faltered.

Azriel laughed. "No, I've known her since she was a cub. Kita's very sweet, really." He knelt down and held out his arms. Kita approached and pushed her huge head into his chest as Azriel scratched behind her ear. "What is it, girl?"

Kita emitted a series of soft growls.

Azriel looked up at Camille. "Hermes is in trouble. We have to help."

"Wait a minute," Jasper was incredulous. "You understand her?"

"Actually, yeah. It's a talent I've developed—sort of."

Albert shook his head. "This is getting weirder by the minute."

"Yeah," Azriel smiled as he petted Kita. "I sure wish she could talk, so people could hear her the way I do."

Kita headed deeper into the woods and halted, looking back waiting for Azriel to follow. They trailed behind her, past the border of the woods and into the thick of the forest. About a half mile in, Kita led them to a small clearing. There, suspended above the ground, Hermes snarled in fear and frustration, tangled in a sling trap. The more he tried to free himself, the further twisted he became in the net. Kita rumbled softly from the back of her throat. Azriel interpreted. "She says she saw three man-cubs set this trap and tried to warn Hermes of danger, but he couldn't resist the chunk of meat. One of them, she says, looked fat and juicy. She wanted to bite him."

"What would Eddie Breck want with a cub?" Albert wondered.

"Whatever the purpose, it couldn't be for anything good. He's foul!" Camille replied, her cheeks flushed with anger.

Jasper handed Azriel his pocketknife. They made quick work of cutting the rope and untangling Hermes from the netting. He scampered to his mother, and she licked him on the face, but then Kita picked him up by the scruff and gave him a firm shake before dropping him—a severe scolding.

Camille giggled. "I guess he'll never do that again, will he Kita?"

The mountain lion rubbed her head against Camille and, without warning, headed back into the forest with Hermes following close behind.

Azriel returned home and let Camille, Jasper, and Albert into the living room. "Mom?" he called out.

"In the kitchen," she responded.

"My friends are here. Mind if we go upstairs?"

"Come and talk to me first."

Azriel excused himself. "Sorry—be right back."

He went into the kitchen, where Abelene was baking oatmeal cookies. "Close the door, Azriel. Is Camille here?"

"Yes."

"Albert and Jasper?"

"Yeah. Mom, I was thinking—Albert and Jasper are getting kind of suspicious."

Abelene raised an eyebrow.

"I had a run-in with Eddie again at school—not like I wasn't expecting it. I called a hawk to give him and his moron friends something to think about."

"That was a little reckless, Azriel."

"Yeah, maybe—but they deserved it. So later, when we were in the woods, Kita came to me for help. She said some boys had set a trap and caught Hermes. I think it was Eddie. Mom, Jasper and Albert know something's up. I think it's time to tell them."

Abelene placed the mixing spoon back in the bowl and brushed back a stray strand of hair thoughtfully. "Do you think that's wise?"

"Not sure, really. Camille knows already, and they're my best friends."

"Be careful, Azriel. Even a friend can betray—whether willing or unwilling." Abelene couldn't suppress the memory of her handmaiden and confidante, who had died under extreme torture to protect her. "This isn't a game, son. Their knowledge of you could be dangerous and compromise your safety—and mine."

"Can you test them for truth? See how much they can be trusted."

"You're learning." She smiled wistfully. "All right. Call them in."

Azriel opened the door to the kitchen. "Hey, guys, come in here."

Albert was the first to enter. He looked at the kitchen, at the eclectic assortment of clay jars and hanging herbs. The aroma from the old-fashioned wood stove made his mouth water. Jasper pushed his brother out of the way. He had been blocking the door.

"Wow! Wicked!" he exclaimed as he gaped at the room. He could only describe it as somewhat medieval—witchy.

Abelene took charge. "Sit down, boys. Have a cookie," she ordered. "Hello, dear." She kissed Camille on the forehead.

"There are things you are probably wondering."

"You can say that," Jasper answered quickly as he snatched a cookie. Taking a big bite, his face transformed with sublime pleasure.

"The question remains as to whether both of you can be trusted."

They both looked at her blankly. Albert piped up. "You mean us three."

"No, dear. Camille I already trust. I don't know you two that well—not for this! I need to see into your hearts." Abelene pulled up a chair and faced them. "You first." She smiled winningly at Jasper and placed her hand over his heart. She closed her eyes and allowed his emotions to merge with hers.

"I sense courage and fortitude, young man. Hmm—loyalty. That's your strength." Jasper smiled in response. "But..." she continued, "you have a temper. You're rash, often acting before thinking. That's your weakness. However," Abelene assured, "you have a deep instinct for right and wrong—and you're quite protective of those you love. You will not betray us." She released her probing. Jasper sighed, relieved.

"Now, you're next," she said as Albert tensed. "Don't worry, son. If you are true, you have nothing to fear." She placed her hand on his heart.

"Hmm, a thinker! Never would have guessed. Analytical. A seeker! Good!" She probed further. "Interesting. You're very private—hard to read and not easily swayed or taken in by deception. That's a strength. There is one thing, though." She removed her hand and stared Albert in the eyes. "You doubt yourself, even when you know the truth. This often makes you hesitant to act, even when you should. You're second-born, so your tendency is to follow instead of lead. That's a weakness. Albert, you're stronger than you allow yourself to be. Trust your judgment—believe in yourself." She nodded, pleased and looked up at Azriel. "He can be trusted. He will not betray us."

Jasper and Albert glanced at each other, somewhat baffled. A twinge of fear tingled across their shoulders. They knew they were in uncharted territory.

"Azriel, may I speak with you privately?" Abelene nodded toward the living room. Away from the others, she spoke in a hushed whisper.

"Mom, what's wrong?"

"Listen, what you're doing is still dangerous! Reveal only what you need to. For now, it will only be an unbelievable tale. See if they can be trusted with a little. You will know. If they prove themselves, then give them more—but be careful."

"I will, mom. I promise."

They returned to the kitchen to find Jasper and Albert gorging themselves on cookies. The plate was almost gone. Camille watched them with disgust, her arms crossed. "Doesn't your mother feed you?" she exploded.

Abelene laughed. "It's all right, dear—there's plenty more." She donned a hot mitt and removed another tray from the oven.

Albert and Jasper stood, embarrassed. Jasper gulped. "Mrs. Kingsley, those were the best cookies I've ever had!" Albert agreed.

Abelene smiled. She handed each two more cookies and nudged them toward the door. "There you go, now out with you!"

"Thanks, Mom." Azriel beamed.

Once up in his room, Azriel faced his friends. "Camille knows some of what I'm about to tell you, but not all. You must be sworn to secrecy. Do I have your word?"

Albert and Jasper both nodded.

"If I try to explain everything, you'll no doubt think I've gone off the deep end. So it's better that I just show you." Azriel reached under his bed and removed an old, tattered tome and a crystal plate. The leather-bound volume had strange cursive writing embossed into the cover. Jasper stared at it with curiosity.

"What is this?" he asked.

"It's an artifact from my home world," Azriel explained. "It will explain much."

"Not likely." Albert gingerly opened the book and grimaced at the foreign text. "It's unreadable." He glanced up at Azriel. "What did you mean—home world?"

"Well… " he shrugged. "I'm not really from around here."

Jasper piped in, "That's not too far of a stretch. I've always thought you were like, from Mars or something."

"Actually, a bit further. Here, let me show you." He held up the crystal tablet. It was roughly the same size as the book with what appeared to be ancient runic letters neatly etched into its border. "This is a translating stone. Watch this!"

Azriel placed the stone plate over the book's cover. The cursive script swirled and rearranged, morphing into readable text.

"The History of Aralia." Jasper read. He peered up at Azriel. "Weird. Where's Aralia?"

"Here—sort of," Azriel said apologetically. "Best if you read from the beginning." He opened the book and placed the tablet gently onto the first page. New text replaced the old, and he began to read.

History of Aralia
The Battle

Two worlds occupy the same space. One, the world of the Ferrishyn; the other the world of men. Once they were but one world.

Many thousands of years ago, Aralia stood in its golden age, when the land was perfected, and all manner of the arts and culture were at their peak. The Ferrishyn lived by the laws of High Magick and brought peace and prosperity to all. But it had not always been so. In the dark years, the land was plagued by fallen wizards who seduced and enslaved the people with their fell magick. Disorganized, and leaderless, Aralia fell prey to rogue wizards and witches who kept the people in bondage and fear, maintaining their power through evil sorcery and isolation. Anarchy ruled Aralia for many years, until the great Wizard Eltanin came out of hiding. Calling forth a small army of common folk, he challenged the evil Sorceress Morta to magickal combat. For two days they battled, neither gaining the upper hand. Tiring, Eltanin began to lose ground and his defeat was imminent. But the battle attracted the attention of the neighboring provinces, and soon a crowd came to witness the conflict. Their hope of freedom rested with Eltanin. When all seemed lost for him, a few—seeing their hopes dashed—rose up, preferring death to another day of bondage. They released their magick and strength into the great Mage. Empowered by hope, he rallied and fought Morta with renewed vigor. Others, seeing the change, began releasing their power into Eltanin. Imbued and fortified by the unified strength of the people, he defeated Morta utterly. Dead, her soul was consigned to the darkness, imprisoned in an unreachable realm.

With his victory, the people realized that though individually weak, united they were strong. Soon, more of the people rallied behind Eltanin. He was joined by another great wizard: Rastaban. Together, they marched upon the city of Triondor, where the Evil Lord Korloth was cast down from his lofty tower and banished to the outer darkness, from whence there is no return. With a second victory, Eltanin was joined by six other powerful Wizards. They were the Lords Rastaban, Altais, Nodus, Edasich, Thuban, and Giausur. Together, they formed the Clave of Wizards. As more of the people were freed, the larger Eltanin's army grew. The evil lords, feeling their grasp on power weakening, joined forces and challenged Eltanin in a war to settle all accounts. The place of battle chosen, they would meet in the grey wastes on the morning of the summer solstice. Thus, it could not be said by the vanquished that they were defeated by inclement weather. All would see in the clear light of day the glory of the victorious.

On that day of reckoning, Eltanin had raised an army of twenty thousand warriors. They were joined by every province from the east, and every powerful wizard, witch, and sorcerer who had tasted freedom and were loath to relinquish it.

At the rising of the sun, the dark lords came, followed by every manner of fell and foul beast and demon, magically summoned from the bowels of Aralia. Through forbidden magick, the evil lords used necromancy to raise an army of the undead. The lords of the East quaked with fear, knowing that they faced their doom. Seeing their fate, Eltanin called for a meeting of the Clave. In desperation, he offered to raise the Elemental Dragons to battle for freedom. The Wizards of the Clave paled at his suggestion. Raising one Elemental was dangerous enough and could be the demise of the summoner; to raise all four was suicide. To control all the Elementals would require a powerful wizard indeed. Eltanin possessed one weapon the other wizards did not know, for he knew the secret names of the Earth Elemental, and of Water, Air and Fire.

The armies drew swords against one another, and the ground grew thick with the blood of the fallen. The clave of wizards fought victoriously, abandoning Eltanin to his folly. The battle raged on, and the tide turned on the Lords of the East. When nearly defeated, Eltanin succeeded in his dread ritual of raising the Elementals. From all four corners of Aralia, they came—Earth, Water, Air, Fire—and their presence filled the sky, blotting out the sun. So stricken by their countenance, Eltanin lost control of the Dragon Elementals, and they would have set upon him for having the audacity to raise them. But in their foolishness, the dark lords attacked the Elementals. Being the embodiment of natural law and the balancing forces of creation, they would not suffer the sacrilege. As one, they turned on the dark lords and destroyed every manner of creature drawn up from the pit of corruption.

But the dark Lords weren't yet defeated. Combining their strength, they summoned the Dragon of Death, an evil and malign creature equal to the Elementals. Apart, they could not defeat death, so to create a more potent creature, they merged as one. The combined Earth, Water, Air, and Fire Elementals became one—the Quintessence—the Dragon of Light and Life.

Life and death battled through the night, the fate of all Ferrishyn resting upon the outcome. Finally, the Dragon of Light bound the Dragon of Death and banished it back into the bowels of the earth, from whence it came.

Knowing why they were summoned, the dragon Elementals promised Eltanin that they would return in a time of dire need, before resuming their places at the four directions.

Aralia, now cleansed of evil, healed from the terrible battle and became prosperous under the wise counsel of the Clave. The people were taught the ways of High Magick and through will alone created a golden world, free from want and oppression.

Jasper paused in his reading. "Wow, Azriel. This is heavy stuff!"

"Yeah." he answered, subdued.

"And you're one of them—one of the Ferrishyn?"

"That's right. It's not just my name—it's my race."

"That's kind of cool, really." Albert smiled and nodded. "So you're not human?"

"Actually, in most respects, I am. Open me up and you couldn't tell us apart. Some minor differences though—like the ears." He pushed back his hair to reveal their shape. "And as my mom says, we're wired a little differently. I'm not even sure if it's all physical."

"So what else can you do?"

"I can see through clothing."

Jasper suddenly covered his crotch and glared at Azriel. Camille stifled a laugh.

"Only kidding. But I can see in the dark."

"That's pretty neat!" Camille grinned.

"Let's read on."

Part Two

The Rift

During the eighty-seventh year of King Tordrid's reign, a rift appeared in the sky from which a great light illuminated the countryside. From that light descended a city that came to rest in the uninhabited regions. The Clave sent representatives to investigate the strange event and discovered a race of men emerging from the great metropolis. To the representatives of Aralia, they requested sanctuary, saying their own world had been destroyed by a natural cataclysm. It had never been determined from where they came, nor did the High Wizards have any clue. For their far-reaching knowledge of the heavens, they should have known about events in the cosmos. Some thought they had arrived from Aralia's future, somehow breaching the barrier of time, but this could not be proven, nor would the newcomers provide any answer.

The representatives—Adepts in Magick—unable to find deception in the newcomers, brought their request to the Clave. After deliberating for many days, the General Assembly of Wizards cast their votes. It was determined that the newcomers would be allowed a place to dwell, under certain conditions. They would have to learn the ways of the Ferrishyn—those of peace and of Magick. Further, they could cause no harm to the planet.

The humans gladly agreed to the terms and made a sacred pact with the Clave of Wizards. Soon, however, the humans proved false. They were either unwilling or unable to learn Magickal Lore. For every Magickal nuance, they could mimic the end result through the use of technology. They could not raise stone from the ground for their dwellings; instead, they decimated the forests for wood and shattered mountains for stone. They did not call on the elements for rain; instead they diverted rivers for irrigation. They did not rely on the abundance of food and game; but instead, introduced destructive herds of cattle that damaged the ground and dirtied the rivers. After many years, they became a plague upon Aralia. The pact between Ferrishyn and Human was deemed broken by the Clave. High Wizard Eltanin himself, was sent to the humans with a request that they find another planet to inhabit, that they were no longer welcome on Aralia—but in defiance they refused to leave. Thus, a solemn council was called to order by the Clave to determine what course of action should be taken.

"Hey, what's that?" Camille asked.

"What's what?" Azriel shrugged.

"The picture." She pointed to the enigmatic image of an eye scrawled on the page.

"I don't know."

"It's got to mean something."

"How should I know? Here's something weird, though." Azriel removed the translating stone from the page. As he did, the eye disappeared. "Strange, huh?" He placed the stone on the page again. "Let's just finish reading this."

Within a month's time, it became apparent that the humans would not submit to the will of the Clave, for it was determined they would destroy Aralia if they persisted in their methods, and the newcomers were unwavering in their will to stay. The Clave, resolved to bring an end to the matter, called upon Eltanin to perform a ritual meant to send the humans back to their own world. Only Eltanin had the power to accomplish such a feat, for he had the promise of the Elementals to return in a time of dire need. It would require months of preparation to gather all the essential elements from Aralia and the lands beyond. In that time, the Humans built fortifications and erected weapons to threaten the peace of Aralia.

On that fateful day of reckoning, all preparations were completed. The day of the Summer Solstice was at hand and Eltanin readied himself to perform the dread ritual within the Temple of Luminance, which stood upon the Heart of Aralia—the place of power where thousands of years before, the Elemental Dragons were first summoned.

Eltanin spoke the names, summoning the Dragon Elementals to his will—but unbeknownst to the Clave, he planned to betray Aralia. He summoned also the Dark dragon of Death, releasing it from its eons-long prison to wreak havoc upon the humans—never the intention of the High Wizards. Drunk with power, he split the world in two, creating another world to punish the humans; he rent the fabric of space and time, separating the Heart of Aralia, tearing it, and its power, from its place.

After the destruction, Aralia was changed to its very core. It is assumed Eltanin vanished into the new world he had created, taking the Heart of Aralia with him. It is also certain that he destroyed the Clave, keeping all power for himself. The name of Eltanin shall be cursed forever.

Over time, it became apparent that in the destruction and reshaping of Aralia, Eltanin had also taken the Elementals with him, for Magick was waning from this world.

The chapter ended. Azriel looked up from the page and stared at his friends, gauging their reaction.

"Geez, Azriel. This guy Eltanin is really one bad dude." Jasper marveled.

"No, Jasper, he isn't. This story is a lie."

"Well, how would you know that?"

"Because someone I trust has told me so. See, it's true that Eltanin did split the world in two. He created another dimension from time and space, but he did so only to save the humans. It was the Clave who betrayed Eltanin. Their purpose was to destroy the humans by raising the Dragon of Death and sending them into oblivion. They had duped Eltanin into performing the ritual, but left one key detail out of the equation. No one knew where the humans had come from in the first place. The Clave had woven a spell of deception over Eltanin. Only in the end did he realize their duplicity. In order to save the humans, he split the worlds before the Dark Dragon of Death could consume them."

"So why read a book filled with lies?" Camille asked.

"Because this is the official history of Aralia. This is what all Ferrishyn believe. They're being lied to."

"Are you sure?" Albert interjected.

"Positive."

Jasper asked, "Azriel, what have you to do with all this?"

He sighed heavily. "I'm Eltanin's heir. I'm destined to undo the damage done by Eltanin and the Clave. I must restore the worlds to one."

"Azriel, that's nuts!" Albert stammered.

"Yeah, absolutely," Azriel agreed.

"And how are you supposed to do this?"

"Haven't a clue."

Camille picked up the translating stone and examined the edge. On it were etched strange runes that bordered the plate. "What do these say?" She inquired.

"Don't know," Azriel shrugged. "I can't read Ancient."

"This is a translating stone, right?"

"Sure…"

"Well, why not write it down and use the tablet to decipher it?" She offered.

"Camille, you're brilliant! Don't know why I didn't think of that myself?"

"I'll give you three guesses," Jasper interrupted, smiling.

"Jasper, shut up!" Azriel growled as he grabbed a sheet of paper. He made quick work of copying the text written on the tablet. Once copied, he placed the translating stone on the page. The writing swirled and changed to English.

If seeing is believing, then truth is in the eye to behold
Touch me with your intent and the story will be told
Speak only the word and the truth will unfold.

"Interesting." Azriel glanced up at Camille. "Let's see what it does."

He placed the plate over the icon of the eye.

"See," he commanded.

The tablet remained inert.

"Okay, that's not it," Azriel mused. "View," he said. Again nothing.

"Try touching it," Camille suggested.

Azriel placed his hand on the plate. "See… view… wait a minute. I know! Truth!"

The tablet suddenly began to glow. Sparkles of light coalesced above the plate, and an image formed into a three-dimensional representation.

Six cloaked men huddled around a table in what appeared to be a secret meeting. One seemed to be the leader. He addressed them in quiet whispers.

"My friends," he began. "There is no other solution to this problem. Eltanin will be none the wiser. Allay your concerns, Giausur."

"But Lord Rastaban," Giausur argued. "This solution seems too extreme. What if something goes wrong? What if he discovers the ruse?"

Rastaban smiled confidently. "Altais, would you enlighten our friend here?"

Altais cleared his throat. "Yes, my lord. I have been successful in placing a cloud of enchantment over Eltanin. His mind is befuddled. He will never suspect our true intention. There is nowhere to send these humans—these invaders who destroy our world. They will be released into the void where they will die. Sometimes sacrifices must be made."

One of the men sighed heavily.

"Thuban, do you have something to add?"

"Lord Rastaban, I'm not so sure about this solution. Things can go terribly wrong. This isn't simple creative Magick we are performing. Raising the Dragon Elementals is Magick of the most potent kind. Lose control, and we doom ourselves."

"Wrong," Nodus interjected. "The impetus of destruction will be upon Eltanin. No great loss. He has become too powerful and has restricted us from exploring aspects of Magick he deems forbidden. He wants all power to himself. If the ritual goes wrong, then let obliteration be upon his head."

"Let's not forget who holds the Dark Dragon captive. Only *we* know its location and how to control it." another wizard stated.

"Wisely spoken, Edasich," Rastaban agreed. "One way or another, three days hence, we will be free of Eltanin and the cursed humans. Then we will be the ones in power."

The image faded from view. Azriel, Camille, Jasper, and Albert sat in silence considering the implications.

Azriel spoke first. "That certainly confirms what I already knew. But it raises other questions."

"Like what?" Albert asked.

"Like who wants the truth to be seen. These images are in opposition to what's written in the Book of Aralia. Someone went through an awful lot of trouble to make sure the truth was known. See? Look at the picture of the eye. It was hand-drawn. Only someone with powerful skills could produce such rune magick."

Jasper was quiet for the moment.

"What's on your mind?" Azriel inquired.

"This is all very strange stuff. But whatever it is, I want to be part of it."

"Yeah, me too," Albert added. "Do you think you could teach us the magick we need to help you?"

"I'm not qualified," Azriel pointed out. "But my mother is. I'll speak with her."

They all nodded in agreement.

"For now, though, you all must be sworn to secrecy." Azriel placed his hand on the magickal book. Following suit, they all took his lead, swearing an oath of secrecy.

The following day, Azriel stayed home from school. Uncle Nick arrived early in the morning in a beat-up rugged old Jeep with plans for a day trip. On a beautiful, crisp autumn day, it promised to be a perfect opportunity for a drive up into the mountains. When asked why, Nicodemus explained.

"There is a seldom-used trail that leads into a cavern only I know about. There's something there I need."

"What are you looking for?"

But Nicodemus would offer no further explanation, other than Azriel's assistance would be required. Azriel made a quick call to Camille, explaining the situation. He finished the call and peered up at Uncle Nick just as Abelene walked up, carrying a basket for a picnic.

"I think she's mad at me."

Nick chuckled. "Why?"

"Some of the boys have been harassing her. We always walk home from school together."

"Oh, I see!"

Azriel sighed. "It's nothing like that, Uncle Nick. We're just friends."

"Whatever you say, Azriel."

North of the old mining town of Wallace, a primitive road led up the mountain to Murray, nearly a ghost town, though some residents managed to hang on for posterity's sake. Other than a bed-and-breakfast and a quirky old museum, it had little to offer. It had passed its boom when the gold ran out in the late 1800s. Taking a westbound dirt road—two miles that jostled the bones mercilessly—Nicodemus pulled over and stopped the car.

"We hike from here."

Abelene peered up the trail that quickly disappeared into the dense foliage, grateful she had worn rugged clothing and heavy boots. Azriel holding his mother's hand helped her up the steepest sections as they followed Nicodemus. For an older man, he had incredible stamina, and by the time they reached their destination, Azriel and Abelene were quite winded. The trail ended, and Azriel glanced at Uncle Nick somewhat baffled. There didn't seem to be anywhere further to go. Thick, impassable brambles blocked their way.

"Where to from here, Uncle Nick?"

"Abelene, would you do the honors?" Nicodemus asked.

"Delighted," she smiled. "Azriel, what do you see?"

He peered into the thicket, using his developing senses. From one section, barely detectable, a slight glow limned a section of bramble.

"There! I see it!" Azriel beamed.

"Good! You're learning!" Abelene encouraged. "Now watch." She waved her hand with a subtle gesture. "Vanish!" she ordered. The thicket faded from view, to reveal a small opening barely large enough for a man to crawl through. Azriel scowled thoughtfully.

"Uncle Nick, how did you find this place?"

"Well, Azriel, during the 1870s, the gold rush reached Murray. I, of course, staked a claim and was prospecting like so many other fools who thought they'd get rich finding the mother lode. But I wasn't here for gold. Something else I was after. Come. I'll show you."

Nicodemus removed a flashlight from his pocket and got down on his knees. He disappeared into the narrow passage. Abelene crawled through, followed by Azriel. The aperture opened into a hidden cavern. Azriel's eyes widened as they adjusted to the dim light.

Quartz crystals of all sizes and shapes jutted from the walls, reflecting back brilliant sparkles. In between, thick veins of gold lined the surface.

"Uncle Nick, is that what I think it is?"

"Yep! The mother lode!"

"But why didn't you mine it?" he stammered.

"Two reasons. News of its discovery would have devastated this mountain. The old miners would have murdered each other—and perhaps me—to get to it. Gold fever—it makes men mad with greed!"

"What's the other reason?"

"Indeed. This cavern holds a treasure far more precious than all the gold you see here."

Nicodemus led them to the back of the cave. The surface of the wall was festooned with clear crystals of varying sizes—perfect and magnificent. Within the center however, a particular cluster stood out from the others. Embedded deeply, it glowed with a blue sheen. Azriel examined it closely, with curiosity.

"It's blue!" he commented.

"Exactly." Nicodemus confirmed. "Blue quartz crystal is so rare. In fact, it doesn't exist in nature—at least not here. Quite common on Aralia, though."

"So why didn't you just take it the last time you were here?"

"It resists my touch. See?" Nicodemus placed his hand over the crystal cluster, and it began to glow more brilliantly. The closer he came to it, the more it repelled his presence. "Now go ahead. You try."

Azriel shrugged. He placed his hand over the cluster, fully expecting the same result, but his hand easily passed through the field of power. "Ouch!" He quickly extracted his hand and examined the slice on his finger. He glanced at the crystal and noticed it was absorbing his blood until it disappeared into the stone.

"It's sharp!"

"Indeed," Nicodemus chuckled. "You must will it into your hands. No hammer and chisel must ever touch it."

"Why?"

Abelene answered. "It's the embodiment of Air Power, derived from Earth Power—the foundation. It embodies the pure essence of the Air element. You must use your will—the purity of thought—to release its bonds."

"Why me? Why not you?"

Abelene smiled tenderly. "Because this task was appointed to you. It's not my place."

Azriel sighed. He wasn't surprised, though. Lately, everything seemed to be his burden. "Okay, I'll try."

"No, Azriel," Uncle Nick commented. "There is no trying—only the knowing that you can."

Azriel cupped his hands beneath the crystal cluster. As his mother had taught him, he cleared his mind of all extraneous thoughts and focused on the crystal. He envisioned pure light and the perfect quality of air as one might experience on a summer morning. The cluster soundlessly separated from the cavern wall and floated into Azriel's waiting hands. Oddly, the rock appeared to have little, if any, weight to it. He smiled at his accomplishment.

Nicodemus removed a blue velvet bag from his pocket and instructed Azriel to place the ethereal treasure into it for safe-keeping. As he did, a rock tumbled down from the ceiling, glanced off his shoulder, and landed at his feet. Azriel looked down at the golden mass. He picked it up with wonder. It was heavy—at least three pounds.

"Uncle Nick, can I keep this? I might need this someday."

He looked at Azriel thoughtfully. The boy's perceptions were sharpening. Azriel would eventually need the gold for his final task, though Nicodemus was certain Azriel couldn't possibly know what that task was—at least not yet. He answered seriously. "Yes, Azriel, that nugget is yours. You've earned it today, as it seems to have chosen you. Keep it safe."

The task complete, they squeezed through the tiny opening at the base of the cave. With a wave of his hand, Nicodemus invoked a spell. "Conceal!" he muttered. The opening suddenly filled in, appearing like a solid wall of stone. As before, the spot was thick with brambles. Azriel smiled, gaping at the passage now completely hidden from view.

"Simple concealment spell," Nicodemus offered, "But quite effective! It's resisted curious eyes for 150 years."

"You'll have to teach me that one," Azriel said hopefully.

"Don't be an ass, Azriel. You already have the power. Have you learned nothing? You've been imbued with Earth Power. It's there. Just believe it is!" Nicodemus smiled amiably and tousled Azriel's dark hair. "Now, if I'm correct, your mother has packed a wonderful lunch."

They found a clearing and ate a delicious meal, as was usual for Abelene's culinary prowess. After gathering up all the remnants, they headed home, back to Harden Lake. Three-quarters of the way home, Azriel began to feel uncomfortable—not the discomfort of physical fatigue, but the anxiety of a sudden pit in his stomach, the feeling that something was amiss. Abelene, sensing her son's agitation, turned around in the front seat and probed.

"What is it, Azriel?"

"I don't know, but something's wrong."

"Clear your mind and reach out with it. Sense the ebb and flow of events. What's the first impression you receive? Let it fill you."

"Camille. She's in trouble. Jumbled images. I'm sensing danger. We need to get home. I think I know where she'll be."

The air had turned crisp and refreshing. Camille donned her backpack after the 2:30 bell and headed home through the woods behind the school, enjoying the solitude. Albert and Jasper usually walked with her, but today they were both serving detention for causing pandemonium in the biology lab when they released all the rats slated for euthanizing and dissection. Most of them were rounded up, save two. Jasper and Albert would not be released from detention until the missing rats were found.

Still about a half mile from her home, Camille suddenly got the feeling she was being followed and quickened her pace. For one thing, the usual twittering of birds and the myriad creatures of the forest stilled their cacophony of noise. The sudden silence frightened Camille even more, and she broke into a frenzied run. Before she had gone ten paces, she heard heavy footsteps. Quickly intercepted, she was surrounded by Eddie, Cory, and Dirk.

The three ruffians surrounded her from all sides, preventing escape. Eddie got up in her face. "What are you doing out here all by yourself. Your friends ain't here to protect you?"

"Leave me alone." Camille tried to push her way out, horrified that she couldn't control the tremor in her voice.

"No, I don't think so, witch! You cost me a lot of money yesterday."

"So it was you who set that trap," she spat. "I'm glad I did!"

Eddie pushed her roughly. She rebounded off Cory, who pushed her back from behind.

"Well, the way I figure it, you owe me five hundred dollars. That's what I was going to get for a live cub."

"Get away from me!" Camille shouted and tried to push her way out, but the boys circled her tighter, blocking her in.

"Hey Eddie, what are you going to do to her?" Cory smiled.

"I don't know. Maybe we should scare her a little," Eddie said with a crooked grin. "Or maybe…" He tilted his head, studying her. "Look at her shaking, Cory. Didn't expect that, did you?"

Camille's breath came in quivering gasps. Terrified, she couldn't repress her tears.

Dirk spoke up. "Come on, Eddie. You scared her enough. Leave her alone now."

Eddie spun around, a feral edge in his eyes. "I'll say when she's had enough."

He turned back toward Camille and stepped closer, crowding her space as she tried to pull away.

But before he could press the moment any further, they heard the thunder of heavy paws from the path. In the next instant a mountain lion burst from the brush and slammed Eddie to the ground.

In absolute terror, Cory and Dirk ran screaming from the woods.

Kita had Eddie pinned to the ground with her massive paws. She stared him in the eyes as he struggled, a low growl rumbling in her throat. Strangely, she began speaking—to Camille's astonishment.

"Listen, you. I've had just about enough of your meddling in my domain."

Eddie's eyes widened and he started to whimper.

"Give me one good reason why I shouldn't bite you! So fat and juicy, you'd be so tasty!"

"Kita, no!" Camille pleaded. Winded, Azriel ran up with Abelene and Nicodemus.

"Now listen to me, fat human! Camille is mine! You leave my cubs alone and stay out of my forest." Kita enunciated slowly for effect. "If I ever see you here again, I will eat you and then pick my teeth with your bones!"

Kita released her hold on Eddie, and he scrambled up from the ground. It didn't go unnoticed that, in his terror, he had peed himself. Camille held her shaking hands to her mouth. She giggled—then began to cry in earnest now that the danger was past.

"Now leave!" For good measure, Kita let out a roar that resounded through the forest. Eddie ran screaming through the woods in terror, crashing through jutting branches and bushes.

Kita gently butted her head against Camille. "He will not be back." She gave her equivalent of laughter.

Camille got down on her knees and wrapped her arms around Kita's neck gratefully. Relieved, she cried.

"You're wetting my fur."

Camille laughed. "Sorry."

Abelene had observed the whole incident and glanced sideways at her son. She could not, however, hide her displeasure.

"Azriel, what have you done?"

"What do you mean?"

"Don't be coy, son. It's not in the nature of a mountain lion to speak!"

"I didn't do anything." Azriel insisted. But then a look of realization clouded his face. "Wait a minute. Maybe I did! But it's not like I really meant it. Yesterday, when we released Hermes from the trap, all I did was mention to Jasper that I wished he could hear Kita the way I did."

Nicodemus glanced at Abelene, gauging her reaction. She crossed her arms and glared at Azriel.

"What you did was foolhardy and dangerous. You've endangered Kita."

Nicodemus came to Azriel's defense. "Be easy on him, Abelene. He has more Earth Power than I ever expected. This wasn't intentional, but he does need to control his words.

Abelene's stance softened. "Perhaps you're right."

Kita nudged Abelene for a scratch behind the ears. She purred and spoke.

"Mother, don't be angry with my brother. He has given me a gift."

"I could never forgive myself if anything ever happened to you, Kita. By speaking to that boy, you've endangered yourself."

"Do you think anyone would ever believe him?"

Abelene thought for a moment considering Kita's question. She smiled. "Probably not. Just be careful and stay out of sight for a while. I don't want you to become a hunter's trophy."

"I'll be careful, mother."

Just then, they heard a child's voice. "I hid like you told me to, Mama."

Hermes scampered up and rolled on the ground. Kita gave him an affectionate lick on his muzzle. He then pounced on Azriel. "Thanks for getting me out of that trap!"

"Oh, dear." Abelene held her hand to her mouth and giggled. She picked Hermes up and cradled him. "Now listen, little one. You should never talk to anyone else but who you see here. Do you understand? Others will try to harm you or capture you. They will lock you in a cage as an oddity."

"I promise, Grandmother." Hermes licked her on the face. She smiled and placed the cub at Kita's feet.

"Come, son," Kita purred. "You've had enough excitement for today." She turned and headed back into the brush, disappearing from sight.

"Well, that was interesting," Nicodemus grinned.

"Indeed." Abelene countered. "I've come to a decision. Azriel's abilities are much too dangerous without further training. I will begin teaching him and his friends the proper use of magick. Do you agree, Nicodemus?"

"Yes. It's time."

"Then the first thing you can teach me is how to put an effective curse on Eddie," Camille interjected with a scowl.

"Now dear, you've been a witch long enough to know the first rule of witchery. Harm none. The second law states that any action will return to you threefold—and usually amplified. You know that, Camille. Trust that Eddie's actions today will return to him. It's the law of the universe."

Azriel thought it would be great to see Eddie covered with warts and exploding pustules all over his body. "Yeah? Well, I think he should…"

"Hold your tongue, Azriel." Abelene ordered. "Your words have power. And if you speak something horrible on that boy, it's likely Camille will be blamed for it. She's already a target. What all of you need to learn is how to protect yourselves. I will begin your training tomorrow after school—that is, if you can manage to keep Albert and Jasper on a short leash!"

Gift of the Amulet

Chapter 9

Three months had passed since the incident in the woods, and it was the last day before winter break. Eddie sat on the bleachers in the gymnasium, with Dirk and Cory on either side. He brooded as he bounced a basketball, serving a five-minute penalty for roughing up a teammate. He had come under tremendous ridicule from his classmates for relaying the story of his encounter with the mountain lion.

Dirk sighed. "Are you still going on about that?"

"I told you. It really happened!" Eddie grumbled. "Not like you guys were much help—bailing out on me when I could've been killed."

"Better you than me," Cory scoffed.

Eddie punched him in the chest. "Up yours!"

Dirk reasoned, "Look, everyone knows animals can't speak. You were scared out of your mind. You could have imagined it."

"Yeah," Cory added. "And you shouldn't have told everybody! Now they all think you're nuts."

"Fine. Well, I'm going to prove it!" Eddie scratched his chest. Over the past few months, he had broken out in an ugly rash that refused to go away.

"Still bothering you, huh?" Dirk asked.

"Yeah, and I know that witch Camille has something to do with it."

"Give it a rest, will you?" Dirk moaned. "You're building all this crap up in your mind."

"What? Do you like her?"

"No!" He argued.

"Then why are you defending her?"

"Because you're obsessed. Look, I know she's weird, but all that witch stuff you keep blabbering about just doesn't happen. You're starting to sound like an idiot."

"Yeah, well, I'm gonna get even with Camille and her stupid friends. And that Azriel? I hate that guy. He's gonna pay too."

Dirk shook his head and sighed. Lately, Eddie was beginning to truly get on his nerves. It seemed that Eddie was heading for trouble, and Dirk didn't want to be part of it. Yet he always grudgingly became part of whatever Eddie had planned. And the last time—when they accosted Camille in the woods—their actions verged on criminal behavior. The last thing Dirk wanted was to be an accessory to a crime—paying merely for not having the spine to stand up to Eddie.

"Look, I gotta go," Dirk said.

"Class isn't over yet." Cory retorted.

"Screw it." He stomped off toward the locker room to shower and change.

"What the hell is his problem?" Eddie groused.

"Haven't a clue," Cory shrugged.

Camille waited at her usual spot for Azriel, Jasper, and Albert to arrive for their walk home. Although a slight dusting of snow blanketed the ground, the weather had warmed considerably. She noticed Dirk walking up to her and turned away, hoping to avoid him.

"Hey, Camille."

"What do *you* want?" Her eyes simmered.

"I don't want any trouble; I just mean to warn you."

"Of what?"

"Of Eddie. I think he's losing it! And he's really got it out for you and Azriel. Just be careful, okay?"

"Why are you telling me this?" Camille hedged uncomfortably.

"I just don't want any trouble."

"Why do you even hang out with him?"

"He's my friend."

"He's an idiot!"

Dirk snickered. "Yeah, sometimes. Just be careful." He smiled and walked away as Azriel strode up.

"What was that all about? Was he bothering you?"

"No, not really." She stared at Dirk thoughtfully as he disappeared into the crowd of students boarding their buses. "Weird, really. He was actually nice to me. He wanted to warn me about Eddie. Apparently he's on the warpath again."

"That's nothing new," Azriel shrugged. "Oh, here's Albert and Jasper. Let's go. My mom has more lessons planned for us this afternoon."

Abelene waited impatiently for Azriel to arrive with his friends. She was pleased with their understanding. Surprisingly, Jasper and Albert were absorbing their lessons in Magick at an impressive pace. It was now time to take them to a higher level of understanding. She had prepared the den for the next lesson by drawing the curtains and lighting candles on every end table and shelf. Adding to the ambiance of the cozy room, a festive Yule tree stood adorned with tiny lights and ornaments, strung with popcorn and cranberries. The following day would be the winter solstice and Abelene had a nice celebration planned for later. As was usual, she also had a snack prepared, as it was difficult for them to learn on an empty stomach. They would need their strength for what she had prepared.

Azriel finally arrived home and Camille, Jasper, and Albert filed in behind him. Abelene had decided to forgo the usual pleasantries and led them wordlessly to the den. Four comfortable pillows were laid out on the floor, with plates of cookies and milk before each one. Taking the lead, Azriel sat on one and the others followed suit. Watching as they began to consume the offerings, Abelene smiled and left the room. Baffled, Jasper glanced at Azriel.

"What's going on? Why all the mystery?"

Azriel answered. "Much of performing Magick is about setting the mood. I'm sure my mother has something special planned."

"I love candlelight," Camille confided. "My Aunts always light candles before performing a ritual. Azriel's right. Setting is everything."

They sat in anticipation, chatting while they finished eating. Albert downed the rest of his milk. At that moment, Abelene returned wearing a purple cape and carrying a box. She placed it on the floor and sat opposite her students. She stared at each individually, gauging their readiness.

After a few minutes of silence, Albert began to fidget uncomfortably.

"Mrs. Kingsley…" Albert began.

"Shhh!" she held her finger to her lips. "Be still."

Azriel was familiar with the techniques of quieting the mind. He assumed a comfortable position on the pillow and closed his eyes, draining his mind of every stray thought. Camille followed Azriel's lead. It took longer for Albert and Jasper to catch on to what they were supposed to be doing, but soon they joined Azriel and Camille in the exercise. When Abelene sensed they had achieved a state of stillness, she began to instruct.

"Who can tell me the first Law of High Magick?"

Surprisingly, Albert responded. "Do as you will, but in all things harm none."

"And what does that mean to you?"

"Well, I guess that you can do pretty much anything you want as long as you cause no harm to anything or anyone. That includes animals and the planet itself." Albert said with more confidence.

"And how would that apply to yourself?" Abelene probed.

Camille answered. "That you should cause no harm to yourself. My aunts taught me that you should never think bad thoughts about yourself or put yourself down, because it takes away your power. Like when you cast a spell—if you have doubt in yourself—the spell will be ineffective."

Abelene smiled, pleased with the answer. "Jasper, can you tell me the second Law of High Magick?"

He thought for a moment before answering. "The second law states that whatever action or thought you invoke will return to you for good or evil—usually amplified. That's why the first law is so important about harming none—because you could do harm to yourself."

"Good!" She beamed. "If you learn nothing else, these two laws are the most important. In everything you do, always consider them before any action you take. That is the way of High Magick. You are ready now for the next level of understanding. Now you may ask: what is magick, really?" She gestured with outstretched hands. "Most people on this planet have a skewed idea of magick—wizards with sparks flying from their hands—witches flying on broomsticks—Hollywood stuff. Because it is made out to be fantasy, not many believe Magick exists. How wrong they are. Magick is everywhere—in the trees and in the ebb and flow of life-giving energy. It is more subtle than any sort of showy nonsense."

Albert interrupted. "Yeah, but what about you and Azriel? I mean, he made a mountain lion talk!"

"That's true," Abelene smiled amicably, "but only because it is part of what the Ferrishyn are. For thousands of years, we have studied and learned the principles of Magick. It's ingrained in us, written down in our genes. Humans, however, deny the very existence of Magick and use other means to control their world. Belief is the strongest force you have available to you. But you must go beyond believing. You must know it's there. As Camille said, doubt is the greatest destroyer of magick. Here's the big secret," Abelene smiled slyly. "Humans have the same ability and potential as any Ferrishyn. It just needs to be developed." She moved closer, taking them into her confidence. "Imagine what would happen if everyone on this planet had the same thought at the very same time! Can you imagine what could be accomplished?"

"But that could have a really bad effect if everyone thought something dark and evil," Jasper interjected.

"That too," Abelene said sadly. "That's why this world is so mixed up. So many people believe so many things."

"So how do you get past it?" Camille inquired.

"Indeed. It must begin with the individual. Small steps, Camille." Abelene slid the box at her side toward Jasper. "You begin by truly knowing who you are. Jasper, would you hand those out?"

He removed an ornately framed round mirror from the box; however, its surface was black rather than the usual silvered glass. They each now held one in their hands.

Abelene continued with her instruction. "You may think you're merely flesh and blood, but you are so much more. These scrying mirrors you hold can help you see beyond flesh to the eternal part of you that lives forever. They will unlock the lessons and experiences you've had in the past that made you what you are today."

"Wait a minute," Albert inquired. "Are you telling me I've lived other lives?"

"Without question," Abelene smiled tenderly. "That part of you that lives eternal is a great storehouse of information—you only need to learn how to tap. Once open to you, your world—your multiverse—will never be the same."

"You mean universe, right?"

"No Albert, I meant multiverse. You need to get past your three- and four-dimensional thinking. Like a deck of Tarot cards, one stacked on top of the other, many dimensions exist simultaneously forming, merging, dissolving, and reforming—but all part of the one. I know you have seen the Book of Aralia, Albert. From a single dimension, Aralia and Earth were split. They exist side by side, but unseen by the other. Now..." She paused. "Take your scrying mirrors and prop them up. As before, you need to quiet your minds. When you're comfortable, begin by staring into the mirror. Look past your reflection to what lies beyond. This will take some time so don't be frustrated. It takes practice to bring forth the images." Abelene smiled. "Be patient with yourselves. That's your lesson for today. I'll return in an hour, and then you can tell me how you did."

As promised, Abelene returned after an hour. She was now dressed in a velvet cranberry gown trimmed in deep green. Her hair was crowned with a delicate spray of mistletoe and Scotch pine, tied with golden ribbons. The room darkened, the candles growing dim, and Azriel was still immersed in the scrying mirror while Albert and Jasper talked quietly among themselves. The boys looked up, stunned. Jasper stared in awe.

"Wow, Mrs. Kingsley. You look beautiful. Will you marry me?" he blurted. Albert and Azriel laughed.

So entranced, they didn't notice Camille sat with her back to the wall, weeping silently. Abelene took note and spoke quietly. "Whatever you have seen in your scrying mirrors, keep it to yourselves for now. Reflect on what you've learned, and let it emerge within you. Not everything will make sense to you. Shortly, I will speak to you individually." She smiled. "There are refreshments in the kitchen. Help yourselves." She glanced over at Camille. "I will speak with you first."

Once alone, Camille fell into Abelene's arms and cried on her shoulder.

"Oh dear! What happened, Camille?" She cooed.

"I saw dark, terrible things."

"The past?"

"No. The future!"

"Are you certain, dear?"

"Reasonably so," Camille insisted. "Abelene, you know some of my family history. Auntie Pen told you as much. So, as you can imagine, I've been taught a lot. I've been scrying since I was nine years old. I've always seen images of my past lives. This is nothing new to me. What you don't know is that I'm a thirteenth-generation witch. Aunt Daffie told me that makes me special. I'll see things others cannot."

"Share with me."

"I'm frightened, Abelene. Even afraid to speak it. You have said that words have power. I don't want to give what I've seen momentum."

"I understand. Take my hand, Camille."

Abelene produced a thin birch wand from her pocket and held it above their heads, motioning clockwise. "Now repeat after me." She commanded.

"Visions dark, words of doom—remain forever in this room!"

The spell now set into motion, Camille was visibly more at ease.

"Now tell me what you've seen." Abelene implored.

"Azriel's in danger—we all are. I saw shadows from the future. Soon, dark forces will come against Azriel. And you're in danger too, Abelene. Your secret is no longer safe."

Abelene smiled with understanding. "Dear, none of us are ever completely safe. Can you be more specific?"

Not really—only impressions. But Azriel is going to unleash something so horrible it will bring the world to the brink of disaster. And I..." Suddenly, Camille began to cry again.

"What is it, dear?"

"I've seen my own death—a couple of years from now!"

Abelene paled. "And this you're sure of?"

Camille nodded miserably.

"Oh, honey!" She held Camille in her arms and rocked her gently. "Now listen to me. One thing you should know about future events is that they are never set in stone. The future is only a possibility—probability. If one alters a present action, the outcome will certainly change."

"How can you be so sure?"

"Because I've seen it—done it! I've looked into the future many times and changed the outcome of things I didn't like."

"Could you change big things—like wars?"

"That's harder to change, because it involves so many people. Remember what I said about belief? When so many people are releasing thoughts of aggression and hatred, that event—that probability—becomes inevitable. But when it involves a more personal event, present actions can be taken to prevent a future incident. So my advice to you is not to worry. Fretting over the future can cause it to take the form you least desire. Together we can make sure you'll be safe. After all, the future is still a matter of choice."

Camille relaxed in Abelene's arms with her assurance.

"Are you okay now?"

"I'll be okay. It'll just take some time," Camille sniffed.

"Word of advice?" Abelene's voice was filled with comfort. "One should never dismiss a vision. Pay heed to it, but never obsess over it. Visions are often lessons or warnings. Remember it, but don't let it haunt you. Now, Miss McElven, I have something to cheer you up! Would you call in the boys?"

Camille rose and summoned Azriel, Jasper, and Albert back to the room. They all found a comfortable spot on the couch. Abelene smiled broadly at them. "Tomorrow is Yule—the winter solstice. The sun is born from the Mother, and the days will grow longer. Be of good cheer through the longest night of the year!" She grinned deviously. "Rumor has it that the Holly King will be visiting my humble abode quite soon! Actually, I think I hear him now!"

From outside, they all heard the merry tinkling of bells. They looked out the window and saw fresh snow falling. Like a scene out of Dickens, a sleigh was pulled by a pair of chestnut mares. Their reins were festooned with festive bells, tied with red and green ribbons. In the sleigh rode a man wearing a deep green robe lined with ermine. He wore upon his head a wreath of holly, woven with red berries and all manner of winter evergreens.

"Whoa!" he said merrily, tugging gently on the reins. Hopping sprightly to the ground, he unloaded a rather sizable sack and hefted it onto his shoulder. Before heading to the house, he removed two golden apples from his pocket and offered the treats to his horses. They nickered playfully as they chomped the apples. The Holly King patted each horse on the cheek and headed to the house.

"Cool!" Jasper said wide-eyed with wonder. He felt like a child again. Spirits lifted, Camille couldn't help but smile with anticipation as she heard a knock on the door. Abelene answered the door, and the stranger burst in.

"Happy Yule and merry meet to you all!"

Azriel beamed up at Uncle Nicodemus. He had truly outdone himself. Abelene kissed her guest on the cheek in welcome. He began rummaging through his sack, tossing packages to whoever could catch them. Delicious sundries—chocolates, fruits, and gaily wrapped nuts—were gathered up and placed on the table for a Yule feast.

"Now, a special gift for each of you." Uncle Nick reached back into the sack and ceremoniously handed each of them a finely crafted walnut box tied with red and green velvet ribbons, as Abelene looked on joyfully.

These were no ordinary boxes, but were hand-carved with strange, arcane runic symbols around the edge. Camille sat at the table and opened hers first. She gasped in awe at the beautifully wrought implements. Jasper and Albert also couldn't contain their amazement at the splendid gifts. Azriel beamed at Abelene. Of course, an explanation was in order.

"What are these?" Jasper whispered. He lifted out a finely etched silver blade with a black onyx handle. In his other hand, he held a sort of knife he had never seen. Fashioned with a creamy white handle, the blade—also etched silver—was shaped into a sickle, much like a crescent moon.

"These, my young apprentices, are the first tools of your craft. You have all learned very well, and it's time to advance your training." Abelene said, pleased with her charges. "Camille, would you explain these items?"

She was speechless at first, faced with such an elaborate gift. They had to have been quite costly. She gently lifted her double-edged dagger from its velvet-lined recess and held it up for all to see. "This is an athame. It's never for cutting—only for directing energy and casting spells. It's a ritual knife that must be treated with respect and reverence."

Abelene nodded, pleased. "I couldn't have expressed it better. Well done, Camille." She lifted the white-handled knife from Azriel's case for all to see. "This oddly shaped knife is called a boline. It is the preferred tool of the druids, used for everything from harvesting herbs used for potions, to inscribing magickal runes. Once these tools are dedicated to their use, only you should handle them, since they will be infused with your energy."

"They all look alike." Albert noted.

"Almost," Abelene smiled pleasantly. "I've taken the liberty of having them personalized. Look closely at the handles."

Camille turned her boline toward the light. That's when she saw, etched within, the image of the lioness.

"Yes, Camille. Within you is the strength of the lioness. She is the hunter and provider. She protects her pride!" Nicodemus explained.

"Hey Albert—what's on yours?" Jasper asked.

"A bear!"

"Indeed!" Abelene grinned. "The bear is strong and clever. Ever wise, he will always give good counsel if you study his ways. He will stubbornly pursue his goal, regardless of personal cost. Fierce on the one hand, and yet gentle and content when eating a comb of honey—even while being stung by indignant bees!" She giggled and turned to Jasper. "And what is yours?"

"A horse!" he looked in awe at the magnificent rearing stallion scrawled on the hilt of his boline.

"That's right, son," Nicodemus answered. "The stallion will bravely charge into battle without regard for personal safety. Yet he will bear a burden on his back without complaint. He is noble and untamed, with an unfettered spirit."

Azriel stared pensively at the artwork scribed on his knife's handle.

"What's on yours?" Camille inquired.

"A dragon." The magickal beast stood with magnificent wings spread, radiating power.

Abelene said gently. "The dragon is all-wise and all-knowing—a fierce warrior and an astute scholar. It is the giver of strength and sage counsel. It rules the elements and fills the fool with dread, but the wise with wisdom."

Abelene held her hands out, as if in an embrace. "I am so proud of all of you. You are all on your way to becoming strong and wise in the Craft. Happy, happy Yule!"

She waved her hand with a flourish. "Reveal!" Six goblets suddenly appeared on the table, filled to the brim with honey mead. "Let us toast the Mother of Life and the Holly King, who bring life, sustenance, and happiness to the Earth! Happy Yule!"

As one they all raised their glasses and repeated cheerfully, "Happy Yule to all!"

Chapter 10

Beltane. The last day of April brought renewed vigor to the surrounding woods. Winter had passed, and although February and March had brought record snowfall, the thick mantle of white had melted quickly in due course. Crocuses, as well as daffodils, had peeked through the remnants of snow—lovely harbingers of spring and renewed warmth to the region. The promise of summer had settled into Abelene's soul, and she was unusually buoyant as she prepared to light the Beltane fire for an evening celebration in the clearing beyond her home. A table had been set up, as well as a maypole festooned with flowers and gaily colored ribbons. All manner of delicious foods were set out for a wonderful feast. Penelope and Daphne were busy tying handmade talismans onto an oak sapling nearly ready to bud. The cloth bags were stuffed with spring flowers and tied onto accommodating branches. Jasper, Albert, and Julia—their younger sister—also joined them and attached their offerings to the tree in honor of the coming summer. Julia was now part of the fold. Abelene had tested her for truth and found her to be sincere, astute, and perhaps a bit devious. She liked the girl immediately. A quick study, Julia was now nearly at the same level of understanding in the craft as Jasper and Albert. It helped of course, that she and Camille were becoming good friends.

In a festive mood, each donned robes in the druidic fashion Abelene provided for the celebration. Ready for the feast, they all seated themselves at the table. Nicodemus, Daphne, and Penelope to the right of Abelene; Jasper, Albert, and Julia to the left. But Camille and Azriel were nowhere to be seen.

Abelene stood and addressed the small company of friends.

"Tonight we celebrate Beltane.
The cold hand of winter has turned, and the soft breath of summer is upon us.
The earth awakens from her slumber.
Life stirs. Seeds quicken. The fields grow green once more.

By the old ways, this is the season of union—
the Lord and the Lady,
the God of Abundance and the Goddess of Fertility,
joined as one to bless the land with life.

From their union comes all growing things—
the lamb in the field,
the bud on the branch,
the warmth of the sun upon our faces.

Behold… the Lord and Lady now approach."

Azriel and Camille emerged from the woods hand in hand, dressed in white robes. Both wore wreaths of flowers upon their heads. As a representative of the Maiden, Camille held an exotic bouquet of flowers, while Azriel—the symbol of the young Lord— held a lit firebrand in his hand. Aunt Pen and Daffie looked on proudly at their niece.

With ceremony, Azriel handed the torch to Abelene. She raised it high toward the sky. "Let this Beltane fire be a symbol of the Lord and Lady's union, the coming summer, and the long days of warmth to fill our souls with light and joy."

Abelene held the firebrand to the woodpile and soon it ignited into a wonderful warming blaze. Everyone clapped to welcome in the summer. Azriel and Camille took their assigned seats at the head of the table.

As one, they all lifted their goblets of fruit nectar and rang out, "In honor of the Lord and Lady!"

They began to eat, enjoying the fellowship of friends. Camille smiled, pleased to be the center of attention as representative of the Maiden. She beamed at her aunts. Azriel, however, scratched his head. The wreath of flowers itched, and he longed to remove it, but protocol required him to leave it on. Also, it didn't go unnoticed by Azriel that Camille was taking her role as Lady quite seriously, every so often glancing at him with adoration.

Jasper couldn't help leaning over and giving Azriel a good-natured jibe. "So when's the wedding?" He whispered.

"Shut up, Jasper," Azriel responded through clenched teeth. Julia, sitting next to Jasper, also needled Azriel with delight. She put on a deep, sultry voice. "I think you two make a cute couple." Everyone laughed and Camille blushed.

"Shut up, Julia," Azriel growled amid more laughter. She giggled devilishly and glanced conspiratorially at Camille. Azriel knew it was going to take a long time to live this one down.

Altais sat in a nondescript black SUV, waiting. Little activity took place on Harden Avenue, a quiet residential street not far from the high school. Students, released from their studies, walked home amid boisterous conversation and laughter. Altais sensed he was getting closer to his quarry and needed to confirm his suspicions. A rumor had been circulating, one that could lead him closer to his objective. He scratched at his right palm; the faint scar still tingled from the impression left by the cube Rastaban had placed there. Absorbed into his flesh, it had increased his abilities tenfold. His senses and perceptions had sharpened. Yet even after raising spying demons from the bowels of the earth, a part of Harden Lake remained impenetrable to his sight—a mystery. Powerful magick had been raised around the deep forest, resisting his touch thus far.

Altais was fairly certain that Penelope and Daphne knew something, but remained mum under his questioning. He also knew that pressing them further would open himself up to suspicion. He could not afford to allow them to uncover his true identity. In time, the truth would reveal itself. Human magick was at play here. He sensed it—old magick from ancient days was being used to confound him. If these humans only knew their potential, they would have long ago vanquished the evils of their world—but Altais preferred they remain ignorant. It was to his advantage that they barely touched upon their magickal ability—nearly as powerful as that of the Ferrishyn. Thus, the Clave of Wizards still held their advantage.

Altais glanced at the rearview mirror and watched as three boys walked down the street. Altais quietly stepped out of his vehicle, a pad and pencil in hand, waiting for them to pass by.

"Eddie Breck?" he asked.

"Who wants to know?" the boy responded.

"Barclay Alvers, from the Press." Altais mimicked a deep country drawl.

"Yeah, that's me. What do you want?" Eddie asked with suspicion. Cory and Dirk eyed Barclay nervously.

"I was wondering if you could confirm a rumor I heard recently—that of a talking mountain lion." Barclay flipped open his pad, ready to jot down Eddie's response.

Dirk rolled his eyes. "Oh, for crap's sake. Not this again!"

Barclay smiled inwardly. He was getting closer.

"Look, I'm going," Dirk grumbled. "You coming, Cory?"

"Yeah, let's go."

They continued down Harden Avenue, leaving Eddie with the nosy reporter.

"So, what can you tell me about it, Eddie?"

Eddie glanced up at Barclay, sizing him up. A thin man with a finely chiseled nose, his dark eyes were acute—even menacing—but Eddie was glad for someone who would finally listen to his story and take him seriously. He told Barclay everything he knew.

"So, Mister Eddie Breck, how can you explain that which you know to be an impossibility? I mean, after all," Barclay chuckled, "Everyone knows animals can't speak—except maybe by... magick!"

"Yeah, well, it seems crazy, but I'm sure Camille McElven had something to do with it. She's a witch, you know. Everyone knows it."

"Indeed! A witch, you say?" Barclay feigned surprise.

"And then there's that Azriel Kingsley. He's a strange one," Eddie glowered. "He's got this thing with birds—like he can control them." Eddie omitted his humiliating experience of the year before—his unfortunate encounter with a flock of birds in the schoolyard.

"Kingsley? Interesting name." Barclay rubbed his chin. "And where does your friend live, Eddie?"

"He's no friend. Actually, I hate his guts! He lives in those woods." Eddie pointed. "Up there—between that mountain and a stream that runs through it."

"What else do you know about him?"

"Not much, really—except he's really secretive, like no one knows much about him or his mother. He's got this weird old uncle, too. I think his name is Nick. He drives around in these old cars. The guy's gotta be loaded. I've never seen him in the same car twice."

"Interesting," Barclay mused. "Well, Eddie, you've been quite helpful. I suspect we'll be seeing more of each other."

"Yeah? For what reason?"

"I'm working on a story. I could use your help."

"Then you believe me?"

"Why, yes, Eddie. I do! There are more marvels in this world than you could possibly imagine. You just need to open your eyes. I could teach you. Give you power over your enemies."

Eddie stared up at Barclay. The offer was enticing. It could be his chance to get back at Azriel. "Yeah... how?" he inquired.

Barclay smiled. "I will see you again. You have my word."

Later that day in the privacy of an expensive hotel room, Altais stared into the full-length mirror beside the bed, forcing his will upon it. Pale with exertion, he waved arcane symbols with his hands. The room darkened, yet within the mirror it began to brighten and transform. A quantum shift soon formed, and within moments Rastaban appeared. Like Altais, he scrawled archaic ciphers into the air, his movements leaving a writhing, luminous trail dissipating moments later. Altais stepped through the portal into the underground chamber—the secret lair of Draconis—the Clave of Wizards. Rastaban spoke a word of command to the mirror.

"Immobilatum," he commanded. The portal remained open and immovable.

"It used to be easier," Altais sighed, and wiped his brow with a silk handkerchief. "All one had to do was speak a portal into existence, and there you were," Altais lamented.

"True. Many things have changed. Some for the better, and some for the worse," Rastaban stated. "So, what have you to report?"

"Nothing so much as perhaps a lead."

Rastaban nodded and sat at the conference table. As was his habit, he poured a drink for himself and Altais.

"So, my friend, what have you unearthed?"

"Yes, I've been digging around a bit. I've found some interesting occurrences. For one, a strange rumor of a talking mountain lion in the forest adjoining Harden Lake. A young man told me of an incident in which he was accosted by the beast. Something else, though. I've told you about the niece of two of my charges. Eddie accused the young lady of being a witch. As you know, I've been keeping an eye on Miss McElven. She has extraordinary potential she doesn't even realize. Yet I'm sensing something else."

"And what would that be?" Rastaban inquired.

"An unseen hand guiding her. Something beyond the instructions of her Aunts Penelope and Daphne, who as you know are part of my coven."

"It's a dangerous game you're playing, my friend."

"They suspect nothing. To them, I am simply Barclay. There's something else though."

"Yes?"

"The young man I spoke to, mentioned someone—a classmate by the name of Azriel Kingsley. It seems this Azriel has a strange power over animals—birds in particular. It suggests a force we haven't seen since the old days when Eltanin headed the Clave."

"Could he be the one?" Rastaban mused.

"Perhaps, my Lord. You know the legends. Eltanin's heir will be imbued with all the powers of the elements. He will be able to control every force of nature—even the elementals themselves. He will be able to defeat the Clave with his power."

"It is indeed troubling, Altais—but there is something else we haven't considered. If the Avatar is among us now, perhaps instead of trying to destroy him before he gets too powerful, we can use him—bend him to our will—recruit him to our side."

"It's possible—but not likely. He will already know of our plans. He would have begun his training by now. There is another way, however."

"Continue…" Rastaban did not hide his impatience.

"The young man I spoke of—one Eddie Breck—seems to harbor a particular hatred. He's strong—filled with rage. We could use him. He already trusts me, since no one else would believe his story. Perhaps I should befriend him."

"I would advise caution, Altais. All you have right now are rumors—nothing concrete. Still, keep a watchful eye. Find out more about this Azriel. Where does he live, where is he from, who his mother is. As for the boy, Eddie—stay in contact but do not attempt to train him. Not just yet. You know as well as I do that humans can be wildly unpredictable. An asset can become a liability if one is not careful. We cannot afford to have our presence known—at least not yet. We must remain in the shadows—for now."

"Agreed. Now I must return."

"Good. Keep a watchful eye, my friend. Until next time."

"Yes, my Lord." Altais smiled before stepping through the mirror, into his hotel room. For a moment, Rastaban peered back from the other side, then nodded before motioning with his hands. The silvered glass morphed and swirled until only Altais' reflection remained.

Gift of the Amulet

Chapter 11

As much as Azriel loved an adventure, he wasn't at all happy to be returning to the Isle of Man. He knew there would be another test—another quest to challenge his sensibilities. He barely had a week after school let out to prepare before having to embark on the journey. This time, however, Abelene accompanied Nicodemus on the excursion. Azriel ached for Camille who had cried the day before they left. Last summer she spent most of her days learning at Abelene's side. This summer she would spend alone. She would not be bored, however, since Abelene left instructions for Camille, Julia, Albert, and Jasper to learn. The series of lessons would prepare them for the coming year. He vowed that next year Camille would accompany him. Azriel wouldn't openly admit it, but he missed Camille more than he should; in fact, had grown somewhat dependent on her friendship—on her calm, grounding sensibilities. So far, aside from his mother, she was the only one he could at times bare his heart to—the only one he trusted with his deepest fears.

The ferry docked at the quay abutting the town of Douglas for which Azriel was grateful. The sea had been choppy, and the relentless up-and-down motion of the waves made Azriel slightly nauseous. He sighed when his feet touched the rugged beams of the dock.

Two figures waited for them to disembark from the ferry. One of them Azriel recognized. The other was cloaked with a cape and hood, hiding her features.

Abelene rushed to the woman, arms extended. They embraced.

"Amaryllis, it's been much too long!"

"Aye, indeed it has, my sister."

The caped figure stepped by Azriel's side and poked him squarely in the ribs—hard enough to make him yelp.

"Hey!" he blurted.

She peeked from beneath her cowl, lifting it just enough for Azriel to see her features.

"Oh—Hi, Felisa!"

She purred a greeting and remarked, "You've gotten taller since I last saw you—almost a man!"

Azriel's cheeks reddened self-consciously as she hugged him.

"Felisa, do you have designs on my son?" Abelene chuckled.

"He's quite a fine-looking young man, Lady." She answered coyly.

Azriel's cheeks darkened even further. He moved to Uncle Nick's side—and away from the women who it seemed to delight in torturing him.

He whispered through clenched teeth, "Uncle Nick, can we go?"

"What's the matter Azriel? Do I make you—uncomfortable?" Felisa cooed.

He grumbled under his breath, "I liked you better when you were just a cat!"

"Meow?" She teased.

"Uncle Nick—please?"

Nicodemus suppressed a smile and cleared his throat. "Er, perhaps we should get moving. We do have a long journey ahead of us."

"Indeed," Amaryllis interjected. "But, I've made it easier this time. Don't want to wear out the boy before we send him on his second quest. Rosemary should be here any minute."

True to her word, within moments Rosemary drove up in an old British metro cab. Azriel winced at it doubtfully, eyeing the Metro cab as if it might collapse under its own weight. He couldn't conceive of how they would all fit into the tiny wagon—particularly with luggage—but Uncle Nick quickly set to securing the bags to the luggage rack.

Azriel smiled and bowed slightly to Rosemary. "Lady Rosalu—" She stopped him midsentence with a sharp glance.

"Oh, sorry. Hi, Rosemary. I didn't expect to see you. How's your father?

"In the hospital, I'm afraid." she lamented.

"What happened?" he asked incredulously.

"Aye, indeed," she sighed. The old fool can handle snakes, alligators, ferrets and all other strange beasties, yet he gets himself in trouble with a stray dog!"

"Huh?"

"He tried to feed the mongrel."

"And…"

"That mongrel dog bit him on the arse! Now my poor papa, he's in need of rabies shots!"

There was a moment of stunned silence—then suddenly they all broke out in laughter.

Rosemary sighed again. "Stupid old fool." She giggled. "Come on, get in."

Azriel was about to get into the front seat when Abelene glared at him disapprovingly. Repentant, he held the door for her and she slipped in next to Rosemary.

Nicodemus and Amaryllis filed into the back leaving little room for Azriel and Felisa. Azriel peered at the tiny space with trepidation. He knew what was coming. He winced painfully and sat next to Nicodemus. It left little option for Felisa except to sit on his lap. She scrunched inside and wrapped her arm around Azriel's neck to make herself as small as possible. He glanced at Uncle Nick with a pleading expression.

Rosemary made a questionable u-turn and headed toward Castleton. Weighed down and over the recommended capacity, Azriel mercilessly felt every bump and rut in the road, augmented by Felisa sitting on his lap. After a particularly brutal pothole, Azriel and Felisa banged heads, their teeth clicking in unison.

"Ow! Azriel blurted.

"Sorry, love. Did I hurt you?" Felisa purred. "Let me kiss it better."

"Felisa!" Amaryllis scolded as they passed a secluded stretch of countryside. "You could make this easier."

She clucked her tongue. "Oh, very well!" Felisa snorted with displeasure.

In moments she transformed into her feline form, nestled within her now-useless cape, and curled up on Azriel's lap purring smugly as more space magically appeared.

A short trek to Castleton, Rosemary pulled up to the now familiar storefront. The ornate black trim glistened with new paint, and the ever-present bronze statue of a mermaid graced the sidewalk. Rosemary, with deliberation, unlocked the door and ushered her guests into the main room. As usual, the contents of the display cases glittered and sparkled, teeming with beautifully crafted objects of silver and gold. Azriel still held Felisa, nestled within her crumpled robe. She jumped from his grasp, alighted and padded to a small niche behind one of the cases. Transforming back into her human form, she huddled behind the counter. Peeking up, hiding herself, no one seemed to notice her dilemma.

"Ahem!" She glared at Azriel.

"Huh?" he answered.

"Robe." She said flatly with a look of consternation on her face.

"Oh! Sorry." Covering his eyes he held out the garment. Felisa brusquely snatched it from his hand and quickly dressed.

Azriel smelled food wafting from behind the curtain that hid the chamber he had entered only once before. Rosemary pulled the drapes aside and Azriel fully expected to see the altar and Ankh suspended from the ceiling, but instead, found a sizeable rough-hewn table and benches gracing the center of the room, Mr. Parkins and Billy tended the hearth where a suckling pig roasted on a slowly turning spit.

Azriel looked at it in sympathy. "Aw, geez Mr. Parkins. You didn't cook up Herman did you?"

He chuckled. "No laddie, Herman's a pet. This here fella is food!"

Azriel sighed in relief. He noticed that Mr. Parkins now had a strange looking contraption firmly attached to where his missing hand had been. Much like a Swiss army knife, it had several folded attachments. A hook, blade, fork, spoon, and a saw were all neatly tucked into a utility compartment.

Billy, meanwhile, set the table with heaping bowls of mashed potatoes, dressing, carrots and leeks. Seeing Azriel, he strode up grabbed him and playfully wrestled him to the ground. "Good to see you again, mate!"

Azriel laughed heartily. "And you too, friend."

He offered a hand and pulled Azriel to his feet. "Now time for some lunch!"

They all seated themselves while Mr. Parkins made quick work of slicing up the roast pig with the knife attached to his cuffed stump.

"Um, Mr. Parkins?" Azriel asked.

"Yes lad?"

"I thought you were in the hospital."

"Aye, I was. Only for an injection. Though I must say it hurt worse than the bite on me arse." He scowled and jabbed the knife into the roast for emphasis.

They all sat and ate the sumptuous meal amid the comfort of a warm fire and the camaraderie of friendship. Not often did the members of the Order of the Ankh meet just for the sheer joy of basking in each other's company. After the thoroughly enjoyable meal, more serious matters quietly asserted themselves. While Billy and Mr. Parkins cleared the table, Rosemary led Azriel to one of the display cases.

"Ye can have any one of these objects. Yer choice."

Azriel looked down, examining all the beautifully crafted items. Diamond-encrusted rings, ruby-studded pendants, silver and gold goblets dazzled his eyes. He was drawn to one object in particular— a golden belt buckle fashioned into a dragon's head. Its eyes were marquise-cut emeralds that sparkled in the dim light. Curiously, one object was tucked into the rear of the case, conspicuous because of its unexceptional appearance. Merely a whittled stick about two feet long with a "Y" junction at its base—or top—Azriel wasn't sure. He remembered his experience with Pog. The old dwarf tried to tempt him with finery and distract him from his first quest. It would seem this test was no different. He knew this next test would have something to do with water—unlocking the name of the water elemental. But what would a strange-looking stick have anything to do with it? The goblet—maybe. But it somehow seemed false as though it were meant to tempt him. The magnificent belt buckle wrought into a dragon's head—that too seemed a deception, though it called to him like a siren wooing a sea-worn sailor. No, he had to go with his heart—even if it made little sense to him.

"I'll take that stick," Azriel said after much deliberation. "Though I don't know why. It seems the foolish thing to do among all this wealth!"

"No, son of Luminance," Rosemary beamed, slipping into her persona as Rosaluna, her accent falling away. "You chose wisely."

She handed him the object from the case.

"What is it? What does it do?" Azriel inquired doubtfully.

"You'll learn in time." Rosemary smiled amicably.

Azriel shrugged and stuck it into a loop on the side of his backpack.

Rosemary offered to drive her company to Cregneash, but much to Azriel's consternation, Nicodemus preferred walking. He grumbled to himself as they set out on a road the locals called the Bypass to Ballakaighen Road. As they continued through the morning to a right bend that became Fisher's Hill, Azriel grew somewhat agitated—not for the actual walking but for the parching thirst in his throat. The clouds had parted, and the sun had broken through. Azriel stripped off his jacket while Abelene and Amaryllis quickly loosened their shawls and tied them around their waists. It did, however, present Felisa with a particular problem, since her woolen robe was making her too warm. With nothing but her bare skin beneath, she found herself in quite a quandary. Felisa did not hide her displeasure at becoming overheated.

"I'm getting too hot," she complained.

"You know what to do, Felisa." Amaryllis offered.

"The way is much longer for a cat."

"I'll carry you if you get tired."

"Oh, very well then." The robe covering her body suddenly crumpled down into a heap, and Felisa in her feline form emerged from the opening, shaking herself off. Abelene stooped down to pick up the robe.

They continued on their way for some time, walking by Shore Road as it skirted the coastline. As they passed a small inn, Felisa meowed loudly in discontent. Amaryllis smiled and lifted her from the ground.

"Can we stop here?" Azriel asked hungrily.

"We ate only two hours ago, Azriel, and besides, the food here isn't very good." Uncle Nick replied with an annoyed edge to his voice. The food at Cregneash is much better. We'll stop there."

The road split and they continued on the left fork. It was at least another half hour before they reached their destination. Azriel recognized the small tavern he had visited once before on his first trip with Uncle Nick. Entering the establishment, the company quickly seated themselves in a far corner. Nicodemus was looking forward to a large bowl of herring and potato soup. The inn was renowned for it.

The old innkeeper strode to the table and greeted his guests affably. Azriel remembered the old man. His ruddy cheeks were still as red and pockmarked as the first time Azriel had met him.

"So, what ye be havin'?" he looked directly at Abelene and raised an eyebrow. She was quite lovely. He glanced at each face until his eyes rested on Amaryllis. His eyes narrowed, and his face darkened. "Yer not welcome here, Amaryllis McBrae!"

She stood to her full height and gazed levelly at the older man. Cradled in her arms, Felisa hissed menacingly at the tavern master.

"What problem would ye be havin' with me, Mister O'Sullivan?" Amaryllis said, taking on his local dialect.

"Aye, indeed," his voice rumbled. "The last time ye showed up here, all hell broke loose! Everyone knows ye placed a hex on me. Me patrons got sick, and me cast-iron pot that's been in the family fer three generations cracked in the fire."

"Nonsense!" Amaryllis laughed lightly. "Perhaps, ye should be considerin' yer own cookin', ye silly old dodder!"

His face reddened further. "Then how do ye explain the pot? Ye brought an evil spirit with ye, ye did!"

"Superstition, old man!" her voice became firmer.

"Oh, ye think so, do ye? There been one series of disasters after another here. Lost a whole set of dishes when that shelf just popped off the wall. How do ye explain that, Amaryllis McBrae?"

"A loose nail, perhaps?" she retorted hotly. "I'm thinking yer fat and lazy and don't look after yer inn as well as ye think! Ye create yer own disasters, if'n ye know what I mean, Mister O'Sullivan."

Abelene stood up from the table and faced the old innkeeper. "Now, now, Mister O'Sullivan. It makes little sense to blame your misfortunes on someone else." She smiled winningly. His temper waned a bit. Abelene often had a calming effect on people.

"But she's a witch. Everyone knows that."

Abelene chuckled lightly, her gray eyes flashing. "Maybe, *I'm* a witch, sir." She patted him on his ruddy cheek. "Just be a dear and get me and my companions some food and drink. I promise you'll be handsomely rewarded."

The man became flustered by Abelene's attentions. To hide his embarrassment, he quickly scurried toward the kitchen and began preparing bowls of food and mugs of ale for his guests.

Nicodemus leaned over to Abelene and scolded. "Now, Abelene. It wasn't necessary to bewitch the old fool."

"I didn't!" She grinned. "I merely used my feminine charms. Quite effective, wouldn't you say?"

Azriel stared at his mother in uncomfortable disbelief, somewhat embarrassed. This was a side of her he'd never seen. He shook his head and took a seat.

"Something to say, Azriel?" she said lightly.

He just stared at her blankly.

"I may be your mother, but I am still a woman! Sometimes one must use what assets one has, yes?"

"If you say so." He muttered. He brooded to himself. He didn't know why it had bothered him so much. Oddly, he stewed with an irrational pang of jealousy, but let it pass.

Mister O'Sullivan returned with a platter heaped with stews, tankards and bread. He also placed a bowl of creamy milk on the floor for Amaryllis's cat. After the delightful meal, Amaryllis faced the tavern keeper squarely.

"It would seem yer havin' a wee bit of bad luck lately."

"No thanks to you, Amaryllis McBrae!"

"Oh, don't be sore." She patted his arm. "I have something for you."

She removed an item from her purse and handed it to the old innkeeper.

Watching, Azriel asked, "What's that, Amaryllis?"

The object was merely two sticks placed in a cross, with colorful woolen yarn continuously wrapped around each quarter piece until it created a diamond pattern of sorts. "Aye," she answered. "It's called a crosh cuirn." She turned to Mister O'Sullivan. "Now, ye nail that to yer front door. It will keep those mischievous fairies away from yer establishment. It will protect ye."

"And why would ye be doin' me any kindness, lass?" he whispered, meant only for her ears.

"Aye, indeed," she whispered back. "Just because I spurned yer advances doesn't mean I don't *like* you, Mister O'Sullivan. But perhaps the next time ye seek to court a lass, ye should dress more appropriately instead of these slovenly old clothes." She tugged lightly at his soiled collar then wiped her fingers on her dress dramatically. "And when ye court a woman, ye bring flowers, or chocolates, or something lovely. And it wouldn't hurt fer ye to lose some weight!" She poked him in the belly.

He blushed involuntarily and clutched the crosh cuirn nervously in his hand. Amaryllis curtsied impishly and rejoined her company. Abelene, who had exceptional hearing, had heard the entire exchange between Amaryllis and Mister O'Sullivan. She approached the flustered man. Looking up at him with sultry eyes, she swiftly paid him for his services, adding an extra ten-pound note for his troubles. He tugged at his grimy collar nervously.

"Now sir, the next time we come to dine at this fine establishment, I'll expect that you treat my sister Amaryllis with a bit more kindness."

"Yes, Ma'am." He muttered. She turned and smiled winningly at Amaryllis. "Now we should be off while we still have sunlight."

Azriel was glad to be leaving the tavern and the craziness of the goings-on there behind. Both Amaryllis and his mother were acting in a peculiar way that confused and annoyed him. Sure, Abelene was always able to get Azriel to behave and perform the way she would like through gentle persuasion, but the actions of both women were downright manipulative! And they were only able to tame poor old Mister O'Sullivan for the mere fact of being women. It was a sobering lesson. Azriel swore an oath to himself that he would never allow a woman to control him like that. He brooded as he walked the slight decline that led toward Amaryllis' home through the rugged countryside.

Abelene and Amaryllis lagged behind, whispering and giggling like schoolgirls. Felisa joined them running up from behind a thicket. She donned her robe again and joined in the secretive chatter.

Uncle Nick strode up beside Azriel. The boy's steps were deliberate as he plodded on, absorbed in his musings.

"Deep thoughts, Azriel?" Nicodemus inquired, hiding his amusement.

He grumbled.

"Come, Azriel," Uncle Nick chuckled. "Man to man—tell me."

"How do they do it?" he whispered through clenched teeth.

"Do what?"

"Look, that barkeep was about to throw Amaryllis out on her butt! And then a couple of words from my mother, and he's eating out of her hand! How do they do it?"

"Ahhh, I see!" Nicodemus emoted a perfect *eureka* moment. "It's their female wiles—their charm. Men will do the most foolish things to gain a woman's approval—stupid things."

"Is that why you never got married?"

"Mostly," He acquiesced. "I'm immortal—almost." Uncle Nick smiled. "It wouldn't be—proper, and…" he shrugged. "Most likely, too painful. Not that I didn't pick the fruits from a willing lady from time to time."

Azriel's face reddened and Uncle Nick laughed.

"You see Azriel," Nicodemus continued. "I've seen greater men than old Mister O'Sullivan fall to women's guile and get thoroughly destroyed. They are dangerous creatures—and quite lovely. You've heard the story of Samson and Delilah."

"I thought that was just a silly fable."

"Oh, he was real enough. A prince among men. And strong? Let me tell you, the man could lift a stone ten men couldn't budge. Strong beyond legend—strength spoken of in awe and disbelief. He could fight off an army of a hundred trained warriors without even raising a sweat. But..." he held up his finger dramatically. "He was superstitious. Samson believed all his strength derived from the fact that he had never cut his hair. It was all in his head, though. Er, no pun intended. And it didn't help that his mother and father reinforced his belief. With or without hair, he would have been just as strong! Only when the crisis came, he didn't trust in his own power. So as the story goes, after many wondrous deeds and killing many Philistines—his sworn enemies—he fell in love with a beautiful woman. Delilah, however, was false, having taken a bribe from the Philistines to betray him by discovering the source of his power. In that way, they would take him prisoner. After a few failed attempts at his secret, Delilah did the usual things a woman does when unhappy—pout, brood—the usual petulance. Finally, giving in to Delilah, he spilled the beans and told her. Of course, that night while Samson slept, Delilah sheared his head like a sheep. When he awoke, he had lost his power."

"Then maybe his hair *was* the source of his strength," Azriel asserted.

"No, but his own belief that his long hair was his power led to his undoing. Of course, the Philistines captured him, took out his eyes, and humiliated him without mercy. It all ended very badly after many years—when his hair grew back. Vanquished, Samson was put on display during a large dinner party for the Philistine nobility at the temple of Dagon. In one last feat of strength, Samson collapsed the temple he was chained to and killed them all— including himself."

"Just because his hair grew back?" Azriel asked, puzzled.

"Forget the hair, Azriel. It was his will that enabled him to take vengeance upon his enemies."

"I don't understand."

"Don't be so dense, boy. What is stronger? Is it the sword, or the arm that wields it? Is it the rock, or the sapling that grows through it? Is it the heart, or the mind that tames the heart?"

"I get it, but what does this have to do with women?" Azriel didn't hide his petulance.

"It all gets back to the will, Azriel. Women make our hearts stronger than our will. They can exert their charms on the mind, and the heart doesn't have a snowball's chance in hell. Only..." Nicodemus sighed.

"Yes?"

"If you have a good woman, your heart can wax strong and it will overcome the confusing traps of the mind. Like magick, your heart will know the things your mind can't—or won't! A bad woman will confuse the mind with logic—or their form of it—and create doubt—that is the heart killer!"

"You really haven't answered my question, Uncle Nick."

"No, I suppose not."

"So what does it all mean, then?"

"I suppose that you should trust your heart when it comes to women."

"Now I'm even more confused."

"Where women are concerned, Azriel. Confusion is something you'll just have to get used to." Nicodemus chuckled.

Their conversation served to teach Azriel an important lesson and distract him from the relentless walking. He was surprised to find they had covered most of the distance to Amaryllis's home. The huge boulder that served as her home loomed before them, sturdy and solid. By now the sun was just setting, and Azriel shivered slightly from the sudden drop in temperature.

Upon entering, a stack of wood already filled the cold hearth, and with a mere thought, Amaryllis ignited the bundle. In moments, a cheerful blaze warmed the room. Felisa set about putting a kettle on the fire to boil water for mugs of hot cocoa. Soon they all sat around the fire drinking cocoa laced with rum.

Azriel sat a little apart from the others, lost in his own thoughts, sorting through his conversation with Nicodemus. He didn't notice at first that Uncle Nick had been watching him, staring at him casually. It didn't take long for him to become rather uncomfortable with his Uncle's scrutiny. Finally, he blurted out with more irritation than he meant.

"What?!"

Nicodemus smiled. "You have quite the day cut out for you tomorrow."

"Yeah?"

"Indeed." Uncle Nick nodded thoughtfully.

"What am I supposed to do?"

"That's for you to discover."

"No riddles? No clues?"

"All you need do, young master, is to ask the right questions, and the water elemental will reveal her name."

"Well, what am I going after this time?"

"A pearl!" Felisa interjected.

Amaryllis shot her a disapproving glance. "Felisa!" She scolded.

"Well, he needs to have some direction!" She shot back, hands on hips.

"I guess." Amaryllis sighed.

"A pearl?" Azriel probed. "Any old pearl. That shouldn't be too hard."

"Oh no, son." Amaryllis laughed lightly. "Not just any old pearl, but the pearl of great price—the pearl of truth!"

"Sounds difficult." He muttered.

"It is! One can only find it if he is worthy. It means moving beyond yourself. You must forego your selfish needs and be charitable to others. Use your intuition, Azriel, and you will find the answer. It's not something you can buy or barter. You will find it if you move outside yourself."

"Now I'm thoroughly confused." Azriel scowled. He knew that probing further would only lead to more ambiguity, and he fell silent.

Felisa yawned and stretched. "I'm tired." she stated sleepily. Without further ado, she kissed Azriel on the cheek. "You'll be okay," she encouraged, whispering in his ear. Her robe suddenly dropped to the floor, and she padded out from the rumpled collar transformed into her feline form. She brushed affectionately on Azriel's legs before curling up by the fire.

Amaryllis looked down at Felisa lovingly and smiled. "Well, I guess that's our signal to retire. Azriel, you have a big day ahead of you. A good night's sleep is what you need now."

Azriel had slept fitfully, disturbed by strange dreams of water and mermaids. In one of them, a small girl became separated from her people. A great storm blew up from nowhere and she was tossed about, caught in treacherous currents that buffeted her, knocking her unconscious. Finally, after the storm blew over, the mermaid was tossed up on shore, half dead. Then, in opposition, his dreams morphed into being stranded in a boundless desert, dying of thirst. A dreadful wind parched his mouth and chafed the skin. Exhausted and near death, he came upon an oasis. The palm trees, however, were desiccated and wizened from lack of water. Beyond the dying oasis was a strange outcropping of black rock. Though crumbled in most places, a single spire of basalt rose to the sky like a needle. It seemed to pierce the sun. Around him, the nomadic residents dug holes in the ground in futility, for the well and small pond which had sustained them had dried up, the life-giving water having sunk into the ground. One by one the camels and horses died, and people dropped to the ground with exhaustion, pleading for help. Azriel jolted awake in a cold sweat. He shook off the feeling of dread and lay in the silent darkness, thinking about the images still lingering in his mind. He knew the dreams meant something—perhaps a clue to his next quest.

Two extremes seemed to be at play here. Too much water—or too little. Either one could kill. The dream, however, brought back the memory of Rosemary and the bronze statue of a mermaid gracing her storefront. It had to be a clue. Still tired, Azriel finally drifted off into a more restful sleep.

The sun crested the horizon, and the day promised to be warm and delightful. Azriel awoke to the mouthwatering aroma of sizzling bacon. Stepping out of the bedroom while pulling a shirt over his head, he nearly collided with Felisa who scurried about preparing breakfast.

She giggled. "Good morning to you, Azriel." She absently licked batter off her hand as she poured the mixture onto a hot griddle.

"Hi, Felisa. It smells good!" Azriel smiled.

"It *is* good." She giggled and removed a teapot from the stove. Just then, a tiny mouse darted from the pantry onto a shelf. Quicker than lightning, Felisa snatched it up and popped it in her mouth, chewing absently as she poured the tea.

Horrified and slightly queasy, Azriel stared at Felisa. "Promise me you'll never do that again in my presence," he said.

"A girl has to eat," she replied, a bit bruised.

"Yeah, well that was—disgusting!"

"I'm sure you've heard a tiger never changes his stripes! Well neither does a cat!" Felisa snapped defensively.

"Will you two stop that bickering!" Nicodemus blustered from the other room. Felisa giggled impishly and served up breakfast.

Half the morning was gone by the time Azriel reached the Fairy Bridge. This time, his backpack was loaded to the gills and heavier than he would have preferred, but he trusted that everything he carried would have some purpose in fulfilling his journey. As before, the bridge arched over the stream, appearing weatherworn and quite in need of repair. He waited for a few passersby to move out of earshot. He looked both ways to make sure he was alone before calling out.

"Pog?"

Almost immediately, Azriel heard a slight pop, and Pog stood before him. With a flourish, the old gnome bowed deeply and greeted Azriel.

"Well, laddie, top of the mornin' to ye!"

"It's good seeing you too, Pog. I thought I would have seen you yesterday when we arrived."

"Aye." He shook his head. "But I had a matter that needed attending to."

"Must have been important."

"Indeed. Some stirrings on the island. Yer being followed."

A sudden chill crept up Azriel's spine.

"Aye, not to worry. I fixed them good."

"Who's following me?"

"Not a who, but a *what*. One of the Clave sent a Mauthe Dhoog after ye. Been trailin' ye since ye arrived here."

"What's a Mauthe Dhoog?" Azriel asked with trepidation.

"It's a spectral hound from hell. They've inhabited this here island since the split. A vile creature with eyes of steel. Someone summoned the creature from the pit. Not to worry though. A Mauthe Dhoog is quite ferocious but not too bright. Ye see, laddie—it has a taste for dead skunk. I set the bait and lured the creature into a clever trap. It won't find its way out for a thousand years!"

"Yeah, but that means someone knows I'm here."

"That's inevitable, laddie. Not with the way ye been leakin' yer magick all over the place. Ye been leavin' a trail of breadcrumbs. Talkin' mountain lions indeed—very foolish!"

"That was an accident."

"Aye," he sighed, "it was. We need to work on that. But don't ye be concernin' yerself, son. I been coverin' yer trail fer some time now."

"Thanks, Pog."

"I'm only here to help. Can't have ye turnin' up dead before ye can be of any use!" Pog chortled. "Now what do ye have here?"

Pog removed the oddly shaped stick from Azriel's backpack and examined it thoughtfully.

"Actually, I'm not really sure what it is." Azriel mused.

"It's called a dowsing rod."

"A what?"

"A dowsing rod, laddie. It's fer findin' water."

"How does it work?"

"It doesn't work at all. You're the one doin' the work. It's just a tool. Now take the two ends in yer hands."

Azriel held the forked end of the stick and pointed the long end toward the ground.

"Now point the dowser toward that rock."

A large boulder was embedded in the ground near the bridge. Azriel pointed the dowsing rod toward the huge rock and waited. Nothing happened.

"What's it supposed to do?"

"Find water!" Pog answered.

"It's not doing anything."

"That's to be expected. Now point it to the river."

Azriel turned toward the water, and pointed the dowsing rod. A strange tug from the stick pulled him forward. The end began gently bobbing the closer it came to the river.

"Ahh, laddie. Yer a natural. Now ye can go on yer quest!"

"Doing what?" Azriel scowled.

"Why, finding water where it doesn't exist! On yer way now."

"Is that it?" Azriel scrunched up his face in consternation.

"That's all there is to it. Do it right and you'll get the answer to the question."

"I'm not even sure what the question is." Azriel couldn't contain his frustration.

"Think laddie. What is it you seek to find?"

"A pearl—I think."

"See!" Pog smiled broadly, "Now ye have yer answer."

"Great." He muttered, his tone flat with sarcasm. Azriel shrugged and started crossing the bridge. But suddenly he stopped short and turned his head staring at Pog.

"No tricks this time laddie. It's safe."

"That's refreshing!"

He stepped forward and suddenly a plank disappeared ahead of Azriel. He turned and glared at Pog.

"Only kidding, laddie. Habit ye know."

The plank reappeared and Azriel was on his way. He spent a good part of the day getting used to the feel of the dowsing rod. He followed the invisible trail suggested by the device, but every time he thought he was close to his quarry, he came upon a well. It seemed there was no lack of water on the island. Late afternoon, the dowsing rod again pointed to the ground. He followed another trail when he found himself in the middle of a sheep pasture. An old sheep hand strode up to him and watched in disbelief as Azriel scratched his head.

"What do ye think ye be doin' there, boy?"

"Dowsing for water." He answered without looking up.

"Are ye daft, boy? The only water you'll find in this here field is sheep piss. Now off with ye! Ye silly git!" The old farmer brandished a pitchfork and chased Azriel off his land.

He ran off but then turned questioningly.

"Wait a minute. I'm sure there's water here."

The old farmer laughed heartily, obviously ridiculing the boy. "Son, you're not from around here, are ye?"

"No. What does that have to do with anything?" Frustrated, he gave the old farmer a steely glare.

"Well, anyone here knows that all ye have to do is dig a mere meter or two and you'll hit water! The land here is rife with underground streams."

Azriel gaped at him and mumbled an apology.

Walking toward the setting sun, Azriel found himself on the road leading back to Castleton. By now he was hungry and rifled through his backpack for a snack. Disappointed, he found no food, but there was a small purse with a few ten-pound notes. Azriel made his way to the center of town, where he followed his nose to a small tavern and the delicious aromas wafted through the old oaken door. He seated himself at a small table in the corner and waited for service. The waitress was young and pretty, with golden curls and a vivacious smile, perhaps a year or two older than Azriel. She leaned over giving the table a quick swipe with a cloth. Azriel couldn't help resting his gaze momentarily at her ample bosom which seemed to bulge through a blouse cut a bit too low. He glanced back at her face, blushing in embarrassment.

She suppressed a giggle and asked, "What would ye be havin'?"

"I don't know. What would you recommend?"

"Ahh, a newcomer. Well, love, the roast mutton is quite good today—mashed potatoes and gravy with a side of greens. My name's Muriel by the way."

"Okay—Muriel." He shrugged. "I'll have the mutton."

"And what's yer name, love?"

"Azriel."

"And would ye be havin' some ale with that—Azriel?"

"No thanks, just some hot cider."

The young women returned shortly with a heaping plate of meat and potatoes smothered with rich, dark gravy. Azriel ate with gusto while the waitress watched him with amusement. Her eyes never left him. The mutton was a bit gamey for his taste, but overall, the meal was quite enjoyable. He washed it down with the cider and quickly paid the tab to avoid Muriel's continued scrutiny. As he stood to leave, she waylaid him at the door.

"Leaving so soon?" She smiled seductively as she chewed noisily on a piece of gum. "I get off at eight o'clock."

Azriel stammered, but before he could get a word out, the barkeep—a broad man with a thick golden beard—strode over and pointed to the tables.

"Get yer arse back into the dining hall. Patrons are waiting to be served."

She glared at the older man and shouted back. "Father, ye ruin everything! I was just havin' a wee bit of fun."

"Move," he said firmly.

With a scathing look, she stormed back into the dining hall and pulled out an order pad from her pocket.

As embarrassed as he was by her advances, Azriel had a sudden compulsion to come to her defense.

"I apologize for me daughter. She's a shameless flirt."

"Oh, no sir. We were just exchanging pleasantries—that's all. I'm new here. Muriel was just offering to show me the sights."

"And a bit more, I'd wager."

"No sir. Nothing like that."

From across the room, Muriel smiled gratefully at Azriel before heading to the kitchen.

The evening was warm and balmy, promising to be a pleasant night to sleep on the beach. Azriel headed past the quay to the narrow beach below. The strip of sand was deserted, except for a solitary figure facing the ocean. Azriel thought to give the woman a wide berth and began walking the other way, when he realized it was Rosemary. He came up behind her and waited.

Sensing his presence, she turned and looked at him sadly, wiping tears from her eyes.

"Rosemary, what's wrong?"

"Sit down next to me, Azriel."

He sat on the soft sand, facing the sea. She stared into the waves and her tears began anew.

"What happened today? Why are you crying?" he asked with concern.

"What happened was long ago, Azriel. You see, I miss my family and I'm feeling a wee bit melancholy."

"I'm listening."

Rosemary took Azriel's hand. She found his presence comforting.

"Many years ago, when I was a wee lass, I got separated from my family. A terrible typhoon blew in from the west; waterspouts were everywhere, and I got caught in the wake. I tried and tried to swim deeper but got overtaken by the strong current. Desperate to reach me mother, I swam until all my strength ran out. I was knocked unconscious by floating debris and washed up on shore. The following morning, Mr. Parkins found me and took me in. For a week, he nursed me back to health. But I had been too long out of water. I could not return."

A look of realization dawned on Azriel's face. "Then the visions I had last night were true! That was you—the little mermaid I dreamed of!"

"Now ye know the truth, young master. I was born an undine. But you see, an undine cannot be out of water fer more than a day otherwise we become human and can ne'er go back. Poor Mr. Parkins didn't know the truth of it, in fact he saved my life. He meant well and followed his heart. He and Mrs. Parkins were childless and welcomed me as a gift from the sea. They raised me as their own, taught me how to speak like humans do. Then when his lovely wife fell ill and suddenly died, I was the only one that could ease father's heart. But, alas, I am permanently altered, Azriel. I can never return home."

"Never?"

"No—never." She sniffed.

"But what about using magick? Surely there is some spell or word that can transform you back. Did you ask Pog?"

"No dear. There are some things, Azriel, even the most powerful Magick can't touch."

"I don't believe that!" Azriel stated firmly.

"No," she said sadly. "Undines are magickal creatures of the ocean, and bound to the laws of water and nature. Once removed from our element, our magick quickly fades. Once human, I was bound only to earth magick."

"I'm sorry, Rosemary."

"Aye. It's not so bad. There is much here to learn and I've accepted me fate, but there are nights like this, when the moon is full, that I become sad."

Azriel grew reflective, thinking about Rosemary's dilemma. "Would you really go back if you could?" he asked.

"An odd question, Azriel."

"Not really. Think of all the people you know here, how many look up to you. I'm just thinking that you've been away for so long; it may not be what you remember. It's sort of like when I think about my father. I never knew him. He died before I was born. Even though that's a missing part of my life, it's not like I can say I miss him. How can I grieve for what I never had in the first place? He was the King of Aralia, which made him powerful, I suppose. But what if he was a tyrant? If that's the case, then it's better off I didn't know him at all."

Rosemary glanced sideways and smiled at Azriel. "So pragmatic for such a young man."

"You might think so, but it's the only way I can make sense of everything that's been going on. Like these quests Nicodemus keeps sending me on. I do them because I'm supposed to, but I really don't know why—other than learning the names of the Elementals. I have no idea what the end result will be. I just keep thinking that maybe in the end, my purpose in all this will become clear. For now, I just have to trust that it will."

"Abelene has taught you well."

As they spoke, dark, ominous clouds began blowing in from the east. They felt the first stirring of the storm when a gust of warm wind blew up a spray of white sand.

"We should go, Azriel. I would not suggest ye staying on the beach tonight. Ye will not be happy. The weather here is unpredictable."

On the way back to the alley where Rosemary's shop was situated, the sky suddenly opened up, and they had to duck under the eaves to keep from being drenched. By the time they arrived at the shop, Azriel needed to towel off and get into some dry clothing he had stored in his backpack. Rosemary put on a kettle for tea.

Warming up by the fire, they sat across from each other speaking of common things, the mundane everyday details of life on the Isle of Man—everything but what was really on Azriel's mind. In the middle of the conversation, Rosemary's eyes suddenly became unfocused as if she were elsewhere momentarily, then she returned. She smiled. Azriel thought it all rather weird and risked the question.

"Er, Rosemary, you just went—somewhere else, like you weren't present. Are you okay?"

"Just fine, Azriel. I was just letting your mother know that you're all right—that you're in good hands." Her accent dropped, again speaking in formal tones. He suspected she was now speaking to Lady Rosaluna.

"Wait a minute. Do you mean to tell me my mother is checking up on me?" Azriel's face burned with humiliation.

"Well of course. That's what mothers do. Do you want Abelene to worry?"

"So how do you do it—talk over great distances?"

"I felt her touch my mind. It's as simple as opening my mind to her presence."

"That doesn't sound that simple at all. It sounds dangerous, actually. I wouldn't want anyone rattling around in my head."

"Yes, but you would be the one in control. You can either choose to answer a call or not—just like a cell phone. It's easy for magickal creatures like us. Besides, that's how undines communicate. I could teach you if you want."

Azriel considered the offer. Something like that could be quite useful in any given situation. "Can you read minds?" he asked quickly.

"No," she smiled. "It doesn't work that way. One has to be trained to be a transmitter and a receiver. It's for communication only. Beyond that we don't delve. People are entitled to their privacy. And there's something else to consider. The mind is a complicated place. It's quite easy to misinterpret one's intentions."

"I don't understand." Azriel shook his head.

"Okay." Rosemary stared up at the ceiling as she thought. "Let's just imagine for a moment that you and I are about to share a custard cream pie! Now you look in my mind and see me giggling as I ponder that delicious pie. How would you interpret my happiness?"

"That's pretty simple," Azriel said. "You love cream pie and you're anticipating the happiness you'll feel when you cut a slice and eat it."

"Aha!" Rosemary held up her finger. "But what you didn't see was what was in my heart. You see, at that moment I'm feeling a wee bit devilish. You didn't see that I was about to pick up that pie and mash it in your face!" To illustrate, Rosemary pushed her hand into Azriel's face and gave a good rub. He squirmed away, laughing. "And that brings up my next point."

"And what would that be?" Azriel drained the rest of his tea.

"It's about this quest you're on. You need to understand what the element of water means. Without water, there is no life."

Azriel suddenly remembered the dream he had of people dying in the desert.

"Next to air, water is the least dense of the elements. Like mutable currents, it symbolizes the realm of emotion and intuition. Your mind will fool you at times, but your heart will always tell the truth—if you are truly in touch with it. Water is as ever-changing as emotion, and it's the very essence of love and compassion. Water can bathe and nurture—but it can also drown! That's why you must rule over your heart, not let your heart rule you. That's not to say that you shouldn't listen to your heart, but it is always a good idea to—test the waters, so to speak." Rosemary smiled winningly.

"What about you, though. Water is your natural element. You were born an undine."

Rosemary's smile wavered. "Aye indeed," she sighed. "I'm a fish out of water. But whatever form I take—whether human or undine—what truly matters is what's in the heart."

"So what about my next test, Rosemary? I'm supposed to find this pearl of great price, but I'm baffled. Everywhere I go on this island, I find water! So what's the point?"

"There is no point." Rosemary giggled at the look of consternation clouding Azriel's face. "This only you can solve, Son of Luminance. In this matter, you must follow your heart. That's the best advice I can give."

"Okay." Azriel conceded. "But I'm going to find a way to help you—if I can."

Rosemary tilted her head considering Azriel. Her heart swelled with love and gratitude for him. "You're a dear, sweet young man. I believe you'll succeed in anything you set out to do." She suddenly had a flash of intuition, a magickal gift inherent in her species. Rosemary took his hand. Her voice took on an ominous tone. "There will come a time, young master, when you will have to make hard decisions. For when the blood within you stirs, your heart will answer first. Those who stand with you will remain—yet the burden will be yours alone to carry. What is lost returns at your call and will endure, changed into radiance."

"I'm not sure I understand."

"No, I suppose not. But you will, when the time comes you will know what to do." Rosemary kissed Azriel gently on the forehead. Her gesture was maternal, like his mother, but he detected a hint of sadness—like she knew something terrible she was loath to reveal.

"What are you not telling me?"

"Do not trouble yourself with meanings. Such words only find their shape when they must. Sometimes, Son of Luminance, it is better for us to not know the future—otherwise our hearts can become immobilized by fear. Courage, Azriel. You will not fail."

Her words did not help to allay his anxiety. His mind was filled with questions and doubts.

Sensing his turmoil, Rosemary placed her hands on his shoulders. She spoke gently. "I also know something else, Azriel. You are strong and brave, equal to any task put before you. I know this because I sense your heart. You have a great capacity to love. It will be enough. Trust me in this."

"I think I understand, Rosemary—or should I say Lady Rosaluna?"

She smiled serenely.

Rosemary led Azriel to a spare room at the back of the shop. It was warm and the bed was comfortable. Tired and frustrated by a fruitless day, Azriel drifted off to sleep. Like the night before, his peace was disturbed by fragmented dreams. Again, he saw Rosemary in her true form. The tiny mermaid washed up on the shore battered and bruised by the freak storm. She lay unconscious through the night, her tail morphing in the moonlight into ordinary legs. This time, however, through her ordeal, he experienced her terror and hopelessness as she was pulled further away from her family. He saw kindly Mr. Parkins as a younger man pick up the toddler and wrap her in a warm blanket as he cradled her to his heart. He brought the child to his wife who wept with joy over having a beautiful little girl to nurture.

And as before, the scene suddenly shifted and Azriel found himself in the desert. The undulating sands and dust devils nearly swept the air from his lungs. Choking and sputtering, he wrapped a cloth around his mouth. All about him, victims of the drought were strewn like refuse, half buried in the mounting sand. Their bones had been stripped bare from the continuous assault of the abrasive wind. The once abundant oasis had been bereft of life. Stricken by the indifference of nature, Azriel sat by one of the skeletons and stared at it with pity. Beyond him, like before, the stone needle rose up into the sky. He glanced down at the ground before him. Oddly, he saw movement in the sand. He dug at the spot and uncovered a tiny fish burying itself in the ground. It was covered with slimy ooze and as he watched, it began to shrivel and dry out until it resembled an ancient fossil. It served as a grim reminder of how fragile life truly was. Azriel pondered this when he began to hear a voice calling him from the distance.

"Wake up, sunshine!"

Azriel shook himself awake and glanced out the window facing the alley. Light filtered through and he glanced at the alarm clock on the dresser and then drowsily at Rosemary. The clock read 5:30 am.

"My, my!" she giggled. "Ye were dug in like a tick! Get up and join me for a swim."

"Are you serious?"

"Aye, indeed." she yanked at his arm. "Come on, the mornin's wasting! The sun's shinin'; the sky is blue, birds are singin'. Ye don't want to waste such a perfect mornin'! Now move yer arse, Azriel!" She bubbled good-naturedly.

Azriel was less than delighted, but he figured there would be no arguing with Rosemary. He quickly dressed in a bathing suit he found on the bed. It would have been stupid to ask where it came from.

A short walk from the shop, he followed Rosemary to the beach. She didn't hesitate when she reached the shore. Dropping her towel, she dove into the waves without even testing the water. Taking her lead, Azriel dove in after her. But gasping with the sudden bite of the frigid water, he quickly rose up and yowled with shock. "Are you crazy? This is ice water!"

Rosemary couldn't suppress her laughter. "Oh, quiet, Azriel. Do ye want to wake up the entire island?"

"You could have warned me." He shivered.

"Aye, and ye could have asked," she countered.

Azriel grumbled and examined his fingers to make sure they weren't turning blue.

"Oh, don't be such a baby. Swim, Azriel, swim. You'll warm up."

It took a while, but he did become more accustomed to the water temperature and was even beginning to enjoy himself. They caught a good wave and rode it in, sliding up onto the sand. The morning quiet and serene, they dried off quickly and hurried back to Rosemary's shop, but not before stopping at the bakery for pastries and coffee. Rejuvenated, Azriel was now ready to face the day.

Gift of the Amulet

216

Chapter 12

Everywhere, water. Half the day was spent in a frustrating, futile attempt to locate water where there was no need. Azriel was beginning to feel like he had been played for a fool. A pointless exercise with the dowsing rod, he was nowhere nearer to completing his task. Tired, hungry, and with the onset of blistered feet, Azriel planted himself under the welcoming shade of an alder tree. He quietly unpacked the lunch Rosemary had given him and absently munched on a sandwich. While he was nearly finished with his meal, a pair of woodcock meandered from a low copse of thicket and eyed Azriel suspiciously. Happy for any company, even a couple of silly birds, Azriel spoke softly to them, coaxing them to come closer. He broke off tiny pieces of bread crust and tossed the crumbs in their direction. Gobbling them up, the game birds came closer and unafraid, sat by Azriel's feet seemingly begging for more of the tasty morsels.

"Yer getting pretty good at that, laddie." Pog walked up from behind and found a seat next to Azriel.

"Man, am I glad to see you!" Azriel sighed with relief.

"Having a rough time of it, are ye?"

"I don't know if I'd say that, Pog." He tossed the last tiny morsels of crust toward the birds. They scrounged them up, and sensing that there was no more, grudgingly flew back to the copse of thicket.

"Then what are ye sayin', laddie?"

"This whole thing is pointless."

Pog reached into his pocket and produced a sizeable crystal ball cut from pure quartz. He handed it to Azriel.

"What's this?" Azriel scowled as he examined the beautiful, perfect sphere.

"It's pointless." Pog shrugged. "Doesn't necessarily mean it has no purpose."

"So what you're trying to say is that there's some purpose to me scudding about, searching for water when there's no need here?" Azriel replied hotly.

"Of course! You've practiced long enough. Now it's time to put your skills to the test."

"Well, that's certainly not going to happen here."

"What do ye mean, laddie?"

"I've been thinking. There's no use for me here. These islanders have all the water they need but…" Azriel hesitated.

"Go on, laddie." Pog prodded.

"Well, I keep having this recurring dream about Rosemary—and something else."

"Ye don't say."

"Yeah. I see myself in a desert. All around me people are dying because the oasis they subsist on has dried up. It would seem that if I need to be anywhere it's got to be in that desert."

Pog squirmed where he sat. "Ah, I don't know, laddie. The world is filled with deserts. Ye don't even know which one. And besides, how would ye get there?"

"I figured you could take me there. After all, you're always popping in and out at will."

Pog glared at Azriel and crossed his arms. He stood and faced Azriel squarely, eye to eye. "Now that's just a wee bit presumptuous, wouldn't ye say there, laddie. Besides, I wouldn't be able to get there without some reference point. Yer bayin' at the moon, son. It would be impossible."

"That's bullcrap, and you know it, Pog. If you've taught me anything, it's that nothing is impossible!"

Suddenly, an angry bull charged through the thicket several yards beyond. The gamecocks Azriel had just recently fed scattered from the bushes in a frenzy. The bull stopped a few feet before Azriel, squatted, and farted out a massive pile of stinking dung.

"There's yer bullcrap, laddie." Pog smiled, pleased with himself.

"Will you stop that!" Azriel exploded. He took a deep breath and calmed himself. "Look, Pog. I'm supposed to be learning how to be a wizard, right?"

"Aye." The gnome agreed.

"Well then, what good does it do if I can't help anyone? Those people in my dream are dying."

"They're not yer responsibility, laddie," Pog said flatly.

Azriel's face reddened with suppressed anger. "I disagree. If I didn't know about them, then you would be right. But I *do* know about their plight, and I have the power to help them. If I sit back and do nothing then I'm as useless as…as…that pile of crap over there. And you would be no better!"

Pog nodded thoughtfully and smiled to himself. "Aye, laddie. That's what I wanted to hear. You've passed the test. Ye see, Azriel, the most important quality of being a good wizard is compassion. To sit by when others are suffering is the worst thing one could do and perhaps one of the vilest traits of humanity. You, son, are a young man of good quality. Of course I'll help ye. It won't be easy though. Matter of fact, it will be downright difficult but—not impossible. But be warned, laddie. This rests squarely on yer shoulders. Now what I want ye to do is hold that crystal ball in yer hands. It's not just any ordinary crystal ball but a dream orb."

"A dream orb?" Azriel questioned. "I've never heard of it."

"Of course ye haven't, laddie. It's very rare. There's only three in existence."

"Yeah? Where did you get it?"

"Not fer ye to know right now, son." Pog said firmly. "Now close yer eyes and think of yer dream. Ye have to be very certain about the details. After all, ye don't want to get lost now, do ye?"

With this, Azriel had no problem. The recurring dream was quite vivid in his mind, in particular, the outcropping of stone and the dark needled spire of basalt.

"Now open yer eyes." Pog instructed.

Azriel did as Pog suggested and peered into the dream orb. Within its crystalline structure, the image from his mind was planted in vivid detail into the sphere. Another change had taken place. Azriel was no longer sitting by the tree, but now sat in a chair at Pog's table. Aside from two bowls of delicious-looking stew, a pile of dun-colored cloth and a few large jugs of water were strewn haphazardly on the floor.

"First we eat!" Pog rubbed his hands together happily. "You'll need yer strength."

The venison stew was quite delicious, and they both finished the meal in short measure. That being done, Pog snapped his finger and the bowls disappeared. He then handed over one of the dusty looking cloths to Azriel. He could see that it was in fact a loose-fitting robe with a wrap for his head.

"You'll need to dress appropriately for the desert, laddie." Pog commented. Azriel watched as Pog dressed and copied, with a fairly good approximation, how the dwarf wrapped the turban around his head.

Pog gathered up the containers of water strewn about and placed them at Azriel's feet. "Now, laddie, you'll need to take the dream orb in yer hands and fix that image into yer mind."

Azriel removed the crystal sphere from his pocket and stared into it.

"Good!" Pog exclaimed. "Now you must project yourself into the Orb. Picture yourself by that stand of rock and remain calm. The first time can be a bit unsettling."

Nothing happened at first, but soon the air around them began to change. Azriel's body pulsed with the drawing in of energy, scintillating with an ever-increasing vibration. Without warning, a blinding flash of light disoriented Azriel, and he swooned with power as he shielded his eyes. He was unprepared for the onslaught of intense heat and wind buffeting his body and nearly cried out with the sudden change. He choked and gagged on the dust swirling around him. Pog immediately wrapped the end of his turban over his mouth and nose tucking it into a fold of his head wrap. Azriel followed suit and stared up in amazement at the black spire of rock that seemed to soar above him.

"Wow, what a forbidding place," He shouted above the screeching of the desert wind.

"Aye, laddie. The locals call it the devil's leap! They avoid this place like the plague."

"Why?"

"The Manisir are a very superstitious people. Their legends say the devil lives in these here rocks and spreads famine throughout the land."

"Oh, that's comforting."

"Somethin' else ye should know, laddie."

"And what would that be?"

"The Manisir are a very ancient tribe of Bedouins. Their traditions go back hundreds if not thousands of years. They have a legend of the Angel of Death. His Name is Azriel, so I wouldn't be throwin' yer name about if'n I were you. It might be taken the wrong way."

"I'll be careful."

"Aye, but what they don't know is that this outcropping of rock is the source of their water in a roundabout sort of way. It's fed by the fourth cataract of the Nile. Then the cavern beneath has an underground spring with a subterranean river that flows to the oasis."

"Then why are they dying?" Azriel inquired.

"That's a good question."

As they spoke, Azriel heard a loud crack and looked up as several sizeable boulders sheared off the face of the spire.

"Look out!" Azriel pushed Pog out of the way and dove for cover shielding his head with his arms as the boulders crashed to the ground followed by a shower of scree and rubble.

"Devil's Leap, my ass!" Azriel blustered. "This place is a nightmare!"

"Aye, indeed. We had best get to work."

Azriel agreed and removed the dowsing rod from his pack. He pointed it to the ground. In the distance he could barely make out the dying oasis. Walking away from the outcropping of rock, he sensed the slight bobbing of the dowsing rod growing weaker the further away he moved from Devil's leap. At some point it stopped detecting any water at all and Azriel doubled back. For the brief time they were there, Azriel was already thirsty. He opened a jug of water and gulped it down.

"Not too fast, Azriel. It must last a while."

"Right," He agreed sheepishly. "He handed the jug to Pog who availed himself of the sustaining water. Azriel continued following the underground trail. It led him closer to the forbidding rock. He climbed over a few boulders until he was completely surrounded by the oppressive stone. At one point, the dowsing rod dipped down with a particularly strong indication. Azriel could see why. A few yards before him a deep hole opened to a seemingly bottomless chasm. He peered down into the hole and shied back. It was dark and unwelcoming.

"Pog, I found something!"

The dwarf had a bit of difficulty scaling the boulders but soon was by Azriel's side.

He looked into the cavity and smiled. "Smell that, laddie?"

Azriel inhaled deeply and then it dawned on him. "I smell water!"

"Aye! And plenty of it!" Pog picked up a sizeable stone and dropped it in the hole. From the sound of the clatter it didn't seem too far down. Pog dropped in another and gauged the distance.

"I'd say it's only a short way down, but we'll need a rope."

Pog removed a cloth bag from his belt and reached in. He removed a flashlight and an impossibly long length of knotted rope from the sack. Azriel watched amazed and shook his head. The sack was far too small to house the items Pog withdrew from it.

"How did you do that?"

"Just a wee bit of Magick." He held it up for Azriel to examine. On first inspection it appeared to be merely an ordinary velvet bag but on the side, finely embroidered, it read in fancy script, *needful things*. Bemused, Azriel opened it and looked inside, peering into the empty sack.

"I don't get it. There's nothing in it."

"Of course there isn't. We have everything we need! Now laddie, if'n ye'd just tie the rope to this boulder here, we can make our way down."

Azriel secured the rope onto the sandstone and tugged on it a few times for good measure before dropping it down to the chasm below.

He shone the flashlight into the cavernous hole and could indeed see that the bottom didn't appear to be that far down. Bracing himself, Azriel lowered his body one knot at a time until his feet touched firm stone. He sighed with relief. He then shone the light upward toward Pog. The tiny gnome was surprisingly agile as he shimmied down the rope.

"There we are, laddie." He smiled candidly. "That wasn't so bad."

Azriel shone the flashlight up and down the narrow chamber to gather his bearings. It seemed as if they were in a tunnel of sorts. It wormed and twisted in a confusing maze of side chambers and dead ends, seemingly carved over time by the wind. He perked up his ears and faintly heard the sound of dripping water.

"Seems it's coming from that direction." Pog pointed at a particularly ominous-looking tunnel. Azriel stared into it and began to sweat. He didn't particularly like closed, dark places and shrank back with consternation.

"Nothin' to worry about, son. Ol' Pog's here with ye."

Azriel exhaled explosively and steeled himself as he followed Pog down the wind-swept passageway. They seemed to be walking down further into the oppressive stone. Azriel shone the flashlight onto the path to find firm footing. He suddenly held his hand back, forcing Pog to stop short.

"Look!" Azriel aimed the light a few feet ahead. "Footprints!"

Together, they crouched down and examined the telltale traces on the dusty surface. They indicated a creature—certainly not human— by the barefoot impressions left there. It had three toes on each foot, and whatever it was, it appeared to have left in a hurry.

They followed the trail for some time. It twisted through oddly meandering tunnels that at times doubled back and twisted in strange angles. At one point the tunnels ceased to be natural and took on the appearance of being purposely carved from the sandstone. They came to a dead end where the footprints they had been following simply ceased. Azriel tested the wall, pushing against it, expecting it to be an illusion. It held quite firmly. He scanned the wall, shining the light up to the domed ceiling, up and around to the other end of the chamber. He noticed the footprint began again on the opposite side and disappeared into the tunnel in which they had just emerged.

"Clever." Pog commented.

They continued following the trail, this time looking for signs of deception, but the prints seemed to descend ever downward. Azriel wrapped his cloak tighter around his body as the temperature decreased. It was a sure indication that they were deep into the earth. The path they followed suddenly shifted to the left into a small crack in the wall. Pog easily slipped through, but Azriel had to squeeze himself into the passage, nearly abrading his shoulders. He grunted as he crouched shimmying through, crawling on his elbows.

It opened to a massive chamber. Surprisingly, in contrast to the cold tunnels, the cavern was warm and moist. Azriel was astounded to find an enormous lake of water. The sound of dripping liquid, almost musical and bell-like, echoed off the walls causing the sensation of being lulled into a somnolent state. Azriel swooned with a sudden desire to sleep. He stretched and yawned. Pog, however, knew of such enchantments. Subtle and powerful, the spell would soothe the victim to sleep, where unwary, they could be attacked and killed. Pog roughly grabbed the flashlight from Azriel's hand and shook him by the shoulders. "Cover yer ears, laddie."

Azriel stared uncomprehending at Pog. With little option, Pog slapped Azriel across the cheek. "Cover yer ears, son. Do it now!"

As if emerging from a dream, Azriel shook himself awake and promptly cupped his hands over his ears.

"What the hell was that?"

"A powerful enchantment, laddie."

The magickal resonance, now muffled and ineffective, Azriel heard, barely perceptible, the sound of sobbing from the far end of the chamber. Pog took the initiative and reached into his cloth bag. He withdrew a pair of earplugs. "Here, son, put these in yer ears."

Freeing up his hands, Azriel was now able to shine the flashlight in the direction of the sobbing. The creature emitted a strangled scream and covered its eyes.

"The light! The light! It hurts! Turn it off! Turn it off! Too long I have been underground." It bellowed.

"Release the enchantment." Pog ordered.

Still weeping, the creature waved its hand and the lulling sound from the chamber ceased.

"That's better." Pog said. He removed a small oil lamp from his cloth bag and lit the wick while Azriel removed his earplugs. The lamp cast a soft, comfortable reflection on the still water. "Norga, come closer. We won't hurt ye." Pog offered.

The creature crept cautiously toward them, stopping every so often, uncertain of their intentions. Azriel stared, astounded at the creature's appearance. It was small, with a shuffling gait. Its large feet were webbed between the toes, and its face was unlike anything Azriel had ever seen. With skin mottled olive and gray, it had large green luminous eyes and a gaping maw for a mouth. Terrified, it continued to sob as it came nearer.

"Don't hurt Norga," it wept.

"Yer a long way from home." Pog stated gently. "Where is Bloog?"

"He's gone—dead. It's just me now." It shook its head sadly.

"What is it?" Azriel whispered to Pog.

"*It* is a she." He said, staring at the cowering creature. "She's a Fenodoree—a magickal denizen of the swamp. I wondered why I haven't seen ye fer some time now, Norga."

"They took my home," she sniffed. "They killed Bloog, drained the swamp, and nearly killed my children." Norga began to bawl piteously.

"Who did?" Azriel asked gently.

"Men with big machines. They tore down my trees and covered my home so they could build a road."

Azriel stared with pity at Norga. "Where are your children now?"

"Here." She emitted a soft chirping sound that echoed over the water. The still underground lake began to seethe with activity and ripples disturbed the surface. One by one, tiny heads peeked up from the water. Azriel looked amazed as hundreds of the creatures peered up at him. They giggled and smiled at their mother as she slipped into the water caressing them. Their arms and legs were unformed. Only their heads were similar to Norga's. From the tails of most of them, tiny legs were beginning to bud from the sides.

"I had no choice but to bring them here. The world of men has become unsafe for one such as me. I had to protect them."

"But why here?" Pog asked. "Surely there are better places than this."

"Look at me, my friend. I am dying. Soon they will be alone with no one to care for them. There is no place anymore for the Fenodoree."

As Pog and Norga spoke, Azriel stood and examined the cavern. He now understood why the water source feeding the oasis above ground had dried up. Norga had created a dam of boulders and stone blocking the flow of water. Its path diverted, it could never reach the men above ground who so desperately needed it. Azriel glanced back at Norga and the little fenlings surrounding her. She smiled and chirruped as they surrounded her playfully. Something occurred to Azriel as he took a handful of water and drank. It was perhaps the purest water Azriel had ever tasted. How was she supposed to feed her children?

He strode back to where Pog stood watching and mused a bit. "Norga," he inquired. "There's nothing in the water to feed your babies. How are you doing it?"

She sighed heavily. "I create the food." To demonstrate, Norga waved her webbed hands and wiggled her long fingers just barely above the water. Suddenly there appeared a swarm of tiny guppies and marshy vegetation. Norga's babies disappeared under the water and swirled into a feeding frenzy devouring every tiny fish and bits of algae. "When I'm gone, I'm afraid all my children will starve." She began to weep again.

Azriel's heart ached for the miserable creature. He sat down and pondered her dilemma. What to do?

"Norga," he inquired again. "You do know that taking all the water is killing the people who live above you. They're dying of thirst."

"And why should I care about the world of men?" She raged. "They took my home!"

"They didn't know better," Azriel countered.

"Yes they did." She cried miserably. "My mate, Bloog, confronted them—tried to speak with them, but instead they shot him. Thought he was a monster!"

"I'm sorry, Norga."

"Sorry, you say. But there's nothing you can do about it. I will die and so will my children! The Fenodoree will be no more."

Azriel glanced at Pog. He had an idea, but it would take some doing. "We need to talk." He whispered to the gnome. They walked some steps away from Norga and conferred.

"Pog, there's a place I know of—though I can't say I've ever been there. I studied about it in school. It just might work."

"What are ye talking about, laddie?"

"There's a really large swamp on the east coast of North America between Georgia and Florida. It's called the Okefenokee Swamp. Not a very hospitable environment for men, but perfect for Norga. It would be dangerous though."

"How so?" Pog asked.

"It has alligators."

"Hmm." The little man mused as he rubbed his beard thoughtfully.

"Anything's better than this." Azriel waved his hand toward the water.

"So how would ye get them there, laddie."

"Couldn't you do it?"

"Aye—but I won't."

"That's rather cold…"

"Ye must be the one to do it."

"But I don't know how!"

"Ye won't know unless you try." Pog stated flatly.

"As a matter of fact," Azriel thought of how he could possibly broach the subject delicately. "My mother has told me the stories of Aralia since as far back as I can remember. She told me that after the worlds were split, wizards lost the power to create portals. How is it that you can, and what makes you think that I have the power?"

"Yer forgetting something, son. Yer mother crossed over from Aralia to here."

"Yeah, and it almost killed her. You're also evading the issue," Azriel said hotly.

"What I can do is my business, laddie. As for you, yer Eltanin's heir. You, laddie, are the culmination of a long line of wizards. Don't you know that all the powers of your ancestry have waited for your birth? The prophecies speak of one with Eltanin's power—one who would be born to restore the worlds. Trust me, laddie. Ye have the power. There is one catch, however. Opening a portal leaves a signature—easy to trace for any adept wizard. I told ye about the clave. I'm now convinced that they are looking for ye, so you must be careful. Never, ever teleport from your home or anywhere ye can be found easily. Here won't matter."

"What about you?" Azriel was suddenly concerned. "You opened a portal from your home."

"Aye, but I've learned to hide my movements quite well. Besides, we used the dream orb—undetectable. And just where do you think I live?" Pog crossed his arms.

"Somewhere underground near the bridge." Azriel stated matter of fact.

"You might think that." Pog laughed. "But you'd be wrong."

"Then where…"

"Not fer ye to know right now, laddie. Now, it's time to begin."

"Wait a minute. How did Norga get here?"

"Conventional means."

"Huh?"

"She swam," he said plainly, annoyed by Azriel's propensity to be quite dense sometimes. By this time Norga had paddled back and stood by them listening to their conversation.

"Could you…" she stammered, not believing her ears. "Could you possibly take me—my children—somewhere else?"

"I've never done it before." Azriel apologized.

"But you could try." Norga brightened and her eyes brimmed with joy. "No one has ever done such a thing for Norga. You are good to Norga—so gallant!"

Azriel glanced at Pog pathetically. "Okay, so what do I do?"

Pog smiled and cleared his throat. "Now laddie, what ye need to do is fix yer mind on where ye are." He watched as Azriel concentrated. "Good! Good! Very good. Now think of where ye wish to be. Now, ye've never been there before, but ye do know the general direction."

Azriel fixed his thoughts on the topographical map he had seen in his textbook.

"Are ye seeing it, laddie."

"Got it."

"Now think of space and time. Think of how long it would take ye to get there and reduce that to a span of a second. Then you must shrink the space between in yer brain until it doesn't exist."

Reducing the time between wasn't as difficult as Azriel had imagined, but reducing the space between was more challenging.

Pog detected Azriel's trouble and added, "Think of a balloon, laddie. You are on one side, and the swamp is on the other. Now if ye took yer fingers and pushed in from both sides, the space between would lessen until they touched, right?"

With that imagery, Azriel finally saw space for what it was— flexible. He stepped into the water with that imagery fixed in his mind. The air before him suddenly wavered and he had to shield himself from the light as it shifted and shimmered. Looming before him, it seemed as if the fabric of matter parted and a doorway opened. In awe he stared unbelieving through the portal. On the other side, if one would call it that, thick sedge grass and cattails rose from a boggy fen. Norga's eyes widened in wonder, and she chirruped to her children. Obediently, they gathered around her.

"Well done, laddie." Pog beamed with pride at Azriel's accomplishment. "Shall we go?"

Tentatively, not trusting his senses, Azriel stepped through the portal and immediately found himself up to his knees in thick viscous muck. He looked down as he continued sinking. "Great." He muttered in disgust. He was followed by Pog, who somehow managed to produce a small canoe as he passed through. Azriel glared at him.

"Don't give me that look, laddie. Ye need to think ahead."

Norga swam through the portal followed by hundreds of happy little fenlings. They giggled cheerfully as they leapt out of the water snagging the gnats and dragonflies that hovered above the fen. "Yummy!" they cheered.

They all gathered playfully around Azriel and rubbed their heads against his body. Seeking refuge, Azriel grabbed the side of the canoe ready to hoist himself in.

"Wait, laddie…"

Azriel pushed down, and as the canoe tipped over, Pog went sailing out of the watercraft and landed with a splat, face down in the boggy marsh.

He sputtered and swore. "Have, ye ever heard of inertia, son?" Azriel couldn't help but laugh at the old troll.

"Aye, I guess I deserved that one." Pog snapped his finger and they both magically appeared back in the canoe, albeit wet and muddied.

"Well, laddie, we had best be going."

Norga swam up to the canoe and leaned on the side.

"Must you go?" She asked sadly.

"Aye, Norga. Yer safe now, and there's still one more thing we need to be doin'."

"Wait a bit longer. I must give the boy a gift."

"That's really not necessary." Azriel countered.

"No, Azriel. I insist."

She turned and dove into the water with her children following close behind. She was gone for what seemed a long time and Azriel glanced nervously at the portal fretting that it would close. She rose from the bog clutching something under her arm. It was perhaps the largest freshwater mussel Azriel had ever seen. Norga rinsed it in the water and held it out to Azriel. He stared quizzically at it when Norga wiggled her fingers with a flourish. The mollusk opened up slowly to reveal an enormous pearl. It wasn't round but a fist-sized concretion of iridescent nacre. He stared at it wide-eyed.

"For you, Azriel. I will never forget you." She chirped once and bowed her head before swimming off, disappearing into the swaying reeds.

Pog stared at the disappearing ripples of water. "Ye did a good thing, laddie. I think she will be safe now."

"Yeah, but she said she's going to die soon."

"Of course, as all creatures must. But now she can die free of worry, knowing her children will be safe."

Pog paddled the canoe through the portal and floated back into the underground cavern. The portal still remained open. "Now release yer thoughts—just wish it away." Pog instructed. In moments the portal dissolved, and they climbed out of the canoe. They rinsed off the mud encrusted on their clothes. "Now one more detail." Pog raised his hands and motioned with a gesture as though he were sweeping two curtains away from each other. The dam of pebble and stone was swept aside and water came gushing through. Pog and Azriel had to scramble to avoid the rising water and hurried back through the tunnels to where the knotted rope still draped from the opening above.

The sun blazed down on them as they emerged from the small opening. However, they weren't alone. Two camels sat, patiently chewing their cud in the shade of the rock. They were saddled and the jugs of water Pog had brought were neatly tied to the sides. Azriel didn't need to ask. Nothing Pog did surprised him anymore.

Pog held out his hands as he approached the camels and patted them gently. "The Bedouins call these beasts the ships of the desert. A good camel is worth its weight in gold."

Azriel scrunched up his face dubiously. "I've never ridden one of these things before," he stated flatly.

"Nothing to it. Just get on the saddle." Pog demonstrated by deftly mounting the beast. The saddle was a rather simple device. Carved of dark wood, it straddled the camel's hump firmly. A soft pillow sat on top with bangles draping down the side. Pog balanced himself on the finely brocaded pillow and tapped the camel lightly on the rump with a riding crop. Obediently, the beast rose from its back legs as it remained kneeling on its front legs. Pog lurched forward slightly and the camel rose up the rest of the way. "See, Laddie! Nothing to it."

Azriel gave a rather poor approximation of Pog's actions. As the gentle beast rose, he nearly fell off the saddle but managed to right himself.

They headed north toward the dying oasis. When they were not far from their destination, Azriel could make out, through the rippling heat waves, scattered dun-colored mud brick hovels where he assumed the locals lived. Erected between them were tents laid out in a haphazard fashion. Pog halted his beast and produced a small, bejeweled bottle from his pocket.

"Here, laddie. Take a small sip of this."

Azriel removed the stopper and sniffed before thrusting the bottle away from his nose. "I don't think so. It smells disgusting."

"It doesn't taste as bad as it smells. Just do it, laddie." Pog insisted.

"Why?"

"Do ye have to be so difficult?" the old gnome growled. "Ye just need to trust me."

Azriel nearly gagged on the fluid. It took every ounce of his will to swallow. "Trust you?" he shot back. "It tastes like cat piss!"

"Aye," Pog took a sip and shuddered. "Probably some of that in it too. But you'll see why in a minute. I brewed that potion meself, so don't ye be complainin'."

As they neared the settlement, an old man approached them. He leaned heavily onto a weathered staff and shading his deep-set eyes with his hand, peering up at them. His wrinkled face was deeply etched with hardship and the passage of time. Dressed desert-style, he was wrapped in a dusty white Bedouin robe, and his turban sat precariously on his head.

Pog whispered to Azriel. "You must greet him with respect. He is the chieftain of his tribe."

The old man addressed them, but not without a little suspicion. Two younger men behind him stood protectively, rifles in hand. He bowed slightly. "As salaamu Alaykum."

Without thinking, Azriel responded, "Wa alaykum as salaam." He nearly held his hand to his mouth in surprise. He understood now why he had to drink the nasty potion Pog had given him. Curiously, he understood the old man and could now speak his language.

The old man spoke frankly. "You should leave this place while you can. There is a curse upon this land. It is a place of death."

Pog answered gravely, "Why haven't ye led yer people elsewhere, friend."

"This is our ancestral home. We were born here and we shall die here. Water is life, and the well has run dry. Our camels refuse to go further and our children are dying. You must leave."

"But we are here to help," Azriel stated. From the rear, he heard the keening and ululations of a few women in mourning. Azriel peered ahead, following the grief-stricken voices.

"Today, one of the grandmothers has gone to meet Allah." The chieftain explained sadly.

Pog ordered the camels to kneel and deftly alighted from the saddle. Azriel followed suit and began to untie the jugs of water from the sides. He offered the jugs to the chieftain. His eyes widened at such a generous gift.

"May the blessings of Allah be upon you both! You must be angels from heaven."

"No sir, we are just ordinary men. We came here to help," Pog insisted.

"I am Habib." The old man placed his hand on his heart and bowed with dignity.

"I am Pog, and this young man is—er—Prince of the Ferrishyn. But I adjure you, sir. Our names must be held in confidence."

"It will be done as you have asked," Habib assured them. He signaled to the men behind him, and they were immediately by his side. "Give water to the children first, and then to the women." He stared thoughtfully at Azriel. "What you have done, Prince Ferrishyn was wise and foolish, for now you are without water.

Surely my people will stave off death for a while longer, but alas, death is inevitable. It is the will of Allah."

"Please, sir," Azriel asked politely. "Show me where the water had flowed."

The old man led them to the center of the oasis. Above them, date palms were showing signs of drought. The fronds, once a vibrant green, had withered and were showing every indication of impending death. Beyond, a few herdsmen were tending to livestock. The sheep and goats were lethargic and many lay panting on the sand. Any grass that remained had withered or had been nibbled down to the roots. The water source was a pond that had dried up. Only cracked mud, baking in the sun, remained as an indication that water had ever been there. Azriel knelt and examined the mud. Oddly, a small fish had dried up and appeared to be fossilized in the caked mud, just like in his dream. He was overcome with a compulsion to pry out the piece with the fish embedded and place it in his pocket. "Sir," Azriel glanced up at him, "the water will return. Of this I am sure."

The old chieftain laughed dryly. "Son, we have been digging here for days. Are you a prophet of Allah, or do you mock me?" he said dangerously.

"I would never do such a thing, sir." Azriel answered carefully. "All I ask is that you trust us."

Habib sighed. "It must be a test from Allah. If it is his will, then let the water return." He bowed graciously. Azriel removed the dowsing rod from his pack and pointed it toward the ground. Pog followed alongside.

"Ye handled that well, laddie." He whispered conspiratorially. "You'll make a good diplomat someday."

Azriel continued to point the dowsing rod at the ground, starting at the dried-up lake. It bobbed once, but thereafter remained motionless. He walked aimlessly to the far end of the oasis and felt another tug pointing to a deep depression in the ground. Walking down the incline, the signal became stronger. As he reached the bottom, the stick began to bob furiously. Azriel called out joyously, "Habib, we need shovels over here!"

The old chieftain cocked a hoary old eyebrow dubiously but ordered two of his strongest men to dig where Azriel pointed.

They trotted over each with a shovel in hand, and began to dig in the caked-up earth. At first they shoveled half-heartedly, not expecting much. They had been randomly digging throughout the day and had resigned themselves to the fact that Allah had abandoned them, but soon signs of moisture began to show through the soil. Encouraged, the two young men began to dig furiously, putting their backs into it and a trickle of water burst through the ground. A few more shovels full and the water began to bubble up like a fountain. As it broke through the parched earth, it suddenly gushed forth. The depression began to fill up with precious and pure water. Many of the nomads watching dropped to their knees and bowed their heads to the ground praising their God for hearing their prayers. As the water overflowed, it began to form a stream that swiftly filled the other basin. Cheers of rejoicing filled the desert and soon Azriel and Pog were roughly grabbed and raised up on the shoulders of the happy crowd. Many rushed to the water and began to drink their fill.

That night, amid fires blazing beneath a glorious crescent moon, a feast of thanksgiving was prepared by the Bedouin tribe in Azriel's honor. He and Pog sat in the chieftain's tent, being served a sumptuous meal. A goat had been slaughtered and roasted on a spit. Most of the time, eligible young women of the tribe vied for Azriel's attention, feeding him platters of dates and roasted goat atop generous portions of couscous. Habib smiled graciously and scolded his young daughter for her less-than-demure behavior.

"Halimah, you are smothering our honored guests." Habib chided.

She was young and pretty, flashing her dark eyes seductively at Azriel. Being the chieftain's eldest daughter gave her certain authority over her four siblings—other young maidens trying to win Azriel's affections. She smiled winningly at Azriel as she offered yet another cup of fruit juice.

"My Prince, would you care for more food?" Her dimpled cheeks shone in the firelight.

"Oh no, Halimah. I couldn't eat another bite." He smiled back at her. The other girls in the tent giggled and began whispering conspiratorially to each other. Azriel blushed and was beginning to feel uncomfortable with such lavish attention.

Habib clapped his hands twice. "My daughters, you have all behaved shamelessly tonight! You will give an old man heart failure!" His scolding was a bit more severe than he truly meant, and his daughters laughed impishly before showering Habib playfully with kisses. He chuckled heartily. "Now off with you all!"

"Yes, Ada!" they laughed as they exited the tent.

Habib still chuckled as one by one they left. Love for his children shone in his eyes. He said half-seriously, "Allah must be punishing me. What does an old man do with five daughters? They will wither my pancreas!"

While he spoke, one of the tribal elders entered the tent with an elaborate hookah. He placed hot coals on the bowl and began drawing on the mouthpiece until he was able to emit billows of fragrant smoke. He sat beside Habib and handed him the hose. Habib drew deeply on the mouthpiece and inhaled before releasing a cloud of smoke. He then handed the hose to Pog, who also partook of the communal pipe, before passing it to Azriel. He stared at it doubtfully. "My mother would object to me smoking," Azriel whispered to Pog.

"Laddie, it would be an insult if you refuse even one puff. The elders are taking you into their counsel. It's an honor."

Azriel shrugged and drew on the mouthpiece as he had seen Pog do. He inhaled the shisha into his lungs and immediately coughed, gagging on the thick smoke. Swooning, he nearly turned green. The elders present with Habib broke out in unbridled laughter, having a great time at the boy's expense. Azriel smiled sheepishly and handed the hose back to Habib. The old man smoked again and finally asked Azriel a question.

"So, Prince of the Ferrishyn, where is your kingdom?"

Azriel thought for a moment searching for a fitting answer. "It's a long way from here, sir."

Habib stared at him thoughtfully. "And do you have a name?"

Azriel leaned over, conferring with Pog.

"Tell him, Laddie."

"It's Azriel, sir."

The Bedouin chieftain raised an eyebrow and nodded. "It is good you have kept your name secret until now. For my people, Azriel is the Angel of Death—but what is in a name, yes? You have brought us life and for that, we will be forever grateful." He handed the hookah hose to the elder by his side. "I think there is much more to you than you are revealing. Perhaps you are Djinn."

"A Djinn?" Azriel asked.

"Djinns are not of this earth. It is said they come from a parallel world, removed from the world of men. They are powerful, and can do what no man can do. You..." he pointed with the pipe nozzle, "You have used your magic stick to find water. You are a Djinn sent by Allah."

Azriel glanced sideways at Pog, looking for direction. In a sense, the perceptions of the old chieftain weren't far from the mark. Pog answered gravely. "What ye say is true, Habib, and I," —he bowed his head— "I am his teacher. But Azriel had a vision of yer people's suffering. He insisted we help ye, so we came from afar to bring water."

Habib nodded with understanding, then whispered to one of the elders. He left the tent and returned shortly after. An ancient woman held on to his arm, and she nodded with respect to Habib and then to Azriel before taking a seat on a soft cushion. Habib introduced her. "It is my honor to have you meet Jezeera. She is a holy woman of my tribe. She had foretold of your coming, but I didn't believe her." The chieftain shrugged. "May Allah forgive my lack of faith."

Jezeera stood before Azriel. Her face appeared eternal, as though carved out of the native rock. The irises of her eyes were glazed over with a white film, yet she seemed to be staring, not at Azriel, but through him. That's when he realized she was blind. It was altogether unsettling to feel as though she were examining him, testing his spirit. She spoke in a wispy voice as though far away—like from a dream.

"There is a legend among my people. It is said that before time existed, a powerful Djinn by the name of At-Tinnan sought to purge his realm from a vast evil. In the heat of this terrible battle, other evil Djinns raised Azi Dahaka from the pit of Jahannam."

Azriel interrupted apologetically. "Jezeera, who is Azi Dahaka?"

"He is the Dragon of Death, who dwells in the deepest pit of Hell," she answered, her voice ominous. Azriel shuddered.

"For a night and a day, At-Tinnan did battle with Azi Dahaka, but death could not be defeated, for no mortal—not even a Djinn—can vanquish death. How does one kill a god? At-Tinnan was the most powerful Djinn ever to have lived, but try as he might, all he could do was wound death. In so doing, havoc was wreaked upon the earth, and the world was utterly destroyed. All At-Tinnan could do was banish Azi Dahaka back to Jahannam from where he came. It is said that At-Tinnan dealt a wound to Azi Dahaka that never healed. To this day, the Dragon of Death rages in anger and grief over his maiming. For a piece of him—a scale that covered the dragon's heart—was lost, never to be returned to him."

From under her robe, Jezeera removed a flattened chest and held it out to Azriel. He took it in hand, and stared at it nervously.

"Open it!" Jezeera ordered sharply. Azriel raised the ornate lid and examined the contents. A black scale, the size of a saucer, rested within. He touched it thoughtfully and pulled his hand back from the enormous power radiating from its black surface. It felt like metal, and it was incredibly cold to the touch.

"It is said that anyone possessing this artifact will be saved from death, Prince Azriel." Jezeera spoke emphatically. "I am a seer—a mystic. I can see into the hearts of men and read their destiny. But yours, dear prince, is closed to me. Yet I sense great purpose. The scale of the dragon will protect you in a time of dire need."

"It's too great a thing for me, Grandmother," Azriel spoke quietly. His head swam with the implications and suddenly his heart quaked with fear.

Jezeera smiled knowingly. "I am nearing the end of my days, young prince. I did not know until today to whom I would bequeath this talisman of power. But your coming was a sign. You have given my people life. And so, it is fitting that you be protected from death when you face him. Now I must go. I require sleep." She rose with a grunt and was tenderly supported by one of the young men.

"Jezeera—wait." Panic rose in Azriel's throat. "Is there something I must do? Your words fill me with dread. What of my destiny?"

She chuckled lightly. "Can one ever truly know the future? There are always many possibilities—many futures. It's the one you choose that matters. In the end, you will know what to do." She grasped his hand and gave him a broad toothless smile. Her grip was surprisingly strong. "Have courage, Azriel." She bowed and with that, she exited the chieftain's tent.

Azriel and Pog sat in silence while Habib continued to smoke. "Jezeera always tells the truth, Prince of the Ferrishyn," the chieftain said. "Do not shy away from your future, but embrace it. It is Allah's will."

There didn't seem to be much more to say. A tent had been set up for Azriel's use, and Habib graciously bid them good night.

As they settled in for a well-earned rest, little was exchanged between Azriel and Pog. Azriel finally spoke as he nestled down into the comfortable blanket. "You're unusually quiet, Pog."

"Aye. Much to think about, laddie. This was completely unexpected."

Sleep evaded Azriel, and reclining, he propped his head on his hand watching Pog. He finally voiced his unspoken thoughts.

"Will I have to face the dark dragon?"

"Aye. But then again, that will be yer choice."

"Is that all you can say?"

"Too soon you have been given this knowledge, Azriel. It is unfortunate. Now ye live with fear."

"Any sane man would be afraid," Azriel sounded angrier than he intended.

"True, laddie. We are all afraid at some time or another. Ye will learn to conquer yer fear."

"How?"

"Sometimes one's purpose can be greater than one's fear."

"I didn't ask for any of this, Pog."

"Ye cannot choose yer destiny. But know this: there is no problem I've ever seen that didn't, in time, present itself with a solution."

"Will I succeed?"

"I don't know. It hasn't been written." Pog sighed. "Do ye want to succeed?"

"Well of course I do," Azriel spoke through a clenched jaw.

"Then, laddie, that's a good start. Now get some sleep."

Azriel awoke the following morning to the sound of activity. He stretched and yawned, glancing up at Pog. The old gnome was already dressed and stood waiting.

"You could have awakened me," Azriel said lightly.

"Aye, but ye needed the sleep."

Azriel dressed quickly and walked out of the tent. Placed before the opening, bowls of food and other gifts were carefully lined up by the flap as offerings. A few feet beyond, Halimah sat cross-legged on a small woven carpet, waiting patiently. Elaborately dressed in native Bedouin garb, she wore gold bangles and a beautiful, beaded headdress that hung delicately just above her dark eyes. She quickly poured a cup of rich coffee from a finely crafted urn and handed it to Azriel like an offering to a god.

"Good morning, Prince Azriel," she smiled graciously. "I have prepared you a good breakfast." She pointed to the bowl of dates and fruit. Next to it sat a platter of meat and goat cheese. She served up a portion, and waited for Azriel to partake before serving herself.

"Shukran, Halimah." Azriel bowed his thanks and began to eat. The coffee was quite strong, and the food was surprisingly fresh. As he ate, Azriel watched the goings-on in the community. Miraculously, the oasis was well on its way to recovery. Already, patches of green were beginning to sprout from the ground and the trees looked much healthier than they did the previous day.

"Father said to take care of you as our honored guest." She flashed a winsome grin. "If you ask my hand in marriage, my father will not refuse."

Azriel nearly choked on his food. "Aren't you a bit young?" he gasped.

"I am almost fourteen—already an old lady. Soon I will be too old, and no one will want me." She pouted.

Azriel quickly looked around but Pog had already disappeared milling about the Chieftain's tent.

"Halimah, you're incredibly beautiful, but marriage isn't in my future any time soon."

"I would be a good wife," she offered.

"I'm sure you would, but I'm not ready. I'm not much older than you, and I'm not even done with school."

"Oh." she looked down, disappointed. "That's okay," she shrugged. "I just thought it would be nice." She tried one more time. "You'd be wealthy. My father has put aside a great dowry."

Azriel looked down at his food without answering.

"I know. There's someone else you love, perhaps." she said with a hint of jealously.

Azriel hadn't given that idea much thought, but he immediately thought of Camille—and wondered why she came to mind. He pushed that thought away and answered, "No, not really."

Her eyes narrowed. "There *is* someone else. I know it, even if you don't, Prince Azriel." She said lightly, then laughed as he blushed.

They finished eating and together they sought out Habib who sat quietly conferring with Pog. Azriel already had his pack on his shoulders and stared at Pog impatiently. The old gnome looked up at Azriel and grinned. Azriel kicked a little sand at Pog's feet and whispered, "You could have warned me about her."

"And miss all the fun, laddie? I wouldn't think of it."

Azriel shot him a sour look.

"Well, we'd best be going. Habib has promised to look after our camels."

Without thinking, Azriel removed the dowsing rod from his pack and gave it to Halimah."

"For you." He smiled.

She gasped. "Your magic stick!"

"May you never be without water again." Azriel stated. He quickly showed her how to use the dowsing rod. "It takes a bit of practice, but it's really not that difficult." He smiled.

"You have given my people a great gift, Prince Azriel. I will never forget you."

"Nor I, Princess Halimah."

"Princess?" she answered quizzically.

"You are the chieftain's daughter, are you not?"

"Of course."

"Well in my world, that makes you a princess."

She beamed a smile at Azriel. "One thing before you leave," she said. "Jezeera was right, but she didn't tell you everything."

Azriel bristled.

"When the time comes that you face Azi Dahaka, you must use the dragon's scale to your advantage. Wear it over your heart, and you will not fail. You will not be harmed."

"How do you know this?"

"I have seen it."

"Really?" he asked dubiously.

Halimah looked down. "Jezeera isn't the only seeress of the tribe. As her powers fade, mine grow stronger."

"Okay—indulge me," He said somewhat skeptically.

"You don't believe me," she countered with aplomb. "Fine then. Give me your hand."

She sandwiched it between her own delicate hands and closed her eyes. "Interesting. You have something in your pocket." She smiled. "A fish!" she grinned, surprised. "It's encased in mud, and though it appears to be dead it is quite alive."

"That doesn't seem to be very likely. It's dried up and hard as a rock—it's a fossil."

She laughed lightly again. "No, Azriel—it is merely a fish out of water, but it is not for you. There is someone you know who needs it. She's very important to you—and quite sad in a way. Give it to her. It's a message."

Azriel was impressed. Halimah opened her eyes; they gleamed mischievously. "Do you believe me now?"

He looked down and shuffled his feet, kicking up a little sand. "Yes, Halimah, I believe you, and I'll do what you say." He looked up and smiled at her. "I hope we will meet again."

She looked away—thinking, searching, listening to some otherworldly suggestion and then looked back at Azriel. "We will," she smiled wryly. "You can count on it."

Azriel smiled and commented. "You're different than I would have expected from a princess of the desert. You seem... well... modern."

She giggled. "Don't be fooled by appearances, Azriel. I've been educated in England. I have other mentors as well. She glanced over at her father, who spoke in low whispers with Pog. Out of hearing range from Halimah and Azriel, Habib and Pog were deeply entrenched in a private matter that needed discussing. Habib bade Pog and Azriel a formal goodbye, with blessings for good health and long life, before bowing majestically. Azriel smiled at Halimah and said, "I guess I need to gather my things."

He, along with Pog, strode to the tent and packed the stray items that were still there. In particular, Azriel made sure he had the dragon scale securely packed in his bag. He was about to reemerge from the tent when Pog stopped him.

"No, laddie. This is where we depart. Take out the dream orb." Azriel obediently removed it from his backpack.

"Now ye remember how to use it, right?"

"Uh-huh." Azriel answered. He closed his eyes and pictured where he intended to go. When he opened them, the image of Amaryllis' home was clearly implanted in the Orb. And, like before, Azriel and Pog touched the orb and projected themselves within the image. With a quick manipulation of space-time, Azriel and Pog disappeared.

Halimah waited by the tent and called in. She held a small basket filled with dates and other traveling foods, having prepared it for their departure.

"Azriel?" Halimah beckoned from the closed flap. Hearing no response, she called again.

"Azriel!" Not hearing any answer, she peeked into the tent and gasped. "Father, they're gone!"

Habib peered inside and smiled with wonder. "See, child. I was right. They are Djinns."

Azriel suddenly appeared in Amaryllis' living room. Felisa was curled up by the fire, but his sudden appearance made her fur bristle and she hissed menacingly. She leapt behind the couch, and emerged fully dressed in her human form.

"You scared me half to death, Azriel." She seethed. "I think I've just lost one of my lives!"

"Sorry," he shrugged.

Everyone seemed to have emerged from their bedrooms at once. Amaryllis and Abelene were both wearing warm robes, and Nicodemus yawned and stretched wearing a nightshirt and a stocking cap. He looked ridiculous, and Azriel couldn't help but laugh. It hadn't occurred to him that it would be the middle of the night on the Isle while it was still morning where he just was.

Abelene looked at the kitchen clock. "Well, it's about time you got here. I was worried sick! You've been gone for nearly a week!" She scolded frantically. "Where have you been?"

"Um, Mom, aren't you forgetting something?"

"Like what?"

"I'd like you to meet Pog." He held his hand out in introduction, but Abelene merely crossed her arms and glared at him. Azriel looked down at his side, but Pog was nowhere to be seen.

"Pog?" Azriel called. "Pog!" he looked with quick jerking motions around the room. "Damn!" he muttered. It was Uncle Nick's turn to laugh. "It's just like him to disappear when things get awkward," he chortled.

Azriel spent the next hour over tea, explaining all that he had seen and done. His explanation centered on three objects. The dream orb, the pearl given as a gift by Norga, and the scale from the Dark Dragon of Death. When he opened the wooden cask holding the artifact, Nicodemus stared at it intently. He tapped his forefinger on his bearded cheek as he considered the powerful object. His brow furrowed in consternation, as if trying to recall something important. "Hmm, he never told me about that," he muttered to himself.

"Uncle Nick, what's wrong?" Azriel inquired.

"Oh, nothing." He dismissed his musings. "I never knew about the injury to the Dark Dragon. It's not in any of the writings, and I wonder why it was never mentioned. It could be important. Now let's see this pearl of yours."

Azriel removed it from the pack and placed it on the table. Everyone gaped at the magnificent gem. Felisa's eyes widened; she gaped in wonder. "It's so big!" she marveled. Abelene nodded, very pleased.

"I didn't even have to look for it. Norga just gave it to me. Heck, it's not like I did anything so fantastic to deserve it."

"Not in your eyes, Azriel." Amaryllis corrected him. "But for Norga, you ensured the survival of her children."

"I wasn't looking at it that way. I just felt sorry for her."

"Remember what I said about compassion, Azriel? That is the true measure of a man. Helping those people in the desert—and saving Norga—was more important to you than the task we set up for you. You took the right path and learned the bigger lesson."

Azriel nodded. "Oh, there's something else." He removed the Orb from his pocket and placed it on the table.

Quickly Nicodemus looked at the Orb and then back at Azriel. He stuck his hand surreptitiously in his pocket and furrowed his brow. "Where did you get that?" he asked suspiciously.

"Pog gave it to me," he said tersely in his own defense and then grinned at Abelene. "Mom, you'll never have to fly again."

Later that day, they gathered around the altar in Lady Rosaluna's secret room behind the curtain in her shop. All were dressed ceremoniously, and as before, Mr. Parkins and Billy were present. Azriel stood in the center and looked around, disappointed that Pog was missing. He found that rather curious considering that he really wanted to introduce Abelene to his mentor.

They stood waiting. Azriel shuffled his feet nervously, wondering what the delay was all about, when a young woman rushed in through the curtain. She was hooded and huffed, out of breath.

"You're late." Lady Rosaluna didn't hide her impatience. The woman slipped her cowl down over her shoulders and smiled apologetically.

"Sorry!" Muriel grimaced. "Me father is an impossible man, don't ye know! He wouldn't let me leave the kitchen until all the dishes were clean!"

"You!" Azriel blurted in amazement.

"Aye, Azriel. It's me. Perhaps ye might have noticed *this* if ye weren't staring so intently at me *bosom* in the restaurant!" She held up a golden ankh from a chain around her neck and let it drop.

Azriel's face reddened with embarrassment as Muriel giggled, but Abelene stared at him with disapproval. Nicodemus coughed as he suppressed a laugh while Azriel sheepishly avoided his mother's eyes.

"Shall we get down to business?" Rosaluna chided the group.

They gathered in a circle around the altar. On it rested the tools of magick Azriel now carried with him. His athame—the ritual blade—glowed slightly in the candlelight; beside it the chalice, wand, and pentacle. Rosaluna nodded and faced Azriel. She bowed ceremoniously. "Son of Luminance," she began. "What have you brought as an offering?"

"I have brought the pearl of great price."

"And how did you come by this?" She questioned.

"It came to me unbidden. It was a gift of gratitude from one I helped, Lady."

"Yet you left your task unfinished. You strayed from the path you were given," she said, her voice laced with displeasure.

Azriel was baffled by her response. It seemed unfair. He had accomplished everything he set out to do and then some. He thought for a while of an appropriate answer in his own defense, but realized he didn't need any.

"I did not stray, Lady. What better task is there than to help those in dire need? It's true I wasn't looking for the pearl, but it occurs to me that I wouldn't have found it by selfishly seeking it. It came to me when I got my mind off my problems and concentrated on someone else's. Norga's gift was a gift of love. What better result, then, could I ask for?" He looked down at his feet and added, "If I was wrong, then I don't regret the choices I made."

Rosaluna smiled. "Son of Luminance, what you say is the truth. You can be on a path and still lose your way. You have learned the ways of water. Water will choose the path of least resistance, yet it can patiently beat against an obstruction and in time wear down any obstacle. Water is the way of the heart! And your heart, Son of Light, beats strongly within you. You have passed the test. Now remove your Amulet and place it on the altar."

Azriel did as commanded.

She nodded with approval. The Earth dragon glowed with emerald power, but the other three remained inert.

"Now take up the pearl and place it in the chalice."

Azriel dropped it carefully into the cup, until it was fully submerged in the water.

"Touch the tip of your athame to the water."

Azriel lowered the blade carefully into the chalice. Immediately, the cup began to roil furiously as the water within seethed and billowed great clouds of steam. When the cloud dissipated, Azriel looked in the chalice, surprised to find a mussel shell wrought of gold.

"Take it, Azriel." Rosaluna commanded.

He was surprised by its weight. There appeared to be a clasp and hinge holding it together, and like before, he opened the tiny cask. Water gushed out from it, yet etched on the bottom was a name.

He looked around at all the faces present. They held their breath in expectancy, waiting.

With a voice of command, Azriel called out.

"Salacia!"

Within moments, Azriel's Amulet began to glow, and the represented creature to the right of the Earth dragon writhed and reared its head with a roar. It flapped its wings several times and settled back down transformed. It no longer appeared inert, but glowed with a silvery blue luminescence.

With the speaking of the name, a torrent of power flowed through him like the currents of a mighty rushing river. Unlocked were the secrets of the depths—hidden creatures and monsters never having seen the light of day. Opened to Azriel was the spirit of the oceans and rivers—the briny medium from which life first emerged; the sustaining flow of rivers and streams that maintained the life from which it gave birth; the tumultuous downpour of rain that nurtures the grains and fruits of the planet—not only the element of water but its commingling with the Earth elemental. In their union lay the stuff of life. This new awareness filled Azriel's heart and spirit to overflowing. The power so infused him that tears bled from his eyes as the wholeness of the universal mind filled him. The overwhelming sense of rightness bore witness to Azriel's new understanding. He now perceived the mechanisms that heaved forth life, not only on Earth and Aralia, but also throughout the many universes—life being the rule not the exception.

And then, as the brilliance of his knowledge filled the room with palpable light, it was suddenly assaulted by a dark presence that dimmed the light and roared its challenge. They all heard it, a malevolence brimming with enmity for all that bloomed and brought forth abundance. Withering decay was on its breath, the antithesis of growth and existence.

In a voice that was surprisingly mellow and compelling, it spoke directly to Azriel.

"I know you, Azriel. I have known you from the beginning. We are destined to meet."

"Who are you?" Azriel shouted.

"I am your opposite. We are equals."

"What do you want?"

"I want what you want. Release me! Release me from my eons-long prison." His voice hissed, pleading with a sighing sound.

"Never!" Azriel replied firmly.

"You will release my brothers and sisters—this I have seen. But you will need me as well."

"You lie!" he shot back. "The elementals bring life. You will bring death. I will defeat you!"

"The voice chuckled with mirth. "You cannot defeat death; you must know that, Azriel."

"I will find a way and restore the worlds."

"Hmm." the dark dragon responded thoughtfully. "We both have the same goal, Azriel. Greetings, brother, and farewell until we meet again. And we *shall* meet again." The voice said with certainty and then faded. Light returned to the room.

"By Shenach!" Abelene's voice quavered with fear. "What have we unleashed?" Her eyes went wide with worry for her son.

Nicodemus found a chair and slumped down as though the air had been bludgeoned from his lungs. He held his hand over his mouth and stroked his short beard as he scowled, concentrating on this most recent event.

"Nicodemus?" Abelene voice went shrill in her panic.

"Rest easy, Abelene," Nicodemus said in a comforting tone. "Azriel is in no immediate danger."

"How do you know that?" Felisa asked, not quite convinced.

"Something the Dark Dragon said."

"Yeah, and what's that?" Azriel inquired impatiently.

"He said to release him from his eons-long prison. That means he's been kept bound for these tens of thousands of years."

"Who possibly can imprison the dragon of death?" Abelene asked incredulously. "It would take someone with incredible power to do that."

"Yes, it would, dear Abelene," he mused more to himself.

"Well?" she insisted.

"Eltanin was the most powerful wizard that has ever lived, but don't forget that he was nearly defeated when he rendered the worlds asunder. He was left broken and diminished. This can only mean one thing. It is as I have always suspected. The Clave has the dragon imprisoned and is using his power to their own ends."

A chill went down Azriel's spine.

"Not to worry, boy." Nicodemus said affably. "You are in far less danger than the Clave. Should they lose control over the Dark One, they will surely be destroyed. His vengeance will be great!"

"But that doesn't make any sense," Azriel held out his hand in consternation. "If as you say, the Dark Dragon is being held captive, why do people still die every day?"

"Indeed, Azriel. Like the dragon elementals that give life, the dragon of death was created at nearly the same time. Inexorable and unbreakable laws were set up from the beginning. The laws governing death are just as unalterable as the laws governing life! The dragon did not lie, Azriel. One cannot defeat death. You are bound by the same laws that bind the Dark Dragon."

"Then it's hopeless." Azriel's shoulders slumped.

"Nothing is hopeless," Nicodemus said with certainty. "One problem has nothing to do with the other."

"Then I must face the Dark Dragon? To what end?"

"In due time, yes you will, Azriel, but to what end—that, even I do not know."

Abelene strode up to her son and embraced him. "Oh Azriel!" she wept. He could feel her body quivering with fear. Her heart was pounding in her chest. "What a terrible mess I've gotten you into." She sniffed.

"Mom, it's not your fault."

He gently extracted himself from her embrace, looking around the room hiding his embarrassment. "It's as you've always said. I was destined to be born at this time. There's nothing I can do but continue to learn what I must so I'll be prepared—when the time comes."

Nicodemus rested his hand on Azriel's shoulder. "You're a very brave young man; braver than I've given you credit for."

Azriel gave him a wan smile and then approached Rosemary.

"Um, Lady Rosaluna, may I speak with you privately?"

She looked at him quizzically and shrugged. She led him outside the curtain into the small alcove. She lit a candle and they both sat at the small table.

"I have something for you. I think it's important."

"Oh?" she said, her curiosity roused.

Azriel removed the fossil from his pocket and placed it carefully on the table before her. "I told you about Halimah," he said candidly. "She said that the fish in that piece of rock is not dead and that a message is there for you."

Rosemary picked up the piece and examined it, speculating on its meaning. She tested its weight in her hand and knitted her brow.

"An odd gift, Azriel."

"I suppose," he shrugged. "When I found it, I really had no idea why I dug it out in the first place. It was sort of a compulsion."

"It seems pretty well dead to me. The poor creature's a goner!" Rosemary stated blandly.

"All I'm telling you is what she told me."

"Well then, let's see if she was telling the truth." Rosemary stood and walked out of the room. She returned moments later with a bowl of water. "If it is alive, it needs water." She carefully placed the rock in the water and watched as it sank to the bottom.

At first nothing happened and Azriel blushed for looking foolish. Perhaps Halimah had played a trick on him, a way of getting back at him for turning down her offer of marriage. But as they both watched intently, the rock suddenly twitched as mud began to dissolve and drop a layer of sediment in the bottom of the bowl. Miraculously the fish, now freed from the rock, released a bubble of air from its mouth, and began breathing. Like awakening from a long sleep, it seemed to shake itself awake and began swimming in circles around the perimeter of the bowl.

Rosemary gasped in wonder. Mr. Parkins emerged from the curtained room with the others and peeked into the bowl. "What've ye got there, daughter?"

"A fish!" she giggled. "From the desert."

"Not just any fish, lass. That's what's known as a lungfish. When a lake dries up, they can bury themselves in the mud for months, even years. When the water returns, they come right back to life. Remarkable creatures."

"Azriel says there's a message for me here, though I can't say what it all means."

"The only message I see is that the little beastie might do better in a proper tank with some food. He'll be all right until the mornin', though. It can breathe air and water," Mr. Parkins chuckled.

Rosemary smiled and looked up at Azriel. "See what you've done. Now I've one more thing I need attending to in the morning!"

Chapter 13

Returning home was far less complicated this time around than navigating security at the airport. It would be difficult to explain some of the objects Azriel now carried in his luggage. It was easy to picture Abelene's kitchen and imprint it in the dream orb. They had timed their departure from Amaryllis' home to arrive there in the morning.

"What a wonderful way to travel!" Abelene said, sighing gratefully. "It's good to be home." She immediately set about putting a pot on the stove for tea. "Nicodemus, would you be a dear and get the cups out of the cupboard?" Back in her element, Abelene enjoyed slipping back into her domestic routine. Azriel immediately set about building a fire in the hearth to offset the chill lingering in the house. Though it was late August, heavy clouds blanketed the sky and to Azriel's dismay, it smelled as though autumn rode faintly on the wind. He hoped that summer would hold out for at least a few more weeks. After ensuring the fire blazed properly, he excused himself and went upstairs to his bedroom. He was tired; certainly not through any lack of sleep, but from the lassitude that comes from too much worry and the frustration of questions without answers. Like one trying to contemplate the true nature of infinity, ultimately, one must accept that perpetuity exists and move on from there. It does little good to dwell on it. Nevertheless, Azriel needed answers.

He kept his treasures in a beautiful wooden chest he had handcrafted in his wood shop class. He removed it from under his bed and unlocked the clasp. Within it rested the gift from his mother—the finely crafted Ritual Athame and Boline. He also stored the pentacle, wand, and chalice gifted to him when Azriel was initiated into the Order of the Ankh. Now he would place the dream orb and the dragon's scale within the chest to keep them safe. Also tucked into the corner of the cask was the sizeable gold nugget he had found, along with the unusual crystal formation, kept inside a dark blue velvet bag from the same place. He frowned when he looked at the bag. He knew it would play a role in his next challenge to learn the name of the Air Elemental. Right now, he didn't want to think about it. He had much bigger concerns. He picked up the dragon scale and pondered its use. Exceedingly cold in his hand, it emanated enormous power. But it also seemed to resist his touch as though shrinking from Azriel's mortality. The mystic Jezeera said that one day, Azriel would have to face the Dragon of Death. What did that mean? Did it suggest that Azriel would have to do the impossible by slaying death? Death cannot be defeated, so what purpose would there be in facing the Dark Dragon at all? Either way, the thought terrified Azriel like no other.

He closed the chest and placed it back under his bed. Another object rested beside the chest and Azriel carefully removed it. He slid his father's sword from its scabbard. He had not examined it for some time now, and noticed with a peculiar sense, that it didn't seem quite as massive as when he first beheld it. The finely crafted blade shone with the usual purple gleam and on each side of the razor-sharp edge, was etched arcane script that had no comparison to any written language on earth. The grip and guard, though utile, were also ornately carved in a fluid style. The design seemed to represent the four elements. Inset within the pommel, however, was a rather unique jewel. The stone, a deep black gem, though highly polished, seemed to reflect no light. Yet when Azriel gripped the handle, a faint spark of light ignited from within it. And it seemed to respond to Azriel's touch. Nevertheless, the weapon was a complete mystery. One thing Azriel did know without question was the story Abelene had told about his father acquiring it from a European market, and that it hailed from the Middle Ages, was a complete fabrication. What reason would his mother have to lie about it? In fact, why was it that she never spoke much about his father? He knew nothing of him except that he was King Berrill of Aralia and then he died in some unnamed war. That was another piece of conflicting information. Abelene was always quite vague about the circumstances of his father's death. She was even vague as to the true reasons for her translocation from Aralia to Earth. Abelene was completely tight-lipped on the subject.

Azriel needed answers. He hoped he would find them in the History of Aralia. He picked up the ancient tome and began thumbing through the pages until he found the place where he left off. Picking up the crystal translation stone, he placed it on the page and began to read. He found that he lately had to rely less and less on the stone. He had found in one section a phonetic pronunciation guide and rules of Aralian grammar. Certain words began to become familiar to him, and though challenging, he was beginning to understand the language and its written form. When he read aloud in Aralian, it seemed to roll off his tongue quite naturally.

He began to read another section of the book. The chapter had a heading that merely read "legends".

An Account on the Formation of Aralia

First there was a Thought, then an Idea. From out of nothing there became a something and it said, I Exist. For many eons, before the first stirrings of life and before man began to count time, the Consciousness dwelled on that one thought and basked in its Oneness. And for untold time it was content with the pure knowledge, but then the Consciousness conceived another thought and that Idea became Time. But once the Thought was put into reality it could not be recalled because it had been created. Soon the great Consciousness became discontent for there was nothing to fill the Time.

And thus the Great Mind conceived of another thought. It wanted to experience everything it could, and be everywhere at once, so the Consciousness became a mote that was infinitely large and inconceivably small since space had not yet been created. But then the Great Mind did conceive of space, but was discontent because it was empty and barren.

The Great Mind could not tolerate the emptiness so it filled the emptiness with Its presence by heaving Itself out into the space It created. In exultation the Consciousness became dust and the dust became stars and the stars became galaxies; all conceived from the thoughts of the Great Mind. But the Consciousness was not content, for the stars served no purpose but their own. To give them purpose, the planets formed around them and took form.

As the planets aged, the Great Mind at first was content, but then found again that the planets served no purpose, so within the oceans he planted another thought. He gave that thought natural, unbreakable laws and roused the elements with Its own Consciousness, so someday they could also say "I Exist."

From the merging of the elements there came a spark that was felt throughout the infinite and Life came to be.

The Great Mind then created guardians over the new life. He gave the Guardians consciousness and wrote within them the laws to govern the new life. One to each element, the first was for Solid Firmament, the Foundation for all others. To the next, the Liquid mutable element, and that which first brought forth Life. To the next, It gave dominion over the winds which carried the most basic elements that anchor the stars. And to the last, It gave the energy of life itself, the spark of fire that ignites Life. Thus the Elementals were born of Earth, Water, Air and Fire.

The Consciousness took delight in Its creations and emanated joy as the Waters nurtured the Creatures, and the Soil anchored Green things, and the Air fed the living things, and Fire provided the mighty spark of Life.

But soon the Consciousness conceived a flaw in Its creation for it continued to grow without constraint, and soon all life cried out in pain for they could not stop growing and would soon destroy that which nurtured them.

So the Consciousness summoned the Elementals and asked them to stop the life they were creating, but they answered the Great Mind by saying, "We cannot, for the Laws are written within us. We can only do what we were created to do."

Then the Great Mind conceived of a solution and brought forth from Its Consciousness, Darkness and Death and presented it to the Elementals. The Great Mind said to them "I give to you, then, your Brother, whose name is Death. It will devour your creations, but in so doing will ease the pain of your creations and bring balance. He is not your enemy but your Brother, for his decay and destruction will ensure that all life will continue."

As one, Earth, Water, Air and Fire embraced their brother and welcomed him as an equal.

Azriel pondered this legend written by the ancient ones. He had never thought of death as anything good, for with death came sadness and loss. In fact, everything he ever learned was a fusion of opposites. Good and evil, light and dark, life and death. It seemed that evil, darkness and death always had a negative connotation. But this story seemed to take on a different meaning. The fact was that life could not have existence without death, or unchecked, life would become a destructive force. Death was a necessity, and if this was true, then in and of itself, death wasn't evil, it just was, paradoxically, a fact of life.

Yet the thought of the dark dragon terrified Azriel. He could accept the concept of death, but that didn't mean he had to embrace it. For whatever purpose this eventual meeting would serve, Azriel needed more information. One thing he did know was that he would someday have to undo the damage that Eltanin and the Clave of wizards had wrought upon Aralia those many thousands of years ago. The Amulet he wore obviously had something to do with it. It was now half awakened, but he was still vague as to what the end result would be and it raised that infuriating, nagging question. What purpose will it serve?

He now knew two of the four names—Lagina-Tierra and Salacia—Earth and Water. He discovered, quite by accident, that when he invoked those secret names, the amulet would writhe with their power, and the two dragons would glow with their movement. Within his mind, he could hear two tones in resonant harmony, like the beginnings of a song, and then it would fade beyond his hearing. He could almost sense their presence watching him, but just beyond his perception he also knew the other presence watched as well—and waited.

His reverie was interrupted by a gentle tap at the door.

"May I come in?" Camille's voice was muffled behind his closed door.

"It's unlocked," Azriel answered.

She opened the door and peered in. "Are you all right?"

"Why do you ask?"

Camille crossed her arms. "Well, I figured you would at least call when you got home." She didn't bother to hide her displeasure.

"Sorry Camille." He glanced up, then back at the book. "I just have a lot of stuff to sort out. This time around got kind of weird." He answered, his head still planted in the book.

"Well?" Camille said impatiently.

"Well, what?" Azriel shot back.

"Look at me!" She demanded.

"Okay." He said heatedly and gave Camille his full attention. His face blanked momentarily with incomprehension. She was almost unrecognizable. Camille's usual outfit would have been a pair of jeans and tee shirt, her head covered with a ball cap, but this time she wore a tight-fitting lavender dress that accentuated her emerging shapeliness. Her blue-black hair was tied back, a cascade of curls and ribbons spilling down her back. Her deep blue eyes were enhanced with a touch of makeup. She looked very—un-Camille-like.

"Er—you look nice," Azriel responded, a bit flustered.

"Nice?" She simmered. "Is that all you can say?"

"You—look beautiful?" he ventured.

Steaming, she picked up the autographed baseball on his dresser and hurled it at him. Azriel ducked as it grazed his head and glanced off the wall.

"Hey! What did I do?" he said, glaring up at her defensively, obviously confused.

"What did you do?" she seethed. "You're gone the whole summer. Not one call—not even one letter. I was worried about you. Then I dress up for you—because I missed you and wanted to look pretty—and all you can say is *you look nice*." She mimicked his vagaries with a caustic edge.

He held out his hands helplessly and shrugged. "I said you looked beautiful. What more do you want?"

"Azriel Kingsley, you're absolutely impossible!" she spat through clenched teeth. She wheeled around, tears forming, and stormed out of his room, slamming the door.

"Camille, wait!"

She ran down the stairs and flew into Abelene's arms in a torrent of tears. "Your son's an idiot!" she blubbered miserably.

"Now, now," Abelene said, rubbing Camille's shoulders. "Tell me what happened."

Azriel came down the stairs from his bedroom cautiously. He could see Camille in the kitchen, waving her arms and complaining to his mother. He was about to enter, but was waylaid by Uncle Nick, who led him by the shoulder to the front porch. When they were out of earshot, Nick asked, hiding his amusement, "So—do you want to tell me what happened?"

"I don't know, Uncle Nick!" Azriel answered, thoroughly perplexed. "She comes into my room all gussied up and then goes psycho on me. Are all girls that crazy?"

Uncle Nick coughed to hide a laugh. "Mostly," he answered.

"I didn't do anything. I just said she looked nice. Then I told her she looked beautiful." He defended himself with agitation.

"Hmm," Nick mused. "Remember what I told you about women, Azriel?"

"Yeah, mostly."

Nicodemus sighed. "Azriel, women are complicated creatures. They can be at once subtle and at other times quite blatant about their needs. They will expect you to read their cues and respond accordingly."

"That's completely nuts," Azriel remarked flatly.

"Perhaps. But as men, we can easily get wrapped up in something—or distracted by our thoughts—and forget to pay attention to the signals a woman might give us."

"That makes no sense. My mother always tells me what's on her mind directly—and without me having to figure it out!"

"Really," Nick said with a note of sarcasm. "You may think you know how your mother thinks, but you're only seeing one side of her. She isn't as one-dimensional as you might think, Azriel. She's multifaceted and as complex as any other woman—perhaps even more so. You saw *that* in Cregnaesh, remember?"

"Okay, I'll give you that."

"Now as to your little friend, Camille. She's exploring her feminine side, and wanted you to notice—and make a fuss over her. Didn't you miss her in the least when you were gone this summer?"

"Well of course I did," Azriel said in his defense. "It's just that I'm not used to her being all—girly."

"Listen, Azriel—you're sixteen, nearly a man. Likewise, Camille is about the same age—almost a woman—and maybe a bit older than you upstairs." Nick poked at Azriel's head to illustrate his words. "I think she would like your friendship to evolve—if you know what I mean."

Azriel blushed nervously.

"Now if I were you, I'd tell her that she looks absolutely stunning and that you missed her terribly while you were away."

"Don't you think she knows that already?" Azriel snapped impatiently.

"It's not enough, Azriel. She needs to hear it from your lips."

Azriel scowled and looked down at the ground. He sat down on a chair and faced Nicodemus. The old man continued. "Son, how do you really feel about the young lady?"

"I think she's great. She's a lot of fun to be with. She's my best friend."

"I asked you how you feel, not what you think, Azriel."

He looked down and shuffled his feet.

"Let me put it to you differently, son. How would you feel if you never saw her again—or if you saw her kissing a young man other than you?"

Azriel's cheeks turned crimson with irrational anger.

"Ahh, see?" Nicodemus chortled. "There *is* something there. Perhaps, Azriel, you need to be more honest with yourself. Sometimes, son, you could lose what you desire because you fail to act when the opportunity arises. That's not just in matters of love, but in all your life decisions. You need to keep your eyes open, Azriel. Don't let your pride blind you."

While Nicodemus spoke with Azriel, Abelene took the opportunity to explain certain matters to Camille. She told every detail of Azriel's journey from the Isle of Man to the African Desert—his rescue of Norga and restoring of water to the tribe of Bedouins. She even told Camille of his encounter with the Seeress Jezeera, and later, when learning the Water Elemental's name, his enigmatic conversation with the Dark Dragon. Abelene discreetly left out certain details of Azriel's meeting with Halimah, the chieftain's daughter.

"So, you see, Camille, Azriel has much on his mind. You must forgive him." Abelene giggled softly. "Men are generally taller than women, wouldn't you say, Camille?"

"Yeah, I guess, but I'm not really following."

Abelene smiled conspiratorially. "I think the path between a man's brain and his heart takes a bit longer to travel—and is strewn with roadblocks. You must be patient with men. They're not as bright as most women and are easily distracted when it comes to matters of the heart. Now I think that Azriel cares for you very deeply—but hasn't admitted it to himself yet. And some men are afraid of attachment."

"But why?"

"Oh, the usual—independence, self-sufficiency, stupidity. It takes a long time for some men to admit they need a woman to guide them. Without us, Camille, men usually make a mess of things."

"Well, that's certainly true," Camille brooded.

"Just make sure you don't push too hard. You don't want to send Azriel packing, do you?"

"No, of course not!" She said fearfully.

"Trust me, dear. Azriel will come around. Just be patient, deal?"

"Deal." Camille smiled and nodded.

She looked up suddenly and blushed. Azriel had entered the kitchen. She hoped desperately that he hadn't heard any of her conversation with Abelene. He fidgeted with his hands nervously as if trying to decide what to do or say. She stared at Azriel, just as confused by his odd behavior.

Abelene cleared her throat. "Is there something you want to say, son?"

"No!" He blurted. Impulsively he grabbed Camille's hand and tugged her out of her seat. He yanked her toward the front door and she resisted at first—but not before turning her head back to glance impishly at Abelene. Camille beamed a smile of victory. Abelene held her hand to her mouth to prevent a giggle from escaping her lips.

Azriel tugged Camille along at a fast walk, well past the confines of the house and toward the woods.

"Azriel, where are we going?" she demanded. He didn't answer, but continued tugging her along with purpose, not letting go of her hand.

"Azriel, stop!" As amused as she was, his behavior was a bit troubling. "Azriel Kingsley, I am not taking one more step until you tell me where we are going."

"To the clearing," he answered quickly. He made it obvious that he would not say another word until they arrived. When they did, Camille recognized it as the place where Abelene had taught her many secrets. Azriel, being as gentlemanly as he knew how, brushed off the stone bench of a few leaves and offered the seat, then sat beside her. Camille folded her hands primly on her lap and waited for Azriel to say something—anything.

"Well?"

"Well what?" Azriel answered.

"Why did you drag me all the way out here?"

He hesitated, then sighed, lowering his head. "I'm sorry," he mumbled.

"Oh?" she replied. Her manner was cool.

"You really do look pretty—stunning, actually. You just caught me off guard. I've just never seen you look so beautiful."

Camille's cheeks flushed.

"You know you're my best friend, but I never really thought of you as… as…"

"As what?" Her eyes flashed dangerously.

"Well, as—a girl!"

"Then maybe it's time you get used to it, Azriel. And maybe…" she looked down penitently. "Maybe I wasn't being entirely fair either. Your mom told me everything that happened while you were away. You really helped all those people?"

"Uh-huh," He answered absently.

"She told me about Jezeera, the Seeress."

"Yeah?"

"And she told me of the Bedouin princess, Halimah." Her voice was laced with suspicion.

"Her too?" Azriel failed to heed the warning stirring in his mind.

"Is she pretty?"

"Oh yeah—beautiful." He answered without thinking.

Camille's eyes began to well up with tears, and Azriel cussed under his breath for not recognizing the trap. He quickly backpedaled and added, "Um, but…but she could never be as pretty as you are, Camille." Beads of sweat began to form on his brow.

"You mean it?" she sniffed.

"I wouldn't lie to you," he added.

Relieved, Camille impulsively threw her arms around Azriel's neck. "I really missed you, Azriel," she cried.

"I know. I missed you too." He gently rubbed her back. "So, what did you do this summer?" he asked, purposely changing the subject.

"Not much, really. Stayed home mostly with my aunts."

"What about Albert, Jasper, and Julia?"

"I saw them a few times," she shrugged, "But then they went on a family vacation, so I had a lot of time to myself. It was lonely, but I did learn something pretty neat. It took me only two months." She waited for a response and stared at Azriel. He stared back. "Well, aren't you going to show me?" he said.

"It's not that good. I just don't want you to be disappointed."

"Come on, Camille, the suspense is killing me." He teased.

"Well, okay." She glanced up nervously. Camille stood and faced Azriel. She closed her eyes and placed her hands together as if she were molding dough or clay. As she flexed her arms together, Camille began an invocation, whispering softly. Azriel noticed perspiration forming on Camille's face with her exertion—and oddly, a drawing in of power. Being fully acquainted with powerful magick, he had seen it displayed by his mother, Amaryllis, Lady Rosaluna; and even Pog. What Camille was doing was not ordinary human sympathetic Magick but something far more advanced—something she shouldn't have been able to do. Yet the scintillating energy was unmistakable.

Camille smiled, pleased with herself. She spread her hands and uttered, "Genero Phasmatis Bestia!"

An animated creature coalesced before his eyes—a golden lioness, strangely luminescent and slightly transparent. It stood regally and then crouched as if stalking some imaginary prey. Azriel gaped, truly amazed. "Camille, how did you do that?"

She giggled. "I stole my auntie's spellbook. It's very old—thirteenth century. Supposedly it was copied from a far older book that originated in ancient times."

"Well, you should be proud. It's very good—really advanced! Here. I'll do one for you." Azriel motioned deftly with his hands while whispering in a language Camille had never heard before. He spread his hands and a silvery-white dragon appeared. Much like the illusion Camille created, Azriel's dragon was ghostly and magnificent. It spread its wings and flew around the lioness—not in any sort of threatening way, but playfully—while the lioness chased after the dragon, swatting at it like it was a ball of string. Camille laughed as the phantasmal images frolicked around their heads.

With a gentle motion Camille waved her right hand and said, "Abeo!" In a puff of smoke, both creatures disappeared.

"That's remarkable. How'd you learn that?" Azriel inquired.

"It's an illusion spell."

"Well, I know that. That's not what I meant. It's just that you shouldn't be able to do that. Most humans struggle with the skill.

Actually, there's only one human I know who can create an illusion that well."

"Who?" She asked genuinely interested.

"Uncle Nick—but he's been practicing Magick for ten thousand years."

She smiled proudly. "Well that just goes to show you, Azriel Kingsley; you don't know everything about me. Auntie Pen told me I'm a thirteenth-generation witch, and that makes me special, I suppose. It's sort of like it gives me extra abilities. I honestly didn't know I could do it until I tried. I can create my lioness just by thinking about what she looks like."

"No, Camille—it's more than that. You can project your lioness because she is inside you—she *is* you. She's the part that makes you strong and fearless."

Azriel had been staring into her eyes as he spoke. He was suddenly lost for words. Immersed in her face, he noted every detail: her porcelain skin, the way her cheeks blushed when she looked at him. He was captivated by the largeness of her eyes, and the impish way her lips curled up at one side when she smiled, and how a wisp of her glossy black hair always seemed to brush against her cheek. Azriel's heart stirred, pounding in his chest. For so long he had ignored his feelings, living in a state of denial.

She faced Azriel squarely, staring into his gold-flecked grey eyes. She pointed to the ground, then drew in the air a tight arc over their heads. "Genero Flora!" she intoned. Around them, a canopy of lilies and orchids suddenly appeared. She took a step closer until she was face to face with Azriel.

"Kiss me," she whispered. Her vibrant blue eyes stared into his, filled with yearning.

"What?" he stammered.

"Kiss me!" she said a little more forcefully. Her breath quickened as she reached up, lips slightly parted. Part of Azriel wanted to run. How did he allow himself to be put in this position? He wanted to kiss her, but he also knew it would fundamentally change their friendship in a way that could never be undone. True, he felt closer to her than any of his other friends, but his heart quaked in his chest.

This was the only time Camille had ever frightened him. He nervously brushed a stray lock of hair away from his forehead and then gently kissed Camille on the cheek.

Her shoulders sagged. "No, not like that," she chided. "Like this." She reached up and pressed her lips firmly on his. Azriel's eyes widened in panic. At first he resisted, but suddenly found that he felt something he wasn't used to. It wasn't unpleasant. In fact, a strange stirring overtook Azriel, and he returned her kiss with tenderness. Camille trembled in his arms. She closed her eyes and rested her head against Azriel's shoulder.

She sighed and whispered, "Thank you."

Now tell me that you love me. Camille took a sudden intake of air. She hoped she hadn't spoken it out loud, but Azriel still held her to his heart without any noticeable reaction. She remembered Abelene's warning about not pushing too hard. She certainly didn't want to send Azriel running. She smiled with contentment. She knew that in time Azriel would speak his heart.

The days were growing shorter as the woods surrounding Azriel's house became a palette of color. The fragrant air was crisp, and frost carpeted the ground. As had become her habit, Abelene was preparing a feast a few days ahead for Samhain—otherwise known as Halloween. Lately, Azriel and Camille spent most of their time together, and it didn't go unnoticed by Jasper and Albert that a subtle change had taken place between them. Of course, Julia had figured it out long before her brothers even noticed the change. She smiled to herself as she watched Camille and Azriel bent over a spellbook. They were giggling over a particularly malicious spell. As had become her custom, Abelene continued instructing her charges in the use of magick. Julia caught on quickly and in some ways, had surpassed her brothers. Camille was a natural and needed little instruction. Being a thirteenth-generation witch certainly gave her a quicker understanding and an edge over her friends, but as Abelene had explained, it wasn't impossible for any ordinary witch to produce the illusion spell—just more difficult. It took greater concentration and control. Albert and Jasper were another matter, however. Since they were older, they had to unlearn many things the world had taught them as absolutes. It wasn't that they lacked talent. What they lacked was faith in themselves. By now, Julia had mastered the illusion spell with Camille's help. Azriel and Camille were the most advanced of the group, and they assisted their friends by individually pouring their energy into each to help produce images of their animal spirits. Camille gathered in the magickal energy as she placed her hands on Julia's shoulders. When the creature coalesced, none were surprised that it was a crafty fox—the trickster. It suited Julia perfectly since she had shown herself to be quite clever and cunning—and not averse to pulling the occasional prank or engaging in wild mischief. It came with the territory of having two older brothers, who teased her without mercy. But she often plotted her revenge on them, and it was usually mean and sometimes a bit over the top. She proved that after Albert had turned her hair green by mixing food coloring in her bottle of shampoo. She reciprocated by putting fresh dog crap under his pillow. He awoke in the middle of the night, gagging, howling his rage, and hurling a string of curses at Julia's locked door as he pounded on it. Of course, in time the incident blew over as often occurs with sibling rivalry. As much as Albert and Jasper were horrible to their sister, let anyone outside the family hurt her and they would rise to Julia's defense. In fact, Albert had recently served a week of detention for roughing up a boy who had insulted Julia.

Abelene watched as Albert and Jasper struggled with the illusion spell. It required imagination, and she feared that the two boys just didn't have any. They were good at other things. The boys had proven themselves more than capable with any spell that included destruction and mayhem. They seemed to derive great joy from blowing things up.

Continuing her observation, Abelene became aware of a surge of power as Azriel directed energy into Albert. As instructed, Albert flexed his arms and shaped the air. He spoke with a voice of command. "Genero Phasmatis Bestia." He spread his hands, and to his chagrin, the savage grizzly he sought to create looked more like a fuzzy teddy bear. Everyone in the room broke out in riotous laughter, but Abelene scolded them.

"That was a good start, Albert!" she said encouragingly. "And Jasper, you shouldn't laugh—you have yet to produce one."

"I can't," he sulked. "I'm having trouble concentrating."

"Okay, then let your mind drift and allow the first thing that comes into your mind to form in the air." She placed her hands on his shoulders, infusing him with power. "Now, let the power you generate show you what's in your heart," Abelene instructed.

Jasper closed his eyes, drawing in the magickal energy, then released it from his hands. When he opened his eyes, he stared with astonishment. A girl, miniature in form, floated before him. Though ghostly, she had flaming red hair and smiled adoringly at him.

"Hey, isn't that Becky Stouse?" Julia asked, looking with wonder and amusement at her brother.

"Yeah," Albert replied. "She's in his chemistry class. She's hot!"

Jasper sat mooning over the image he created, smiling wistfully. As he watched, the apparition began to unbutton her blouse.

"Jasper!" Abelene scolded with disapproval. "Abeo!" she uttered quickly, with a wave of her hand. The image vanished.

Julia smacked her brother. "You're such a pig!"

"Way to go, Jasper," Azriel commented while holding in his laughter.

Camille and Julia turned and glared at him.

Abelene merely crossed her arms. "At least we know what has him so distracted. Chemistry, indeed!"

A brief moment of embarrassed silence, and they all roared with laughter—at Jasper's blushing as much as at Abelene's exasperation.

"Now, in two days it will be Samhain." Abelene quickly changed the subject. "You should all be here by around six. Nicodemus will be here too. I understand he has quite a surprise in store. Now off with all of you. Shoo!" She motioned and smiled at the roomful of teenagers. She left the room shaking her head.

Azriel lit the bonfire in the yard behind his house. Jack-o-lanterns glowed with ghostly faces in a circle surrounding him and his friends. Also attending were Camille's aunts, Penelope and Daphne. They all wore black capes, and Abelene addressed them solemnly.

"Tonight is the night we honor our beloved dead, those who have lived and departed this world. At this time of year, more than any other, the veil between the living and the dead is thinnest. It is at this time that we eat in remembrance of them and invite them to join in the feasting." Abelene was about to add more when she tilted her head as if listening to something. She sensed an onrushing surge of power emanating from somewhere in the house. A brief flash of light appeared in the kitchen window. She smiled broadly and exclaimed. "Well, I think Uncle Nick is here with his surprise."

From the back door, Rosemary and Mr. Parkins filed out, followed by Amaryllis, Felisa, Billy, and Muriel. Though it was an unexpected pleasure, Azriel was nevertheless disappointed that Pog was not among them. He found it curious that Pog remained so reclusive. Rosemary and Amaryllis approached Abelene and embraced her warmly. Billy strode up to Azriel and roughly grabbed him.

"Hello, mate!" He laughed merrily as he clasped him on the shoulder.

"How did you guys get here?" Azriel wrinkled his brow and smiled crookedly.

"Rather odd, really," Billy explained. "Nicodemus has some kind of magick ball. Calls it a Dream—something or other."

"A dream orb?"

"Yeah, that's it."

Azriel glanced at Nicodemus with an odd look on his face. "Nice of you to tell me."

"And ruin the surprise?" he chuckled.

"We could have saved a lot of traveling time, don't you think?"

"Oh, don't be so boorish, Azriel. Half the fun of a journey is getting there."

"Yeah, I guess," he smirked. Azriel took the time to introduce everyone to each other. Muriel and Felisa stood by him as he made another introduction.

"Hi, I'd like you to meet my girlfr—" he caught himself. "Um, this is Camille." He blushed slightly while Camille smiled secretly, pleased at Azriel's *almost* admission. Muriel, though quite charming and friendly, could not quite conceal the slight look of disappointment on her face. Jasper, Albert, and Julia joined the group of young friends. Julia, forgetting her manners, stared with curiosity at Felisa. Her feline features were unmistakable. Annoyed at such scrutiny, Felisa hissed at her. A few feet away, Amaryllis turned and scolded. "Felisa! Behave!"

"This isn't a freak show!" she snarled back.

"Wow! Cool." Albert and Jasper said at the same time. Felisa rolled her eyes with exasperation.

Azriel then pulled Muriel into the circle and introduced her to his friends.

"Hi!" Albert said affably, but Jasper stood with his mouth agape, stammering, totally smitten by Muriel's golden curls and dimpled smile.

"Jasper? Hey, Jasper!" Azriel coughed a laugh and snapped his fingers a few times in front of his stunned friend's eyes. "Hey, buddy! Wake up!"

"Oh—yeah. Hi," he said weakly." I was staring..." He turned and walked away to hide his embarrassment.

Muriel glanced at Julia, Felisa, and Camille, giggling in the way girls often did when presented with an awkward situation.

"I think you caught my brother's attention," Julia smiled crookedly at Muriel. "He'll be impossible to talk to the rest of the evening. I've seen this before."

From the other side of the patio, where the adults spoke quietly among themselves, Abelene suddenly clapped a few times to get everyone's attention. "Come!" she said cheerfully. "Time to bring the festivities inside."

They all headed toward the house. Azriel was surprised to find a long table overflowing with delicious foods. A golden-brown roasted turkey with all the trimmings, fruit, nuts, and delicious pies adorned every inch of usable space.

"Mom, how did you..."

"Why, magick, of course. It's really quite a simple matter." Abelene beamed.

"If you say so." Azriel shook his head with amazement.

They all took their seats. To his chagrin, Jasper was seated directly across Muriel at the broad table. Looking down, he refused to meet her eyes.

Oddly, at the head of the candle-lit table was an empty chair. Julia asked no one in particular, "Are we having another guest?"

She didn't have to wait long for an answer. Abelene stood holding a goblet of wine. "Tonight, here and throughout the world, many cultures celebrate Samhain, otherwise known as the Day of the Dead. In Mexico, for example, they actually set up a feast at the graves of their loved ones. They call it *Día de los Muertos*. It's not a day of sadness, but a way to remember with joy the people of the past. In this way they remember those they loved who have departed this world. For us, we leave this place setting empty to invite our dead to join in the feast." Abelene raised her glass. "To our honored dead!"

They all raised their glasses in the toast. "To our honored dead," they said in unison.

The feast began in earnest. Azriel couldn't help but think of the father he never met and wondered who he was and what he was like. Likewise, Camille thought of her parents too. She remembered little of them, having been young when they disappeared. She was, however, grateful for Aunt Pen and Daffie, the only remaining family she had. Then a thought occurred to her. She did have a much larger family, in a sense. They were seated all around her. Camille smiled with contentment and filled her plate.

After dessert was served, they all joined in playing games and bobbing for apples. They sat entranced by the fireplace while Nicodemus told scary stories. While he wove a gruesome tale, Rosemary had disappeared for a while and then returned. As she did, all lights were extinguished except for the candles, which blazed inside carved pumpkins placed strategically throughout the living room. Rosemary was followed by Abelene and Amaryllis. Dressed in black gowns and capes, they stood regally before the guests.

Rosemary was made distinct by wearing a silver crown with an upturned crescent moon as the emblem of her office. Together they were a representation of the triple goddess—the maiden, lady, and crone. Somehow, perhaps through a trick of the light, Amaryllis, as the crone, seemed to appear much older. The celebration suddenly took on a more solemn atmosphere.

"I am Lady Rosaluna," Rosemary spoke without preamble. "I call Camille, Jasper, Albert, and Julia to stand before me."

They stood, glancing pensively at one another, and approached the Lady.

"I have been watching you from afar. Abelene has reported your progress, and I believe you are all ready for the great work ahead of you." She smiled gracefully. From the ancient days, a powerful brotherhood was established to battle against the coming darkness and to restore the shattered worlds to wholeness. It is the responsibility of those who know the true nature of this world to be warriors against the dark powers of the Clave. You are being called to join the Order of the Ankh—but know this. It is not a frivolous commitment, but a secret and serious one. You all are entrusted with the restoration of the world. It is an honor for you to be asked into the fold, and you join a short list of great men and women throughout history who have looked forward to the day of restoration."

With ceremony, Abelene and Amaryllis placed a silver chain with the emblem of the Ankh over the heads of the young adults standing before them.

"You now have the duty to continue your studies and learn fully the ways of magick." Lady Rosaluna added. "You all will have help whenever you need it. This is my commitment to you." She smiled winningly. "Now be welcomed by your brothers and sisters!"

The induction ceremony ended, Billy, Muriel, and Felisa joined them in a tight circle. Billy shook hands with Jasper and Albert. "Welcome aboard, mates. Any friend of Azriel is a friend of mine!"

Meanwhile, Camille sat down and toyed with the tablecloth pensively. Muriel sat next to her. "Well, ye seem out of sorts, Camille." she piped.

"Oh, it's nothing really. I'm just a bit overwhelmed, that's all." Camille smiled tentatively. "And I'm afraid for Azriel." she whispered. "He's in an awful lot of danger, isn't he?"

"Aye, dearie. But we all are, don't ye know." she replied in a thick brogue. "But he's strong and has a good heart." Muriel smiled. "He defended me virtue to me father, he did."

"What do you mean?" Camille eyed her suspiciously.

"Now don't ye be worryin', lass. I was just showin' off me charms, flirtin' with him, but he was a proper gentleman. Me father—he called me a floozy, but Azriel told him I was a proper lady."

"Oh, he did, did he?" Her eyes flashed.

"Besides, I can tell he's sweet on you, don't ye know. He may not say much, but I think he'd defend ye honor to the death!"

"That's what I'm afraid of." Camille shook off a sudden chill.

"Now, yer friend, Jasper—he's another matter. I haven't been able to get him to talk to me all evenin'. Just shuts up like a clam!"

Camille snickered. "Yeah, he gets kind of stupid around beautiful girls."

"Aye." Muriel sighed tragically. "I guess I'll just have to fix that. He's a rather cute bloke—so let the fireworks begin!"

Muriel stood abruptly and walked with purpose to where Jasper was chatting with Azriel and Felisa. She put her hands on her hips and spoke, her voice quite cross. "Jasper Cunningham! Ye come here right now and talk to me!" She pointed to the ground for effect.

"Um…um." he stammered helplessly and took a step toward her.

"Ye might as well get used to it. I'm not goin' away and we'll be workin' together, don't ye know." She said with exasperation. "Now just because ye think a girl is pretty doesn't mean ye avoid her. Grow a backbone, man!"

"Well, I…" he hesitated as his cheeks turned crimson. By now, the din and chatter in the room lessened as most turned to watch with amusement.

"All right, then. If ye won't, then I will! After all, someone has to break the ice, don't ye know!" Muriel stepped forward, grabbed Jasper by the collar, and planted a long passionate kiss, full on the lips. His knees nearly buckled under him as everyone broke out in uproarious laughter.

"Wow! That's one hell of an icebreaker," Jasper gasped.

"See that! He speaks!" Muriel crossed her arms comically. "Now, you and I are goin' to finally talk!"

Whatever transpired between Muriel and him, Jasper wouldn't say. Later, however, he did press Azriel as to when he would be returning to the Isle of Man. Azriel didn't need to ask. Muriel and Jasper had apparently made some arrangements to meet again. It was obvious by Jasper's eagerness that sooner would be preferable to later.

The celebration over, Azriel watched Amaryllis, Felisa, Billy, and Muriel depart by way of Uncle Nick's dream orb. With a shimmer and a ripple in the air, they simply vanished from the room.

"Wow—wicked!" Jasper stared at the vacant space amazed, and with a touch of regret. Shortly after, Camille left with her aunts Penelope and Daphne, followed by the Cunninghams. This left Azriel and Abelene alone at last.

She stood by the sink and began washing the dishes, while Azriel aided her by drying and putting them away. As he placed a stack of plates in the cupboard, he paused and thought for a moment.

"Um, Mom?"

"Yes, dear."

"Why do you bother with all this cleanup?"

"What are you saying, Azriel?"

"Well, couldn't you just snap your fingers, make everything go away, and be done with it?"

"Why, yes I could, dear," She said and began humming to herself.

He stopped and screwed up his face in chagrin. "Then... why don't you?"

"That would be cheating, dear."

"Cheating? Didn't you make a whole feast appear just like that?"

"That was different, Azriel. I certainly couldn't be in two places at once. Besides, I *did* cook the meal. I just told the food where it needed to be when it was done." She continued humming as she scrubbed another pot.

"Then why don't you tell the pots and dishes where to go?" he asked with a touch of annoyance.

"Azriel," she said sternly, "I *like* washing the dishes."

"Yeah, well I don't. Seems like a big waste of time."

"It's my time to waste," she retorted in a patronizing voice that always infuriated Azriel. He grumbled under his breath.

"Watch your tongue, Azriel," she scolded.

They continued the chore; Abelene washing, Azriel drying and stacking. When they were almost done, Azriel stopped and started thinking.

"Mom?"

"Yes, Azriel."

"Tell me about my father."

She paused for a moment, then resumed scrubbing a particularly stubborn spot from a cast iron pot.

"What would you like to know, dear?"

"Everything. What was he like, what did he do—how he lived—and died? I want to know about the sword that's been under my bed for years. Oh, and by the way, don't tell me Uncle Nick bought it at an antique store in Europe. I know it's not true. It belonged to him, didn't it? It was my father's sword."

She turned and looked sharply at Azriel. "It's not something I like talking about."

"I need to know."

She sighed, sat at the kitchen table, and waited for Azriel to join her.

"Many years before you were born, the people of Aralia lived in peace for untold generations. After the Split, the world was left in disarray. The Clave of wizards had been fragmented by the event, and turmoil rose from within. At the time, five Great Houses ruled the various kingdoms scattered throughout Aralia. They were the houses of Varn, Porin, Telynech, Gorlyn, and Ferrishyn. Of the great houses, Ferrishyn was the least, ruling a small island nation to the west. The four other houses—never giving much thought to King

Ozric or the Ferrishyn kingdom—were content to fight among themselves. Because he was a fair and gentle man, the other four Houses thought Ozric weak and unfit to rule. Their ill-conceived opinions of him arose from the fact that Ozric ruled with fairness and humility, and had built a more democratic nation—with a Council of Advisors and the Tynwald—a gathering of the minor Houses. In that way, all would have an equal say in his government. The other four houses thought a king should rule with more authority, and they spurned his ideas of a self-governing kingdom. Soon, conflicts arose throughout the world. Petty differences and squabbles between the houses escalated to a boiling point, and open war was imminent. When it appeared that war was unavoidable, Ozric—exercising his right—requested a grand council of the five Great Houses. Grudgingly, they agreed to meet in a neutral place. With great ceremony, a pavilion was set up at the plains of Shenach—a desolate place, marking the division where the kingdoms of the four Great Houses converged. They underestimated Ozric's cunning, however, for they did not know he kept a powerful secret. You see, Azriel, after Eltanin engaged in the ritual to raise the four elementals, he bequeathed the great sword Errin-lil to Ozric—his nephew. Eltanin knew the mortal danger in which he would place himself, and wanted the sword to be kept safe should evil befall him."

"Wait a minute," Azriel said, wide-eyed. "My sword?"

"The very same, Azriel," Abelene answered.

"So, what's so great about this sword?"

"It's the sword of power—the beacon of hope," Abelene stated gravely. "When the world was new, and the first Kingdom of Aralia was unified under Eltanin's rule, he forged Errin-lil—the Lightbringer—from a precious metal found only in the heart of Aralia. It was not a sword of war, but of peace. Anyone rightfully bearing the sword would be invincible—but only one who was the legitimate heir of Eltanin could bear it. It would destroy anyone else who touched it. For many years after Eltanin's demise, it was thought that the sword had been irretrievably lost.

"And so, Ozric waited out his gambit and planned for the day the council would convene. The day finally arrived, and the Kings of the Great Houses converged upon the plains of Shenach. And as expected, there were hours of threats, posturing, and open declarations of war. Three of the kings refused to negotiate in good faith. When Trevor of House Gorlyn saw the merit of peace between the kingdoms, and thus defended Ozric's position, the three kings of the other houses turned on Trevor. They promised to unite and destroy him. Ozric, having had enough and seeing no choice, finally rose from the conference table and spoke with authority. 'If you cannot cease the hostilities between you, then I will bring war upon all of you!'

"Stunned to silence, the three opposing kings stared at Ozric with incredulity. Then they all laughed in derision. King Flen of House Porin faced Ozric squarely, he said with contempt. 'You, a minor king of a minor kingdom, will defeat us all? You have gone insane! The four houses could easily raze your kingdom to the ground! By what authority would you utter such a wild boast?'

"'By this authority!' Ozric unsheathed his sword and raised Errin-lil for all to see. It erupted with white fire as he held it aloft. The four kings paled and gasped in recognition of the sword of power.

"But Flen, a pompous and self-righteous man, sneered at Ozric and challenged him. 'It's a fake. Everyone knows that sword was lost 500 years ago. You are not man enough to wield the sword of Eltanin.'

"It was Ozric's turn to laugh. 'If that is what you believe, Flen, then take Errin-lil from me and strike me down—but I wouldn't if I were you. It could prove—damaging to your person. Only Eltanin's heir can wield the sword."

"Flen growled with disdain. 'Rubbish. Only a fool believes such nonsense!'

"'If you say so,' Ozric said archly. He sheathed the sword and held it out, hilt first toward the man. 'Don't say I didn't warn you, Flen.'

"The King of Porin grasped the hilt of Errin-lil and slid it from its scabbard. He raised it overhead ready to strike Ozric down, but when he did, the sword, as was its nature, erupted with white light. The kings of the great houses watched in horror as white fire consumed Flen's right hand up to the elbow. It scorched and withered his limb until it was nothing but a blackened stump. Ozric lifted the dropped sword and placed it back in its sheath. As Flen writhed on the ground in agony, the remaining Kings stared pale faced with fear at Ozric.

"'Now,' he said calmly. 'Does anyone else wish to challenge me?'"

Abelene paused in her storytelling and watched Azriel's reaction. He was transfixed by the story, which put much into perspective, but it did nothing to explain what his role was in all of this. Azriel still wondered why he possessed the sword.

"Shall I continue?" Abelene asked.

"Yes, please do." Azriel replied somewhat breathless.

"After that incident," she continued, "it was easy for Ozric to bring peace between the Houses." The Houses Varn, Porin, and Telynech reluctantly agreed to peace knowing full well what the consequences of their refusal would be. But with House Gorlyn, King Ozric forged an alliance with King Trevor. The House of Gorlyn was well known for siring some of the most powerful wizards and sorcerers due to their bloodline also descended from Eltanin as third- and fourth-generation cousins. To cement the union of House Ferrishyn and House Gorlyn, Ozric took Torianna, the niece of King Trevor, to wife. A powerful sorceress and wise in the ways of magick, together Torianna ruled alongside Ozric as they governed the Five Kingdoms with wisdom and peace.

"In time, they bore a son, Alialdor, and he in turn took Carril of House Gorlyn to wife, but in time, King Ozric died of extreme old age having reigned for 749 years. And as rules of succession applied, Alialdor took the throne and inherited Errin-lil. Alialdor and Carril also bore a son, and he married a daughter of House Gorlyn, and it remained as such for many generations."

Abelene ceased her narration and glanced at the table. Her eyes were distant and troubled.

"Mom, what's wrong?" Azriel asked quietly.

"The telling becomes difficult from here, Azriel. It breaks my heart to recount it."

Azriel took her hand to comfort her. She smiled sadly. "In time, after the Rending of Aralia, magick, as you know, began to fade throughout the land. Simple magick became difficult and the Great Houses weakened. Only the line of Eltanin remained strong. The House of Gorlyn faded as well. Only one sorceress every few generations was born with the capacity to remember the Old Magick.

"But where the Ferrishyn line is concerned, through each successive generation, kings grew increasingly corrupt, craving power. They began delving into forbidden magick and twisting the Laws that had always been the cornerstone of Aralian society. Soon, a Prophecy began circulating throughout the land—one who would come, restore Magick to Aralia, and reunite the split worlds as one again. It was said that he would bring peace and the Laws of Magick would be written in his heart. The Prophecy had been unearthed from what many believed were the ruins of Eltanin's tower. Moreover, it had been written in Eltanin's own hand. The belief in this prophecy further empowered the Ferrishyn kings, and they grew prideful and arrogant. Many became tyrants, and a bane to the people. Worse still, their union with the daughters of House Gorlyn became a mockery. They used their sorceress queens as ornaments—to grow more powerful and to preserve their years—for like magick in the land, their own spans of life had faded as well.

"Then, two generations past, King Aldorag of House Ferrishyn set his envious eyes on the kingdoms of the east and the great wealth they possessed. He took up the sword Errin-lil, the Lightbringer, to bear it upon the kingdoms of the east."

"But why would he do that?" Azriel asked, stricken to the heart.

Abelene's eyes burned with anger. "Greed and power often do terrible things to a man's heart. It becomes cold and stony, unable to love anything but earthly treasure. The heart becomes even resistant to the love of a devoted wife and mother. In that way, Aldorag's heart became hard and unyielding, despite all the vast kingdom and possessions he held. He marched a great army to the east to conquer and oppress. It wasn't enough for Aldorag that he was overlord of the west. He wanted dominion over the entire world. But then a strange thing happened. Aldorag sought to use Errin-lil to slay his enemies, but it turned on him. In the heat of battle, the sword which had served the countless heirs of Eltanin—refused to be an instrument of evil. It saw the darkness in Aldorag's heart and, rather than be used for evil, consumed him to preserve its own purity. Errin-lil betrayed Aldorag and scorched his flesh to ashes. The war between East and West ended and Errin-lil, the Lightbringer, was returned to House Ferrishyn. The sword and the kingdom fell to..." Abelene's expression darkened and she locked eyes with Azriel. "They fell to his son—Berrill—your father."

Azriel's chest tightened as though he couldn't breathe. The impact of the story affected him far more than any other Abelene had ever told him. She seemed reluctant to continue, but she steeled her resolve.

"Berrill had inherited his father's throne, and as an heir of Eltanin, sent out royal messengers to retrieve a daughter of House Gorlyn. They returned with a young woman who was already proving to be an adept sorceress." Abelene smiled ruefully. "I—the most powerful sorceress born of my house in five generations—handed over like a prize."

"So you had no choice in the matter?" Azriel suppressed a surge of anger at his mother's plight.

"No. It was my duty. I had to honor the alliance that had been in place for thousands of years."

Azriel glowered with his head down. The idea of an arranged marriage repulsed him. "Did you ever love him?" he asked.

Abelene sighed with resignation. "Not in the very beginning, but in time, I learned to love your father. He wasn't like Aldorag. In the beginning, he was kind, with all the right intentions. He wanted to undo the damage his father had done to the Ferrishyn kingdom, but it is difficult to wipe clean years of oppression and turmoil, and to earn the people's trust. It was even harder not to fall to the sway of corruption. The people were tired of being ruled by the petty whims of a king. And there were other problems as well. Berrill, along with his advisors began to delve into Eltanin's prophecy. They discovered a detail that had previously gone largely unnoticed. Oddly, for all those years of religious scrutiny and devotion, not one scholar had turned the scroll over to view its reverse—a single page bearing a star chart and Eltanin's calculations. It pointed to yet another prophecy: when all the planets aligned in the constellation of the Dragon, a ruler would be born who would unite the split worlds and abolish the present system. He would restore true Magick as Eltanin's heir, and the kingdoms would be no more, for there would only be one. Furthermore, men and Ferrishyn would rule themselves, for the unerring laws of life would be written in their hearts.

"At first the prophecy meant nothing to your father—merely an exercise of the mind. There were other matters to contend with. As Overlord, Berrill's grip on the kingdoms to the west was failing. Society had fractured into different factions, and the Great Houses began to rebel against him. After the tyranny of Aldorag, the houses sought to dissolve the alliance by any means possible. There was turmoil from within as well. Berrill's council of wizards and advisors had a new problem. They learned that I was pregnant. They twisted Berrill's heart, turning his joy in his future heir to distrust and envy. The stars were read, and it was determined that the child I carried would be born when the planets aligned with the great dragon. They turned your father's heart against me. He feared the child in my womb would someday wrest his throne away from him. He so coveted his power that he listened to his advisors and sought to do away with me. They drove him mad! But there were others loyal to me and the prophecy. The kingdom soon became divided and a rebellion against the throne ensued. After an assassination attempt on Berrill, he accused me of being behind the uprising and had me imprisoned. He had one of my handmaidens tortured for information, but she had none to offer and died in agony—faithful to me, even to the end." Abelene's eyes now filled with tears.

"In an effort to squash the uprising, Berrill—filled with darkness and revenge—took a full complement of men to kill all the rebels, but his palace guard refused. For many—underpaid lowly soldiers—it would have been brother against brother. In the end, they turned on your father, and he was murdered. The entire kingdom exploded into violence and mayhem. I, too, would have been murdered, for I carried the next heir, and the people were done with kings. But those who were loyal to me broke me out of my prison. There was nowhere I could escape where my enemies could not find me, so to preserve my life and the future of the worlds, I performed the ritual that thrust me—and the baby I carried, you, Azriel—into this world. I brought with me what I could—your amulet, the Book of Aralia and Errin-lil, the sword of Eltanin. So now you know the whole story." Abelene stared at her son with tears running down her cheeks.

Azriel was cut to the heart by his mother's tale, but something nagged at him—a skipped detail, an omission perhaps. "Is that everything?" he asked blandly.

Abelene hesitated, then stared Azriel in the eyes. "Yes, son. That's everything." she said sadly.

"The sword—Errin-lil. It's dangerous, isn't it?"

"Only in the wrong hands, Azriel."

"Something happened you should know about," he ventured.

Abelene looked up sharply. "What?" She held her breath.

"Well, I was handling the sword the other day, and when I held it, the stone on the pommel began to glow faintly."

She hesitated, thinking deeply. "That would make sense, I suppose."

"How?"

She smiled at Azriel's consternation. "It's because you're not fully empowered yet. You have still to learn of Air and Fire."

"Mother, it scares me!"

"And it's good that you're afraid," she said quickly. "Wielding power is a frightening responsibility. It's important that you always examine the motives of your heart. Your heart can be easily betrayed by the logic of the mind. You may think at times that you are acting out of good, but every action has a consequence. That is why you must become adept at peering into the future. Always examine the possible result of any action you may wish to undertake. Never act out of hate and vengeance, Azriel. It is the first step into darkness. Once down that path, it is difficult to return. Let that be a warning."

Azriel sighed heavily.

"Oh, Azriel." She looked at him with love in her eyes. "You have always shown a good heart and have always acted with the best of intentions. I am so proud of you, son. You're a joy to my heart."

It was very late and he was tired. But Azriel found that the story affected him deeply. The sorrow and burden he felt were nearly unbearable. Much as he held in his grief, when he kissed his mother good night, he fell against shoulder and heaved a sob. It was too much. Abelene held him tight and wept for his pain. She never meant to hurt him with the history of his bloodline. The last time he cried was when he was a child, over telling a lie—but this was different. The weight of the worlds rested on his shoulders; his unquenchable sorrow was a result of unasked-for responsibility and the burden of the task before him. Abelene cried—not only for Azriel and his lost childhood of innocence, but for herself. Her little boy was gone. Azriel was becoming a man.

Gift of the Amulet

284

Chapter 14

Azriel was actually glad to be back at school the following Monday. It helped take his mind off magick, strange prophecies, and powerful swords. Camille noticed a subtle change in Azriel. He was unusually tender with her when they met in the morning for their usual walk to school, but she said nothing. She knew that in time, he would tell her what it was all about. He immersed himself in his English assignment and finished it well before his classmates. Having nothing much to do with the remaining time, he thought it would be fun to translate his paper into Aralian for the sheer pleasure of it. He scrawled the cursive symbols on the page and smiled with satisfaction. Meanwhile, Camille, sitting next to him, finished her paper as well. She, however, decided it would be delightful to torture Eddie Breck, who was seated three desks ahead. She surreptitiously projected the illusion of a fly buzzing around his head. She was getting quite good at it, now able to add the annoying buzzing sound of the insect around his ears. With a twinkle of mischief in her eyes, she added another, and then another, until Eddie's head was surrounded by a swarm. He began slapping at his ears and face.

Azriel whispered under his breath, "Camille, stop it!"

"No! It's fun!" she replied impishly.

"Don't instigate him."

"Why not? Payback, you know! Besides, he'll never know it's me."

Suddenly, Eddie bolted from his desk and began frantically swatting at the air and at himself. Jerking wildly from the imagined attack, he ran out of the classroom and down the hall, screaming, with the swarm of angry flies chasing closely behind him as the class erupted in laughter.

Azriel turned and stared at Camille, speculatively.

"Are you having fun?"

"Yes! Lots!" she grinned devilishly.

"I've never seen this side of you. You're vicious!"

"Yeah, isn't it great?"

Azriel sighed and shook his head.

When school let out in the afternoon, as usual, Azriel waited for his friends at the front entrance so they could walk home together. When Jasper and Albert walked up, Azriel and Camille were engaged in a disagreement. They hung back and listened.

Azriel argued. "Look, Camille. Just because you have a little power now, doesn't mean you're supposed to flex your muscle. Messing with Eddie Breck was stupid. Why invite trouble?"

"Why?" she retorted, "I've put up with his crap for the past three years, and I'm tired of it. It's about time that I give him a taste of his own medicine."

"There's a time to use power and a time to refrain. Have you forgotten everything my mother taught you? Your Aunts?"

She faced him nose to nose, with hands on hips. "Azriel Kingsley, who put you in charge?"

"Do you think I'm saying this just to give you a hard time? I'm looking out for you, Camille. I—I—care about you, and using your magickal skills to torment someone, even if you hate his guts is a poor use of your abilities. Save it for a time when it's necessary."

"I hate to interrupt when the show is getting so good, but I think Azriel is right, Camille," Albert interjected. "First rule, right? Harm none."

"I didn't touch Eddie Breck. I just messed with his mind a bit. What's the harm in that?"

"What's the harm? Jasper joined in. "You may not have bruised him, but you did violate him. What if he figures out that you were the one who made him think he was being attacked by flies? The guy's unstable. He'll come after you or one of us. No, you didn't hurt him in any way, but you could cause one of us to be hurt, yourself included."

Camille sighed with resignation. "I didn't think of it that way. I guess you're right. I'll stop tormenting him. But if he ever comes near me again, I won't stay my hand."

The next couple of weeks left Azriel little time for anything but study, and when his schedule finally eased, he began searching the Book of Aralia for more information about the Sword of Eltanin. He didn't find much—only something that didn't make sense. Every so often, he found a hand-scribed image of an eye. When he placed the crystal tablet over the symbol, it normally projected an image to illustrate a point in the narrative. But in some places it projected only black static, as though whole sections had been erased. He had yet to figure out how to see past the blackened images.

He sat with Camille on his bed and showed her the latest reflections the book projected. He'd skipped ahead to the last section, bypassing several tedious chapters of Aralian history. The segment he read now concerned his father—King Berrill. It described, from a certain point of view, Berrill's inheritance of the throne, his coronation, and wedding to Abelene of House Gorlyn. It recounted the growing discontent among Berrill's subjects, followed by paragraph after paragraph of politics and economic minutiae from the western kingdoms.

"Here, listen to this," Azriel said to Camille. He read aloud.

"On the thirtieth year of Berrill's reign, Queen Sorceress Abelene of House Gorlyn conceived a child and carried the next heir of Eltanin's line. She consulted her astrologers and discovered that her child would be the Lightbringer and Uniter of the fractured worlds. She secretly sought to depose the king and place herself on the throne as queen regent until her son would be born and come of age to rule the Western Kingdoms. Having discovered the plot, King Berrill had Abelene imprisoned for treason."

Azriel paused. "That's where the book ends—the remaining pages are blank.

"Well, that doesn't make sense." Camille scowled, thinking.

"Actually, it does—at least partly. My mother told me it was true. She *was* imprisoned, but not for the reasons stated here. My father feared my destiny. He so wanted to hold onto his power that everyone—including my mother—fell under suspicion. Eventually, my father was murdered, probably by his own men."

"That's terrible!" Camille gasped.

"And it gets worse. When the rebellion broke, my mother would've been next, but a few loyal to her freed her from prison and helped her escape. So it would make sense that the book ends here. She made off with it from the royal records to preserve it when she fled to this world. It's important—even if some details are inaccurate. This relates my entire bloodline until my mother's escape from Aralia. But *these...*" he pointed to the eye symbol. "These were added later. What I can't figure out is *who* added them."

"Have you asked Abelene?" Camille inquired.

"She said she didn't know, or else she's just being deliberately evasive."

 "But why would she do that?"

"I think there's lots of things she knows but won't tell me. One thing for certain is that there's more to her than meets the eye. I've realized lately that every time I think I have her pegged, something happens that makes me see that I don't know her at all!" Azriel laughed. "Here, let me show you something. I think it'll put a lot into perspective."

He placed the crystal plate over the last eye symbol scribed into the book. Like every time before, it projected a moving image from the page.

Abelene sat in a green velvet dressing gown, imprisoned in a suite high above one of the palace towers. It was not the usual prison, but rather a comfortable sitting room, with a bedchamber and many amenities one would expect of a royal suite. But nonetheless, it was still a prison under lock and key. Beyond, the door was guarded by two of Berrill's men. Oddly, a choker enveloped Abelene's neck. It was finely wrought silver, but inset within its filigreed design was a glowing red stone, its aspect baneful and malignant. That proved to be the case when she tried to use magick to unlock the door, and the choker began to tighten around her neck, strangling her breath. She gasped for air. The moment she recanted, the stone released its hold on her. The obvious intent was to prevent her escape by magickal means or otherwise.

As was the usual daily event, a chambermaid brought her a meal in the afternoon. The guards, following orders, would check under the plates for any weapons or magickal items, and as was typical, every day they would sift through the food as well. The guard, fingering through the food, suddenly began to convulse as the quick-acting poison entered his skin. He dropped to the ground, foaming at the mouth. The other guard pulled his sword, ready to strike down the chambermaid, but before he could react, an arrow flew past her and pierced the guard through the heart. She breathed heavily and lowered the cowl hiding her face. Beads of perspiration trickled down Lady Elsinore's face. Three cloaked men filed unseen through the hall leading to Abelene's chamber. One searched through the fallen guard's pocket and removed a set of keys. As quietly as possible, he unlocked the door to Abelene's prison. Approaching her, they all fell to one knee in respect.

"Milady, we've come to release you." The young man bowed his head.

"Elrid, you're my hero!" Abelene smiled graciously to the Captain of the Guard.

Elsinore spoke breathlessly. "My Queen, please turn so I can get that cursed thing off your neck." She held in her hand an elaborate key. The end of it had a round disc with several notches that lined up with the slot. She carefully placed it in the receptacle on the back of the collar and pressed twice. The necklace began to glow and floated from Abelene's neck into Elsinore's waiting hand. She tossed it aside with disgust as Abelene sighed with relief.

"Thank you, my cousin." Abelene embraced Elsinore with gratitude. "You took an awful risk."

"I could not let you rot in here. I swapped clothes with your chambermaid. No one ever suspected."

"Come, Milady," Elrid said. "We have an escape route."

"Not until I find my husband. I owe him that."

"As you wish, Milady." Elrid looked at one of his men and shrugged. They drew swords and led the way out of the tower into the main hall. From outside the palace, Abelene heard angry shouts of the multitude screaming their rebellion against House Ferrishyn.

The sounds of steel against steel echoed through the chamber as the murderous horde broke into battle. Agonizing screams resounded off the walls as the mob was cut down by Berrill's soldiers.

"Did you do what I asked, Elsinore?" Abelene asked anxiously, her eyes wide with terror.

"Yes, Milady. The ritual has been set up in the east tower.

"Good. We must go to the throne room first."

They scurried through a confusing maze of halls and chambers, two guards in front and Elrid covering Abelene's back. Outside, it sounded as though the rabble of outraged citizens was getting the upper hand by sheer numbers. A steady thumping of a battering ram against the main gate resounded through the hall and shook the castle. Abelene hurried to the throne room and approached the great seat. Above and behind the throne, two hooks supported Errin-lil, the ancestral sword of House Ferrishyn. She carefully removed it from its place on the wall. She was terrified to handle it, expecting it to char her body to cinders, but the stone on the pommel flashed briefly as though it sensed her presence, or perhaps the child she carried, and would allow Abelene to keep Errin-lil safe for the future king. She sheathed the sword and wrapped it in linen for safekeeping. Resting on a table next to the throne was the Book of Aralia. She snatched it off the pedestal and handed it to Elsinore. She ran ahead from there to her personal chamber and removed a small carved box from her jewelry chest and stuffed it in her pocket. As she turned, however, she heard footsteps coming from one of the halls. Frantic, she, with her complement, fled to the east tower. As she turned the corner, she saw her husband at the far end of the hallway approaching fast. Behind Berrill, hot on his heels, five soldiers with swords drawn were chasing him down. Startled by the pursuit, Abelene stood tall and raised her arms to release a spell. In one hand she held a dagger; the other she shaped into a claw.

"Inferno!" she called out, the incantation releasing her power. The five soldiers suddenly ignited into flames. Their screams were horrifying as they writhed on the ground in pain and died.

"My wife," Berrill exclaimed in surprise. His eyes had a murderous wildness in them she had never witnessed before.

"My husband." Abelene replied. There was a hard edge to her voice. But she could not get out another word. From behind the king, another complement of soldiers rounded the corner in hot pursuit.

The image suddenly grew fuzzy, and the exchange between Berrill and Abelene was muffled, becoming inaudible before the projection darkened to a black cloud.

"See," Azriel commented. "This happens every time I view this. I don't know if it's deliberate or just a flaw, but there are three minutes where nothing is visible."

Camille looked pale. She was holding back tears. "Poor Abelene," she whispered. "I never knew she had gone through so much."

Azriel placed his arm around Camille's shoulder protectively. "Are you all right to watch the rest? It gets pretty brutal from here," he asked, his voice protective.

Camille wiped away a tear. "No, I'm okay. I need to see what happened."

Just as Azriel had predicted, a full three minutes passed before the projection from the tablet resumed.

Abelene stood in the center of a room. Surrounding her, seven full-length mirrors faced her. Errin-lil was now strapped securely by a harness to her back. She cradled the Book of Aralia against her chest. Five men stood guard at the door of the tower chamber. It was locked and barred, but from outside it was obvious that mayhem still plagued the castle. The sounds of battle bled through the doors, and someone shouted from beyond, "The king has been murdered! Find the assassin!" Suddenly, there was a pounding on the great door.

Elsinore was frantic. She embraced Abelene in tears. "Milady, you cannot delay. You must go now!"

The pounding and shouts behind the door grew louder.

"I wish I could take you with me, my cousin," Abelene wept. She took Elrid's hand. "My loyal friend, flee the kingdom and keep Elsinore safe. Protect her! When all is safe, protect the throne. You and Elsinore must rule in my stead."

"I am your servant, Milady. You have my vow."

"You must all stand back now." Abelene ordered. She stared at Elsinore with tears in her eyes. "Farewell, dear cousin. I will always remember you."

Abelene raised her hand, facing one of the mirrors. In her hand she held a rather large perfectly shaped crystal. As she invoked the words of release, the crystal began to glow, dim at first, but then with blinding intensity. It cast a beam of light into the mirror facing Abelene. It reflected to the mirror behind and to the left of the sorceress. The beam bounced from mirror to mirror until Abelene was surrounded by light. It grew with intensity, and the room pulsed with power and an audible throbbing.

Finally, Abelene released the final words of the incantation.

"Solvo Letalis Animus." Abelene shrieked as the mirror facing her shattered into thousands of slivers. Her body was drawn into the blast and emerged in an explosion of splintered glass from the opposite mirror, as the shards sliced into her body. Five more times she suddenly emerged from one mirror to be absorbed by the other until she was surrounded by a whirlwind of splintered glass. And just as suddenly, Abelene vanished from the room.

The moving images faded into stillness, and both Azriel and Camille stared at the blank page.

"Abelene went through Hell, Azriel." Camille wiped the remaining tears from her eyes.

"Yeah, I know," he said quietly. "I look at some of the things she had to go through, and my troubles seem rather insignificant."

"I wouldn't say that." She smiled sadly and looked down at her hands. "You're truly remarkable, Azriel."

"So you say, but I feel more like a tool. It's like I have no choice in what I must do. So far, what I've done is child's play compared to what I know is coming."

"Did you ever consider that maybe you were chosen for a reason?"

Azriel laughed sardonically. "Not much choice in that, is there? Something else, though. Did you ever consider that everyone I'm involved with has some part to play in this as well? I know I'm being prepared for this great task. I'm gaining in power; I'm finding the tools I will need to accomplish this end, but it all seems small compared to what I will have to face. I never asked to be some mythical master of time and space. I mean, think about it. What will uniting two separate worlds do to the people who will have to live in this transformed world? All I see is chaos in the aftermath."

"Maybe that's not for you to be concerned about. Perhaps the result will be far different than you expect," Camille offered poetically. "You should be concerned about now. The future will unfold the way it's supposed to, regardless."

"Which has me thinking," Azriel said, a distant look in his eyes. "I still have two names to learn. I think sooner would be better than later. This winter break, I'm going back to the Isle of Man and I'm taking you with me."

Camille gazed at Azriel with what amounted to adoration. "I thought you'd never ask!" she beamed.

"By the way," he added. "I have one more thing to show you."

Camille looked quizzically at Azriel as he reached under the bed. He removed it and laid it gently across Camille's lap.

Her eyes widened. "Is that what I think it is?"

He nodded seriously. "It's the ancestral sword of Eltanin—Errin-lil, the Lightbringer."

Camille gasped in awe to behold such an object of magickal power.

"It's so powerful. I can feel it!"

"Yeah, so can I. The problem is, I have no earthly clue as to what I'm supposed to do with it."

"I'm sure you'll figure it out, won't you Azriel?"

"Hmm," he answered absently as he turned a page in the Book of Aralia. He knitted his brow with consternation. "Wait a minute…"

"What's wrong?" Camille asked.

"This wasn't here before. The page was blank. How can that possibly be?" He posed the question more to himself, not expecting an answer.

"Well, it is a *magickal* book, is it not?"

"Yeah, but…" His words trailed off as he glanced at the text. He began to read silently.

Camille waited for him to read aloud, then finally crossed her arms with annoyance. "I'm still here, Azriel."

"Oh, sorry," he muttered sheepishly. He read the new passage aloud.

"In the year 20,366, the great Sorceress Abelene of House Gorlyn, crossed the chasm of space and time and would have been lost to the void had not the Wizard, Nicodemus read the signs of the prophecies. As a pupil of High Wizard Eltanin, he had studied for six thouand years the codices and ancient scrolls of Thoth to prepare for the day that the future of Aralia and Earth would be sealed. Nicodemus opened the dimensional portal to allow Abelene and her unborn child, the Son of Luminance, through. He, along with the Ancient Order of the Ankh, nursed Abelene back to health and attended to the birth of her son."

Beneath the new text, an emanation of light suddenly swirled and coalesced into the now familiar eye.

"There's definitely something really strange going on." Azriel scowled.

Camille shrugged as if the occurrence was perfectly natural. "Maybe you weren't ready for the message until now. Did you ever consider that?" she said with grave pragmatism.

Azriel sighed. "I guess we should see what it has to tell us."

He placed the tablet on the newly-scribed page, and as before, it began to project new images.

There appeared what seemed to be a massive stone building with a single turreted tower. A wall of mountains surrounded the structure, and strangely, there didn't seem to be any access to it by conventional means. No road from the forbidding mountain range led in and out. Totally isolated, the structure appeared to have risen out of the native rock, which glowed a fiery red in the setting sun. Once behind the craggy peaks, night descended quickly.

Nestled against the tower was a polished stone courtyard, roughly square, carved from the same red rock as the surrounding mountains. But within that square, permanently etched in black, was a circle, and inset within, a pentagram about twenty feet in diameter. Five figures stood at each cardinal point. Azriel gasped in recognition. At the apex of the star stood Nicodemus. He held a black orb that glowed with ruddy golden light, his face intense as he stared with extreme concentration into the stone. Amaryllis stood to his left. In her hand she held a censer, billowing with aromatic smoke. Beside her stood Lady Rosaluna, holding a chalice of water. She looked no older than Azriel was now. Next to Rosaluna, Mr. Parkins as a younger man with all his limbs intact, held a brazier of fire. But beside him stood a mysterious figure. The old man, thin and gaunt, seemed incredibly ancient. His hair, silvery white, hung below his collared robe, and he sported a beard that fell in cascades to his chest. He held a spray of flowers in his hands. The cowled figures faced the center as representatives of the four elements, chanting in a language Azriel now recognized as Aralian. Perfectly centered in the pentacle, a sphere rested on a black velvet cushion. It seemed to be flawless, and began glowing as the chanting built in intensity.

Nicodemus, his face soaked with perspiration, still peered into the black stone he held. "It's time!" he instructed.

The steady chanting continued to build as a palpable pulsing in the air. The words took on a cadence and rhythm that morphed into a harmonic resonance. Nicodemus, at the point of quintessence, the apex of the pentagram, raised his hand and directed the accumulated energy the five were creating into one focused beam of power, and released it with a word onto the perfect crystal sphere in the center. It detonated, spraying the invokers with a rain of fine crystal grains.

Where the sphere had been, now lay Abelene. Nearly dead, her clothes were in tatters. She sprawled in the center of the pentagram, battered and bruised, bloodied from the many cuts and contusions she had received at the culmination of her ritual.

Nicodemus quickly went to Abelene's aid, with Lady Rosaluna and Amaryllis attending to her with purified water, ointments, and bandages. The strange old mystic also knelt next to Abelene and touched her distended belly.

"The child lives." He proclaimed in a deeply melodious voice. "Attend to her." He stood and bowed slightly to Nicodemus, then vanished.

Nicodemus gently lifted Abelene into his arms and carried her inside the tower, where a room had been prepared for her recovery.

She remained unconscious for days on end as Amaryllis and Rosemary attended to her. Her wounds healed quickly, but when she finally awoke, madness had overtaken her as a result of her terrifying experience. Passing through the seven mirrors had left her mind shattered and fragmented, haunted by the horrors she had witnessed in the transition. Only the continued presence of Nicodemus and Amaryllis kept her from going completely insane. Finally, after weeks of nurturing, Abelene's wits returned to her.

The projection shifted, and Abelene was now in the travail of childbirth. She screamed in agony through a difficult delivery. Amaryllis and Rosemary nurtured her through the ordeal, wiping her brow and guiding her through the final moments.

A blanket covered her legs, and Amaryllis waited to receive the child into her arms.

"He's coming! One more push, Abelene. Just one more!"

Her final stores of strength nearly spent, Abelene gave one final shove with a loud groan. Smiling with tears in her eyes, Amaryllis lifted the squalling infant up for Abelene to see. "Look at your beautiful son!" She wrapped the baby in a warm blanket and placed him gently into Abelene's arms.

The travail of giving birth seemed to be quickly forgotten as Abelene stared with adoration into her baby's eyes. He had a shock of black hair and stared back into his mother's face. Abelene smiled with joy. "Your name is Azriel," she cooed.

The projected image faded from view. Azriel stared at the empty space with wonder, but Camille wept openly. She fell into Azriel's arms. "Oh, Azriel," she wiped her eyes on his sleeve. "You were such a beautiful little boy."

Overwhelmed by what he had witnessed, he closed the book. It was enough to digest for one day.

After Camille left, Azriel sat alone in his room, pondering the magnitude and meaning of what he had seen. Abelene was far from ordinary by any stretch of the imagination. It was hard for him to accept that his mother would have gone through so much to preserve Azriel's life. Her sacrifice left Azriel profoundly moved. It also served to steel his resolve to accomplish the tasks set out before him. He vowed to no longer rage against his destiny, but embrace it, to whatever end it would lead to.

Azriel walked down the steps to the living room. Through the open archway to the kitchen, he saw Abelene scurrying about in the act of preparing dinner. She seemed so content to be performing the mundane tasks of domesticity, that Azriel smiled to himself as he watched. She stood over a pan of gravy, humming an old Aralian folk song as she seasoned the mixture and tasted it, assessing the flavor. Her back turned to him, Azriel quietly walked up behind her. When she turned, she nearly dropped the spoon with astonishment. Azriel smiled at her and gave Abelene a strong hug. Surprised at his warmth, Abelene had a bemused look on her face, wondering where this sudden, rare surge of affection stemmed from.

"Is everything okay, son?"

"Never been better." He maintained his hold on her with his cheek against hers. Azriel whispered gently, "I love you, mom. I just needed to tell you."

Gift of the Amulet

298

Chapter 15

Altais stared at the full-length mirror in his hotel room. How he hated this form of travel. Passing through the mirror always left him disoriented and unsettled. Also, there was always the fear that one could get stuck between planes should the sorcerer at the other end lose his concentration, but Rastaban had called for a meeting of the Clave, and his command was not to be ignored without dire consequences. Altais waited impatiently for the mirror to coalesce. Best to get it over with. The others of the Clave would arrive by conventional means or otherwise. As he watched intently, the mirror began to darken and swirl. In turn, Altais motioned with his hands the symbols and sigils required to open the portal. Rastaban stared back at him from the other side, and, bracing himself, Altais stepped through with a shiver.

"Greetings, brother." Rastaban nodded ever so slightly. Thuban, Edasich, Nodus, and Giausur were already seated at the conference table central to the meeting room. As usual, Rastaban seated himself at the head of the table and decanted a drink of fine cognac for the last arrival. Altais took his place at the second position next to Nodus.

Rastaban glanced at all of them, but did not speak. Altais shifted in his seat uncomfortably. Rastaban was obviously troubled by something.

"My Lord?" Nodus broke the silence.

"Of late, I have been deeply disturbed by something," Rastaban began without preface.

"My Lord?" Giausur asked.

"There's something we may have overlooked."

"And what would that be, My Lord?" Thuban questioned anxiously.

"Why is it that for twenty thousand years, we have not located Eltanin? For twenty thousand years we have searched for the reversal spell that would restore the worlds to destroy it, and have not found it. Why?"

"I don't understand your concern, My Lord," Nodus commented.

"Perhaps we've been looking in the wrong place, or maybe it doesn't exist at all." Rastaban mused.

Altais had been listening, chewing on a thumbnail, but said nothing.

"You're strangely silent, my brother," Rastaban said to Altais.

"I've been digging around, as you commanded, my Lord. I may have something useful."

"The boy you've been speaking to?"

"Yes. He's told me some interesting things, not the least of which are his troubles with a classmate who seems to exhibit some unusual powers."

"Speak," Rastaban ordered.

Altais cleared his throat briefly. "About sixteen years ago, we felt the first stirring. We sensed Eltanin's presence for a moment. There was also a surging of power that rippled through the universe and beyond, through the dimensions. We know Eltanin is here. We also know the Son of Luminance dwells on this world. We also know he is well concealed."

"That is old news, my brother." Nodus interjected.

"Ah, so true. But in questioning that boy, Eddie, I've discovered some things. Of course, this Eddie is a dullard and a fool, but he is useful. He trusts me." Altais said with an evil laugh. "Something he said caught my attention. There's one he calls Azriel who lives in the foothills of a place called Harden Lake. Much mystery surrounds him and his mother. They are secretive and reclusive. Then there's the place that surrounds him. There is magick there. It's very subtle, meant to confound the senses. I have not been able to penetrate this magick. It suggests powerful sorcery being used to protect them— human sorcery."

"We're not concerned with human sorcery, Altais." Rastaban scowled.

"Perhaps we should be, my Lord. There was something else the boy mentioned—an uncle by the name of Nick. He seems to be somewhat of an enigma."

"I'm not following." Giausur piped in.

"What if he is that renegade wizard, Nicodemus?"

The ground suddenly shook as the dark dragon imprisoned beneath them stirred. The Clave looked at each other fearfully.

"We killed all the human sorcerers five centuries ago," Nodus said with certainty.

"But Nicodemus was never accounted for. It was never confirmed that we killed him when we destroyed his tower."

"Wrong!" Thuban muttered emphatically. "I was there, Altais. I witnessed with my own eyes when his tower collapsed on him, burying Nicodemus alive. He is dead."

"What if he's not?" Altais countered. "Of all the human sorcerers, he was the most powerful. It would be like him to interfere with our plans. He knew of us. We know he was trained by Eltanin, and he knew our purpose. The stakes are high, my Lord. It would be wise not to ignore this."

Rastaban placed a finger on his beard and tapped thoughtfully. "Perhaps you are right. Our plans could be thwarted by the wrong conclusion." He rose from the table. "I think it is time for us to move forward, Altais." He faced his subordinate. "I want you to take the boy, Eddie, into your confidence. Don't reveal too much; show him some of your powers—nothing special, of course, but give him something to think about. You may find out more. Meanwhile, it is time to face the dragon. He may know something we do not."

Altais' face blanched. "No, my Lord. It is too dangerous. Our grasp on him grows tenuous."

Rastaban chuckled. "Your fears are unfounded. Our grip on him has never been stronger."

A single vault separated the council chamber from the caverns below. No key could unlock the massive door; only a word from Rastaban would break the seal. The Arch Wizard muttered an incantation, one the rest of the Clave knew, but would never dare to use. The vault door opened with a creaking groan and Rastaban led the way down to the hidden cave below.

It was a dark and foreboding place. With a thought, Rastaban ignited the torches strategically placed in sconces along the way. The stairway, partially man-carved and in other sections natural, led down to the deepest chamber in the subterranean caves. As they approached, ruddy light emanated from the vast opening. A piteous roar shook the walls, and sulfurous fumes nearly bowled them over as Rastaban faced the dragon.

It was black as uncut jet, towering above the frightened wizards. Its venomous yellow eyes darted from one to the other with burning contempt, but its eyes finally rested on Rastaban with such malignant hatred that any normal man, wizard, or otherwise, would have withered with fear. The only thing that protected them from the dragon's wrath was a towering transparent pyramid that kept the dragon contained. Around his neck and left ankle, a glowing chain kept him bound. One flaw, however, marred the dragon's perfection. A single scale torn from his broad chest still bled from a battle that took place eons ago. It was that flaw that weakened the dragon and kept him vulnerable.

Rastaban removed a small crystal pyramid from his pocket and toyed with it as he spoke. "I require information," he said with deference.

"The day of your doom approaches, Rastaban—for you and your Clave of wizards." The dragon's voice was surprisingly rich and melodious. "It was only by chance that you captured me. Your power is not as great as mine."

Rastaban smiled. "Trickery or not, you are mine to command."

"Ah, yes. Indeed, it is as you say," the dragon mocked him. "But I am patient. And I still function as creation would have it. You have not defeated me, Rastaban. The laws of death and decay have not been broken, as is my purpose. My prison is only temporary. And when I am released, you will learn fully how those laws of death apply to you."

"Empty words, I think. These walls and chains have bound you for many eons, and for many more they will hold you firm."

The dragon laughed with contempt. "I grow tired of this conversation, Rastaban." The dragon sat on his haunches and folded his leathery wings. "Now, what do you want?"

"I want the name of the Child of Luminance."

"It is forbidden for me to speak it. No amount of compulsion you could cast upon me would cause me to speak the name. Even if I could, I would not give up a brother."

"A brother, you say?"

The dark beast smiled in the fashion of dragons. "You would be wise to fear him, Rastaban. His arrival spells your doom."

"Words, I think," Rastaban taunted.

"Leave me, or release me. I grow weary of you. Be warned, Rastaban. The day approaches. You will be stripped of all power; you will be consumed by despair. And when that day comes, I will not stay my fury upon you. I will consume your soul and consign it to oblivion!"

"So you have said before," Rastaban smirked. He turned purposely and would have departed, but the dragon spoke again.

"Heed my words, Arch Wizard. When you think you are closest to victory is when you will face your bitterest defeat. I look forward to the day."

The words of prophecy resonated through Rastaban's heart. He would have ignored it altogether, had it not kindled something he had never experienced before—doubt. With a snarl of frustration, he departed the chamber with the Clave following closely behind. Altais breathed a sigh of relief.

Christmas vacation was still a week away, and Azriel looked forward to a few weeks off from school. So far, the first few months of tenth grade had flown by with few problems, except for a run-in with Eddie and his two goons, Bernie and Cory, the day before. Strangely, Dirk didn't seem to be part of his entourage anymore. Not that Azriel was surprised. Left to himself, Azriel found Dirk to be a decent sort. On more than one occasion, they had spoken, cautiously at first. Once, Azriel was even so bold as to ask why he wasn't part of Eddie's gang anymore. Dirk was quite candid about wanting to avoid trouble. He had noticed of late that Eddie was becoming more erratic every day, and didn't need the hassle. Dirk had a future to think about, and being friends with Eddie would only screw it up. In the end, he decided that distancing himself from his former friend was in his best interest.

As to Eddie, Azriel's last encounter with him started with words and led to blows. Although witnesses had seen Eddie throw the first punch, Azriel, Jasper, and Albert had to serve a week of detention anyway. Not that he minded. Eddie sucker punched Azriel as he turned away, trying to avoid yet another run-in. He responded immediately, and it turned into a brawl, with Jasper and Albert beating the crap out of Cory and Bernie while Azriel went ballistic on Eddie. What Eddie had in sheer bulk and brawn, Azriel, the smaller of the two, made up for it with speed and agility. All the past couple of years, holding in his anger exploded into rage, and he beat Eddie senseless. Later, he was sorry for losing control. It had never happened before. Worse, Azriel knew that it wouldn't be the end of it. Things would certainly escalate. Yet serving a week of detention for fighting was a small price to pay for the satisfaction of finally putting Eddie in his place.

Camille hated fighting, and even tried to break up the fight before it started, but Julia pulled her to safety. Inwardly, though, she was quite proud of Azriel and looked at him in a new light. Later that evening at his house, Camille applied cold compresses to his bruised face, while Abelene paced the floor, trying to suppress her anger.

Azriel argued, "Mom, what was I supposed to do? He struck me without warning. Sometimes things are just unavoidable."

"Abelene, it wasn't his fault," Camille added.

"Azriel, I got a call from the boy's mother. You broke his nose."

"Yeah, well, I should have broken more than that!"

"Azriel!" Abelene shouted. "Fighting never solves anything!"

"So, what was I supposed to do? Let him get away with it?"

Abelene pulled at her own hair and growled with frustration. "Next time he threatens you, turn him into a toad!"

"Mom," Azriel said evenly. "Isn't that just a bit cliché?"

Camille let out an involuntary giggle.

Abelene stared at her son with displeasure but suddenly broke out in laughter at her own silliness. "Oh, dear me, what am I going to do with you, Azriel?" she said with resignation. "Next time, don't use your face to stop a fist. You have much too handsome a face to have it marred by some idiot."

"Oh, Mom. Will you stop!" Azriel moaned.

"Abelene's right, Azriel. You do have quite a handsome face." She kissed his bruises enthusiastically as he squirmed with agitation.

"Geez, Uncle Nick was right about women. You're all nuts!"

Abelene and Camille glanced at each other and smiled.

The week passed by quickly. Azriel was released from detention a day early, and hurried home. He was more excited than he had been for some time. All arrangements were made for Camille and Jasper to accompany him and Abelene to the Isle of Man. Rosemary already knew to expect them, and would have her doors locked and window curtains drawn against prying eyes. Azriel's bag was already packed, and he waited impatiently for Camille to arrive. There was a knock on the door, but to his surprise, Uncle Nick stood at the doorway, grinning broadly.

"I've decided to come with you. Besides, I need to speak with Amaryllis," Nicodemus stated sagely.

"Good!" Abelene beamed. "Yule just isn't the same without you, Nicodemus." She kissed him warmly on the cheek. With the front door slightly ajar, Camille was the next to enter. She carried a satchel filled with clothing and Yule presents. Her face glowed with anticipation.

"Well, it looks like we're all here," Abelene said. She turned to Jasper. "How did Albert take it?"

"You know Albert. He's feeling a bit put out about the whole thing, but he *did* plan a date for the holidays. He'd been working on Becky Stouse for months. She finally agreed to go out with him. Cancelling the date to come with us would not have gone over very well. Tough choice, I guess." Jasper shrugged.

"Indeed," Abelene smiled. "Affairs of the heart often win out."

Azriel produced the dream orb from his pocket. "Is everyone ready?"

They all nodded. Azriel closed his eyes, remembering every detail of Rosemary's shop, and implanted the image into the orb. He examined the crystal carefully to make sure he hadn't omitted any detail. Nicodemus and Abelene stood close, and Camille had her arm locked with Azriel's.

"Hold my hand, Jasper," Abelene ordered amicably.

As one, Azriel, Abelene, and Uncle Nick touched the dream orb, and moments later they all arrived at Rosemary's shop.

"Wow, what a rush!" Jasper gasped.

The shop was festively arranged with garlands of spruce and twinkling lights. In the corner, a beautiful Christmas tree overflowed with crystal ornaments and stacks of presents. Rosemary had dressed in a deep crimson velvet gown with white lace brocade. Atop her head was a crown of holly supporting four lit candles. Beside her stood Mr. Parkins in his finest suit. Amaryllis, Billy, and Muriel waited behind them.

"Happy Yule!" they cried out cheerfully.

Muriel flew into Jasper's arms and hugged him. "I've missed ye, Jasper." She examined his face and then Azriel's. Their bruises had faded somewhat, but were still visible. She knitted her eyebrows as her smile faded. "Ye've been scrappin' haven't ye! Now how are we supposed to take a proper holiday picture with ye lookin' all battered?" She crossed her arms sternly. "Let me look at ye in the light." She dragged him over to the Christmas tree and took him by the chin, moving his head this way and that. "Nice shiner, ye got there! Now I won't be havin' yer brains scrambled into mush, don't ye know. So ye stop those fisticuffs, Jasper Cunningham!"

Jasper smiled with chagrin and wanted to kiss her, even with watchful eyes around him. Yet he refrained. He didn't want to be unseemly. But Muriel was certainly cute when she got cross. Jasper couldn't resist. He kissed her tenderly on the cheek.

"Now don't ye try to be butterin' me up, Mr. Cunningham!" She folded her arms again indignantly. Muriel's golden curls bobbed merrily, and her dimpled cheeks glowed as everyone laughed at her.

"Come," Rosemary beamed. "We have holiday nog." She doled out cups of creamy eggnog, spiked with brandy, and they all toasted their reunion. Azriel glanced at the festive room and noticed a tank with a fish swimming lazily. He walked over with Camille and peered into it. Rosemary joined him. "The little beastie has grown since the last time ye were here. I think I'll need a bigger tank soon!"

"Did you ever figure it out yet?" Azriel inquired.

Rosemary looked at him, puzzled.

"The fish. What does it mean?"

"I'm not sure, really. It would seem that you've presented me with an enigma far greater than the one I provided for you," she said lightly.

The following day was Christmas Eve, and the Town of Castleton was atwitter with activity. Festive lights hung from every home and shop. Castle Rushin was well lit with a massive tree decorated in the courtyard. People scurried about to finish their last-minute shopping. Joyful smiles lit every stranger's face as they rushed from shop to shop. Abelene didn't mind helping Rosemary tend to her store, hosting more than the usual customers, and in fact she proved to be quite a crafty negotiator.

It left Azriel and Jasper a full afternoon to see that Camille and Muriel were well entertained. A pleasant snow began to fall, and they spent about an hour gawking at window displays and enjoying their time together.

Nestled in a corner of the town, a small welcoming inn looked like the perfect place to eat.

"Hey, why don't we stop here?" Jasper offered.

"Oh, no. Ye don't want to be goin' in there," Muriel countered. Azriel suppressed a smile, remembering.

"Why not? It looks cozy." Jasper pressed the issue.

"Me father owns it. Now, unless ye want to be answerin' twenty questions and be badgered the entire time we're there, then I would suggest we find somewhere more suitable to eat."

"How about there?" Camille pointed to a sign that read, *The Green Dragon.*

"No, I wouldn't suggest that place either. The bloke that owns it is me father's sworn enemy. He'd probably poison the food!"

"Okay, so why don't you pick the place?" Jasper smiled.

They followed Muriel down a narrow alley into a small café and seated themselves at a cozy booth. It seemed to cater to a younger crowd and a few of the young men and women waved a greeting to Muriel.

They all ordered a hearty stew, piping hot cider, and began to eat. Muriel conspicuously held onto Jasper's hand. A brief glance and nod to Azriel attested to the fact that he was quite pleased and more than a little smitten. And Muriel made no pretense that she already considered Jasper as *hers*.

"So what's next?" Muriel said between spoonfuls of the delicious stew.

"Well…" Azriel answered thoughtfully. "My being here isn't just a pleasure trip."

"Oh?" Camille looked up, fixing her eyes on Azriel.

He gave a wan smile. "I've realized I need to be prepared for whatever comes next—whatever that is. You see, Muriel, I know now that learning the names of the Elementals really isn't about the names themselves, not that they aren't important. But it's more about understanding their nature. Each time I earned the right to a name, I learned the inner workings of what they represent. They can be used, with respect, of course, to my advantage when I need them."

"That's pretty intense, Azriel." Jasper said seriously.

"Don't I know it!" he replied with enthusiasm. "There's more though. When the worlds were torn apart, creating two dimensions, the damage wasn't just superficial. Both worlds are wounded, lacking in vitality. Neither world can defend against the intrusions of their inhabitants. There's more at stake than you can imagine! By understanding Earth and Water, I know now that both worlds are losing the ability to heal themselves. If Aralia and Gaia are not reunited soon, both will be damaged beyond repair."

"Gaia?" Jasper asked.

The waiter appeared and refilled their glasses with hot cider. Azriel lowered his voice.

"Gaia is the true name of this world. It suggests a living organism, not just some dead thing to exploit. I can't speak for Aralia because I don't know what's going on there, but I do know what's going on here—and it's not very good. Humans certainly have needs, but more and more, Gaia is stressed beyond endurance to provide for her children. The majority of humans are clueless, taking what they can for personal gain without giving much back. And I think everyone here understands that by having learned the laws of high magick. It's about giving back and being aware of the laws of nature."

"Spoken like a true scholar!"

"Pog!" Azriel exclaimed.

The little man stood at the head of the table and smiled broadly at Azriel.

"I sensed ye were back, laddie. All I had to do was follow me nose."

Azriel had a bemused look on his face and sniffed absently at his shirt, checking for any odor. "Why didn't you come yesterday to Rosemary's shop?" he asked.

"Er—I was a mite busy, laddie."

"Well, my mom is only two streets over. You can finally meet her."

"Um—no." Pog stroked his beard. "Can't stay but for a wee bit of ale. Hello Muriel," he changed the subject. "And who's this strapping lad I see ye holdin' on to so tightly?"

She blushed. "This is Jasper. He's my—friend." Muriel smiled broadly. "And also, a new recruit to the order."

"Ye don't say? Well, welcome aboard, laddie." Pog shook his hand. "Er…would ye be so kind as to slide over and let an old man rest his keester?"

Muriel nodded graciously and squeezed close to Jasper. Pog sat next to her and ordered a tankard of ale. "Now who's this lovely lass?"

"I'm Camille, sir."

"Sir! Oh, my! I like this one, Azriel."

Camille suppressed a giggle. "Azriel's told me a lot about you."

"All bad, I'd be certain." He took a deep quaff from his tankard.

"Well, not all of it." Camille's eyes twinkled with mischief.

"Ah, a lass after me own heart! Let me know if Azriel ever dumps you. I'll be waitin' next in line."

"Pog! You're disgusting!" Muriel scolded.

"Aye, yer right, lass, yer right."

"Well, for your information, I think you'll be waiting an extremely long time, Pog," Azriel said as Camille looked down, her face aglow from all the attention.

"Aye," Pog sighed dramatically. "Tis a sad fate for me not to have the comfort and charm of such a lovely lass in me old age." Pog drained the rest of his ale and squelched a burp. "Well, best be off. Just one thing, Azriel. I expect to see you in two days. You know where I'll be. Oh, and bring this lovely young lady, with ye. There's some discussin' we need to do."

Christmas came and went. Aside from the usual celebrating and festivities associated with the holiday, Azriel spent much of the day going over a few things in his mind. For one, Pog seemed to go out of his way to avoid meeting Abelene. There was something strange and mysterious about it, and Azriel considered broaching the subject with his mentor. What was it about Abelene that seemed to make Pog scarce every time there was an opportunity to introduce them? Azriel glowered, a little hurt by Pog's avoidance since he had grown quite fond of the little troll for all his quirks and faults. But if it weren't for Pog, Azriel would still be a neophyte in the Magickal arts. The little guy had taught him much, and Azriel had no doubt that he would learn much more from his mentor.

Camille and Azriel spent Christmas with Amaryllis and Felisa. Jasper, however, was absent from the gathering since he had been invited to Muriel's for the holiday meal. Jasper spent the morning fretting over the whole affair and how awkward it would be, but Abelene instructed him in etiquette, and even helped him pick out gifts for Muriel's family.

Abelene was happy to help with preparing the holiday feast. Felisa, however, insisted on seasoning the goose and cooking it since it was her prowess that provided the meal. She took particular pride in having stalked and landed the bird herself. Nicodemus, as was his habit, produced two bottles of particularly fine wine from his private cellar. They all ate the scrumptious meal and had their fill of dressing, smothered in rich gravy with mashed potatoes and leeks. Abelene cooked a delicious mince pie and a plum pudding. Desserts, as always, were her specialty.

Azriel rested on the couch. "I'm stuffed," he said with contentment. Uncle Nick dozed in the easy chair, snoring noisily, much to everyone's amusement.

Camille, Felisa and Azriel enjoyed each other's company, playing a game of producing the most outrageous illusions they could conceive of while Abelene and Amaryllis talked quietly among themselves.

Later that evening, everyone retired to bed. Azriel was amused by the fact that no matter how many guests Amaryllis had, there always seemed to be ample room in her cottage for separate sleeping arrangements. Azriel supposed that since the house was, in itself, magickal, all Amaryllis needed to do was create the extra rooms as needed.

Camille yawned and kissed Azriel on the cheek before heading to her assigned room. Having nestled into a comfortable bed, Azriel lay awake for a while. He reached into his backpack and removed a small velvet bag. It contained the crystal he had found several months before. He intended to ask Pog about it and perhaps get a clue as to its purpose. He removed it carefully from the bag to avoid being cut by the sharp edges. It glowed with a deep blue aura as Azriel stared into the pristine rock formation, yet it seemed to have little if no weight to it at all. He placed it back in the velvet pouch and placed it on the night table. He fell into a restful, dream-filled sleep.

After a hearty breakfast prepared by Felisa, Azriel and Camille were ready to embark on the short journey to the Fairy Bridge, where Azriel knew he would find Pog waiting for them. The morning was cold, bright, and crisp as they left the house. Camille squinted at the massive stone, well camouflaged by Amaryllis' magick. No one would ever suspect that it was a home.

"That's really quite remarkable," Camille commented.

Azriel mused. "I know what you mean. It's funny, though. Nothing really surprises me anymore." He breathed deeply, tasting the salty tang of the air. The waves were unusually turbulent this day, and their crash and boom on the shore were almost deafening.

Camille snuggled up next to Azriel. "I'm freezing." She shivered even though she wore a heavy hooded coat lined with white fleece. The ocean air was just too cold and damp.

"We should go then," Azriel said, then produced the dream orb from his pocket. He implanted the image of the Fairy Bridge into the crystal, and with a touch, transported immediately to the foot of the bridge.

They found Pog skating on the frozen river beneath. He wore a floppy red stocking cap and a red and white striped scarf. He was busily scribing circles on the ice, whistling merrily, oblivious to their presence. Or at least it seemed so.

"Ah, laddie and little lass, come join me for a wee bit of fun," he said without looking at them.

"But we have no skates!" Camille called out.

"Hmm, that's where ye would be wrong, lass."

Camille looked down at her feet. She and Azriel were now inexplicably wearing nicely fitting skates. They gingerly stepped onto the ice, testing it for strength, holding onto each other for dear life.

"Now, don't ye be worryin' lass. Ol' Pog won't let anything untoward be happinin' to ye."

Azriel had some experience skating, having had some tentative overtures to playing hockey, but found he much preferred baseball. Camille, however, had never been on skates and held firmly onto Azriel's hand. She almost slipped and fell, nearly pulling Azriel down onto the ice in the process. He caught her in his arms, their faces close. Camille giggled. It was all so ridiculous, floundering on the ice. But her laughter and close proximity were infectious and Azriel couldn't contain his own laughter.

"You're making fun of me." Camille blushed and smiled, gazing into Azriel's eyes as Pog circled around them, executing a perfect axel. Azriel was, for some strange reason, unaware of anything but Camille. He felt a strong stirring in his heart and kissed her tenderly on the lips. When their lips parted, Camille's breath came in short gasps, overwhelmed by his affection.

"What was that for?"

"Well…" Azriel turned his face away and blushed a deep crimson; his words caught in his mouth.

"Ahh, young love. It just warms me heart!" Pog skated past them with his hands behind his back. Azriel and Camille stared at each other and blushed further before letting the moment pass. By the time a half hour passed, Camille was getting the hang of skating and even managed to maintain her balance unaided a few times, but she still preferred holding onto Azriel's hand—not necessarily for steadiness.

"Had enough?" Pog seemed to float backward on the ice as he flew past them.

"Yeah, I think Camille is starting to turn blue," Azriel answered.

She was almost sorry to stop—the afterglow of Azriel's kiss still fixed in her heart—but she was indeed chilled to the bone.

"Well, we best be goin' then!" Pog produced a wand, and with a flick, they were immediately transported to his home. A cheerful fire blazed in the hearth, and three mugs of hot cocoa sat on the table along with a tray of delectable pastries. The warmth was welcoming and Camille sighed with contentment as she removed her coat.

Pog, ever the gracious host, bowed flamboyantly. "Help yerself to some sweets, Milady."

Camille giggled self-consciously at all his doting.

"Now, yer probably wonderin' why ol' Pog here would want to be talkin' to ye, lass."

"The thought has crossed my mind," Camille smiled.

"Truth be told, I want to see just how committed ye are to what's needin' to be done. Er' laddie, would ye give me and the lass a moment?"

"Pog, is this entirely necessary?" Azriel asked protectively.

"Now don't ye be concernin' yerself, laddie. The little lady is completely safe in me company. Ye need to be concernin' yerself with that er—crystal yer hiding in yer pocket there. Five rooms back is me library. Perhaps ye should be startin' there. And if I catch ye eavesdroppin', I'll make yer ears ten times bigger than they already are!"

Camille held her hand to her mouth to hide a laugh.

"Fine then," Azriel grumbled to himself as he left the room.

"Now that that's out of the way, I need to be askin' ye some questions, all right, lass?"

"Okay." Camille sipped her hot cocoa and peered over her cup. This all seemed very strange.

"Ye sure you know what yer getting' yerself into, girl?" Pog's demeanor suddenly changed. Gone was the jovial little troll. His face became troubled and serious. "Being involved in Azriel's destiny could be dangerous to ye, lass."

"I know," she answered pensively.

"How *much* do ye know?"

"Enough. Azriel is fated to restore the two worlds into one. He must raise the Elementals—release them from their entrapment. He also will have to face the Clave and bring about their ruin. It scares me, Pog. I'm not sure he's ready or if I am." Tears came to her eyes. "Sometimes he seems so strong, and yet at other times, so vulnerable."

"There's something else ye need to know, dearie."

"And what is that?"

"The Clave has the Dark Dragon of Death entrapped. They use his power for their evil purposes. Eventually, Azriel will have to face the dragon."

Camille's hands began to shake. "Don't you think I already know that?" She spoke through her tears.

"Ye need to hear it all, lass. The Clave is very powerful; they will use anything to get to him, including you."

Camille held her hand to her mouth and sobbed.

Pog closed his eyes and tilted his head as if listening to some unseen voice. He took her hand in his and patted it gently. "I sense somethin'. Aye, I do. Somethin' yer not telling me."

She nodded mutely. "Last year, Abelene was giving instruction on seeing into the past using a scrying mirror. But I've been scrying since I was nine. So I used it to look into the future. There I saw…I saw…" She looked up miserably with tears streaming down her face. "I saw my death."

Pog's eyes softened with compassion.

"The future is a very shadowy place. One can never really know it for certain."

"But I saw it. I'm going to die."

"Then why don't ye distance yerself, lass? Stay out of danger."

"I can't."

"And why is that?" Pog's eyes bore into hers.

"Because I love him."

"Not good enough, lass," he said firmly.

"Yes it is!" she argued, suddenly angry. "If I only have a little time left, I'd rather spend it with Azriel, than be apart from him. I don't know why I know this, but in the end, he will need me."

Pog looked down with resignation. "Aye, lass," he spoke almost in a whisper. "Perhaps, in the end, he will." He sighed heavily. "I would have spared you the heartache; prevent ye from bein' part of his destiny, but there is great power in love. It goes beyond conventional wisdom." Pog laughed ruefully. "Ye may not know this, but it was love that caused this whole mess in the first place."

"I don't understand," Camille wiped her eyes with a sleeve.

"Ye see, lass, Eltanin shattered the worlds not out of malice, as the book of Aralia would have ye believe, but out of love for all creatures. When he realized the deception and evil intent of the Clave, how could Eltanin have allowed all humanity to be consigned to the void? They would have perished. And it wouldn't merely have been death of the body, but an annihilation of the soul, Eltanin's included. He did what he had to do to save them. This, ol' Pog is certain of."

"I do understand, Pog. It's for the very same reason that I can't abandon Azriel to his fate. For whatever end, for whatever destiny Azriel must face, I must face it with him."

"It is as ye say, lass. But I needed to be sure. Ye see, Camille. Azriel is Ferrishyn—Elvenkind. You are human. Maybe it all does make sense." Pog thought pensively, digesting that bitter morsel. "Maybe you are part of this for that reason. Together, you are stronger because of the difference."

Pog rose from his chair. He gestured with his hand. "Come with me, would ye, lass?"

Camille followed the old gnome throughout his tunneled house. She found Azriel immersed in an old volume. So engrossed in studying the text, he nearly jumped when Camille and Pog entered the library.

She sat next to him while Pog perused the shelves, looking through the scrolls and volumes of books, searching for a particular volume.

"Are you all right?" Azriel inquired of Camille.

"I'm fine." She answered, but Azriel wasn't convinced.

"You seem upset."

"No, I'm okay. What are you reading?" She changed the subject.

"I found this book on the Elementals. It says a lot about Air. It says here that Air is the embodiment of communication and wisdom. To understand Air is to understand the power of mind, thought, and word. It is the soul and breath of life. Here's something interesting." Azriel bookmarked a page. He removed the velvet bag from his pocket and lowered the cloth from its contents, being careful not to touch the sharp edges it protected. Camille's eyes widened. The crystal formation glowed slightly over its blue surface. Camille, with curiosity, reached to touch it, but it resisted her attempt, repelling her hand away.

"That's very strange."

"I'm the only one who can touch it," Azriel sighed.

"What is it?"

"Well, according to this book, it's called an Æther stone. They are fairly common in Aralia, but extremely rare on Earth."

"What is it used for?"

"It says here that the crystal doesn't form by conventional means, but is the embodiment of Air. It has practically no weight, see?"

Azriel carefully lifted the Æther stone about two feet off the table and dropped it. Camille gasped, fully expecting the stone to drop and shatter. Instead, it floated back down onto the velvet bag.

Azriel continued. "It also says that it has only one purpose, that is, to grant knowledge to one who is worthy. It chooses the seeker and will only be released with that person's touch."

"How did you come by it?"

"Uncle Nick brought me to a cave he had hidden over a hundred years ago. He couldn't touch the stone; neither could my mother. But when I reached for it, the stone just dropped into my hand. It cut me too." Azriel smiled, remembering how it had absorbed his blood. "I guess I imprinted on the stone, or maybe it imprinted on me!"

"It works both ways, laddie." Pog returned to the table holding a small black book embossed with arcane symbols on the cover. He sat across from Azriel and Camille.

"Here ye go, lass." He slid the book over to her. "Ye need to learn everything on these pages. Those spells will protect yer person. But I warn ye, they are not to be used frivolously. They are powerful, but they can be dangerous if'n ye don't know what yer doin'. As a matter of fact, it wouldn't hurt ye to work on these together. When push comes to shove, simple illusion spells won't really help ye at all except fer yer personal entertainment."

Camille looked at Azriel with a wry expression. She waved her hand and produced a fluffy bunny rabbit from thin air. It scampered about the air and planted a kiss on Azriel's cheek.

"Charming," Pog grumbled, his tone flat. He flicked his finger and a giant carrot appeared. As the bunny scampered up to it and began nibbling, the thing sprouted claws and fangs. It chased after the rabbit, terrorizing the poor creature.

"Pog!" Camille screamed, aghast. "That was really mean!"

Azriel suppressed a laugh and Camille scowled at him with disapproval.

"Now it's time for yer next task, though I suspect you'll find it easily. Come," Pog motioned, "Come, come! Oh, and bring that crystal. Yer goin' to need it."

It seemed Pog's underground home went on forever. Camille and Azriel followed Pog through a confusing maze of tunnels that seemed to zigzag through small caves and dimly lit barrows. The tunnel finally ended at a small wooden beamed door. When he opened it Camille gasped in delight. Impossible though it seemed, a beautiful landscape was spread out before them. Cascades of purple wisteria hung from ancient trees. The vista spread out before them in magnificent displays of color. The lush green countryside was like something out of a dream. Central to the garden, a delicate gazebo beckoned invitingly.

"Pog, how is this possible? It's still winter here!" Camille said breathlessly.

"Aye, indeed. The question ye may be wantin' to ask yerself is where exactly is here?"

"But..." Azriel gaped.

"Ye don't know?" Pog smiled broadly. "Well neither do I! Just accept it, laddie, and enjoy yerself. I'll be leaving now. Ye might want to leave yer doubts at the door!"

With that, they stepped through the entry and Pog closed it behind him. The sun shone down on them warming their faces.

"It's enchanting!" Camille beamed.

"I think it *is* enchanted." Azriel took her hand and they ran happily toward the glistening white gazebo. There was a marble table central to the lacey structure filled with bowls of exotic fruits and berries. All kinds of tasty treats were laid out for the taking.

"Oh, my!" Camille giggled. "Should we eat it?"

"Pog did say to enjoy ourselves. Why would he want to trick us?"

"What if it's all an illusion?" she asked.

Azriel picked up a fruit that seemed somewhat akin to a peach. "It sure feels real enough," he said and bit into it. A look of pleasure filled his face. Wow this is amazing! Have a taste."

"She bit into it gingerly at first, but then with more relish. "*I don't think I've ever tasted anything so wonderful.*"

Camille looked up at Azriel wide-eyed. She hadn't spoken, but Azriel heard her as clear as if she had. Not quite believing, he tested, "*Did you speak?*"

"*No, I only thought it.*"

"*Remarkable.*"

The more they indulged in the feast, their minds became increasingly open to each other until they were communicating easily without speaking.

Although the table was laden with more than they could possibly consume, with a sudden insight Azriel understood that it would be wrong to ingest more than they needed. Sated and content, they decided to explore the vast glade. The carpet of green grass seemed to go on forever and the sweet fragrance of the place overwhelmed their senses.

"*I sure wish we had a blanket.*" Azriel thought.

Camille smiled. She had been thinking the same thing. They continued walking hand in hand and came over a rise into a nestled valley. Lying on the grass, a soft quilt had been laid out.

"*That's really weird.*" Camille stared at it. "*I'm sure that wasn't here before!*"

"*Shall we?*" Azriel motioned with his hand.

They seated themselves opposite each other and breathed in the view.

"What do we do now?" Camille spoke.

Azriel answered. "I'm not sure, but I think I'm supposed to use the crystal for something. He removed it from its velvet pouch and placed it between them, but then he suddenly became aware of something. The crystal, which previously had no substantial weight, had now become quite heavy when it made contact with the blanket."

"Very strange." He examined it closely. A faint humming seemed to be coming from the crystal directed at Azriel's mind.

"I hear it too, Azriel." Without thinking, Camille picked up the rock formation and held it to her ear. Azriel gaped at her.

"You shouldn't be able to do that!"

Camille stared at the rock and then at her own flesh with a sudden insight. Like Azriel, her skin was beginning to exhibit a distinct luminosity.

"It's this place. I'm certain of it." She gently placed the crystal back on the blanket and walked toward the tree shading them. She placed her hand on the deep textured bark but found that her hand easily passed through it. She wasn't at all troubled by it. For this place, wherever it was, it seemed natural.

"I think I understand." Azriel stared up at Camille amazed. "The stone is solid to our touch because like it, we have become Æther, sort of like spirits. How else could I understand the Air Element without becoming part of it?"

Camille sat again on the blanket, and like Azriel, stared at the stone. The humming sound became more pronounced, almost musical, though without any melody or cadence. Soon they became entranced by the Æther stone, yet it was in no way unpleasant. It was in fact soothing, comforting. The tones filled their minds until their souls were merged with the stone. It was peaceful and seemed to fill them both with a deep longing. Oddly, the sensing went beyond mere thought, but was a knowing and awareness further than normal comprehension. Azriel was inexplicably feeling Camille's emotions.

When she looked up at Azriel, her face was beatific, transformed serenely into a sort of quiet ecstasy.

"*I love you, Azriel.*" Her thoughts filled his mind and heart. There was such a look of longing on Camille's face that Azriel stroked her cheek tenderly.

"*Go on. Say it.*" He heard a voice in his mind. It wasn't Camille's, nor was it his own. It seemed neither male nor female, but a blending of both. Perplexed, he looked down at the stone.

"*Yes?*" it answered.

"Are you really speaking?"

"Why of course." The Æther stone answered with what amounted to amusement.

"How is it that I can hear you?"

"That's simple, really. It's just that you've only now begun to listen." It replied with humor. *"You must seize the moment, Azriel. Tell her the truth. You've put it off long enough."*

Azriel took Camille's hand in his and smiled shyly.

"Camille, I love you, too. I have for some time now." His words bore into her heart. The admission he denied for so long filled her to overflowing. Reaching forward, her eyes glistening, Camille kissed him.

They held onto each other for what seemed hours, though they sensed timelessness in this enchanted place. It could have been minutes or days. They spoke quietly, but suddenly they were overwhelmed by a deep somnolence and a sense of peace. They fell asleep wrapped in each other's arms with the crystal lying between them.

Azriel slept peacefully, more restfully than he had in months.

He stood by a brook and a celebration of mythical proportions seemed to be taking place. Beyond the green-carpeted lawn, a structure, for what could only amount as a high spired castle, loomed before them. Glistening white, the majestic towers reached toward the clouds. Azriel was surrounded by people he had never met, but his senses told him that he should know them somehow. Looking down at his garb, he was finely dressed in a white tunic and leggings with a superbly crafted belt. Attached to it firmly, the sword, Errin-lil hung at his side. Draped over his shoulders, a deep blue cape lined with ermine hung below his waist. From all areas of the vast lawn, tables had been set up overflowing with fine food and pitchers of wine. Many well-wishers greeted Azriel enthusiastically, some of whom he recognized as departed ancestors. Happily, they bade him welcome as if he had come home from an extended journey. To his astonishment, Camille approached, magnificently arrayed in a dazzling yellow gown. Her raven hair was bedecked with flowers cascading down to the small of her back. And like

Azriel, she wore a deep blue cape on her shoulders. Camille was being led by a complement of maidens toward him. She beamed a smile at Azriel, and he thought his heart would burst out of his chest.

As they stood together, an old man came toward the couple. From his bearing, Azriel resisted the sudden urge to bow in deference to the mythic figure. He stood tall and erect, in defiance of his perceived years. Incredibly old, yet with a vitality that challenged reason, the ancient one faced them with kindly eyes. He emanated peace and tranquility as he raised his right hand in blessing. In his left, he held a gleaming staff fashioned from a metal that reflected purple in the afternoon sun. Encased on the top of the staff sat a black orb held in place by cleverly crafted aspen leaves. The orb glowed with golden fire at its core, much like the stone embedded in the pommel of Azriel's sword. Azriel was sure he had seen this ancient one before. The old one had been present when Abelene had translated from Aralia to Earth. Azriel had seen it in the Book of Aralia.

The ancient one raised his hands and the crowd hushed to silence. He gently ordered Azriel and Camille to kneel.

Smiling serenely, the old one finally spoke. "Azriel of Aralia, rule over your kingdom with peace and wisdom." He placed a delicate crown on Azriel's head. "Rise, King of Aralia."

Azriel stood feeling a bit abashed by the whole display, but the ceremony wasn't over. There suddenly appeared an unusual personage. Tiny by comparison to Azriel and Camille, she was slender and lithe. Though youthful in appearance, the fairy had flowing white hair framing a cherubic face, but her intelligent eyes glowed with blue fire. Her body was covered in a wispy dress that ended at her knees, but her most unusual feature was a pair of gossamer wings, much like that of a dragonfly protruding from her shoulders. In her hands she held a silver circlet that glowed with the same indigo argent sheen in which Azriel was familiar. She handed the crown to Azriel.

The old one spoke again. "Azriel of Aralia, will you accept Camille of Earth as your queen?"

"I will." He said solemnly as he placed the delicate crown on her head.

The ancient one smiled. "Then I bid you rise, Camille, Queen of Aralia."

Azriel awoke still holding Camille as they lay on the comfortable blanket. He stared into her face, so close to his. When she opened her eyes, they were glazed over with tears.

"Oh, Azriel! I'm overwhelmed! I don't know what to say!" They gazed into each other's face with the sudden realization that they had shared in a dream.

"Did we dream of the future?" Camille whispered.

"I don't know." Azriel answered with a sense of wonder.

"It is the future that awaiteth you, shouldst thou complete thy task, Son of Luminance." The voice came from above them. It sounded familiar—the same layered voice that Azriel heard from the Æther stone. He looked down at the blanket, and to his astonishment, the crystal had disappeared. Azriel and Camille turned and looked in the direction of the voice. The first thing they noticed was a pair of tiny bare feet. Looking up, Camille gasped. Standing before them was perhaps the smallest woman she had ever seen. The woman-child smiled impishly at them. Her gauzy wings wavered a bit and she lifted off the ground a few inches and back down again. White flowing hair surrounded a porcelain face, and like the fairy in their dreams, her eyes shone with blue fire.

Azriel and Camille sat up from the blanket, stunned to silence by the small creature's purity and magnificence. She exuded the combined aromas of lavender and sage.

"Do not fear, Son of Luminance. I will not harm thee. I am named Paralda."

Azriel swallowed hard. "What do you call your kind?"

"I am a sylph—a creature of the air. I pray thee, walk with me. For thus that I am permitted to answer thy questions."

Camille ventured, "Paralda, were you trapped in the crystal?"

"Nay, Lady of Radiance, I *am* the crystal. For eons, I have awaited the coming of the Son of Luminance. His touch hath released me from the womb in which I grew, and his hearing of my voice, when heart and mind united, hath transformed me into my true form. For that I am grateful."

As they walked beside Paralda, her feet barely touched the ground. She floated next to them, every so often her wings fluttering to keep her aloft.

"Where are we, Paralda?" Azriel asked.

"Everywhere and nowhere. This one place hath kept Aralia and Earth bound by a singular thread ere the one became two. All that hath been lost remaineth here awaiting the time when the two shall be united. It was for this purpose that thou wast born, Son of Luminance. Shouldst thou succeed, then the Magick torn from both worlds shall be dispersed into the restored world, but shouldst thou fail, darkness shall overtake the wounded worlds from which neither, I daresay, shall recover."

"But why me?" Azriel scowled, burdened by the weight of his responsibility.

Paralda smiled serenely and tilted her head. "If not thou, Son of Luminance, then who? Thou wast born to this purpose. Dost thou spurn thy destiny? Surely great shall be thy challenge, but just as surely, great shall be thy reward. Much hinges upon thy willingness, Azriel."

Camille stopped and stared at the sylph, stricken. "But Azriel could die!"

"It is as thou hast said, Lady of Radiance. Yet, be of good cheer, for Azriel hath been chosen from the beginning for this purpose. When the time cometh, as surely it must, he shall be imbued with all the powers he needeth to complete his task. But understand, Lady of Radiance, thou hast a part to play in this as well. Thine destiny hath been fused by the love that bindeth thee. It shall not fail thee."

Paralda had led Azriel and Camille to the door that gave entrance to the magickal place. "Here we must part. But before thou returnest to thy world, I must impart to thee a gift. My Mistress hath instructed me to givest her name that thou mayest complete thy task. Lady of Radiance, thou art part of this great purpose and shall also receive the gift."

Paralda hovered before them and extended her delicate arms. She touched them both on their foreheads. Azriel's mind exploded into vision as knowledge of the universe merged his heart and mind, as it did to Camille. It felt like a mighty rushing wind sweeping away any doubts that still lingered in their minds and with the final outpouring, Azriel was granted the name of the elemental.

When she was done, Paralda removed her hands from Camille and Azriel, crossed them over her heart and bowed her head. "Son of Luminance, Lady of Radiance, if all goeth well, it is perchance we shall anon meet again." She smiled warmly, and with a shimmering, vanished.

Camille took one last lingering look at the captivating place, sorry to be leaving.

"Well, I guess we should go." Azriel said apologetically. He too regretted the thought of having to return to the real world. It would have been too easy to remain there and forget all the troubles Azriel would have to face. He had never experienced such serenity, but he also suspected that staying too long, one could become immersed in forgetfulness and lose a sense of purpose. Azriel sighed and placed his hand on the doorknob.

"Wait," Camille cooed softly. "Just one more." She wrapped her arms around his neck and kissed him deeply. "Now we can go." She grinned shyly.

When Azriel opened the door, he found Pog sitting on a small bench reading a book.

"Have you been waiting all this time?"

"Er, laddie." Pog removed a pocket watch from his tattered vest and peered at it. "It's only been five minutes."

"But we've been gone more than half the day!" Camille argued.

"Ah, lass, time moves differently on the other side. I trust ye found what ye were lookin' for?"

Camille looked up at Azriel and blushed.

Azriel cleared his throat to hide his embarrassment. "Most certainly, Pog. I've learned the name."

"Now that's a fine lad!" Pog patted Azriel's shoulder proudly.

"Will you be there tomorrow—at Rosemary's?"

"I'm afraid not," Pog said with regret.

"It's my mother, isn't it? What is your problem with her, Pog?"

"Yer buildin' things up in yer feeble mind, laddie." The old troll said dismissively.

"Yeah? Then how do you explain that every time she's here, you're not! It doesn't seem right." Azriel fumed.

"Listen, laddie. What I do with me time is me own business. It's not fer ye to know. Now as to yer mother, she's a fine woman and a grand lady. Someday she and I will sit down and have a long talk, probably about her dolt of a son, but laddie, now is not the time."

Azriel shook his head with exasperation as he and Camille followed Pog back to his lair.

Like before, Azriel was surrounded by robed and hooded members, loyal to the order of the Ankh. Jasper and Muriel held hands, and Camille proudly stood to the left of Azriel, completing the circle. As usual, Lady Rosaluna resided over the gathering. She wore the crown of her office as high priestess and stood before the altar. This time, however, Azriel's green robe of the acolyte was replaced by the blue of the Adept.

"Speak the name, Azriel, Son of Luminance." Rosaluna commanded.

Azriel removed his amulet and placed it on the altar.

"The name is Anvindr." He called out with new confidence.

And like before, the third dragon on his amulet stirred and reared, empowered by the summoning of the name. The glowing purple metal from which it was fashioned transformed before their eyes into golden splendor—as, unbidden, a rushing wind streamed through the chamber. Riding that wind was Paralda, the sylph Azriel had met in the place between. She was not alone, however. Paralda was accompanied by two others. One was attired in green, gold, and russet raiment. All manner of flowers and herbs bedecked her soft brown hair. She remained aloft on supple leathery wings, the color of fallen oak leaves. The other, also floating before them, wore a crown of pearls in her hair the texture of seaweed. She was clothed in a silvery iridescent garment that fell in cascades over her body and she floated on spiny fish-like fins.

Paralda smiled winningly. "Son of Luminance, these before thee are my kin. I present to thee Krinaea, a Dryad and guardian of the deep forest." Krinaea bowed graciously before Azriel. "Also with thee is my sister Maera, a Naiad and protector of the ocean depths." Maera placed her hands over her heart in greeting. She spoke in a gentle voice. Know, dear Son of Luminance, we are here to serve. We offer our assistance to you in any time of dire need. Though we cannot interfere in the lives of men, we can be your eyes and ears when you are blind and deaf." Her smile was serene.

"I have been watching you," Krinaea spoke, her voice as deep and mystical as a primeval forest. "Look for me in the dark places when you are lost. My sister Maera will pull you free from a whirlpool of doubt when you are trapped."

"And I shall tether thee to the ground when thou driftest like a kite without a string." Paralda added. "One more thou shalt meet ere thou completest thy task. This is the most difficult and elusive task of all, but thy reward will be great even unto the preserving of thy life and the one thou lovest." She said cryptically. "Fare thee well." Paralda vanished first, then Krinaea. But Maera stayed behind for a moment and took Rosemary aside. "Why have you not returned, my sister?" she asked gently.

"I cannot. I haven't the power. I am now bound to the world of men."

Maera bowed her head sadly. "Yet, the power still remains within you, dear sister."

"I've lost the ability, Maera." Tears formed in Rosemary's eyes.

"No, dear one. You've only lost your faith. It will return in time. Was not a message sent to you?"

"Yes. But I don't understand."

"You will in time. Dwell with these humans a while longer. They need you." The Naiad turned to depart. "Oh, I almost forgot. Cleodora sends greetings."

Rosemary held her hand to her mouth to suppress a sob. "Tell my mother that I miss her."

Maera nodded graciously and dissolved into the air.

Winter vacation passed quickly, and all had gathered at Rosemary's shop for their departure. Jasper and Muriel stood apart, heads bowed, speaking quietly. Obvious from their demeanor, they were sad to be parting. It would not be until spring that they could meet again. Muriel was comforted, however, in the fact that her family had accepted Jasper with open arms. As a final gesture of affection, Jasper and Muriel exchanged their necklaces that bore the Ankh. Though identical, both had worn the sacred emblem close to their hearts. It would carry their love across the ocean to each other.

Abelene tenderly embraced Amaryllis and Rosemary while Nicodemus prepared his dream orb for the short journey. Within moments, they were translated back home.

Immediately upon their return, however, Abelene had a sudden sense of intrusion. She knew without a shadow of doubt that someone had broken through her spell of concealment. Normally, her home was hidden to the outside world, but now there seemed to be a vulnerability, as though her house was now open to outside scrutiny. She reached out with her senses and examined her domain. Nothing was missing. No one had physically entered the house, yet there appeared an overall impression of intrusion.

"Abelene, what's wrong?" Camille asked with concern.

"Something's amiss." Abelene scowled, trying to locate the offending presence, or its afterimage. Nicodemus scanned the domicile and grumbled under his breath.

"Are you sensing anything?" Abelene asked.

"No." he answered gruffly, "And that's what's bothering me. Azriel, I want you to check your room and see if anything is missing, particularly that sword."

"Uncle Nick," he countered with aplomb. "Don't you think that anyone touching it with any evil purpose would wind up as a pile of ashes?"

"Nevertheless, it wouldn't hurt to check."

Azriel ran up the steps two at a time and checked his room, particularly under the bed. Everything remained unmolested. He called down as he ascended to the main level. "Nothing's missing, Uncle Nick."

But Abelene's agitation had increased.

"Mom, what has you so riled?"

Abelene answered as she stormed through the house. She now wore her ritual robe. She obviously intended to perform some sort of Magick. "I am feeling violated," she snapped as she knelt by the cold hearth, withdrawing a shovelful of ashes and pouring it in an iron brazier. To it, she added a small spoonful of powdered nightshade and stirred it in the ashes with her Athame, softly chanting an invocation. She then added a pinch of copal resin for truth. Camille had been tailing her, determined to find out what Abelene had in mind. She answered Camille's unasked question. "All beings, no matter how great or small, leave an after-image of where they have been. Time is not as static as you were taught to believe. Like rewinding a tape, I can view what has been."

Marching to the front door, Abelene made her way to a spot about twenty feet from the house and waved imperiously to the sky. Suddenly, a stiff wind blew through the trees at which point she held up the bowl of ashes. "Phantasmo obscura, chrono riverti!" she called out in a voice of command. The wind picked up in intensity and blew the ashes out of the bowl. They blew around the property, creating a misty fog that covered the house and surrounding yard. Ghostly images began to appear. Like an apparition, the mailman drove up and deposited a few letters in the mailbox. A stray dog crossed from the front yard and disappeared into the back woods. Then Kita padded in with Hermes trailing behind, and scratched at the door. Getting no response, she quickly left the premises. Then a ghostly sedan drove up and a man—a stranger Abelene had never seen—stepped out of the car. The shadow figure looked in several directions before strolling around the property. He wore a hooded cape, making it impossible to see his features. As he snooped around the property, he tapped an ornate cane on the ground. It didn't seem to be anything more than an affectation, having no other than an ornament. But when he came to the back door, he held up the cane and muttered something. Abelene couldn't hear the words. Since the spell was only a projection of the past, any sound was muffled. The result, however, soon became apparent. The stranger spread his arms and a second apparition appeared as a shadow of the first, proceeding from his body. The shadow easily passed through the locked door and roamed about the house. Abelene and Azriel followed the shadow, mirroring his steps while Nicodemus, Jasper and Camille waited outside observing the stranger. The phantasm floated upstairs into Azriel's bedroom. It looked at items on the shelves and then did something strange. It bent down and thrust half its body through the bed to peer at what lay beneath. It then stood with a start, flinching away from the powerful object hidden there. Ghostly or not, it seemed to back away in fear, then it disappeared. Outside, Camille watched as the shadow returned and fused again with the first figure. In exaltation, the man tossed back his hood and smiled with glee. Camille paled. The ghostly image passed through Jasper and the sedan drove off. Jasper began twitching, wiping at his arms and chest, brushing off the willies in revulsion.

"Ugh, that was just sick!"

Camille would have laughed under different circumstances. But what she now knew was cause for serious concern. This couldn't wait.

"Abelene!" There was no answer. "Abelene!" she cried out, louder.

Azriel and his mother charged out of the house. Pale and frightened, Camille stood panting, her chest heaving.

"What is it?" Abelene quickly banished the spell and stared at Camille.

"I know who that man was. It was Barclay."

"Do you mean the head of your Aunt's coven?" Azriel asked quizzically. "What would he want here?"

Nicodemus stood pensively, stroking his beard, thinking hard. "Barclay is not what he seems." He muttered with realization. "Only a wizard with enormous power could project himself like that."

"What are you saying?" Abelene demanded.

"What it means is that your secret is no longer safe. This wizard was here for a purpose; a bad one I can only assume."

"It's worse, Uncle Nick," Azriel fumed. "He took a marked interest in the sword."

"The sword, you say?" Nicodemus mused analytically. "That can only mean one thing. The Clave now knows that Eltanin's heir is alive and well. We must make preparations."

"Preparations? For what?" Azriel spread his hands inquiringly.

"To leave here as soon as possible. You are no longer safe."

Azriel snapped with anger. "We can't just leave!"

"Oh, you have time yet." Nicodemus responded dismissively. "But it may be a good idea to plan on an extended vacation this coming spring."

"What should we do in the meantime?" Abelene asked fear-stricken.

"Azriel must begin his final task, and quickly. We must also place an impenetrable shield around your property. A concealment spell is no longer good enough. We must all now be on guard. Trust no one." Nicodemus turned and faced the frightened girl. "Camille, that goes for your aunts Penelope and Daphne. I want to meet with them as soon as possible."

332

Chapter 16

The following day a very serious and frank meeting took place in Abelene's living room. Nicodemus had translated back to the Isle of Man and summoned Rosemary and Amaryllis. Naturally, Felisa was with them, as was Mr. Parkins. An unprecedented summoning followed. Abelene stretched her mind over the forest abutting her property and called to Kita.

Azriel had been given a promise by the dryad, Krinaea, that she would assist in times of trouble, and he called on her with a simple token of invocation she had left in his care. Paralda and Maera had left a means of summoning as well. Paralda had left him with a feather from Wakiya, a Thunderbird she herself had befriended. Maera had gifted Azriel with a small nautilus shell. Though ordinary in appearance, it had been etched with a series of runes over its entire surface. She had instructed him to speak her name into the shell, and she would appear. Likewise, Krinaea had given Azriel a golden acorn. All he needed to do now was to hold it in his hand and speak her name. All three of these magickal items he kept in a small leather bag along with the whisker Felisa had bequeathed to him. As simple as these items appeared, they were dear to Azriel, and he kept them safe on a strong leather cord attached to his belt. He held the acorn and whispered Krinaea's name. Within moments, she appeared and curtsied a greeting. "I didn't think it would be so soon that you would require my help, Son of Luminance." She smiled but her voice was solemn.

"I would not trouble you without due cause, Honored Queen of the Wood, but the situation seems—dire."

"Very well, Azriel. I am here to assist."

"We are waiting for a few more to arrive."

"I am patient, Son of Luminance. One develops fortitude when one has lived as long as I have."

"Just how old are you, Krinaea?"

"One never asks a lady her age," she countered with feigned indignation.

"My apologies, lady."

"No need," she smiled. "Let's just say that I was born with the first tree."

"That's a long time."

"Indeed, Azriel. But remember that trees measure time differently."

There was a soft tapping on the door and Abelene peeked out from behind the drawn curtain. She opened the door and greeted Penelope and Daphne. Camille came in with Jasper, Albert, and Julia, and of course sought out Azriel. Abelene was about to close the door when Kita pushed her way in with her head, followed by Hermes, who scampered in behind her. He had grown somewhat, and was now approaching his adolescent stage. His gait was somewhat ungainly.

"Greetings, Mother." Kita's deep voice filled the room. Abelene dropped to her knees and wrapped her arms around Kita's neck, nuzzling cheek to cheek. Watching, Felisa glanced up at Azriel with a quizzical expression.

Azriel answered her unasked question. "My mother found Kita orphaned and raised her from a kitten."

"I knew I liked your mother for some reason." Felisa's face crinkled into a broad smile. She then greeted Kita respectfully with a series of purrs and soft growls in the language of cats. Kita responded politely, then switched to the human tongue. "Remarkable that you can speak the true language."

"Not really." Felisa suddenly morphed into her true form. A sizeable Manx cat padded out of the crumpled clothing lying in a heap on the floor. Felisa rubbed her face against Kita's in greeting.

"She's cute, Mama." Hermes said brightly. "But where's her tail?"

"Now don't be rude, son. You're forgetting your manners."

Felisa crawled back into her rumpled clothing and resumed her human shape. "It's quite all right, Kita, he's young. If he were a bit older I might have bitten his rump for good measure."

Kita produced a rumbling sound from the base of her throat that sounded remarkably like laughter.

The assembly gathered in a tight circle. Kita sat on her haunches and gruffly told Hermes to stay put as Nicodemus formally called the meeting to order.

"As you all know," he began, "there has been an intrusion in Lady Abelene's home."

Azriel arched an eyebrow. This was the first time Nicodemus had ever spoken of his mother in such a formal fashion.

"This was no ordinary break-in by thieves," Uncle Nick continued, "but was done by extraordinary magick. This man was no amateur, and I am convinced he is one of the elusive Clave."

Albert gave an involuntary shudder, but Jasper inquired, "What exactly is the Clave and what would they want here?"

"Indeed," Nicodemus answered darkly. "You all know of Eltanin's betrayers, but what you do not know is that there has been a war going on for millennia. When the worlds were rent apart, the Clave were deposited here on Earth. They immediately sought out centers of power in the hope of subjugating the world. Ancient wizards such as myself and Amaryllis strove against them and thwarted their plans of domination, but they remain ever elusive. They are cunning—their indignities know no bounds. In retaliation for our meddling, many of the Order were horribly executed. I personally lost two dear friends, Melchior and Balthazar, wizards and astrologers of the highest order. It is said that Merlin, my friend and student, was defeated by Morgana, the sorceress, but the truth is much darker. She was acquainted with Rastaban, who would meet with her in her dreams and teach her forbidden magick. Though powerful enough to destroy Merlin, alas, she was only a tool of the Clave. In the end, her reward from Rastaban was to be consigned to eternal oblivion.

"From the very beginning, the Order of the Ankh searched the world for every prophecy known to man, hoping for the coming of the Son of Luminance."

Azriel squirmed uncomfortably in his seat, every furtive glance directed at him.

"We searched Egyptian, Sumerian, and Hebrew prophecies of the foretold coming. We sought out the Oracles of Delphi, the temples of Dionysius—every prediction throughout the world—to find clues to his arrival. But the Clave also sought out prophecies and destroyed them at every turn. They were the force behind the destruction of the Library at Alexandria, the Mayan Codices, and the lost scrolls of Atlantis. It was only when the Scrolls of Eltanin were discovered that we knew the Coming Child of Light would be not of this world, but from Aralia."

Nicodemus leveled a gaze at Azriel. "The Clave has vowed his destruction ere the worlds of Aralia and Gaia are reunited."

"Oh, that's comforting," Azriel muttered blithely.

Nicodemus ignored the comment. "Now the war has led here. This wizard of the Clave has been parading around disguised as Barclay, head of the northwest covens. He has fooled them, all the while searching for clues to the Child of Luminance's whereabouts. Now the secret is out. The Clave has discovered Errin-lil, Eltanin's sword. It is only a matter of time before the Clave works their way here." Nicodemus scowled, his expression troubled. "Penelope and Daphne have already tasted of Barclay's deception, but to their credit, they resisted his questions and revealed nothing. It does raise an issue, however. He found his way here. There is another enemy out there—whether by accident or by design—who led him here."

"What do you propose then?" Amaryllis asked.

"All here must go into hiding by summer's end. There are safe houses throughout the Isle of Man and in Ireland that will offer sanctuary. They are well hidden by powerful magick, and you will not be found. Penelope and Daphne, you must go back to Ireland and hide Camille. It is no secret that the Clave will try to use her to get to Azriel.

"Amaryllis and Rosemary, you must gather our forces and warn them of the coming storm. They will know what to do.

"As to Jasper, Albert, and Julia—this presents a problem. I assume your mother knows nothing about your involvement in all this. Perhaps it is time to bring her into the fold."

"Are you kidding?" Albert blurted. "She'll freak! She thinks knitting is exciting. It says a lot." Jasper snorted a laugh.

"Oh, she'll come around. *I* will ensure that."

"What about Azriel?" Camille asked, unable to squelch the quaver in her voice.

"It is essential that he complete his final task. It's the most important one. Everything hinges upon it."

"It sounds like the boy is running out of time, Ancient One." Kita purred with respect.

"There is time yet, little sister, but I must speed up his instruction." He then addressed Azriel directly. "Your final challenge will be accomplished at my stronghold. It is well hidden and impenetrable. You will spend much of your time there. And Abelene, though you have mastery over magick, you must sharpen your skills even further. I have a library at your disposal. Use it."

Nicodemus paused in his instructions and rubbed his beard thoughtfully. "That leaves Kita and Krinaea. Kita, you must guard against intrusion into these woods and the surrounding forest. And Krinaea, I would not be so bold as to give you orders, Queen of Dryads. I merely ask that your people be called upon to protect these woods. Watch over Abelene's home as well as Camille's and Jasper's until safe passage can be arranged."

Krinaea nodded her acceptance with grace and dignity. "I will grant what you ask, Ancient Nicodemus."

Camille began to cry. "Are we all going to be separated?" she asked, looking in panic at Azriel.

Nicodemus' eyes softened. "Of course I have thought of that, dear child." He removed a small sack from his chest pocket. He began doling out beautifully wrought golden rings to each member of the Order. The bands each had an emerald stone set in the center. "These rings will allow communication over vast distances. You can forget your cell phones; they are too easy to trace. And, besides, the rings never need to be recharged." Nicodemus tried at levity to lighten the mood. "Are we all agreed then?" He concluded.

They all nodded silently. The gravity of the situation hit home. A somber mood crept through the room.

Jasper broke the silence. "Um, Abelene?"

"Yes, dear."

"Do you have anything to eat? I'm kind of hungry."

Everyone turned and looked at Jasper with what amounted to baffled amusement. But Julia picked up a pillow from the couch, wound up mightily, and smacked him in the head with it.

"Jasper, you're such a pig! Is your stomach the only thing you can think about?" Julia fumed.

If nothing else, her actions did serve to lighten the tension in the room. Everyone broke out into laughter as Abelene brought out a platter of pastries and served up refreshments.

The stronghold was surrounded by red sandstone peaks cradling it like an escarpment to keep away outside intrusion. Structurally cut from the same native stone, it had not been erected piece by piece, but magically shaped by Nicodemus from the eroded skeleton of all that remained of a mountain. It had resisted detection from the outside world as there was only one means of access—through the dream orb Nicodemus kept in his possession. When he first discovered this place of solitude, Nicodemus preserved the integrity of the jagged promontory and incorporated the castle's design into the mountains, camouflaging it from the air— invisible in plain sight. Nicodemus had named the stronghold Caer Wylusung for the symbolic strength of the mountain. For six thousand years it had served as his sanctuary where he could observe the progress of civilization. If asked, Nicodemus would admit that he found the place quite by accident when preparing to translate from his home in the Nile delta to a promontory located somewhere in Greece. As he prepared to translate, finger poised over the dream orb, a fire-cured urn on a shelf above him tipped over and struck him on the head. The image fixed in his mind swam before him and he awoke at the base of the red rock spires. A forbidding place, he found it to be perfect for his use. It took him another thousand years to determine that its location was somewhere in the southwest region of North America, today known as the Canyonlands. Though alone most of the time, he was seldom lonely, for knowledge was his closest friend and advocate. Thus his years were spent refining his magickal skills and delving into the deepest mysteries of life and death. Time was his ally and, for all his efforts, Nicodemus, next to Eltanin, became the most powerful wizard, sorcerer, and necromancer that ever lived, human or otherwise, though upon meeting him for all his eccentricities, no one would suspect what power lay beneath his ordinary demeanor.

Over those years spent in seclusion, he had occasional visits from natives on vision quests, and for a time became known as Ga'an, the Grey One—also sometimes known as Coyote the trickster. The natives knew that their Holy Ones dwelt within the mountains and could heal sicknesses and impart wisdom. For them, it took great courage to scale the mountains and find the hidden place. Not all succeeded, but the quest itself was their reward. Often, when they found Nicodemus, they would stay and learn at his feet, to become great medicine men in their own right.

But time clouds memory, and soon Ga'an was forgotten, as well as the secret way to his stronghold. Nicodemus missed those days; things were simpler then.

Azriel stood in the courtyard with Nicodemus, in the center of the massive, scribed pentagram central to the stone platform. He looked down overcome with a sudden pang of guilt. This place was where his mother through her travail and suffering had translated from Aralia to save Azriel's life—and her own.

"You have questions," Nicodemus stated with calm assurance.

"Many," Azriel answered.

"Good. You have passed the first three challenges. It is no longer time for secrets. Ask, Azriel."

"This is where my mother came to Earth, right?"

"Yes."

"How did you know that the time was imminent?"

"I didn't," Nicodemus replied, a touch of humor in his voice. "Eltanin did."

"So, he's alive then?"

"Very much so—but in hiding."

"But why? If he is the most powerful wizard, couldn't he crush the Clave?"

"Maybe at one time. But now his powers are waning as yours wax strong. You must understand Azriel, Eltanin and the Clave have remained hidden from each other for eons. The betrayal of his brothers broke Eltanin in ways that can never be imagined. Rastaban was his closest friend, but he was taken by the dark allure of unlimited power. Who is stronger between them, I can't say. But I do know the time of Eltanin's revealing has not come to pass."

"It is he whom I saw in the Book of Aralia. It showed me the ritual that brought my mother here."

"Yes, that was him. He perceived her travail and knew she would die if he were not there to bring her through. It was only the second time he had come out of hiding." Nicodemus said. He sounded sad.

"What was the first?"

"When he found me." Uncle Nick smiled warmly.

"What happened?"

"Indeed. The time was nearly ten thousand years ago. I was born in a rather ordinary village that abutted the Altean River. To my limited knowledge, it was a peaceful, happy place. But, as is the way of man, wars soon broke out between two factions seeking to overthrow Atlantis. My village was, you might say, caught in the middle, with no interest in politics or border disputes. We just wanted to be left alone. I honestly don't know the cause, but one night long ago, warriors swept through our village like a scourge, hell-bent on murder and annihilation. My mother hid me in a small granary, warning me to bury myself in the barley. I was only three. Throughout the night, in terror, I heard sounds of fighting and screams of the dying. In the morning, there was only silence. The marauders had gone, leaving the bodies of my people to decay in the sun. I roamed aimlessly, looking for my parents, and I finally found them. They were dead."

Nicodemus looked down solemnly, reliving the ordeal.

"I cried for days, tired, thirsty, and hungry. That is when Eltanin found me near death, as he passed through the land surveying the brutal aftermath. To my people, he was merely a seldom-seen hermit who lived in the mountains. Claiming me as his own, Eltanin raised me like a father. Eventually he became my master and taught me the ways of Magick. In time, he released me to explore the world. Shortly after that, Atlantis sank into the sea. Still, we managed to stay connected from time to time, but hardly ever in person—except for once in Egypt, and when your mother came through."

"I'm sorry, Uncle Nick. You went through a lot."

Nicodemus smiled ruefully. "Ancient history," he said with a dismissive wave of the hand.

"Uncle Nick, you once told me that you were Atlantean. How long did your people normally live?"

"Oh, approximately a thousand years give or take."

"Yet you have lived over ten thousand."

Nicodemus sighed. "Yes, in the beginning, magick kept me alive, but even that couldn't hold back the advance of time. That is why my master came to instruct me when I left Egypt. It was through the Lapis Occultus that I was renewed and gained near immortality. It is how I stayed alive all these years—Amaryllis as well." Nicodemus looked at Azriel gravely. "It is why you are here. You must learn the secrets of immortality. It is how you will learn the final name, that is—the essence of fire. Be warned, Azriel. It is the most difficult to learn and control—but the most rewarding for all your efforts. Come, my young Adept. I have something to show you."

Nicodemus led Azriel from the courtyard into the main gallery. A massive hearth sat in the center of the room with a huge oak table, comfortable high-backed chairs, several oil lamps, and shelves upon shelves of books and scrolls. Azriel was immediately drawn to the volumes of magickal texts and ancient tomes.

"Plenty of time for that, Azriel." Nicodemus smiled tenderly. He remembered his own youth and his insatiable thirst for knowledge. He led Azriel farther to another room off to the side of the main hall. The young man's eyes widened with wonder as he beheld a laboratory cluttered with an array of unimaginable objects. Racks of vials filled with unnamed elements, beakers, and flasks brimming with mysterious fluids. In the corner stood a small forge whose purpose, at this point, was inconceivable.

"This will be your next challenge, Azriel. You must learn the science of Alchemy."

"It doesn't seem much different from chemistry class." Azriel shrugged.

"It may seem that way," Nicodemus said tartly. "But it is entirely different. It is all well and good to learn spells and enchantments, petty sorceries and incantations—but here," Nicodemus patted the table filled with strange instruments. "Here is where the heart of the best wizard lies. Here is where you learn to refine the basest metals into the purest gold, and from that gold, you refine your spirit. Once you achieve that end, you create the Lapis Occultus—the Philosopher's Stone." His eyes glowed with passion.

"Sounds complicated," Azriel mused as he touched one of the strange instruments on the table.

"It is, Azriel—and not for the fainthearted. It requires fortitude and patience. There are many things to learn, young master, such as the qualities of hot, cold, dry and moist. Each element shares some of these traits. You must learn them.

"Fire, for example, exhibits many qualities. It isn't just the flame, Azriel. It is the very spark of life—the electricity of the lightning bolt right down to the nuclear furnace of a star! Learn this and you begin to understand the very nature of the universe. Understand the universe, and you then understand yourself."

"How long will this take, Uncle Nick?"

"It will take as long as it must. The path of the alchemist is not an easy one, Azriel. It is prone to trial and error. You will fail more often than you succeed. But in the end, you will triumph and attain the wisdom to deal with any challenge."

Nicodemus removed a sheet of parchment from a dusty bookcase and handed it to Azriel. "Here. This is your first lesson. Memorize it and learn the meaning. They are not just words, young master, but the key to alchemy. Understand it to your very soul, and you will be well on your way to infinite knowledge."

Azriel flattened the scroll on the table and scowled thoughtfully as he read. "What is this, Uncle Nick?"

"They are the words of Hermes Trismegistus, copied from the Emerald Tablet. Very few have fully understood it, but those who did achieved great things."

"So who's this Hermes guy?"

"It is said he came out of ancient Egypt. To the Egyptians he was called Thoth, and they worshipped him as a god. I met him only once. A rather likeable fellow actually—when he was not speaking in riddles. He allowed me to copy this text and now I bequeath it to you." Nicodemus smiled affably and lit a few candles. "Sit, Azriel— read!" he instructed gravely and left the room.

Azriel stared after Nicodemus as he departed and quietly closed the door, leaving the boy to his studies.

Azriel read the text slowly.

This is the truth, the whole and certain truth, without a word of a lie

That which is above is as that which is below,
And that which is below is as that which is above.
Thus are accomplished the miracles of the One.

And as all things come from the One, through the meditation of the One, so all things are created by the One Thing through adaptation.

Its father is the Sun; its mother the Moon
The Wind bears it in its belly, the Earth nurtures it.

It engenders all the wonders of the universe

Its power is complete when it is turned to earth.

Separate the Earth from Fire, the subtle from the gross
Gently and with ingenuity.

It ascends from Earth to the Heavens and descends again to Earth,
Combining the power of above and below.

Thus you will achieve the glory of the Universe.
And all obscurity will flee from you.

This is the power of all powers.

For it overcomes every subtle thing
And penetrates every solid thing

Thus was all the world created,

And thus are marvelous works to come
For this is the process

Therefore I am called Thrice-greatest Hermes
For I am master of the three principles of universal wisdom

This concludes what I have to say about the work of the sun.

Azriel sat back and pondered what he just read. He started over again and reread the ancient text, then sighed heavily. This was going to take a long time.

He spent much of his time between school studies at home and learning the science of alchemy at Caer Wylusung. Nicodemus opened the stronghold to Camille and Abelene as well so they may make use of his extensive library.

Today, Azriel worked in the laboratory, reading through ancient texts and attempting to convert hydrogen to a heavier element. It was the first step toward creating the chemicals needed to convert lead to gold. As inspiration, he had brought the sizeable gold nugget he found at Uncle Nick's secret cave and set it on a small pedestal on the worktable. Earlier he had inquired of Nicodemus why it was necessary to create gold in the first place when he already had all he needed. Uncle Nick blithely told him, "You're missing the point, Azriel. It's not about the gold. It's about the process. Once you learn the secrets of transformation you refine yourself and discover the power within you—within all of us. It might serve you well to remember that we are all stardust, composed from the stuff of the universe."

Azriel pondered Nicodemus' enigmatic answer as he toiled meticulously, heating up the forge, and filling an iron crucible with various powders.

In the library, Camille pored over the spellbook Pog had given her. She was attempting to form a sphere of energy in her hands. She came close with a tiny spark of light, but it fizzled into a puff of smoke. She ran her fingers through her hair in frustration. Abelene watched as she sipped tea in one of the brocaded high-backed chairs with Nicodemus.

Camille tried again. This time a glowing sphere appeared above her hands, trying to coalesce—but like syrup, the plasma dripped through her fingers into a puddle on the floor and vanished. She sighed heavily.

Just then a muffled explosion sounded from the direction of the lab.

"Dammit!" Azriel's voice came from the other side of the door. He staggered out of the lab choking as acrid smoke billowed out into the main hall. Some of his hair and sleeves were singed. Sooty ash covered most of his body and face. Startled, Camille turned to look with concern, but a laugh got stuck in her throat. She tried to suppress it, but Azriel's ruffled appearance and his pathetic look triggered something in Camille. She rang out with peals of laughter and, for some reason, couldn't stop. She tried to apologize and force herself to stop laughing, but the more she tried, the more ridiculous it all seemed. Tears ran down her face, and she held her hand to her mouth to try to muffle her amusement, but for all her effort she just couldn't. Finally with no other choice, she ran outside and howled again with unbridled guffaws and hoots, doubled up and out of breath. She finally regained her composure and reentered the main hall. Azriel stood facing her with arms crossed and a sour expression. "So glad I could provide you with entertainment." He said crossly, his voice lacking any humor. Camille snorted, giggling again and ran outside again to resume her laughing. Azriel sighed with consternation. There was suddenly another muffled explosion from the lab and the sound of tinkling glass.

"Crap!" Azriel groused.

Abelene held her hand to her mouth and ran outside to join Camille. They fell into each other's arms in hysterics.

Azriel stood watching them grumbling under his breath.

Meanwhile, Nicodemus went to a closet and fetched a broom and dustpan. He handed them to Azriel without saying anything.

"I guess that wasn't it," Azriel glowered.

"Now don't be too hard on yourself, Azriel." Nicodemus tried to be consoling. "Don't look at it as a failure, just a lesson in what *not* to do. If anything, you are now one step closer to success."

"Yeah, great." He replied, his tone flat.

"You've only been at it for a few days. You'll probably have many more mishaps before you get it right, so don't get so discouraged. After all, Rome wasn't built in a day."

"Yeah? Well, it sure burned down in a day."

"Good point." Nicodemus mumbled and went back to his reading. Azriel sat on the chair facing him and waited. After a few moments, Nicodemus put down the book and cleared his throat. "It would seem you need a little direction. I think that perhaps you are getting ahead of yourself."

"I don't understand."

"To use an old cliché, you are trying to run before you've even begun to crawl. Forget about trying to refine heavier elements. Start at the beginning again."

"What do you mean?"

Nicodemus paused and thought while tapping his fingers on the end table. "All right, now if you were to begin counting, where would you start?

"One, of course."

"Really?" he said feigning surprise. "Why not zero?"

"Because zero is nothing. It's not a number."

"See, then? That's where your error began."

Azriel's expression signified that he wasn't grasping the conversation.

"Let me put it to you another way, Azriel. Zero is not nothing, but a figure with no defined quantity. It's pure potential. It could be all or nothing and everything in between. Once you understand that, then you can proceed to one.

"But how can nothing be something."

"Ah!" Nicodemus brightened. "That is the greatest mystery of all. How was the universe created from nothing? Was it something or not? Quite the riddle. But the universe did have a start, and it started from Zero—nothing that became something."

"You're confusing me." Azriel shook his head trying to understand.

"That is why you must understand the concept of One as well. Zero and One must be understood together for either to make sense. The Zero became the One. Pure potential thus became an absolute, a singularity—a One. But the question then remains. What transformed it from Zero to One? Understand that and you begin to understand Alchemy."

"Uncle Nick, I'm completely lost."

Nicodemus chuckled. "I wouldn't expect you to get it right away. It's a difficult concept to understand. Think about an unfertilized egg as the beginning—as the Zero. It remains just that without the One. The One is the spark, the movement from which everything else will proceed. The egg exists as potential. You can either eat it and be done with it, or fertilize it and grow a chicken. Zero and One are like male and female, light and dark, hot and cold, dry and moist. Opposites—but their union is the start of the Great Work of the heavens."

"I think I'm starting to understand. Hot and cold, dry and moist—the combinations of any produce the elements."

"See that, Azriel. There is hope for you."

"So what about the idea of Two?"

"Perhaps we shouldn't get too far ahead of ourselves. But let's just start by saying that One by itself does nothing but remain One. Destroy it, rend it in half and it will create the Two that proceeds from One. The Two will always seek to unite back into One, equals and opposite and from there is where all life originates."

Azriel pondered that and chewed on a fingernail. "The book you gave me on alchemy described the union of Three being salt, sulfur and mercury. What is that supposed to mean."

"Yes, sulfur represents fire, the sun, maleness and consciousness. Mercury is feminine, watery, the life force, the moon. Salt is the offspring of the Two balancing them both. Tell me something, Azriel. Is Mercury a liquid or a metal?"

"It's both—I think."

"How can it be both? Surely it must be one or the other!" Nicodemus challenged.

Azriel shook his head trying to clear it. "It just is." He spread his hands in agitation.

"Indeed," Nicodemus smiled. "Because it is liquid and metal, it exists in two states at the same time. Remarkable! That is also why it acts as a unifier or mediator of both sulfur and salt. And thus, Two becomes Three. Understand this to the heart and you will be one step closer to creating the Lapis Occultus, which exists in three states at the same time."

"You mean liquid, solid and gas?"

"A good guess, Azriel, but not correct. The answer would be liquid, solid and spirit—also known as Life Force, the purest potential there is."

"I don't think I'm ever going to get this." Azriel mumbled.

"You will in time, Azriel. I think I've given you enough to think about for now. And speaking of potential, well done, Camille, well done!"

Camille had returned from outside. She beamed proudly as she held in her hand a glowing ball of pure energy. Abelene had worked with her in teaching her how to produce the plasma ball. Camille tossed it back and forth from hand to hand.

"What you see there, Azriel, is pure potential gathered in from the stuff of the universe. It is visible energy." He hesitated and stared nervously at Camille who was now tossing it up in the air and catching the glowing mass.

"Er, dear, would you stop that? It is not a plaything."

"What do you mean Uncle Nick? It seems harmless enough."

"I would prefer not to have the walls of my stronghold collapse around me." He answered firmly. "Let me show you something. Follow me."

He walked outside with Camille tailing behind with curiosity. He then pointed to an outcropping of rock several yards from the courtyard. "Now see if you can hit those rocks over there with that ball."

"Okay." Camille shrugged. She had a pretty good arm and was confident she could hit the target. She wound up and pitched the ball at the stone boulder, and it met its mark. The concussion of the explosion nearly dropped them to the ground. The glowing orb had blasted half the boulder into powder and Camille's ears rang from the blast. She gaped at the destruction. "Good heavens!" she muttered in a half whisper.

"That is what I meant by potential. That glowing ball of plasma you created is a formidable weapon and not to be used lightly. But bear in mind that it has other more creative uses. But for now, keep it under wraps. And Camille, I wouldn't show this to Albert and Jasper, at least not just yet. Can't have them blowing themselves up." He smiled wryly. "Perhaps you and Azriel should practice with this right now. The faster you can produce a plasma ball, the better off you will be should you ever need one in a hurry. But would you please stay outside with this. I'd like to keep my home unscathed." He turned to head back into his study. "Abelene dear, could we speak privately?"

"Certainly." She nodded and followed Nicodemus back into the main hall. She closed the door behind her.

He sat opposite Abelene and poured her a glass of wine, an 1807 muscatel.

"Mmm, delicious!" She held it to the light noting its reddish-brown color and the way it coated the crystal goblet.

"The girl shows remarkable talent." Nicodemus began in all seriousness.

"Yes, she has an uncanny grasp on the magickal realm. She's nearly as good as Azriel."

"Hmm, makes me wonder…" he trailed off.

"What is it, Nicodemus?"

"Abelene, how much do you know about Camille?"

"Her family is from Ireland. She has told me on more than one occasion that she is a thirteenth-generation witch."

"Indeed, but that wouldn't fully explain her extraordinary abilities and her natural affinity for talents that should be beyond her grasp. It took me years to produce a plasma ball. She has done it in twenty minutes."

"So what are you thinking?"

"I have a theory, though I can't prove it. But I would not at all be surprised if somewhere in her ancestry there is elfin blood. She could be part Ferrishyn. That would explain much."

Abelene nodded pensively. "Her surname is McElven, after all. It is entirely possible."

"It does however raise a few questions. Who would she be descended from? If not Eltanin, then who? One of the Clave?"

"It's a good question. But I wouldn't be too concerned. We know where her loyalties lie." Abelene said defensively.

"Oh, I'm not questioning her loyalty." He paused and stared at Abelene with the glimmer of a smile. A sudden concussive sound shook the castle. He looked up in the air and sighed, shaking his head.

"Nick, you did tell them to practice."

Nicodemus grumbled to himself. "Well, I suppose you're right." He replied snappishly. "You're quite taken up with the young lady, aren't you?"

Abelene's eyes sparkled. "She's good for Azriel—keeps him grounded. With his powers, he needs to be with someone on equal footing."

"I agree. It does raise a bigger question. It seems likely that there are more like her throughout the world. After all, Eltanin translated here 20,000 years ago. So did the clave. Perhaps more of your people are here and don't even know it."

"I'm not following, Nicodemus." She shook her head.

"I'm just wondering what will happen should Azriel succeed and reunite the worlds. What then? Has anyone considered that?"

"It's never really been discussed in any of the texts."

"One world, two distinctly different cultures? One bases its existence on Magick. The other is fully invested in technology. This could prove to be—interesting." Nicodemus swallowed the remains of his wine.

"I have wondered the same thing. Will the transformation heal the worlds or will it thrust us into war?" Abelene glanced down at the floor pensively. "Regardless, Eltanin's prophecy will come to be for better or worse. And try as we may, there is no way to properly prepare the world for it. I guess all we can do is let the chips fall where they may and hope for the best."

The room shook again with another concussive explosion from outside followed by another. They heard riotous laughter. Azriel and Camille were obviously enjoying themselves. After another detonation that nearly tipped the wine bottle off the table, Nicodemus deftly caught it before it could crash onto the floor. He dropped his head into his hands and sighed heavily. He muttered, "I can see this is going to be a very long day."

Gift of the Amulet

352

Chapter 17

"Mrs. Cunningham, I've invited you here to take you into my confidence." Abelene poured her another cup of coffee as they sat facing each other at her kitchen table.

"Maggie. Please call me Maggie." The woman was slender, of average height, with strawberry-blonde hair. She had a pale, freckled complexion with stunning, dark green eyes. Abelene could see where Julia got her lovely looks. The girl could have been the younger twin of her mother.

Maggie smiled nervously. She looked around at Abelene's kitchen uncomfortably. It was a hodgepodge of cast-iron cauldrons, hanging herbs, shelves of clay-fired pots and a huge open hearth with a dangling kettle that bubbled merrily. Whatever it was, it smelled delicious. Maggie's own kitchen was sterile by comparison. Walking into Abelene's home was like stepping into a medieval novel with kings and queens, witches and sorcerers—the stuff of fantastic tales she used to love as a child.

Abelene smiled winningly. "Maggie, how willing are you to step outside your comfort zone—how willing are you to accept things that couldn't possibly be?"

"I used to believe in happily ever after, if that's what you're asking. Reality has a habit of setting in when your husband leaves you for another woman, and you are left raising three children on your own." She answered bitterly. She cocked her ear, listening to Julia and the boys having a spat, as usual. They were outside with Azriel and Camille playing a game of some kind. And as usual, Albert or Jasper had probably taken advantage of Julia in some way. She smiled. "They really don't mean it. They love their sister far more than they let on."

"I've been spending many days with your children, teaching and instructing them. They are—should I say—interesting young adults."

"Oh no. What did they do now? Did they damage your house? Steal your car? I have good insurance if they broke anything."

Abelene laughed. "No, it's nothing like that. You see, Maggie. There's a whole other world out there of which you know nothing about. This may be hard for you to believe, but your sons are well on their way to becoming quite adept at wizardry, and Julia, well she's a very capable witch."

Maggie was taken aback. She responded defensively. "Now look, Abelene, I know Julia can be a real brat sometimes, but no one's ever called her a witch!"

Abelene giggled. "You say witch like it's a bad thing." She held her finger to her lips and thought. "Maybe I should tell you the whole story."

Abelene spent a good part of the next hour explaining in detail Azriel and her home world, the rending of Aralia and Earth. Her narration included the tale of Eltanin and the Clave, and how Aralia was now bereft of magick, and why it was Azriel's destiny to reunite the worlds into one.

"So let me get this straight," Maggie interrupted at last. "You're telling me my kids are growing up to be sorcerers?"

"That's right. They're surprisingly talented as well." As Abelene spoke, she removed the kettle from the hearth and doled out two portions of the enticing apple crisp that had been cooking in the pot.

Maggie said nothing at first, digesting everything Abelene had told her. She tasted the hot dessert. It was certainly delectable. Of course, Abelene didn't tell her about certain ingredients that would help open the woman's mind to the truth. She knew it was slightly unethical, but it was imperative that Maggie understand the full scope of this reality.

"You know, Abelene, rumors have been flying around Harden Lake about you and your son for years. I never put much stock in them. What am I supposed to think now?"

"You can think what you want, Maggie," Abelene said pensively, "but keep in mind that I take a great deal of risk by bringing you into my confidence. There's something else I haven't told you. I've had an intrusion into my home by one of the Clave. The secret is out and it's now quite possible that you and your children are in danger. The Clave don't leave loose ends."

"And I'm supposed to be happy you've told me all this?"

"Would it have been better to keep you in the dark, Maggie?"

"No—I suppose not." She said with a pouty expression. "But this is all very hard to swallow. That is, except for this delicious apple crisp. I'm not leaving here without the recipe."

Abelene had to admit that she liked Maggie and her subtle humor. Still, it appeared that Maggie wasn't entirely convinced, and Abelene took to explaining more when the flock of hungry teenagers sifted into the kitchen, attracted by the aroma wafting through the window.

Abelene doled out some to each of them, and they all sat at the table. Maggie crossed her arms and glared at her children. "Now it's all starting to make sense—your secretive behavior, strange things going on in the house—and it's not like any of you are likely to study anything, and there you are, Jasper, with your head in a book all the time. What are all of you reading anyway?"

"Spells, Mom."

She snorted with disbelief.

"Albert, why don't you show her something." Abelene offered. "Do your full-body illusion spell."

"Are you sure?"

"Yes."

"If you insist." Albert answered doubtfully.

Albert waved his hands, muttering an incantation. In moments he morphed into a nearly full-grown brown bear.

"Arrrgh!" Maggie yelped and screamed, flailing her arms and flinging the spoonful of apple crisp across the room. It landed with a splat on the floor.

"Mom, relax. It's still me." The bear held out his paws and gestured.

She cowered in her seat.

"Oh, for crying out loud!" Albert looked up toward the heavens and crossed his furry arms. "Mom, you need to lighten up a bit."

"Now don't you sass me, Albert. You know I'm afraid of bears!"

"Cripes!" he groaned. "Maybe this is better?" he said with sarcasm. His image suddenly morphed into a six-foot fuzzy rabbit. "Maybe I should change my name to Harvey?"

Everyone broke out laughing.

"That's not funny, Albert. Change back this instant." She jabbed her finger in rhythm to her words on the table.

"Fine." He waved in dismissal, "Abeo!" The giant rabbit dissolved with a puff of smoke and Albert reappeared.

Maggie sat staring at her hands. They were visibly trembling.

"Mrs. Cunningham," Camille said gently. "Here this is for you." She reached out into the air. "Rosa, sub rosa." Camille whispered. A beautiful lavender rose appeared in her hands and she handed the fragrant flower to the frightened woman. She hesitated before accepting the gift.

"It really isn't anything to be scared of." Camille offered. "It's just a different way of looking at things. Magick is as natural as planting a garden. It just needs to be nurtured for it to blossom."

"That's a good analogy, Camille." Abelene said with approval. "Maggie, would you like to go on a short journey?"

"What do you mean?"

"It's quick and painless. I'd like you to meet Azriel's uncle. He's also been teaching your children."

"Mom, are you sure that's wise?" Azriel questioned.

"Sometimes full immersion is the only way to bring about understanding."

Azriel shrugged and removed the dream orb from his pocket. He fixed the image of Uncle Nick's stronghold into the crystal. Jasper took his mother's hand and stood by Azriel. They all gathered around making sure they had contact with him. "Hang on," he said and touched the orb.

They suddenly relocated to Nicodemus' castle. They stood in the center of the courtyard and Maggie gaped in wonder. For all its remoteness and arid surroundings, it had an austere beauty she could appreciate. Nicodemus approached them with a friendly greeting, looking very much the wizard he was—except Azriel had never seen him actually wear the traditional robe and magister's cap normally associated with wizards in classic literature. He supposed it was all show for Mrs. Cunningham's sake. He nodded formally to Maggie and then to her children. "Well, it's very good to see my young adepts again. Julie, have you been practicing your quick fix spell?"

"Yes sir," she answered respectfully.

"Show me."

Surrounding the courtyard was a low stone wall with various urns and statues. About twenty feet from them, a fifteen inch stone gargoyle rested on one of the raised pedestals incorporated into the wall's design. Nicodemus gave a negligent flick of his finger and the poor statue tipped over and shattered. Its wings were broken in five pieces as well as its tail.

"Uncle Nick, you broke Mortimer!" Julia whined with disapproval.

"You named the statue?" Nicodemus asked tersely.

"Well," she blushed. "I kind of like him."

"Then you know what to do, dear." Nicodemus said patiently.

"Right." Julia produced a small wand from her sleeve as her mother raised an eyebrow. Though she didn't really need to use a wand, she preferred it for concentrating her will and directing the power toward her purpose. She pointed at the broken pieces and intoned the words to produce the desired result. "Simulacrum refectio!"

As if she had rewound the incident, the broken pieces came together with an audible click. The statue righted itself and floated back to the pedestal. She looked at Nicodemus proudly.

"That was awesome, Julia." Jasper complimented. "But I think I have one better." He flexed his arms and with his hands clawed to invoke his will, there was a drawing in of power and a sudden release. "Animatus Simulacrum!" he voiced with authority.

The tiny gargoyle suddenly shook as if awake from a long slumber, then stretched its green, leathery wings and yawned. It flew over to Jasper and perched on his shoulder. It began nuzzling against Jasper's cheek, purring affectionately. He smiled sheepishly and removed a caterpillar from a nearby bush and fed it to the little guy. Mortimer smacked his lips making yummy noises. It then flew onto

Maggie's arm obviously begging for another treat. Maggie froze in terror while the gargoyle rubbed his little head against her shoulder.

"Hey Mom, he likes you!" Jasper said brightly.

"Yes—he's really—um, cute—um, quite lovely." Eyes wide and a bit horrified, her voice quavered. She removed a small candy bar from her pocket and held it up for the gargoyle. It snatched it out of her hands and greedily slobbered it down, wrapper and all.

Nicodemus grabbed the spell book Julia was holding and smacked Jasper in the back of the head with it.

"You dolt!"

"What did I do? It worked perfectly." He shot back defensively.

"Idiot!" Nicodemus growled through gritted teeth. "Yes, you did it perfectly, but if you had bothered to read ahead, you would have discovered that there's no reversal spell!"

Mortimer licked his lips, belched, farted, and flew back to Jasper.

"Then what are you going to do with him, Uncle Nick?" Jasper smiled sheepishly.

"What am *I* going to do with him? You mean, what are *you* going to do with him. He's your problem now!"

"I can't very well take him back with me." Jasper protested.

"You brought him to life. He's already bonded with you."

"Actually, he *is* kind of cute." Camille smiled and scratched the little gargoyle under the chin. He purred and craned his neck for more. Mortimer practically melted into her hands like putty.

Maggie Cunningham glared sternly at Nicodemus with her arms crossed. "And you trust my kids with using magick? Are you nuts?"

Nicodemus held his hand to his mouth and coughed to hide a laugh. He spread his hands apologetically. "Well, I…"

Her eyes narrowed and she pressed her lips together with obvious disapproval.

Ever the diplomat, Nicodemus spoke gently. "Mrs. Cunningham, your children are actually quite talented, maybe a bit impetuous," he glanced over at the gargoyle now nuzzling up to Julia, "but remarkably talented. That just doesn't come out of thin air. Magickal talent is usually inherited. If there's anyone to blame, it would be you, my dear."

"What the hell is that supposed to mean?"

"Tell me, Mrs. Cunningham, when you were a child, what kind of books did you like to read?"

"How is that relevant?" she sputtered.

"Please, indulge me." He smiled affably.

"Well—I liked tales of knights and damsels in distress, you know, battling dragons and all that." Her face lit up as she remembered. "I loved One Thousand and One Arabian nights, and the stories of Merlin and King Arthur."

"See that!" Nicodemus grinned. "You were already predisposed to things of the magickal nature."

"I suppose…"

"The only difference is that you didn't have anyone to teach you."

"Yeah, but things like that don't happen in real life! I mean really…" Her words trailed off as she suddenly realized how silly she must have just sounded. Obviously, to the contrary, magick *did* happen. "I can't believe I'm saying this." Maggie grumbled. "Could you teach me?" her face suddenly became very hopeful and childlike.

"Hmm—well—I don't know." Nicodemus rubbed his beard indecisively.

"Oh, please?"

"Are you prepared to throw all logic and reason out the window?"

"That should be easy enough." she replied tersely. "After all, I've been raising three teenagers."

Jasper, Albert and Julia all gave scathing looks to their mother for her veiled insult, but Nicodemus quickly agreed that Maggie's training should begin as soon as possible. Decision made, they all headed into the stronghold.

A table had been arranged with all kinds of fruit and pastries. Mortimer flew in behind Jasper, and immediately dove toward the table. The gargoyle had revolting manners. It ravaged the fruit gluttonously, belching as it glommed down as much food as it could cram into its mouth. Maggie stared at it, somewhat horrified.

"That—that's disgusting." She held her hand to her mouth holding down her revulsion.

Camille came to the rescue. "Mortimer!" she shouted with authority. By now his hind end was sticking out with his head buried deep into the bowl of fruit. He poked his head out with what amounted to a look of guilt on his face.

"Get over here!" Camille pointed sternly. Mortimer flew over to her and hung his head in shame. "Now sit! Don't move." It lifted its clawed hands and started rubbing at its eyes, whimpering. It sulked as Camille patted its knobby little head. Camille smiled affectionately and produced a golden apple from her pocket. She held it out to him. Mortimer's eyes brightened and he grabbed at the treat, but Camille snatched it away.

"Take it nice!" she scolded. Penitently, Mortimer gingerly took the apple from her hands and quickly crammed the whole thing in his mouth, chewing noisily. Camille sighed. "We'll just have to work on that, Mortimer. Now behave yourself."

Jasper asked, "Master Nicodemus, the way Mortimer eats, how big is he likely to get?"

"He won't get any larger than the stone he was carved from."

"Well that's a relief." Albert said with a hint of sarcasm.

"Actually, Gargoyles are very obedient creatures, but they need to be taught. Mortimer is little more than a toddler, so to speak. He will take orders, but you must treat him kindly. Do that and he will be the most loyal friend you could ever have. Gargoyles are intelligent, crafty, and protective, but they can be destructive and gluttonous unless they are taught not to be. Punish him when he needs it, but not too long, otherwise he could become sulky and resentful. And keep in mind that he is a Magickal creature. One bite from him and you will be turned to stone for a day and a night. Not to worry though. It's not permanent and they rarely bite unless threatened or provoked."

Abelene looked adoringly at the creature and held out her arm. "Come here, Mortimer," she cooed. The gargoyle looked at Jasper as if asking permission. "Go ahead," he said. Mortimer flew over to Abelene and sighed with contentment. He folded his wings as

Abelene cradled him. Mortimer sighed and quickly fell asleep in her arms.

"He really is quite sweet," Abelene said as she looked down, smiling.

"Now that we have that out of the way, we need to arrange your lessons, Mrs. Cunningham," Nicodemus offered.

"Well I'm sure I can make time in the evenings after work." Maggie mused.

"Work!" Nicodemus said with disgust. "What is it you do?"

She smiled apologetically. "I'm a greeter at the local Megamart."

"How droll!" Nicodemus said with mild contempt. "We can't be having that now, can we? You need to learn, and you need to learn quickly." He strode over to a shelf, removed a few books, reached inside a hidden recess and yanked out a stack of one-hundred-dollar bills. "There's fifty thousand. That should get you by for the next few months. Can't have you splitting your loyalties. I suggest you quit your job immediately." Nicodemus ordered with finality.

Maggie gaped at the stack of bills, thoroughly flustered. It was more money than she would ever see in two years. "I don't know what to say?"

"Not enough?" he said with sincerity. "There's more if you need."

"But how..."

"Listen to me, dear. When one has lived as long as I have, eventually one has little need for money."

"Just how old..."

Jasper interjected. "Mom, you don't want to know. Trust me."

"Now, Mrs. Cunningham,"

She interrupted. "Nicodemus, please call me Maggie as long as we are on a first name basis."

"All right—Maggie. I will come for you every weekday at precisely nine o'clock. Be ready and have your lessons prepared. Azriel will be able to return you every evening. Are we all clear on this?"

They all nodded.

"Now as soon as the time is right, I will begin relocating all of you to keep you hidden and safe. Sadly, I fear we are running out of time. It may be sooner rather than later."

Eddie was in a black mood. Lately he spent more and more time by himself. He no longer hung out with Dirk. In truth it could be said that Dirk no longer associated with Eddie and had found a new set of friends. Now it seemed that Cory and Bernie were becoming scarce as well. The fact that he had come home from school to find his mother passed out on the couch with an empty bottle of vodka by her side only added to his isolation. It didn't help his frame of mind either when, the night before, his father had called again from Japan, where he did business. Like twice before, he was going to be detained for another two weeks. When was the last time he had seen the old man, Eddie wondered? Two, three months? Christmas, that's right! He thought. He had been back for five days and then had to return to Japan on an urgent matter. He had brought Eddie the latest video games from Tokyo. They still remained unopened on his dresser.

Eddie despised his life, resented his father for his continual absence, and hated his mother for her weakness. Anger building, Eddie sat on a bench in the deserted city park wanting to destroy something—anything. As he simmered, a golden-tinged grey squirrel scampered down a tree to gather a few acorns and paused nervously, sizing Eddie up. He stared at the tiny creature with contempt. Eddie picked up a sizable rock at his feet and hurled it at the poor animal. He hit it squarely in the hindquarters. It squealed with pain and darted up the tree for cover—and safety.

"Stupid squirrel," Eddie muttered darkly.

He heard soft footsteps coming from behind him and turned suspiciously.

"Hello, Eddie," Barclay said pleasantly.

"What the hell do *you* want?"

"Now don't be that way. I just want to sit—and talk."

"I don't feel like talking, okay." Eddie snarled.

"*Good.*" Altais thought. His alter ego, Barclay, had done a good job in gaining the boy's confidence. Now it was time for the masterstroke. *I will destroy him so utterly that I can build him back up piece by piece. Mold him like soft clay, shape him—sculpt him into whatever shape I desire, to be useful. I shall become his friend, and he will have no other. Right now, though, I will say nothing. Give the boy the luxury and the solitude of silence.*

He watched Eddie out of the corner of his eye. He could almost see the chip the boy carried on his shoulder becoming a mountain ready to crush him into a pile of guts. Slumped on the bench, back hunched, nearly ready to break with the unbearable weight, Eddie was close to self-destruction. Just the place Altais needed him.

"I hate my life," Eddie exploded. "And I hate this world."

Barclay didn't answer immediately. Timing was everything. He waited until all the rage Eddie harbored was nearly ready to spill forth in a torrent, like a dam breaking.

"Eddie, what would you say if I told you the world is not what you think it is? Everything you were led to believe is a lie, not necessarily an intentional deception, but a lie of omission."

"Why are you talking crap? Life is real enough and it sucks. You're just trying to confuse me with all your big talk."

"That is not my intention, Eddie. But perhaps you will allow me to show you something that will put it all into perspective. All it requires is that you trust me."

"Why should I?"

"Because I'm the only one who can help you right now. I'd like to take you on a short excursion. Let's call it a day trip. Why don't you call your mother and tell her you'll be gone for a few hours."

"She wouldn't care. She's wasted right now, passed out on the couch." Eddie stewed where he sat. He stood defiantly. "Sure, let's go. Show me your big secret."

"Good," Barclay smiled warmly but there seemed to be a hint of cruelty in that smile. "Care to go for a ride?"

"Sure."

He was parked across the street—a new black Mercedes S-Class sedan.

"Get in," Barclay offered.

"Nice wheels." Eddie admired. He sank into the soft leather interior and ran his fingers across the sculpted dashboard with appreciation. He had never been in such an opulent car. His mother's car was a ten-year-old Ford Minivan, not bad, but nothing like this!

Barclay turned over the ignition with a grin and the engine purred with the potential of speed. It only took five minutes to head across to the neighboring town. A ritzy world-class hotel overlooked a pristine blue lake. Beyond it, a dock wrapped around a marina that housed the playthings of the rich and well-connected. Eddie stared up at the grand structure with wonder, dazzled by such wealth as Barclay flipped his keys to the parking attendant.

"Are you hungry, Eddie?" Barclay asked as they entered the main lobby.

"Starved."

"Then let's eat."

They headed to the top floor of the high rise. The five-star restaurant afforded a panoramic view of the lake and surrounding mountains. Eddie stared out at the scene, which started him thinking. He was troubled, yes, but not stupid. Looking down at the menu, he noted the prices. A lunch for two could easily top a hundred dollars. He placed the leather-bound placard on the table and stared suspiciously at Barclay.

"Who are you, really?" There was a touch of scorn in his voice.

"What do you mean?" Barclay asked, genuinely surprised by the question.

"You're a reporter, right?"

"Yes."

"Well, I'm not an idiot. You couldn't afford a place like this on a reporter's salary."

Barclay chuckled. "Very perceptive, Eddie."

"Well?" he shot back.

"All in due time, Eddie. When we're done eating, I have something to show you."

The waitress returned, took the order and scurried back to the kitchen. Ten minutes later she placed two plates on the table. Barclay had ordered a filet mignon and Eddie, a seafood platter. It was perhaps the most delicious meal he had eaten in months. His mother had crawled back into a bottle and rarely cooked anymore. And when she did, it was out of a box or pre-prepared. Either way, it took little effort.

They spoke little as they finished their lunch. Barclay paid with cash and left a generous tip. He then led Eddie to the elevator and punched the button taking him to the sixteenth floor. The door slid open and Barclay turned right to the end of the hall. The double doors opened into a three-room suite trimmed in oak and polished brass.

Eddie gaped. "Now I *know* you're not a reporter, so who are you?"

"Tell me, Eddie. Do you believe everything you see?"

"Real is real, isn't it?"

"That depends on your point of view. You go to the movies, the canisters of film are real enough, but what they contain is an illusion loaded with special effects. Yet while you watch, you believe what you see, right?"

"I suppose."

"What about this?" Barclay waved his hand and in a gentle arc. His attire suddenly changed. He now wore a robe of midnight blue velvet, and atop his head a golden brocaded hexagonal tam. In his hand he held a staff.

"What the…" Eddie pulled back and his eyes flew open. "Who the hell *are* you?"

"My true name is Altais."

"You're a magician, then."

He chuckled. "Magician is such a derogatory title. No, Eddie, I'm a sorcerer—a wizard if you please."

"Bullcrap. There's no such thing."

"Quite the contrary." Altais smiled. "There is a hidden world of which you're not even remotely aware, Eddie. We are part of a secret society, blended in with the rest of the world so no one would suspect. Do not confuse us with charlatans who pull rabbits out of hats and make their beautiful assistants disappear. That is fakery, slight of hand, trap doors. Magick is real—and everywhere. You are among wizards and witches and don't even know it."

"So you can do anything you want, make anything you want?"

"Within certain boundaries."

"So you could have all the money you want?"

Altais snickered. Just what he expected. Shallow greed instead of the true potential of power and control. This was too easy. "Certainly!" Altais muttered an incantation and stacks of money, gold coins, and jewels appeared on the coffee table.

"Holy crap!" Eddie laughed, dazzled by such wealth. "Did you just make all that?"

"No Eddie, I stole it. A little bit here, a little bit there from strong boxes and safes all over the world. It will never be missed—at least not right away." Altais said with mild contempt. "Care to see more?"

"Yeah!" Eddie answered expectantly.

"How about this?" Altais snapped his finger with a wicked grin. With a flash that made Eddie flinch, three beautiful girls, perhaps few years older than him, appeared. Wearing nothing but skimpy bathing suits, they approached him and giggled. "Hi Eddie," they all said in unison. "Oh, he so cute," the sultry blonde said dreamily. "And so strong," The cute Asian one chimed in. "And so manly," the young black woman with tight curls whispered in a husky voice. They surrounded him, pressing their bodies against him and began showering him with kisses as one began unbuttoning his shirt.

Altais snapped his finger again and they vanished.

"Hey, where did they go?" Eddie wiped the sweat off his brow with a sleeve.

"Trickery—illusion!" Altais sneered.

"But…" Eddie tugged at his collar with frustration.

"How about if I show you the truth."

"What truth?"

"Is there anyone you wish to see—perhaps, spy upon?"

Eddie thought for a while. He had not seen his father for three months. What possibly could be keeping him away for so long while

Eddie's mother continued to deteriorate into the useless husk she had become? Yes, he knew what he wanted to see.

"Could you show me my father?"

"Are you sure you want to spy on your father? Perhaps his life should remain private, Eddie." Altais faked his concern but inwardly smiled with glee. This would cement Eddie's enslavement. The boy would have no one else to turn to.

"I want to see him now." He demanded.

"As you wish."

Altais brought Eddie to the master suite where the full-length mirror was affixed to a wall. He prepared to invoke a projection into the mirror, but then asked Eddie, "Do you have anything that belongs to your father? It will help locate him."

"I have this." Eddie reached into his pocket and extracted a folding penknife. He handed it to Altais. "Will that work?"

"Perfectly." He took a glass from the bathroom and placed it on its side, then he inserted the folding knife into the glass, pointing the base like a lens toward the reflecting surface of the mirror. He dropped to his knees and whispered something into the open part of the crystal glass. Eddie thought he heard the word "reveal."

At first nothing happened. But soon the surface of the mirror began to change. Like an upright television, it revealed an image of Eddie's father. He seemed to be sitting on a comfortable couch in a high-rise apartment. This was obvious by the panoramic view of the brightly lit city coming from the window behind him. Gaudy neon decorated the city, words shaped in light, Kanji, the newer Katakana, and Romanized Japanese decorated the skyline of inner Tokyo. His father shuffled through papers, highlighting key passages of work-related documents. Eddie smiled, happy to see his father busy working the evening hours. But his smile faltered when a woman entered the frame, a lovely Asian woman perhaps a few years younger than Eddie's mother, sat beside the man holding two martini glasses. She handed one to Eddie's dad, then pressed her shapely body against his. She kissed him tenderly—and Eddie's father responded without hesitation.

"No." Eddie shook his head in denial. "No!" His anger morphed into tears. "No, no, no!" Eddie could not contain his rage as he watched his father engage the beautiful woman. He couldn't watch anymore. He took a vase from the end table and hurled it with all his strength at the mirror. It shattered, spraying the room with shards of silvered glass. He dropped to his knees and sobbed.

"I'm sorry, Eddie. It was not my intention to upset you." Altais held the boy to his shoulder as he cried. "The truth is not always pleasant, son. Life is filled with disappointment and heartache. But wouldn't it be nice to have power over those who hurt you or torment you? Wouldn't it?"

"How?" Eddie sniffed, utterly broken of spirit.

"Would you like to get back at all those who have hurt you, Eddie? I could *show* you how." Altais suddenly stood tall and flexed his arms over his head. All the shards and splinters of mirrored glass gathered into a writhing mass above the sorcerer's head and suddenly flew back into the empty frame. It seemed to melt, then reformed again into a perfect surface. Eddie paled at the display of such power. He bristled with his first tinge of fear. Thus far, everything might have had a logical explanation, the money, the girls, even the viewing of his father in Tokyo, but seeing the destruction he had caused to suddenly reverse and the mirror restored to wholeness was more than he could accept. He backed away from the mirror and sat again on the couch. Eddie's hands shook.

"Now listen to me, Eddie." Altais reasoned. "You've seen some strange things in the past few years, haven't you?"

Eddie nodded.

"And no one believed you, did they?"

"Not a one. They all think I'm crazy." He said hotly.

"What if I told you you're not crazy? There is an explanation, though you won't like it." Altais flashed a grim smile. Tell me, Eddie. Who do you really despise right now—someone you really hate."

"Well, that's a no brainer. It's that Azriel and his witch girlfriend."

"He's a sorcerer, Eddie. A very powerful one—a wizard, like me. And the girl, Camille; she's no slouch either. Remember those birds that attacked you a few years back? That was no accident. Azriel caused it. And the mountain lion that spoke? That can only occur through powerful Magick. Eddie, I am aligned with five other wizards. Throughout the ages, we have protected humanity against disaster by neutralizing rogue wizards. You have done us a great service by leading us to Azriel. He is dangerous and has the power to destroy the world. It is my duty to stop him at all costs. Now I think it is time for you to meet my Master."

Altais arose from his seat and formed a few arcane gestures over the mirror. Its reflective surface swirled and reconstituted. Without warning he grabbed Eddie by the wrist. The boy tried to wrestle from his grasp but, the wizard's grip was strong, and he could not break free.

"What are you doing?" Eddie spoke angrily through gritted teeth.

"You must trust me." Altais replied, dragging Eddie toward the mirror. With two strides Altais stepped through the mirror and pulled Eddie behind him.

Eddie trembled where he stood. The room was dimly lit by candles affixed to sconces inset into the stone walls. Five men sat at a table with high-backed chairs, more like thrones. They were dressed much the same as Altais in black hooded robes. Only the one at the head of the table seemed different. His robe was lined with a purple embellishment around the seams and there were strange symbols embroidered in the fine silky cloth. But the difference was not in the clothes he wore, but in the emanation of power he exuded. The man rose from his seat and lowered his cowl. He had a kind face, all except for his eyes which were piercing, hard, and unforgiving.

"Is this the boy, Altais?"

"Yes, my Lord Rastaban. It is he."

Eddie shook with fear as Rastaban approached. The ancient wizard stood inches from Eddie and captivated the boy with his gaze. He stared into Eddie's eyes examining him, probing his thoughts. Eddie could not turn but was trapped by that gaze as if he were involuntarily held motionless. Rastaban turned away and chuckled to himself. "Yes, this one will do just fine for our purposes."

Only then was Eddie able to move again.

"Eddie, I have a job for you. Complete it to my satisfaction and you will be rewarded."

Eddie knew he was now part of something that seemed to make little sense, but his eyes told him differently. He was among powerful men, yet for some reason they needed *him*. Although terrified, the thought appealed to him. There was at minimum a pervading sense of menace, yet Eddie liked it. And though he couldn't place a finger on what it was, something dangerous dwelled beneath his feet. He didn't know how he knew, but there was a powerful force nearby that terrified and exhilarated him at the same time. After being so powerless for so long, so impotent against forces beyond his control, Eddie was ready to embrace that dark force if only to give himself power against his enemies. Behind him, Altais peered at Rastaban and smiled victoriously.

Eddie looked back at Altais then at Lord Rastaban. He said evenly, "What is it you want me to do?"

Chapter 18

After two days spent with Nicodemus, it was time to return to Harden Lake. The morning sky was overcast, threatening to rain all day. They translocated back to Maggie's home. Mortimer, perched on Jasper's shoulder, gave a perfunctory look around and flew onto the porch railing. Jasper said evenly, "Now, Mortimer, this is your new home. You must stay on the property and never leave. If anyone ever finds you, they will do bad things to you. Do you understand?"

Mortimer nodded and held up one finger. He flew across the yard to a run-down shed sorely in need of paint. He hung onto the wood planking and nearly faded from view. Like a chameleon, he changed color, blending into the wood. He was now barely discernible.

"Wow, cool!" Albert grinned.

Mortimer flew back to Jasper's shoulder and changed back into his normal mottled green. He seemed to have an expression on his face that bespoke pride.

"Well, we had best be going," Abelene said with a smile. Maggie, laden down with a few spellbooks, handed them over to Julia and embraced Abelene.

"I don't know whether to thank you or curse you for getting me involved in all this," Maggie quipped, "but at least now I know what's been going on around here."

"I understand," Abelene responded warmly. "Now don't be a stranger. If you get hung up on any spells, feel free to ask my help."

After returning home, Azriel did a quick sweep of the house to make sure there were no other intrusions. Was it paranoia? Probably, but Azriel couldn't help feeling exposed. He had always felt safe in his own home, but now he couldn't shake the uneasy feeling. Things seemed normal enough now, but he was deeply troubled by something Nicodemus had said in passing—something about time growing short. When pressed on the issue, Nicodemus replied that he had nothing concrete, but he would have an answer soon—as soon as he double-checked his calculations. After that, he refused to answer any more questions on the matter.

This didn't sit well with Azriel. He hated being in the dark about anything. What made it worse was that the science of alchemy seemed to elude him. He had read over the Emerald Tablet of Thoth so many times for clues to the key to alchemy that his head hurt. It still made little sense to him. He planned to question Pog as soon as it was humanly possible and perhaps get some answers from him. Azriel didn't know why, but his gut told him that Pog could very well offer some insights that Nicodemus was either unable or unwilling to reveal.

The following day, school would resume, and Azriel had a good mind to blow off his classes. But he knew better. Abelene would certainly get cross with him and make his life unbearable for the next several days following the infraction. So with a sigh of resignation, he decided he would go, but perhaps skip out early. He would then head directly to see Nicodemus and resume his feeble attempts at alchemy.

The day started in the usual fashion. Azriel showered and prepared himself for school. He looked at himself in the mirror and noticed the beginnings of a soft beard. It looked terrible. Camille had even complained through giggles that it tickled when they kissed the day before. But he had to admit he was looking more like a man every day. He had mixed feelings about it. Childhood was now behind him. He would soon have to face the challenges of being an adult. But he was also resentful as hell. What normal adult would ever have to face a destiny laid out before him like Azriel's? Thinking about it darkened his mood. No one at his school could ever imagine how complicated his life had become, no one except Camille. Of course Jasper, Albert, and Julia knew some of it, but he only told his deepest fears and concerns to Camille. She seemed to understand him even more than his mother did. Love probably had something to do with it, not that Abelene didn't love him. Certainly she did, and proved it in so many ways. It was different with Camille, though. Tender and intimate. Thinking of her, he decided he would do what he had put off for some time. He removed a shaving kit from the drawer—one Nicodemus had given him a few months ago—and opened it.

Shaving was awkward at first. Handling the razor gingerly for fear of cutting himself, Azriel felt a bit spastic as he applied pressure. He did manage to finish the job with only two nicks on his chin. He put on a little aftershave and cologne, wincing from the sting.

Azriel headed downstairs for breakfast. Abelene had a bowl of oatmeal waiting for him. She looked up from reading and giggled at the cuts on his face. She gently touched the cuts on his chin.

"Staunch!" she commanded, and the cuts closed and disappeared.

They heard a tap on the door, and Camille let herself in.

"Morning!" she said brightly.

"Morning, dear." Abelene returned the greeting and served up a bowl for the girl. "Will Penelope and Daphne be home today?"

"I don't think they have any plans. Why don't you ask them?" Camille pointed to the ring on her finger as a reminder.

"Of course." Abelene shook her head clearing the little lapse of memory.

"Mom, is everything okay?" Azriel asked. Abelene was not usually forgetful.

"Oh, just distracted." she said absently and went back to reading her book.

"What are you reading?" Camille asked with her mouth full.

"Swallow first." Abelene scolded. The girl blushed.

"Well?" Camille demanded.

"It's a book on star movements and trajectories. Nicodemus asked me to look for something about alignments. I haven't found it yet, though." She went back to the book and took notes on a sheet of paper.

Camille and Azriel finished eating. He grabbed his schoolbooks. "I have to go, Mom." He kissed her. "I'll probably be home late. Camille and I will be heading to Nicodemus straight from school."

"Then I will see you there. I have something to discuss with your uncle."

The day dragged, even for a Monday. Azriel fidgeted in his seat watching the clock, waiting for the bell to ring. Only one more class and he would be free to translocate to Caer Wylusung and continue his alchemical work. He thought absently.

Azriel had finally succeeded in transmuting boron into carbon. It sounded simple enough, but it was no easy task. He failed five times before finally getting the desired result. The problem was that the ideas of modern chemistry needed to be partially abandoned. Alchemy required a different thought process and a strict code of conduct. It wasn't merely dealing with substance, but a blending of spirit. Nicodemus had blandly stated that, to understand alchemy, one must assume the innocence of an infant and the craftiness of an old fox.

The bell rang. Azriel gathered his books and headed toward the gymnasium. The basketball court was flanked on either side by slide-out bleachers opposite the entrance to the gym; to the right of the bleachers was the door to the locker room. Azriel was about to enter to change into his gym shorts when he thought he heard his name mentioned. Ears perked up, he listened while he looked around to locate the source. High above him on the top tier of the risers, he heard Eddie talking in low whispers to Cory and Bernie. Azriel was curious about what the lout had to say, and ducked underneath the bleachers directly below them.

Eddie was agitated as his friends sat quietly; a few other boys also listened in.

"Look, I'm telling you," Eddie said heatedly. "That reporter, Barclay, found me in the park. I was really pissed about a few things. We talked and he invited me to lunch at the resort. But then when he invited me up to his suite, all hell broke loose."

"He invited you into his hotel room? What, does he have a thing for *boys*?" Cory snickered.

Eddie glared at him with a level gaze. "Don't be a perv, you jackass!"

"Then what did he want?"

"Well as it turns out, Barclay isn't a reporter. It's not even his real name. He goes by the name Altais, and he's a Wizard."

"A wizard." Bernie shot back in a mocking voice.

"Yeah, butt-crack! I wouldn't have believed it either if I hadn't seen it for myself."

Under the bleachers, Azriel blanched.

"The guy, like, shape-shifted before my eyes. He created money and jewels out of thin air."

"That would be pretty useful." Cory made a side comment to Bernie, snickering.

"Shut up, man. I'm being serious." Eddie growled. "Altais snapped his finger and suddenly there were three hot babes in the room ready to do anything I wanted. Then he made them disappear."

"Likely story. Hey Breck, you couldn't even get a female dog." Bernie laughed. Eddie punched him.

"You think I'm making this stuff up? Screw you, Bernie." Eddie continued his story but omitted what he had seen in the mirror. That was too painful. Beneath him, listening, Azriel began to sweat. Panic rose in his throat like bile.

"The whole thing gets crazier from here," Eddie said darkly. "Altais waved his hands, or something like that, and the mirror in his room changed. He grabbed my hand, stepped into the mirror and dragged me through. Scared the piss out of me. Look, I know it sounds nuts, but it was magic, plain and simple. We were in this other place—underground, I think. Altais then introduced me to this other wizard he called Master—a guy who called himself Rastaban. He was kind of old and creepy—scary, like he had a lot of power and would mess up anyone who got in his way. Then he told me there was something I had to do."

"Yeah, like what?" Cory asked derisively.

"Sorry man, I can't tell you. I swore I wouldn't."

Bernie glanced at Cory then at Eddie. "Man—dude—what kind of drugs are you on?"

"What, you don't believe me?"

"It's not like you've been exactly stable," Cory sniped. "First you say a mountain lion spoke to you, then wizards that do tricks and walk through mirrors. What next? Little green men from Mars? Eddie, you need to get some professional help, man. You're losing it."

The few others who had been listening shook their heads and stepped down from the bleachers with comments like "nuts" and "crazy" escaping their lips. As they walked toward the locker room, Azriel slipped deeper into the shadows.

"Look, "Eddie continued. "I didn't think you guys would believe me. But I know what I saw. And something else, too. That Azriel and his witch girlfriend? Well, their lives are going to get real complicated from here."

"What does Azriel have to do with anything?" Cory asked.

"Something Altais told me. Azriel is a wizard too. Remember all the weird stuff that's been happening around here? Azriel's the reason. The little turd is dangerous. Altais told me to watch out for him."

Eddie continued to rattle on to his friends, but Azriel had heard enough. He slipped into the locker room and exited out the back way to the main lobby where Camille would be waiting. She always did this, since she had a free period at the end of her school day.

Azriel stomped up, obviously distressed, and pulled her by the arm. Flustered she followed quickly behind, struggling to keep up with him.

"Azriel, what's wrong?"

"Shh. Not here!" he whispered looking this way and that so he wouldn't be noticed. He pulled Camille behind a stand of bushes that lined the school.

"Azriel!" she purred, a bit shocked and a little turned on by the thoughts suddenly running through her mind.

"It's not what you think." Azriel said firmly. He removed the dream orb from his pocket, infused the image, and translocated with Camille to Nicodemus' stronghold.

When they arrived at Caer Wylusung, they found Nicodemus and Abelene tinkering with an unusual contraption. Two disks on pulleys, one behind the other, turned in the same direction.

Nicodemus was making adjustments to the gears. Strange symbols were scribed on the surface of the first disk, with configurations that looked much like a star chart of constellations. Behind it, the larger wheel had continuous marks like the succession of seconds on the face of a clock. Azriel, however, was in a heightened state of agitation and didn't bother asking what the device was for. Nicodemus picked up on Azriel's mood.

"What seems to be the problem, Azriel?"

"Uncle Nick, we have a *big* problem."

Nicodemus had never seen Azriel so completely agitated. Whatever it was must be serious. He sat on the high-backed brocaded chair and offered the other two seats to Azriel and Camille.

"Is everything okay between you two?" he asked amicably.

"It's not about Camille and me. Everything's fine in that area. It's about the Clave. Remember Barclay? Well he's been talking to that tool, Eddie."

"How do you know?" Abelene asked.

"I overheard him talking about me, so I hid under the bleachers listening, spying. It turns out Barclay *isn't* Barclay. He's Altais."

Nicodemus looked up as if he had been struck. "Are you sure?"

"Positive. Eddie, that rat, was rambling on about things he couldn't possibly know. I also heard him say that Altais dragged him through a mirror to some secret place where he met Rastaban."

Nicodemus rubbed his beard thoughtfully. "This is indeed troubling. It appears the Clave is preparing to make a move. Perhaps we must hide you before they strike."

"But what about everyone else? Jasper and Albert, Julia and her mom—they're in danger too," Camille stated the obvious.

"They will not do anything to draw attention to themselves, but you are right, Camille. We must move everyone out of harm's path."

"So we should move on it now," Azriel said heatedly.

"True." Nicodemus nodded. "But first there is something I must show you. Abelene, would you reset the wheels to zero?"

She deftly readjusted the strange device turning back both wheels to a starting point. Above it an ornate arrow fixed to the twelve o'clock position pointed to zero. Examining it, Azriel noted that the increments etched into the larger wheel were consecutively marked 1000, 2000, 3000, and so on. Aligned beneath the arrow, two dots—one red and one green—on each wheel lined up. On the smaller wheel to the right of the red dot was a blue dot delineating a position over one of the constellations.

"What is this thing, Uncle Nick?" Azriel peered at it closely examining the constellations on the wheel. He recognized some of the easier ones like Orion, Ursa Major and Cassiopeia. But their positions did not seem to match how they appeared in the sky. They appeared almost random.

Nicodemus cleared his throat and pointed to the red dot on the larger disk. "This wheel," he began, "represents the world before it was split in two. "Now this one," he pointed to the green on the smaller disk, "this marks the point of fracture, when the worlds were split in two. And this one is you, Azriel." Uncle Nick pointed to the blue dot. Now watch what happens."

Nicodemus pressed a button on the base of the device, and the wheels began to slowly turn clockwise. Upon examination, however, the smaller wheel representing Earth moved slightly faster. As both disks rotated, the time piece measured off years. Through each successive millennium the span between the two worlds ever widened. At one point, the two worlds sat opposite each other in their paths. Azriel looked at the dial. At this point, it marked off 10,000 years. As the Earth dimension continued its path, the gap between the two worlds narrowed with Earth approaching Aralia in the advancement of years.

"Now watch!" Nicodemus spoke with passion, his eyes aglow.

The blue dot representing Azriel now was in alignment with Aralia. Nicodemus halted the motion of the wheels.

"See that, Azriel? That is the moment of your birth. As you can see, the stars attested to your coming. In that grand alignment, you were born at the very head of the constellation Draconis. It is your destiny to slay the dragon, destroy the Clave and heal the worlds. Now here is the culmination."

Nicodemus turned the switch and the wheel advanced another few increments until the red and green dot aligned again. He again halted the machine's motion.

"And there you see it—a grand conjunction when both worlds will align. It is at this time, and this time only, when fusing the worlds back to one can be accomplished. If it does not happen, then the worlds will have to wait another 20,000 years, at which point neither world will survive."

Azriel held his hand to his mouth thinking as he examined the placement of the three dots. Something eluded him. "Uncle Nick, why is the time of my birth so significant?"

"Good question." He answered. "The time of the alignment draws near. The day the worlds conjoin will be the day you turn eighteen."

"So what are you saying?" Azriel couldn't mask his panic. "We have less than a year and a half? How the hell am I supposed to do all this in a year and a half?"

"Language." Abelene interjected sternly.

"No wait. I have to finish the final task of creating the Lapis Occultus. I have to release the four elementals from their bondage. I have to defeat the clave. And all this has to be done in one and a half years? Do I have that correct?" Azriel spat with sharp sarcasm.

Nicodemus smiled slightly. "Yes, I'm afraid so."

"Well that's just great. Is there any more good news?" Azriel sputtered.

Nicodemus shrugged. "There is another minor detail."

"Yeah? And what would that be?"

"At the moment you were born. Jupiter, Venus and Mars formed a great trine, framing the head of the constellation Draconis."

"Sorry," Azriel shot back belligerently, "I never studied astrology. You're going to have to explain it to me." He crossed his arms.

"It's really quite simple. Jupiter is the planet of kings and leadership. Venus is the ruler of the heart—of love, and Mars is the warrior—the conqueror. Together they are quite powerful. These three are auspicious planets to be born under, but..." Nicodemus held up his finger. "The fact that they formed a grand trine over the head of Draconis speaks of another matter. The dragon rules over wisdom. And the head of the dragon is the star—Eltanin."

Azriel looked up, startled.

"Son it's no accident that Eltanin is the head of Draconis. If you had studied the stars, you might have realized that the seven wizards of the Clave were duly named for the main stars that make up Draconis."

"I thought the Clave had six wizards."

"Indeed! But you're forgetting that Eltanin had been the head of the Clave before he was betrayed, so the message is clear. Your birth overshadows Eltanin. Your destiny is clear. You, Azriel, will defeat the dragon—Draconis—otherwise known as the Clave, and you will also someday replace Eltanin as head of the new Clave. Eltanin will wane as you wax strong, for you are his heir, Azriel. You were destined from the beginning to replace him."

"But Eltanin was the greatest Sorcerer who ever lived."

"That's true, young Master, but the operative word is *was*. Yes, Eltanin, is indeed powerful—not one to be trifled with, but he was permanently scarred by the ritual that split Aralia into two worlds. It broke his heart, Azriel. He has never recovered." Nicodemus gravely stated.

Stricken to the heart, Azriel's chest heaved as if all the air had been sucked from his lungs. "What am I going to do?" he complained.

Nicodemus retorted with a sharp rebuke. "You can begin by stopping your whining." He pounded the table with his fist. Camille jumped, startled by the old man's intensity. "Next, you must stand firm and ready. Learn all there is to learn. Embrace your destiny and for God's sake, grow a backbone!"

"I'm sorry, Uncle Nick." Azriel muttered penitently.

"And stop apologizing." Nicodemus added. He stormed off to his study with a very distraught Abelene chasing after him. That left Azriel and Camille alone in the main hall.

Camille looked at Azriel with sympathy, then flew into his arms.

"Are you okay?" she asked in a soothing voice.

"I suppose," he replied glumly.

"I've never seen Nicodemus lose his temper."

"I think he's scared."

"No way," Camille protested. "Nicodemus isn't afraid of anything."

"No, he would never show it. His fear usually comes out as anger."

"Are you afraid, Azriel?" She whispered.

"Terrified."

"Terrified of what?" she squeezed his hand.

"Terrified of what will happen if I fail—and terrified of what will happen if I succeed."

Camille gently placed her hands on Azriel's face. "This may not mean much, but I have complete confidence in you and—I love you."

"I know you do, Camille. It's just that…"

"Hey, what ever it is you must do, we'll get through it together, okay?"

382

Chapter 19

A steady drizzle drenched the woods and surrounding forest around Harden Lake. Abelene glanced out the window, sipping a cup of tea, watching the rain. The house was so quiet and tranquil that it was hard for her to imagine that anything could be wrong with the world on such a pleasant, warm spring day. The gentle raindrops nurtured her garden and filled her with longing for Aralia. It had been over sixteen years since her departure and she wondered what had become of her cousin Elsinore and Elrid, Captain of the guard. Did they preserve the kingdom in her absence, or did the palace fall to anarchy through lack of a king? If Elsinore followed her wishes, she would be acting as queen regent in Abelene's stead.

She smiled fondly. She hoped that Elsinore would have married Elrid by now. The captain had always carried a flame for Elsinore, even when she was a haughty, belligerent child, and Elrid, a mere palace guard.

But Abelene had other things to think about. For one, Azriel, for all his quiet strength, seemed so vulnerable lately with such a heavy burden placed on his shoulders. The fate of two worlds would be determined by her son's success or failure. She sorely wished he had been born ordinary so he wouldn't have to suffer the interminable loneliness of one whose actions bore so much scrutiny. Certainly, Azriel was surrounded by friends and so many who loved him, but the fact remained that he was so horribly alone. Though they all perhaps understood his burden in concept, no one could fully comprehend the depth of Azriel's inner conflicts and the constant turmoil of his soul. Lately Azriel was so tough on himself that Abelene seldom had the heart to correct him anymore. Not that it was often necessary. The burden of the future seemed to have suddenly matured Azriel beyond his brief years. She wiped away a tear as she stared out the window.

Krinaea had kept her promise to Nicodemus and guarded the woods that kept Abelene's home secluded—shut away from the outside world. Abelene had poured much of her magick into the trees to the point where they were nearly self-aware, but Earth wasn't like Aralia. The trees didn't obey her like they did before the worlds were torn asunder. Like so many other magickal creatures, Krinaea had been diminished by the rending of Aralia. She still had her Health Sense and could cure plant and creature alike, but Earth held little magick and the trees no longer responded to her. Therefore, Krinaea was more than a little surprised when a mighty oak that stood on the perimeter of the open glade suddenly lashed out and held her fast. She struggled against its limbs; the more she strained against it, the tighter its grip. Krinaea stopped struggling. She tried to think logically. Was it possible that the trees had reached sentience? Speaking in the language of trees, she, Queen of the Dryads, commanded. "Release me, brother Oak!"

But the oak held firm and, oddly, she sensed the tree viewed her as an enemy. Anger like sap rose up in the tree and squeezed her harder. She could not even translocate out of its grasp since her arms were affixed and prevented her from forming the sigils needed for her escape. There was magick here—but from a source she had never encountered.

Frustrated, Krinaea sighed. "Kita!" she called out, sensing her companion was near. She waited for a few minutes and called out again. She knew it was just a matter of time. Since they both guarded the forest, they had naturally become quite close. They had spent lonely hours talking of woodland things and teaching Hermes the skills he would need to survive. By now Hermes was half grown and well on his way to developing into a magnificent mountain lion.

Krinaea sensed Kita's approach. She was silent on her feet and cautiously entered the glade. Kita wasn't particularly fond of open spaces. They made her feel exposed.

"Kita! Up here!" Krinaea called out in a quiet voice. Kita looked up startled and then emitted a soft series of growls, her equivalent of laughter. She sat on her haunches and examined her little friend. "My, my—you seem to have gotten yourself into a bit of a bind, little sister."

Krinaea flashed an ironic smile. "I'm trapped, though I don't exactly know why. Where's Hermes?"

"Nearby. Today he hunts alone. He is no longer a cub."

"You should be proud, Kita."

"I am," she purred.

"Kita, could you find Abelene? I'm sure she could get me out of this."

"It would be my pleasure."

The rain had abated. Kita rose, shook the water off her fur, and turned to leave when an arrow flew out of the thicket, striking her in the shoulder. Kita roared in pain and collapsed onto the ground.

"Kita!" The dryad called out in horror.

As the she-lion fell, vines shot out of the ground and bound Kita until she was immobile. Krinaea's eyes flew open suddenly aware that she was hearing an incantation. Powerful magick was being used—magick she hadn't seen since the old days. A tall arborvitae planted by the stone bench, central to the glade, moved slightly and morphed into a man. A concealment spell! How had she missed it? Krinaea chided herself for becoming old and weak. When she was young, she would never have been fooled so easily. Though diminished, she was still not without power. She strained against her bonds and began to call out, invoking all the woodland creatures around to come to her aid. But the moment she did, the man motioned with his hands. A branch shot out from the tree and wrapped around her face, effectively gagging Krinaea and preventing speech. Now powerless, she struggled and wept.

The man muttered a few words and motioned with his hand. A shrub off to the left vanished, replaced by a boy. Dressed in camouflage, he held a crossbow in his hands.

"A good shot, Eddie." Altais complimented him with cruel laughter. The boy stood over Kita and gloated. Though bound and injured, Kita was not mortally wounded. She looked up at Eddie with contempt. "I should have eaten you the first time I saw you."

Hermes watched from under the dense thicket, immobile with indecision. Mother had taught him from the beginning never to place himself in danger unless it was absolutely necessary. This certainly was a dire situation but there were two man-things against one, and one—the man-cub—held a killing-thing that shot thorns. Could he attack? Hermes looked for an advantage, but didn't see any. He knew he must act. Hidden low, he had the element of surprise. Lying prone on the ground, however, only Kita could see him. She made eye contact with him and shook her head imperceptibly in the manner of cats. The message was clear. Do not.

Hermes crept away and, with adequate distance between them, galloped with all his strength toward Grandmother's den.

Abelene had donned a royal purple dress that fell to her ankles and cinched up a brocaded copper-hued belt. For some reason, though she couldn't put her finger on it, she needed to feel pretty today. She had no plans other than perhaps taking a stroll through the woods and gathering spring flowers and perhaps a peck of wild mushrooms, now that the rain had abated and the sun was shining brightly. She touched her hair and adjusted the ornate comb that held it in place.

She heard a familiar scratch on the front door. Good! It would be pleasant to walk with Kita and Hermes. When she opened the door, Abelene immediately knew something was amiss. Hermes' head hung down in shame.

"Grandmother." Hermes sulked. "Mother has been injured. Two man-creatures have her bound."

"Where is Krinaea?"

"I don't know. She is missing."

Abelene sharpened her senses and reached out to the forest. She detected a wrongness—not merely the intrusion of hunters, but an overall feeling of evil. The force behind it was magickal, yes, but twisted—a fell magick that drew on dark energy so frightening that she almost faltered. She threw on her green velvet cape, grabbed her wand and athame, then flew out the door.

"Take me to Kita, Hermes."

"She's in the open area where you like to sit and smell flowers."

Abelene dashed through the woods every so often snagging her cape on a jutting branch.

"Hermes, listen to me." Abelene puffed with the exertion of running. "Under no circumstances are you to enter the glade, no matter what happens. I will not have your death on my conscience. Do you understand?"

"Yes, grandmother."

"You must remain hidden. If anything happens to me, you must tell Azriel. Are we clear on this?"

"Yes."

They ran several hundred yards and entered the glade. Other than Kita, the clearing was empty. Abelene immediately knelt beside Kita trying to loosen her bonds.

"Mother," Kita said weakly. "You must leave me. It's a trap!" Abelene quickly scanned the area. She heard muffled cries coming from above. She located the sound and to her horror, saw that Krinaea was held captive, bound and gagged by dark magick.

"Mother! Leave now!" Kita said with more urgency.

Abelene spun around at the sound of an unfamiliar voice.

"Greetings, Lady Abelene. For so long I have wanted to meet you." The man stepped out from behind a copse of thicket dressed in a wizard's cape that bespoke his office and the octagonal magister's cap signifying his rank. Tall and gaunt with graying dark hair, she knew his name by description alone.

"Altais. Why am I not surprised that you would be behind all this."

He smiled pleasantly, but his eyes were cold—hard. "I am pleased you know my name, Lady Abelene."

Eddie stepped out from behind the bushes, holding the crossbow. He gaped at Abelene. He had no idea that Azriel's mother was so beautiful. She gazed back at the young man, and her shoulders sagged. She didn't berate him but just looked sadly at him.

"Oh, Eddie. So young you are to be swayed by such evil. Why? Why do you hate Azriel so much?"

Eddie couldn't answer. Somehow Abelene's disapproval struck him through the heart. For whatever reason, the woman's condemnation mattered and he backed away in shame.

"Enough!" Altais commanded. "I will not allow you to sway the boy with your witch's power."

"Like you did, Altais, enslaving his mind with sorcery?" She faced him squarely. She waved her hand above Kita, a subtle gesture, and spoke with command. "Calamus Abeo et salus!"

The arrow protruding from the mountain lion vanished and her wound closed up.

Eddie's eyes widened with such a display of power.

"Well done, Lady. I commend you. Your skills are formidable."

Abelene smiled, but it was humorless. "Enough of this! What is it you want, Altais?"

"I think you know, Lady Abelene." He grinned expansively. "Surely you're not that obtuse in your reasoning."

"Do you think me a fool, magician, that I would so easily give up my son?"

Altais winced as if he had been stung. Abelene's use of the word *magician* was far from a veiled insult.

Altais wheeled around and struck Abelene across the cheek with the back of his hand.

Eddie rushed at Altais and grabbed his arm. "Hey, you said no one would get hurt!" Though Abelene was the mother of his enemy, he saw something in her that he respected, grace and charm, poise and something that bespoke of royalty. She was everything his own mother was not. Eddie's reaction to Altais' violence was automatic.

"Unhand me, fool!" Altais growled and belted Eddie with a closed fist, knocking him to the ground. The boy looked up in shock at the sudden betrayal holding a hand to his eye. It was the distraction Abelene needed. With a quick motion of her hands, she translocated to the opposite side of the glade. She glared at Altais as she rubbed her cheek.

"Is that how you treat your friend?" Abelene squared her shoulders readying herself to face off against her enemy in magickal combat. She drew a wand from her belt.

Altais snickered. "A wand, lady? How thoroughly provincial."

She aimed the wand, not at Altais, but above him. "Quasso!" she ordered. Above Altais, a large branch suddenly snapped and plummeted to the ground, missing him by inches. He barely had enough time to move out of the way.

"Clever girl!" Altais praised her for her ingenuity. He waved his arms and thrust a clawed hand. "Multi Lammina!" he snarled. A dozen blades of varying size and shape appeared and flew toward Abelene. She held out a hand, fingers splayed and shouted, "Tecum!" A nearly transparent forcefield appeared, shielding her from injury. The knives fell harmlessly to the ground.

"Outstanding." Altais complimented. Abelene pressed her lips together. She had the impression that Altais was merely toying with her. She wasted no time and flicked her wand at the knives. They twirled as if they were caught in a whirlwind and flew at unimaginable speed in all directions then returned to Altais. He barely had enough time to defend against them. One grazed him on the cheek.

He wiped the blood away and grinned dangerously. "Vicious!" he commented.

"Tit for tat." Abelene grimaced.

This enraged Altais and he parried her attack. He made a grasping motion with his hand and Abelene's wand exploded with a loud concussion. She held her fingers against the pain. But she kept her poise. She called the power of the stars into herself and released a ball of plasma from her hands. The concussion nearly knocked Altais off his feet.

"Honestly, Lady Abelene, is that the best you can do?" He shot back with contempt.

From two miles away, Mortimer was awakened from a nap in a shade tree by the sound of explosions. He sidled back and forth on the branch, torn by indecision. Jasper had told him to stay put, but he sensed that a friend was in danger. An image of the pretty woman who gave him food and allowed him to sleep against her bosom came to mind. Orders or not, he had to help her. Mortimer knew Jasper would be angry if he left, but his master wasn't there to command him. Mortimer spread his wings and flew south toward the source of the turmoil. In minutes he arrived at the glade to find

Abelene and a stranger in the full throes of battle. They hurled lightning and glowing spheres at each other. There was another there who cowered on the sidelines. He seemed of no significance. But Abelene he knew, and the other was an enemy. Mortimer knew he must defend. He charged toward the stranger with full speed, claws outstretched, intent on mangling his face and gouging out his eyes, but as he approached, an arrow flew by and grazed Mortimer's wing. In anger, he whirled around and saw the boy trying to nock another arrow in the crossbow. Mortimer charged him.

Eddie screamed in terror and dropped the crossbow. He shielded his face just as Mortimer bit him on the shoulder. He instantly congealed into stone. Mortimer resumed his charge on Altais.

Too late, Altais caught the movement out of the corner of his eye and whirled around. "Petrify!" he commanded, and Mortimer suddenly went rigid and tumbled to the ground. It did, however, give Abelene the advantage she needed, and she struck Altais square in the chest with a salvo of fireballs. Enraged, he flung off his cloak, now engulfed in flames.

"I am done playing," he snarled. Altais released the sum of his fury and hatred against Abelene. The attacks came in quick succession—a series of plasma balls and lightning strikes. They parried each other's handiwork, either banishing or mirroring back each spell. Abelene pointed her athame at the stone bench with an incantation. It flew toward Altais threatening to crush him but at the last second he held it motionless in the air, and it dissolved to rubble. Clearly he was gaining the advantage. Spell after spell, he pummeled her with bone-crushing concussions for which she could not defend. Abelene was beginning to tire. Or was she? Altais wondered. He was confused by her smile. Abelene seemed to be grinning victoriously. Altais projected a clamp around her neck, lifting her off the ground. She struggled against the pressure around her throat unable to speak the word needed to banish the spell. Deprived of air Abelene's vision swam and her body went limp.

With the glow of victory in his eyes Altais lowered her body gently to the ground. Defeated, Abelene gasped for breath, unable to rouse her strength. She could not defend against Altais' approach.

He removed a small crystal from his pocket, a glowing golden pyramid, and cast it overhead. It hovered above Abelene. Suddenly, the crystal pyramid expanded in size to engulf her in power. Altais spoke a word of command and Abelene, trapped within the crystal, vanished from the glade.

Mission accomplished, Altais smiled gleefully and sighed.

Enraged, Kita struggled against her bonds with bloodlust coursing through her veins. She needed to kill her subduer—but could not.

Altais looked down at her with feigned pity. "You will be freed in time. And I will be long gone." He strode away stopping only once to pause and stare at the solidified form of Eddie, frozen in his moment of terror.

"Stupid boy," he smirked and disappeared into the brush.

Gift of the Amulet

392

Chapter 20

Azriel hurried home with Camille by his side, their hands clasped. It had been a good day—or so it seemed. For one thing, Eddie wasn't at school, which made a few classes far more enjoyable. The other thing was that he, in a moment of inspiration, figured out the next tactic he would use through alchemy to attain the next level of transformation. Azriel was excited to test his theory. If correct, it would take him one step closer to creating the Lapis Occultus—the elixir of life.

Azriel unlocked the door and let Camille enter. "Mom?" he called. He expected her to be tooling around the kitchen as she always did, but the room was empty, the hearth was cold.

"Mom, where are you?" Only chill silence answered him.

"That's strange," Azriel murmured. "She usually tells me if she's going to be out. He walked around the house looking for her while Camille waited in the dining room. He knocked softly on Abelene's bedroom door. Perhaps she was napping. No answer, he opened the door and peered in. She wasn't there and nothing seemed out of place—except for some reason her ring of communication was left on her night table. He wondered vaguely why she would have taken it off at all.

"Azriel!" Camille cried out. He flew back downstairs, his feet barely touching a step.

"What's wrong?" he asked out of breath.

Camille said nothing, but tears were in her eyes. She held out a note. Her hands shook as she handed it to him.

"What the hell…" He stared down at the note, cold fear rising in the pit of his stomach.

"I found it on the table."

"What's this supposed to mean?" he asked, not really expecting an answer. "*Who* has her?" He gaped at the scribbled symbol, oddly serpentine like a connect-the-dots snake—with the words, "**We have Abelene.**"

Camille shook her head and sobbed. "I don't know what that symbol means."

"My mother is a mighty sorceress. Who would even have the power to take her?"

"Only someone with more power."

Azriel blanched. Camille was right. Azriel ran back upstairs to retrieve his sword and the dream orb. He strapped Errin-lil to his back and returned to Camille's side. She was weeping uncontrollably. Azriel held her—to calm her and himself.

"Come on," he said. "Nicodemus will know what to do." Azriel infused the image of Caer Wylusung into the dream orb. Moments later, he and Camille translocated to the castle. They found Nicodemus casually reading ancient scrolls, sipping from a goblet of wine. He looked up from the text and smiled. "You're early, Azriel."

This couldn't wait, Uncle." He thrust the note under Nicodemus' nose. The old man's expression immediately sobered.

"It was left on the dining room table. What does it mean?"

"You don't know? Pity you never paid attention to your astrology lessons."

"Uncle Nick—straight answers, please!" Azriel couldn't quash his panic.

"The message, of course, is obvious. Your mother has been abducted."

"By whom?" Azriel demanded.

"The Clave. In particular—Altais."

"How do you know?"

"Simple, really. That symbol is a signature of sorts. It is the constellation Draconis. The dot in the corner is in the position of the star Altais."

"Altais." Camille repeated, a chill running through her.

"We must return," Nicodemus said with finality. "And leave the sword here."

Azriel hesitated, then unbuckled Errin-lil and leaned it against the wall.

They quickly orbed back to Abelene's kitchen and stepped outside. To their surprise, Hermes waited by the door. He hung his head, his eyes moist.

"Mother is trapped, and Grandmother has been taken."

"By whom, Hermes?" Azriel asked.

"Two man-creatures came. One battled Grandmother and took her. I tried to bite through mother's bindings, but they are tough and my jaws are weak. I feel shame."

"It's not your fault, Hermes." Camille stroked his fur, trying to soothe him.

"It is. I should have disobeyed Grandmother. She told me to remain hidden no matter what happened. So I hid like a frightened kitten."

"Hermes, take us to Kita," Nicodemus ordered, though his voice was gentle.

"Follow." The great cat answered sullenly.

After a few minutes, Azriel realized where they were headed— but when they reached his mother's private glade, he was unprepared for the devastation that had taken place. Scorch marks scarred the ground. Branches lay strewn where trees had been shattered. To the side, Kita lay bound by roots, imprisoned and immobile. Azriel knelt beside her.

"I'm sorry, my brother. I could not protect our mother." Kita said, her sorrow palpable.

"It's not your fault, Kita. You're blameless in this."

"I should have been more cautious and sensed the trap. You must help Krinaea."

"Where is she?"

"Up in the trees. Find her."

Camille and Nicodemus searched the glade calling for the dryad, but there was no response. Uncle Nick motioned for silence. Barely perceptible, he heard muffled crying and followed the sound. About twenty feet above, the tiny dryad was held captive by the massive oak that had guarded the glade for hundreds of years. Limbs wrapped around her and one clamped over her mouth preventing speech. Tears streamed down her face as she struggled against her bonds.

"Oh dear," Nicodemus muttered. He rubbed his chin, contemplating the dilemma. Meanwhile, Azriel attempted to cut through the vines imprisoning Kita, but for every vine he hacked through, another grew in its place. He could not cut fast enough to free her.

Nicodemus realized what he needed to do. It wasn't exactly a spell, but rather a command he learned during his days as a druid. He perceived that the mighty oak's unnatural awakening was painful for such an old tree and it had struck out at the closest thing to it, trapping Krinaea.

"Sleep Brother Oak, return to your slumber." Nicodemus commanded, and placed his hand on the aged, gnarled bark of the trunk. A tremor ran up the bark, and a creaking sounded from above as the ancient oak released its hold on the Queen of Dryads. Weakened from the ordeal, Krinaea tumbled down and Nicodemus—barely in time—caught her before she struck the ground. He laid her gently on the ground and stroked her tiny head. Krinaea curled up into a ball and sobbed out her grief. She—the Queen of Dryads—had never suffered capture and defeat. She had failed to protect Abelene, as was her charge. So bitter was her failure that she could not face Azriel or Nicodemus.

"I must return to my realm and face my shame. I am no longer Queen. I will pass my burden to one of my sisters," she wept disconsolately.

"You will do no such thing," Nicodemus replied firmly. He pulled Krinaea to a sitting position, but she hung her head in shame, auburn locks hiding her face.

"No dryad has ever suffered such defeat. I have never known sorrow—only joy. I am broken, Master Nicodemus."

He gently lifted her up and smoothed her wings. She wept on his shoulder. "Now, now," he said soothingly. "I fear we are all facing a time of sorrows. But we cannot let it consume us, can we? Otherwise, we will be powerless against the evil coming against us all."

"Uncle Nick," Azriel called from across the glade. "I need your help."

Nicodemus placed Krinaea on her feet and stood. He strode over to where Kita still lay bound. Krinaea flew beside him. Frantic, Azriel sawed at the vines with his boline, but with every vine cut, another would replace it.

"Hmm, this is quite puzzling," Nicodemus mused.

"Not really," Krinaea shook her head as she wiped her eyes. It is banevine from the old country. Altais must have scattered the seeds here. Normally it's quite harmless—unless awakened by blood."

"How do we get rid of it?" Azriel asked.

"It's really quite simple," Krinaea replied. "It lives briefly—one day only, but it cannot abide darkness. Master Nicodemus, may I have your cloak?"

He removed it, and Krinaea spread the black fabric over Kita completely covering her. They all heard a crackling, like the sound of walking on dry leaves. The vines sloughed away and Kita rose to her feet. Nicodemus retrieved the cloak and Kita shook herself off.

"That was unpleasant," she growled.

"Azriel, over here." Camille called out. Mortimer lay prone on the ground, rigid as though in death. Krinaea flew to her side.

"Is he dead?"

"No, only petrified. See?" Krinaea touched the little gargoyle on the chest and a soft glow emanated from her fingers. "There. That's better."

Mortimer shook himself awake. He began emitting grunts and growls and chirping noises while gesturing angrily to the edge of the clearing. He flew over to the petrified form of Eddie and firmly kicked it, then backed away holding his foot, snarling and hooting in what could only be perceived as curses in gargoyle.

When Azriel saw the frozen image of Eddie, blind rage overtook his senses. He picked up a large club-sized tree limb from the scattered remains on the ground with the sole purpose of depriving the calcified Eddie of his head.

"Azriel, stop!" Nicodemus ordered.

"Why should I?" The stress of the past hour finally surfaced and angry tears formed in his eyes. He trembled with the violence building within him.

"Because you'll kill him. His petrified state is only temporary. He is still alive."

He pointed to the statue. "That bastard led Altais right to my mother. He should pay for what he did!"

"And he will, Azriel—but not like this." Nicodemus reasoned. "His conscience will be the greater punishment."

He still held the limb poised to strike, his face red with anger.

Krinaea flew between Azriel and Eddie. She pleaded. "Young Master, there's a difference between being a warrior and a murderer. Which will you choose? Murder is a path from which there is no return."

Azriel screamed in frustration, hurling the limb into the woods.

"You've chosen wisely son." Nicodemus placed a comforting hand on Azriel's shoulder. The old sorcerer glanced to the side and noticed Kita affectionately licking Hermes on the face. She was gently chiding him. "No, son. Trying to save me would have only led to you roaming the forests of our ancestors. Then I would miss you."

Nicodemus spoke up. "It is time. Abelene's abduction was a message from the Clave. They have played their hand, and now it is time for us to play ours."

"I don't understand, Uncle Nick."

"No, I don't suppose you will understand what I have to say, son. But you must heed my words. The time is not right for you to rescue Abelene."

"What?" Azriel's voice resounded through the glade.

"Listen to me, Azriel. Right now, you are ill-equipped to face the Clave. You have not yet come into your full power. Altais is powerful, yes—but Rastaban is even greater than he."

He shouted at Nicodemus. "But what about my mother?" Azriel could not squelch his anger.

"If the Clave had wanted her dead, Altais would have done so. They fear what you will become, Azriel. They are trying to pull you off task. If you fail to finish what you started, then the Clave will defeat you, and there will be no stopping them. Their plans of world domination will come to full fruition."

"But they can harm her, Uncle Nick."

"I doubt that son. They are using her as bait. If you go to her now, you will be playing right into their hands. Trust me on this."

"So we do nothing." Azriel burned with indignation.

"Oh, I never said that. We must now gather our forces and prepare for battle. Things will get very dangerous from here. The Clave has many clever tricks and will use everything in their power to draw you out before you are ready. We must turn the tables on them and disrupt their plans, frustrate them until they make a mistake. Then we will strike."

Chapter 21

It could only be assumed that Abelene's house was no longer safe for Azriel. He gathered the most important belongings from his room and placed them carefully into a suitcase. He packed the Book of Aralia along with every magickal component he had gathered over the past three years. One small chest contained the enigmatic black scale from Azi Dahaka, the Dark Dragon of Death—Eltanin's nemesis. In another he kept his wand, chalice, and pentacle; in yet another his athame and boline etched with the symbol of the dragon. Each object he packed had special meaning, a lesson learned or a gift earned. He had experienced so much in the past few years, and there had always been help along the way. Nicodemus, Amaryllis, Felisa, Billy, and Muriel; more recently Krinaea, Paralda, and Maera. He had friends on other continents too; the Bedouin Chieftain Habib, the old Seeress Jezeera, and of course the Princess Halimah, a prophetess in her own right. So many had taught him and had given him special insights. But nothing could have prepared him for the most recent events. Abelene was gone and Azriel could do nothing about it.

Azriel fumbled at his belt just to make sure he had the summoning items for reaching his new friends. From Krinaea, Queen of Dryads, a golden acorn. From Paralda, Sylph of the air, a feather, and from Maera, Naiad of the ocean depths, a rune-encrusted shell. He patted the bag containing these items to make sure they were secure. Azriel added one more item. He took the ring from Abelene's night table and added it to the pouch to keep it safe.

Azriel pensively removed his amulet from inside his shirt. Three dragons glowed with power. Earth, water, and air transformed into their substantive properties, yet one remained inert—fire—the most elusive. One more to go, he thought. This amulet seemed to be the crux of all that happened. His empowerment was like the awakening of a great beast, but that beast was the Clave.

The Amulet.

He cherished and yet resented it at the same time.

Azriel double-checked all the items and zipped his suitcase closed. He was about to exit his room when he considered the small, framed picture he always kept on his night table. He picked it up remembering. It was a marvelous day he had spent with his mother when he had been around ten years old. They had gone to Silverwood amusement park and had a great day of rides and floor shows. Toward evening, they stopped at a dress-up booth to be photographed in costume. Abelene had chosen the Wicked Witch of the West, complete with pointy hat, red-and-white striped stockings, and a gnarly-looking broom. Azriel had dressed as a flying monkey. It was certainly a silly photograph. They both looked ridiculous, but it was a good day, a wonderful memory, and now suddenly precious to him.

"Mom," Azriel whispered as he touched the photo. He swallowed down the lump in his throat and then unzipped the suitcase, securing the photo inside.

Azriel walked downstairs slowly, then stopped in the kitchen. He paused for the poignancy of the moment. This, more than any other room, was Abelene's domain. If Azriel ever needed her, nine times out of ten, he could find her there either cooking or merely sipping tea, pondering something deep in her thoughts. He always could rely on her being present.

Abelene was gone. That thought kept pounding at Azriel like a battering ram. He never felt so powerless, and even with all his friends to support him, he experienced loneliness so profound he wanted to weep.

He walked outside and locked the door. Like his mother had taught him, Azriel walked the perimeter of the house and cast a spell of safeguard over it. A gut-wrenching thought invaded his mind. He had a sudden sick feeling that he would never see his home again.

Tomorrow he would meet in the glade. Camille would be there with her aunts, Penelope and Daphne. Jasper, Albert, Julia, and their mother Maggie—they would be there too. Pog would come with Nicodemus and together they would all go into hiding—exiled from their homes. Like Azriel, they were no longer safe from harm by the Clave. From now on Azriel knew his life was fundamentally changed. He also no longer had the luxury of time on his side. The next year and a half would be filled with preparing for the inevitable.

With his suitcase in hand, Azriel removed the dream orb from his pocket and translocated to Nicodemus's stronghold.

The old wizard greeted Azriel warmly and embraced him with sympathy. In Azriel's absence, Nicodemus had set up permanent quarters for him and showed him to the room. It was palatial—kingly. The sword, Errin-lil, was mounted on a bracket behind the oversized bed.

"Uncle Nick, isn't this just a bit ostentatious?"

"It was the best I could do on such short notice," Nicodemus replied with a touch of irony. "Leave your things and follow me to the dining hall. Dinner awaits."

They ate quietly of a surprisingly delicious stew, but Azriel didn't have much appetite. He picked at his food. Nicodemus said little, but finally spoke up. "Azriel, now more than ever, you must maintain your strength. Please eat."

"Uncle Nick, under the circumstances, I'm not very hungry."

"Here then." Nicodemus poured him a goblet of wine. "It will stimulate your appetite and calm your nerves."

Azriel took a sip and winced at the flavor. He hadn't yet developed a taste for good wine. He placed the goblet back on the table.

"Uncle Nick, I keep feeling like I should have been there. Maybe I could have prevented all this."

"There's nothing you could have done, Azriel. I know this may not make any sense to you, but somehow I think all this has some as of yet unnamed purpose. Abelene has a part to play in this destiny. We all do, even that little scoundrel, Eddie."

"You should have let me kill him," Azriel muttered darkly.

"No Azriel. Revenge serves no purpose. In all your dealings with men and elves, you must always take the high road. If you are set on retaliation and killing, then you are no better than the Clave. Rastaban's heart was twisted by his lust for power. Once long ago, he was a good wizard, wise and beneficent—like Eltanin—but his own thoughts betrayed him to the darkness. Now his need for power has corrupted him; it has taken hold of him like a narcotic. He can never get enough and can never be satisfied. He has murdered and plundered all the great wizards who ever opposed him. Eltanin was his closest friend and brother, and yet Rastaban betrayed him, hoping that Eltanin would destroy himself. That of course did not happen. But rest assured, he will murder Eltanin if he ever gets the chance."

They spoke through the early hours of the morning until Azriel was tired enough to sleep, but he tossed and turned in bed, plagued by his thoughts. When he finally succumbed to exhaustion, Azriel's dreams were disturbed by dark images of Abelene imprisoned and in turmoil. He awoke in a cold sweat with a start, the echo of his mother's voice calling to him.

Again, he tried to sleep, but he dreamed of Abelene. Her voice was far away as if she were lost, searching for him. "Mom, where are you?" he called in his sleep. But her voice receded as if being pulled into the void.

"Mom! Come back," he shouted.

Azriel found himself in a deep, cavernous pool. He was up to his neck treading water trying to reach the sandy shore, but a large serpent blocked the way. It hissed, threatening to devour him should he attempt to reach dry land. If he swam one way, the giant snake slithered in the same direction, mirroring his movements. Behind the snake, Abelene lay prone on the sand as if in the repose of death. Azriel needed to reach her, but the serpent continued to threaten, rearing its head, sidling back and forth in the strike position.

"Now this will never do." Norga of the Fenodoree swam up beside him. "Quite the dilemma, wouldn't you say, young wizard?" She croaked. "I think the serpent is hungry." Norga swam circles around Azriel. "Oh, yes indeed, she *is* hungry!"

The serpent suddenly grabbed at its own tail and began to devour itself. But with each bite of its tail, Abelene began to fade. By the time the snake was merely a head, Abelene vanished from sight.

Norga sighed. "Oh, that's too bad."

Azriel bolted upright from his bed. He rubbed his eyes and discovered they were moist. He stared up at the vaulted ceiling and then out the window. The sun had not yet crested the surrounding mountains, but he decided he had enough sleep. He sniffed at his skin and wrinkled his nose at the clammy smell of fear. Azriel decided to bathe. He let the hot water surround him and soothe the tension away along with the dreadful memory of the night's terrible dreams.

Azriel dried off and dressed. He walked out into the main hall and was surprised to find Nicodemus awake. The old man was dressed in the same clothes he had been wearing the evening before.

"Don't you ever sleep?" Azriel asked.

"Only when I need to," Nicodemus smiled wryly. "I've been preparing rooms for our guests. It seems this would be the safest place for them. I certainly have the room, though I must admit that I dread the thought of having to share my castle with a bunch of unruly teenagers."

In spite of Azriel's somber mood, he couldn't help but laugh. Uncle Nick was normally a private sort. It was likely that he would sequester himself away from his guests and lock himself in his study.

"We'll try not to be too hard on you, Uncle Nick."

"Oh, good." Nicodemus barely masked his sarcasm.

"Uncle Nick?"

"Yes?"

"Have you spoken to Pog? I haven't seen him for weeks."

"Yes, I have."

"Well, is he going to meet us at the glade?"

Nicodemus paused, mumbled, stroked his beard, scowled, and then mumbled again. "I am uncertain."

"He's been somewhat elusive lately."

"That is his way, Azriel. You had best get used to it."

They had a few hours to kill before the appointed time when they would all meet in the glade, so Nicodemus whipped up a quick breakfast of French toast and eggs. As they ate, Azriel explained his dreams to Nicodemus hoping he could shed light on the strange meanings.

Nicodemus chewed thoughtfully and smacked his lips. "The subconscious often speaks to us in mystical symbols, young master. The question you must ask yourself is what do the dreams mean to you? What does the snake represent?"

"The Clave, at least I think." Azriel scowled with uncertainty. "But it was eating its own tail!"

"Yes it consumes itself with hunger. And what is that hunger, Azriel?"

"I don't know."

"What does the Clave want more than anything else?"

"Power and control."

"Over what?" Nicodemus quizzed, hoping he could subtly lead Azriel to the right conclusion.

"Well, I guess power over the world."

"But they have that already, son. Who do you think is the driving force behind wars and economic ruin, dark conflicts between ideologies? The Clave feeds on all that is negative, all that would destroy. So, I ask you again, Azriel. What do they have no power over?"

Azriel thought for a few minutes, mulling things over in his mind. Nicodemus sat patiently waiting. Then it dawned on Azriel like a blinding light.

"They have no power over me!"

"And there you have the truth! They can imprison your mother, they can try to keep you from fulfilling your destiny, but they can't take away your free will. That, young master is your strength—and that is their doom!"

Strength returned to Azriel—not a quickening of his muscles but an inner fortitude that suggested that he would be up to the challenge no matter what obstacles would be placed before him. He smiled with a sudden thought.

"What do you find amusing?" Nicodemus wiped his mouth with a napkin.

"I was just thinking. When the Clave took my mother, I don't think they realized that they're getting more than they bargained for. She's not as sweet as you think. She's going to give them hell. Their lives are going to get very complicated. Is it possible she allowed herself to be taken?"

Nicodemus chuckled. "I wouldn't put it past her. Your mother is a very complicated woman. She can be as treacherous and as deadly as that snake in your dream. Rest easy, Azriel. It's not inconceivable that she is setting them up for a very abysmal plunge. There's an old adage that says to keep your friends close, but keep your enemies closer."

"I hope you're right, Uncle Nick."

"Well," the old man said smartly, "shall we go?"

Azriel steeled his resolve. "I'm ready."

They assembled in the glade, laden down with luggage, milling about and conversing in soft whispers as they awaited the arrival of Azriel and Nicodemus. Camille had a compulsion to clean up the area. She took charge, ordering Jasper and Albert to gather up all the broken branches and place them in the fire pit. Mortimer leisurely flew around the open field looking for food. He found a delectable spider and gulped it down, then perched back on Jasper's shoulder. The broken pieces of the stone bench were also gathered in a pile. Not surprisingly, Jasper had perfected the fire spell and concentrated his will on the pile of timber. "Inferno!" he commanded and the pile ignited into a great roaring blaze. His mother Maggie nodded with pride at her son. Though still timid, she was learning magick at an alarming rate, having spent every free waking hour at her studies.

"May I try something?" she asked hesitantly.

Julia grinned. "You don't need to ask, Mom. We're students just like you."

She smiled at Julia and faced the pile of stone. She removed a wand from her sleeve and pointed it at the pile of broken marble. "Refectio." She intoned. At first nothing happened. She tried again more forcefully. "refectio!" There was a sudden inrushing of sound like the wail of a typhoon. The stones pieced together with a thunderous clicking and stood upright, whole and unmarked.

"Wow, Mom. That was great!" Albert said with encouragement. Here, watch this!" He waved his hands with a subtle upward motion. "Tollo sublatum." The stone floated off the ground, weightless. Albert gently pushed it back to where it had once rested on a base. "*Demitto*!" he commanded and it floated onto the two upright slabs of stone.

Camille and Julia clapped proudly. Suddenly Maggie spun around, eyes wide with terror. Two mountain lions had entered the glade. She stifled a scream.

Jasper rolled his eyes. "Mom, it's only Kita and Hermes. I thought we told you about them."

Kita gently brushed her head against Camille affectionately. "How are you and my other cubs?" she asked.

"Doing well, Kita." Hermes flanked her and nuzzled against her leg. Camille giggled. Mrs. Cunningham appeared as though she was going to faint.

"Mom, it's cool. Kita and Hermes are coming with us."

Kita looked up at Maggie and appeared to wink. "I promise I won't eat you! But that one over there, I would consider for breakfast." Kita pointed with her nose at the still solidified form of Eddie.

Mortimer took the opportunity to explain, through wild gesturing, how the boy had shot an arrow at him, and how in retaliation, he bit the creep on the shoulder. Mortimer hovered, glaring at Eddie with his arms crossed. For emphasis he held out a hand at Eddie's face and snapped his finger belligerently. Camille held her hand to her mouth and giggled at the gargoyle affectionately.

"Now that you're all done congratulating yourselves, perhaps we can get started," Nicodemus bellowed more crossly than he truly meant. He and Azriel had translocated into the glade unnoticed.

Camille rushed to Azriel's side and hugged him, then kissed him on the lips. "Are you okay?" She asked with doleful eyes.

"As good as I can be under the circumstances."

Nicodemus looked at the massive pile of suitcases, chests, boxes and bags, shaking his head with dismay. "Have you ever heard of packing light?" He grumbled, then removed a cloth satchel from his pocket and unfolded it with annoyance.

"Reducto!" he muttered. All their belongings suddenly shrunk to miniature size amid wondrous stares. "Albert, would you do the honors?" Albert smiled and gathered all the tiny boxes and packages into the bag.

Meanwhile Azriel glanced around the glade looking for his mentor. "I thought Pog would be here," he said sullenly with disappointment.

"He'll get here in his own time." Nicodemus assured. No sooner had the words escaped his lips than a strange sensation overtook them all. Camille was the first to feel it. She looked around, startled as she felt a massive drawing-in of energy. A pulsing, throbbing emanation gathered at the edge of the glade when suddenly they all had to shield their eyes as a brilliant penumbra of light, more blinding than the midday sun congealed before them. The overpowering brilliance suddenly formed into a solid shape. They all drew back as a massive white dragon towered over them. Maggie fainted. The dragon glowed with outstretched wings, power shooting out sparks of color like a rainbow. It reared its head and roared, belching out gouts of flame.

"Holy crap!" Jasper shouted, his legs trembling.

The glow became at once unbearable, but then the light faded as the dragon morphed into an ancient man. He wore a gleaming white robe and a wizard's cap. Long hair, and beard framed a gaunt face with kindly eyes. The wizard held a staff crowned by a glowing black orb.

"Eltanin?" Azriel gaped in wonder. "Is it really you?"

The old Arch Wizard chuckled. "I do love to make a grand entrance."

Nicodemus bowed reverently with deep respect. "My Lord, it is wonderful to see you again. Great illusion, by the way." They all gathered close to him with reverence and awe. Eltanin had now become a legend to these young sorcerers.

"My old friend." Eltanin smiled warmly. "It has been much too long. We have some catching up to do." His voice was gentle and resonant. "Nicodemus, if you don't mind, please take your charges to the stronghold. I wish to speak to Azriel alone."

Azriel was excited to finally meet Eltanin, but was vaguely disappointed at Pog's absence. He sighed as he looked around. "Well, I guess Pog won't be joining us today."

"Now, why would ye be speakin' such blarney, laddie?"

"Pog?" he gestured, "Where have you been?" Then he screwed up his face with confusion. Eltanin had disappeared.

"Silly twit. I've been here all the time, ye wanker!"

Pog beamed a smile at him and suddenly transformed. Pog expanded and stretched until he stood altered into the guise of Eltanin.

Azriel's mouth hung open with sudden realization. "You're—you're Pog?"

"Aye, indeed, laddie." Eltanin spoke with Pog's voice, then resumed his normal timbre. "Yes Azriel. The deception was necessary for your safety and mine." He glanced at Nicodemus and nodded. The old sorcerer gathered up his refugees and removed a dream orb from his pocket. They all vanished, leaving Azriel and Eltanin alone in the glade.

The Arch Wizard was about to speak when he was interrupted by a horrified scream from the edge of the glade. Eddie had been in the throes of terror when Mortimer bit him, thus turning him to stone. Now, at this moment he reconstituted to flesh and bone, the remainder of his scream emerged from his mouth.

Azriel spun around and glared at him with fists clenched. His eyes were cold with accusation and disgust.

One side of Eddie's face was deeply bruised, his eye nearly swollen shut. It appeared that his cheekbone may have been shattered. He was obviously in tremendous pain and bore it stoically. But tears welled in his eyes.

"Azriel, I—I—didn't know. I'm…"

"Stow it, Eddie. You've done enough damage." Azriel trembled with the violence building within him. It took every ounce of effort to keep from beating Eddie senseless.

Eltanin placed a hand on Azriel's shoulder to steady him. He approached Eddie and the boy shrank back.

"Don't be afraid, son." Eltanin spoke gently, his voice soothing. He towered over Eddie, but his demeanor was calm and assuring, not at all like Altais who had been hard and cruel by comparison. Eltanin gently touched Eddie's broken and ravaged face examining the fractures. He nodded with understanding. Like a doctor gently ministering to a patient, Eltanin touched Eddie's wounds and released a soft emanation of power. The purple swelling of his bruises disappeared, and Eddie could now open his eye again. The fractures to his cheekbone knitted back to solid bone and the pain suddenly abated.

Eddie looked up at Eltanin with gratitude, and he finally allowed his tears to flow. The Arch Wizard looked down at Eddie with compassion and nodded. "You can go now, son." He said warmly. Eddie stared for a few more seconds at the kindly face, and then disappeared into the woods.

Eltanin returned to the stone bench and motioned for Azriel to sit. He held his staff across his lap and looked at the magnificent clearing, drinking in its beauty.

"Do not hate your enemy, Azriel. It clouds your judgment." He finally said.

"Why did you do it?"

Eltanin sighed. "His suffering will be far greater than his wounds, Azriel. He will have to live with what he has done for a very long time."

Azriel nodded. Eltanin spoke the truth. Azriel perceived the enormous age and wisdom of the Arch Wizard. In a way, Eltanin was his grandfather, some hundreds of generations removed, but he felt a kinship nonetheless.

"Three years ago when I met you by the Fairy Bridge, you told me we were kin." Azriel smiled ironically. "You were telling the truth."

"Yes, Azriel Ferrishyn."

"Grandfather, why didn't you just appear to me as you are?"

"Would you have believed me then? An incorrigible old dwarf was easier for you to handle."

Azriel laughed with a touch of melancholy. "You know, I think I'm going to miss that old troll."

"Now don't ye be worryin' yer heart there, laddie." Eltanin replied in Pog's voice. "Ol' Pog will be visitin' from time to time." The ancient one placed a comforting hand on Azriel's shoulder.

"Grandfather, why did you choose now to come out of hiding?"

Eltanin sighed. "Rastaban forced my hand. The Clave's attack on Abelene was the sign I was looking for. We cannot let this go unchallenged. I must confront Rastaban, and you, Grandson, must come into the fullness of your power. I am here to help and guide you toward that end. Your old life here draws to a close, Azriel. You are at the cusp of a new one, with all the challenges, hardships, and rewards that go along with it. Are you ready?"

"I am, Grandfather."

"Then let us begin." Eltanin rose from the seat and stared at Azriel warmly. "I'm proud of you, my grandson."

Azriel looked up at his ancient ancestor and swallowed hard. For lack of words to express the profoundness of his emotions, he said nothing.

Eltanin held his staff before him and the black orb at its crown began to glow with power. "Now, Son of Luminance, if you would take hold of my staff."

Azriel obeyed and made contact with the smooth wooden surface of Eltanin's staff of office. He swelled with the surge of power drawing into him like an electric charge. An onrushing of speed, a release of cosmic energy and Azriel went forward to his next destination. With a blinding flash, he and Eltanin disappeared from the glade.

Epilogue

Nicodemus stood alone upon the high battlements of Caer Wylusung, his cloak drawn tight against the chill of the mountain night. Below him, the world lay sleeping—fragile, unknowing, and for the moment, unchanged.

Above, the stars burned with their ancient indifference.

Dragons had once ruled the firmament of the world, long before men learned the language of fire, and before wizards ever dreamed of bending the elements to their will. Nicodemus remembered them well. Not as beasts, as the stories so often claimed, but as forces— vast, willful, and bound to the bones of creation itself.

It was a mistake, he knew, to believe that dragons were gone. Nothing born of the First Making ever truly vanished. It withdrew instead, receding into silence, waiting for the world to circle back to a moment when it would again be required.

He rested his hands upon the cold stone and exhaled slowly.

The balance had shifted. He felt it now, like a pressure behind the eyes, like the stillness that precedes a storm. Old powers stirred. Old names whispered themselves awake in the deep places of earth and sky.

And somewhere not far from him, a boy slept fitfully, burdened with a destiny far greater than he had yet understood.

Nicodemus allowed himself a thin, knowing smile.

"Soon," he murmured to the night. "Soon enough."

414

Books by the Author

The Chronicles of Abahrazha Trilogy:
The Singingwood
Arcalian Apocalypse
Children of Prophecy

Shattered Worlds Trilogy:
Gift of the Amulet
Dragon Lord
Equilibrium

Summerlands: and other Selected Works

Leo Rising

Echoes of Venus

Michael Anthony Cariola